C y

They almost exploded the world,
believing they were right.

THE PLANET
THANKS
YOU !

PHOTO OF VASILI ARKHIPOV COURTESY OF M.
YAROVSKAYA AND A. LABUNSKAYA

The Last Saturday of October

The Declassified Secrets of Black Saturday

By

Douglas Gilbert

A Novel Based on the True Story

Dedicated to all who serve.

60th Anniversary Edition

Based on the true story, characters in *The Last Saturday of October* were real and are placed in their actual positions of responsibility and authority. Russian names and titles are articulated in the Cast of Characters. Names, dates, events, and photographs may be accessed by consulting the notes section and bibliography of this edition. A glossary of naval acronyms and Russian words used in the story is included after the last chapter.

Table of Contents

Prologue
Russia, September 2017

"What in the world happened to Vasili Arkhipov?"

"What possesses you to ask me such a thing again?"

"Who could believe the spine-tingling rumors about your grandfather?" Yelena asked her son, Sergei. "They're too outlandish to be more than myths or legends fed by phantoms. Every answer brings more questions. He never spoke of his nightmares before he passed, except in his sleep. He always said, 'My secrets will die with me,' but they didn't." Yelena shook the engraved card she held in her hand. "They live on to haunt us even after he's gone."

Glancing up from his book, Sergei's eyes flashed under his dangling spit curl of inky black hair. "What rumors?" he asked, toying with his mother's angst because he loved hearing her stories about her legendary father.

Extending the fancy letter, Yelena declared, "They say he saved the world, and they're inviting us to London."

Sergei's eyebrows lifted his sardonic eyes before he questioned, "Both of us? What's happening in London?"

"He'll receive a big posthumous award. They want us to accept it for him on the anniversary of the day they call Black Saturday. They say he was an incredible hero."

Sergei closed his heavy book and placed it on the table. "That's absurd, how could one man save the world?"

Yelena pointed the fine letter at him and said, "Your skepticism comes from him. He questioned everything. It's Cold War history, and it's time you know the full story."

"The Cold War isn't history. Nothing happened."

"*Nyet*, it was a time of grave risk, unbridled hope, and vast fear. They almost exploded the world, believing it was right. Your grandfather was in the thick of it." Yelena pressed her finger into her thumb for Sergei to see. "We came this close to nuclear war. It's a miracle or destiny or blind luck that we survived. The Future of Life people say it was your Grandfather Vasili watching over all of us."

Relaxing with a grin, Sergei yawned, "Spare me the lecture. Just tell me the story before we get to London."

Yelena (daughter) and Sergei (grandson) with Vasili Arkhipov's Future of Life Award (October 27, 2017). Published with permission from the Future of Life Organization.

Vasili Arkhipov is arguably the most important person in modern history, thanks to whom October 27, 2017 isn't the 55th anniversary of WWIII. **Max Tegmark, President, Future of Life Institute, October 27, 2017, in London.**

Cast of Characters in Order of Appearance

Captain Second Rank Vasili Aleksandrovich **Arkhipov** — 69th Submarine Brigade Chief of Staff and Executive Officer (*starpom*) of the B-59 (also called the legend, Vasya, and Starpom)

Alexandr **Arkhipov** — Father of Vasili Arkhipov

Mariya **Arkhipov** — Mother of Vasili Arkhipov

Captain Second Rank Valentin Grigorievitch **Savitsky** — Commanding officer of B-59 (the old man and the captain)

Lieutenant Victor **Mikhailov** — B-59, Jr. Navigator

Captain Third Rank Ivan Semonovich **Maslennikov** — B-59 Political Officer (Poli)

General Ivan Ivanovich **Maslennikov** — Deputy to the Supreme Soviet of the USSR and a candidate member of the Central Committee after Great War

Senior Lieutenant Vadim Pavlovich **Orlov** — Leader of *Osnaz* RIS group (Oz)

Admiral Vitaly Alexeyevich **Fokin** — First Deputy Commander in Chief of the Soviet Navy, recipient of Order of Lenin and Order of the Red Banner. Coauthor of Operation Kama

Rear Admiral **Yevseyev** — Original 69th Torpedo Submarine Brigade Commander

Captain First Rank Vasili Naumovich **Agafonov** — 69th Submarine Brigade Commander (hero of Polyarny)

Captain Second Rank Ryurik A. **Ketov** — Commanding officer, B-4

Captain Second Rank Aleksei **Dubivko** — Commanding officer, B-36

Captain Second Rank Nikolai Aleksandrovich **Shumkov** — Commanding officer, B-130

General Matvei Vasilevich **Zakharov** — Marshal of Soviet Union, Chief of the General Staff, Deputy Defense Minister. Coauthor of Anadyr and Kama

Vice Admiral Anatoly Ivanovich **Rassokha** — Chief of Staff of the Northern Fleet

Rear Admiral L. F. **Rybalko** — Commander of 20th Operative Submarine Squadron

Captain First Rank Nikolai Vladimirovich **Zateyev** — Commanding Officer of the K-19

Chapter One – The Assignment

The battle line between good and evil runs through the heart of every man. **Alexander Solzhenitsyn.**

September 1938 then September 1962

"Vasili, you damned good-for-nothing, put down that book. All you ever do is read and study. You're too lazy to ever be a decent farmer," said Aleksandr Arkhipov.

Vasili tensed without moving, suppressing his sullen distaste for his father's insult. Glinting like river rocks beneath his tousled soot-black hair, his eyes rose above his book to meet Aleksandr's glare. "You call my studies, my assignments for school, good for nothing?"

Aleksandr pinched the last few crumbs of black bread off the table between his fingers and placed them on his tongue. "School won't bring in the harvest," he replied.

Vasili closed his book and placed his oversized farm hands on the rough-hewn table to confront the injustice. Glancing at Mariya, his silent mother, who never took sides within the rustic log *izba*, he said, "The harvest is in. How much do you think they'll let us keep this year?"

Worried that Vasili's begrudged respect, laced with defiance, might lead to trouble, his father said the only thing that could defuse the situation, "Go slop the hogs."

Viewing his father as he would a total stranger, Vasili stood, his shirt too large and his pants too short. Moving toward the kitchen door, he donned his cap and barn coat, pulled on his *golosh* boots, caked with farm filth, and grabbed the slop pail next to the sink. Without a word, he opened the door and strode into the evening cold.

His face hardened by frustration, Aleksandr turned to face Mariya and growled, "That young man is nothing but trouble when all we have is trouble. I don't know what to do with him. He's out of control."

"He's your blood and your bones," Mariya said with stony resolve. "You will save him before he gets himself in real trouble with the *kommissars*. They'll kill him. You don't need to understand him, just save him."

"I'll send him off to join the army. They're recruiting young men. I'll lie about his age and let them straighten him out, make a man of him," said Aleksandr.

"You'll do no such thing. Rumor is that war is coming, and I won't have him killed in a farm field or a battlefield. Send him to the Navy. That'll be safe enough," Mariya said, nodding her head to convince herself, catching a glimpse of Vasili passing by the window.

"*Svin'i*," he called as he rounded the farmhouse, stomping his way to the hog pen.

Grunting and snorting in anticipation of dinner and Vasili's soothing voice, the two hogs charged the fence. Shaking the food scraps from the slop pail into the pen for the mud-slathered animals, Vasili spoke, "Father says I'm good for nothing. He thinks he's important with his strip of land to till, but the *kommissars* will come from Moscow. You're important so they'll take you, but they won't feed you. You'll feed them. It's your purpose, but farming is not my destiny. They'll take our harvest, too, and we'll starve again this winter. Then we'll see who's good for nothing."

Vasili heard the distant rumble of truck motors, rolling despair across the fields, a sound he knew too well.

Like peasants devouring their food scraps, the hogs gobbled the slop as Vasili continued speaking, "School just started last week, and I've almost finished the seventh-grade reader." While cleaning the fallen autumn leaves from the water trough, he listened to the truck motors closing in. "I read a story about a peasant boy, same as me. He was good for nothing. Spent his days whittling bird whistles out of wood. When the invading army arrived in his village, no one was there except the boy. The German lieutenant trusted him because he believed the youth was good for nothing. The boy told the army officers that he could lead them to a clean watering hole. There's always some truth in the best lie. He led them into an ambush and alerted the resistance with his bird whistle. Now he's a legend, and the Germans drank their own blood. I dream that someday I'll be somebody."

After the trucks rolled onto the farmstead and shut down, Vasili heard a scuffle outside the *izba*.

His father's voice severed him from his dream, "Vasili Arkhipov, bring the hogs."

Vasili unlatched the hog pen gate and uttered an urgent whisper, "Run *svin'i*."

He turned to see his father's ghastly face, reduced to nothing but a peasant's prayer for survival, locked in the clutches of two Communist Party *kommissars*.

Twenty-Four Years Later

September 19, 1962. After a night of heavy drinking in Havana, Fidel Castro's private pilot boasted, "We will fight to the death and perhaps we can win because we have everything, including atomic weapons." The (American) spy at the end of the bar made a mental note and reported the pronouncement to the United States Intelligence Board who included it, word for word, in John F. Kennedy's daily President's Intelligence Checklist (PICL) the next morning. **Special (CIA) National Intelligence Estimate (SNIE) 85-3-62, Doc. 13, Military Buildup in Cuba, 9/19/62.**

Rumors flew above the Arctic Circle, news rode on a truck, intelligence lay sequestered, and the submarine captains received their information last unless they chose to inform their crews. One month prior to the most dangerous day, two men, the old man and the legend, faced off to discuss a grave situation at the Sayda Bay naval outpost, outside the northernmost Soviet city of heroes, Murmansk.

"The assignment's changed," said the legend, Navy Captain Second Rank Vasili Arkhipov. "It's all changed."

His words froze the old man, Captain Second Rank Valentin Savitsky, commanding officer of the B-59, one of four boats in the 69th Torpedo Submarine Brigade. His eyes diverted like electric sensors from the chaos on the pier to survey the legendary hero standing before him, but he saw only a common naval officer wearing a dress blue uniform and clutching a file folder stuffed with the bureaucratic paperwork of a desk job.

"Again?" said the old man without emotion, expecting the worst as he studied the lines of seaborne suffering in the legend's face. His eyes, half-shuttered as if sheltering the secrets of long-fettered ghosts, unnerved the old man, wondering what he was prepared to reveal. Every ship had an old man, but only one brigade had a legend.

The open bridge atop the submarine conning tower provided privacy for conferring over Top Secret matters while all hands, on deck below them, wrangled with a huge stores loadout, mimicking a bucket brigade, two-hand tossing loins of beef, pork, and sausage, salt-cured to extend shelf life. They broke open boxes stacked with tins of meat, fish, coffee, tea, and lard. To prevent infestations of mice, cockroaches, and bedbugs aboard ship, they left the cardboard on the pier and heaved each can, man-to-man, on a human conveyor belt until it disappeared down the hatch to the bilge for stashing between the ribs of the pressure hull. Feigning disinterest in the breaking news, the old man pointed toward his crewmen and said, "They'll sleep with cabbage and rutabaga tonight, and walk on canned potatoes tomorrow. It's good for them to know our voyage approaches." However, he needed to know the thing he was afraid to hear. "What changed?"

"The forward deployment force is reduced to four submarines." The legend shifted his weight as he delivered the consequential reveal, "I've informed the other captains, so you're the last to know." As the brigade chief of staff and second in command, his duties ranged from monitor to messenger, but he worried about a great deal more.

"Sounds reckless, but ballsy." The old man's eyes narrowed as he turned to face Arkhipov. "Which four?"

"Our 69th Torpedo Brigade." The 20th Submarine Squadron combined the brigade of four torpedo boats with a division of seven missile boats plus the submarine tender. "The mission briefing's over, and we've been chosen."

The old man released an audible sigh and blurted, "Splendid, they haven't scratched our operation, but what happens to the missile boats?"

"They'll stand down, stay behind with the tender, and join us after we establish the new sub base." The submarine tender, *Dmitry Galkin*, was the squadron commander's flagship. "But no time for celebration; I must reassign the brigade staff from the tender to ride the subs."

The old man redirected his gaze to the pier and the massive stores loadout, prescribed by the Admiralty in St. Petersburg, that challenged his crew to stuff every cranny forward of the engine room. He better understood now the pandemonium he saw below. Without tender support, all stores were being crammed into the four subs. Toilet paper bundles launched over the spring lines wrapped with metal rat guards to the hatchman with a hoot and a howl. Submariners needed certain things to sustain life below the sea: oxygen, water, food, girly magazines and toilet paper.

"Intriguing move, but risky to deploy without tender support," the old man exposed his private concern.

Sizing up the captain, so open and anxious to express his misgivings about his superior's decisions, Arkhipov wondered if the new old man was ready for the biggest mission of his life and said, "True, but the brass directed a covert passage. We can't have a telltale tub tagging along, can we?"

"*Nyet*, but covert passage will slow our progress. What's the brigade commander think?" Both men reported to the brigade leader, but in different capacities.

"Doesn't matter," said the legend, bowing his head in respect. "He's sick, fighting for his life. Let's hope..."

"What the hell does that mean?" The old man recoiled and cut off the unexpected answer.

Without exasperation, Arkhipov reached out and said, "I was about to say before you interrupted, 'let's hope he recovers.' He suffered a severe attack in Moscow after the mission briefing." He looked away, expecting some indignant reactions based on the data in the old man's file.

The captain's robotic eyes scrutinized the legend, questioning what was happening to him and why, before he said, "I don't know you well, but if this is a farce, you have a keen sense of humor. This is your idea of a joke?"

The legend stepped back, allowing the captain to stew before answering, "*Nyet,* dead serious. Must you question everything I say, and every command decision?"

"It's not what you say that I question. What I question is every damned thing you don't say. What kind of severe attack?" The cryptic answers gnawed at the old man, magnifying his frustration. "Look at me, Arkhipov."

The legend locked his eyes. "Panic attack, or maybe he lost his nerve. Clutched his throat, struggled to breathe. They thought it was a stroke and hauled him to the hospital. Almost lost him." Placing his fists on his hips, the legend added, "Proceed with caution when addressing me, Captain Savitsky, and you may refer to me as Captain Arkhipov."

Nonplussed, the old man retorted, "Very well, Captain Arkhipov, my apologies." He frowned, tapping the side of his neck with two fingers, "*Vodka* involved?"

The legend tapped his own neck twice to confirm, "*Da*, did you ever see the brigade commander not drunk?"

"*Nyet*, but he seemed fine the last time we spoke." Grappling with his dark, innate suspicions, the old man said, "There's always a reason that people disappear for no reason. What did he say?" The old man's scowl intensified. "That man always has something to say."

"One word. 'Madness.'" The legend's eyes flashed, then shadowed. "Just 'Madness.'"

"Must have been one hell of a briefing." The old man clasped the back of his own neck. "I'd like to visit him before we sail, bring him a bottle, ask him some questions."

"Too late, he's been replaced." The statement hung in midair. "Our mission is called Operation Kama. That's what I know." The legend continued, "They transferred him to the infirmary in Severomorsk. Confusion, headaches, nausea, and blurred vision from soaring blood pressure."

"Replaced? Two weeks before we sail?" The old man hated change, especially last-minute shakeups.

"*Nyet*, the sail date changed too." The legend looked down at the crew hustling food stores for the cruise.

"Thank God. We could use more time to train the crew," the old man, relaxing for a moment.

"There's less time. We sail on Monday," Arkhipov reported. It was Thursday. The old man tensed again.

Shipyard workers, called yard birds, complicated the loadout by erecting masking screens to hide the sub from prying eyes in preparation for the upcoming torpedo loadout, scheduled for after dark when US U-2 spy planes at the edge of the stratosphere suffered night blindness.

The captain straightened and shot back through a full glower, "Four days to prepare? That's all we have?"

"That's right, our new brigade commander arrives on Sunday with the brass to inspect the ships and crews."

"The brass is coming here to send us off? Every damned day the brass reaches down to stir things up."

On the pier, the guards interrupted the progress of the ship's crew. Arguments flared, and the chief torpedo man stepped between a sailor and a yard bird, confronting the yard bird, chest-to-chest, chin-to-chin and expressing ugly pleasantries about his mother. When the yard bird shoved him away, the torpedo man punched his face.

"Avast combat," the old man's command voice boomed over the ruckus. Two fierce words from Captain Savitsky ended the fight, and the commotion ceased. All heads turned like owls to see his raised fist shaking at them. His crew knew his boundaries, but yard birds quarrelled with every submarine crew in the yard. No one challenged his authority, and the work commenced again.

Arkhipov ran his fingers over the ship's bulwark as if assessing its mettle for battle. Searching for the right words, he leaned into the captain and spoke in a low voice, "This comes straight from the top, Fleet Admiral Gorshkov and Premier Khrushchev. They're sending the number two naval officer, Deputy Fleet Admiral Fokin, to visit every boat. He wants to see spit and polish, not sailors brawling with yard birds. I'm in charge until they arrive."

The rebuke felt like a face slap, and the captain's cheeks reddened, but he acknowledged the dressing down with a nod and a grimace, asking, "Who's the last-minute brigade commander, you?"

"Not me, they only want the best." Arkhipov had been passed over for the position. "The hero of Polyarny."

"Captain Agafonov will command the brigade?" Savitsky knew of him only by rumor and reputation.

"*Da*." The legend paused, placing his right index finger to his lips, opening his eyes wide enough to bare his trepidation, and delivering the rest of his message with a serious voice, "We'll be outfitted with special weapons."

"*Ni figa sebe*, nukes?" The old man's brow hung like a cliff over his dark eyes. "On diesel subs?"

Arkhipov raised his hand, frowned at the old man, and said, "Special weapons. Be ready, you'll be briefed."

"When I hear the word 'special,' I know it's a dog's breakfast," the old man said. "Every time the Admiralty or the Kremlin seizes on a horrible idea they call it 'special.'"

"Careful with your comments about the Admiralty. A dog's breakfast?" asked Arkhipov, probing the metaphor.

"Nobody knows for sure what's in it, everything no man can stomach, but it changes your day forever."

"Ah, like pig slop. There's more, we'll have riders, special forces on every boat," another secret slipped from the legend's lips like a whisper over water.

Everything shifted. The captain shivered as he felt it settle. "Where the hell are we going with special forces?"

"Top Secret. I'm here to say that you'll be briefed when our new boss arrives; you'll receive sealed orders."

"The more you say, the less I understand about this suicide mission. Massive force reduction with no support, special weapons with no training, special forces for no reason, and a command shake-up with an accelerated departure." The tangle of confusion pointed to disaster, the blind secrecy reeked of ruin, and the new captain relished the opportunity. He scratched his chin and said with a devious smirk, "Sound like a friendly undertaking to you?"

"Of course, have faith. It's the perfect assignment for your first command mission. Sail to a fraternal country to show the flag and set up a forward base. They invited us into their home, and they'll welcome us with open arms. No strings, no consequences. The combination of military firepower and international diplomacy is strong medicine."

Unconvinced, the old man said, "Faith? When was the last time our navy set up a new base on foreign soil? Faith distracts from honest angst. Nothing's easy, things go wrong, and there are always consequences. You issue assignments like sausages but tell me nothing. All this secrecy and confusion are for what, a surprise party?"

"*Nyet.* It's extra protection. Secrecy prevents those who are not invited from spoiling it. All else is a precaution in case the secret is revealed. It's not a suicide mission, just a permanent move. Say your last goodbyes. We're never coming back to Kola Bay, not on the B-59."

The legend gazed over the golden autumn forests rolling up the taiga-covered hills that ascended the rocky Russian coast of Kola Bay to the Khibiny Mountain peaks. Shallow Arctic sunshine cast long mountainous shadows over the ships, the men, and the sea water. The old man had arrived in Murmansk a few weeks earlier to take command of his boat and to prepare for an extended voyage. The mad rush accelerated through the summer. Now, this. "We have no idea where we're heading, do we?" the old man hissed.

"*Nyet.* It's not Russia, but it basks under a Soviet moon and a red flag. For twenty years, you and I have been all navy, surviving budget cuts and force reductions. Now, for the first time since Premier Khrushchev rose to power, our navy finally expands, and we'll go where he sends us."

"You know I transferred my executive assistant out last week; couldn't trust him, so I'm seeking a good man to be my *starpom.* You've handed me enormous tasks with a compressed schedule and no additional help, except for the brass, the kind of help we don't need." The chaotic planning chapped the captain. "It's a bad omen to put to sea with holes in the crew."

"That's the last thing I came to say." Arkhipov drew a breath before he continued, "I've assigned myself to replace your senior assistant as your second in command for this voyage."

Startled, the captain said, "You? My *starpom*? You think I need a guardian, some damned protector? I heard they chained you to a desk after your last assignment."

"*Da*, it's true, like a good-for-nothing man, but that's over. The squadron commander will speak to the doctor, and he'll issue a clean bill of health. Rest assured, you'll receive an official medical report. No issues at all."

Arkhipov felt something creeping up behind him. He whirled around. It vanished, leaving a vague shadow.

The old man noticed the strange, sudden motion. "You all right? You look like you've seen a *dybbuk*." He didn't need a crazy man on his boat for his first mission.

Arkhipov squeezed his eyes shut for a moment, turning slowly back. "I'm fine, just a little tense, but the sea cures all and sets things right. You'll see once we depart."

"You think the squadron commander can twist the doctor's arm to make you well?" the captain demanded.

"For him, it should be an easy twist. The irony is that he'd kill to make this journey, but he's forced to stay behind with the missile boats and the tender." Arkhipov stared at the pier without seeing it as though he watched his dreams rupture and his last chance slip away. "For me, this assignment is a matter of duty and the needs of the navy. I never planned to abandon Russia for another world, but *Rodina-mat' zavyot.* Homeland Mother calls."

"Let me get this right," the captain said, shaking his bushy head from side to side. The doctor will sign a scrap of paper saying you're fit to ride my boat to Lord-knows-where as my *starpom* and serve the brigade commander as his chief of staff at the same time — two masters?"

Arkhipov's tone hardened, "That's right, comrade, the same way he signed your papers stating that you're ready for command. That's how it is."

The captain recoiled again and asked, "You order me to be your captain when you don't even want to go?"

Arkhipov replied, "Operation Kama is big, bigger than our personal problems. We have duties to perform."

"So, it's done?" The captain's gut told him it was all wrong, but it was his first command. The deep mystery captivated his imagination, and his excitement overcame his doubt. He had been chosen and not replaced by some fancy missile boat captain. He would prove that he was worthy. "There can be only one captain aboard this ship. To avoid confusing the crew, when you're on my boat, Captain Arkhipov, we'll call you Starpom. Is that clear?"

"*Da.* It's done. We'll detach from the squadron and the northern fleet and report directly to Moscow, under the command of Admiral Fokin. We'll be fine, God willing."

Chapter Two – Underway

Our voyage began. For the first five days, everything was quiet, the weather was auspicious. But then it became worse, it got to be so that we would feel uneasy if we didn't get drenched once every fifteen to twenty seconds. But we were wearing protective clothing, so Neptune was powerless against us. The sea looked beautiful at night. The water is luminescent this time of the year, especially in the Norwegian Sea... **Lieutenant Anatoly Andreev, Assistant to the B-36 Submarine Commander. A Submarine Sailor's Letter Home, October 1962.**

Freezing fog rolled across black water from the forlorn boneyard of scrapped submarines in Severomorsk and over Captains Valentin Savitsky and Vasili Arkhipov, the *starpom*, standing atop the B-59 open bridge.

"Hell of a thing, leaving home, not knowing where we're heading. Who knows about our mission?" asked the captain, half to himself. "What's the brass concocted this time? Where in the world are they sending us today?"

"Still grousing? Our orders lie in the safe, and there's no turning back from this moment on," Starpom replied. "We'll know soon enough. Nothing more to say."

The captain's grimaced face spat out, "Orders won't tell us why we're bringing a nuke and a kill squad to visit a secret friend. The absurdity of it screams into our faces."

"Aye, it's a maddening mystery, but you'll discover that sea captains never have the answers they need. There's always fog or smoke or some infernal blindness preventing you from seeing what you need to see." Starpom knew the reason, but he was not at liberty to divulge the information to the old man before the appointed hour on their journey.

Changing the subject, Starpom asked, "How did you end up in the navy after Brest?"

Dismissing the question as irrelevant, the captain mumbled, "I lied about my age."

"We all did, but was it your father's idea?"

The captain turned to face his *starpom* and said, "I have no recollection of my parents."

Arkhipov's eyebrows rose as he responded, "You never knew them or you chose to forget?"

"No recollection, and you?"

"My father wanted me to be a farmer, bigger family, bigger plot of land to till. Not my dream. I had to escape, and my mother understood. She sent me away."

"And your father agreed to release you?"

"He decided the Navy would make a man out of me before I returned to the farm. No imagination in that man."

The captain pulled his collar over the wind side of his face and said, "Nice to have parents who want you home when you're on the run, but lacking that, all I want on this gelid morning is to submerge."

Soviet Premier Nikita Khrushchev deployed his submarines under the cloak of secrecy and deception to advance his political agenda, proliferate the socialist revolution, and rectify the international imbalance of military power by replacing it with a balance of fear. No enterprise was too large to undertake, and no detail was too small to manipulate. His sailors were man-boys — conscripts, runaways, adventure seekers, and lifers — bright in a wicked sort of way, filled with lusty enthusiasm, nautical lingo, and a salty, uncivilized, sense of humor.

Their crisp uniforms instilled in them a swagger irresistible to women, and they savored the siren's call for they belonged more to the ocean than to the Motherland.

"Another dark, frigid farewell for our departure," the old man muttered. "A good opportunity for our men to feel cold, wet, and scared. I received your medical appraisal last night. Says you're fit for duty. Are you? Fit for duty?"

"*Da,* you don't believe the report?" Starpom answered the question with a question. "You think I'm crazy, but you know the old saying: The crazies know they're crazy, but the rest of us are undecided." Laughing and guiding the discussion back to the moment at hand, he continued with an assuring smile, "You would be the first to know. Are you ready to take us to the ends of the Earth?"

The captain growled, turned his head, and spit three times over his left shoulder for luck. "Always ready to sail on deadline. Set the special sea detail. Prepare to get underway." Whispered sailor to sailor, the announcement passed by mouth from the quarterdeck at 03:30.

At the outset of their sojourn, the two men could have passed for brothers — handsome, square-jawed, athletic men with coarse, onyx hair, matching widow's peaks, clefts in carved chins, and bushy black eyebrows. Captain Valentin Savitsky appeared older, like the big brother, although they were the same age and rank. Vasili Arkhipov, his unexpected *starpom*, had boarded during the pre-sail pandemonium, still acting as brigade chief of staff, a sniveling, boot-licking position from the old man's viewpoint. When the old man called him Starpom, he said it with a sneer for they were not brothers, and he watched Arkhipov watching him, each man assessing the other. Too many naval officers were drunks like the stricken brigade commander, careless, halfhearted, and lazy, but Arkhipov was different. The old man sensed in him a resolve that needed testing, and he knew how to test a man's balls.

Starpom, son of Alexandr and Mariya Arkhipov, hailed from a peasant farm outside Staraya Kupavna. The Noginsky District of Moscow Oblast had an underground Islamic influence that exposed him to the teachings of the Prophet, terse words with deep meaning. Tall, raw-boned and handsome, he inherited his mother's heart and his father's hands. He joined the navy in 1939 at age thirteen to escape farm collectivization and the horrors of Stalin's first social experiment. Local communist leaders and volunteers from Moscow seized crops and animals for the Motherland and demanded even more from the farmers in their next year's productivity goals. Peasants resisted the government by burying stores in graveyards, burning crops, and slaughtering livestock. The youthful Arkhipov handled extreme situations with a paradoxical combination of forbearance and ferocity, deferring to the *kommissars* who came to call but rebelling with the others when they left. Successful peasants, called *kulaks*, sold their excess products for money and drew Stalin's wrath. He deemed the best farmers to be capitalist enemies of the state, despite their expertise. Staring from his hiding places with revulsion, young Arkhipov had witnessed the attacks. Like rotting produce, *kulaks* were hung from trees near the road to terrorize resisting peasants. Other *kulaks* disappeared by the millions, shipped off to Siberia, and nothing could save them. Many peasants celebrated in secret when Stalin died, hoping in their hearts that he had been murdered. Premier Khrushchev's anti-Stalinist policies provided no relief for peasant farmers as he rose to power.

With little motivation to produce crops that would be seized, the morale and productivity of the surviving, less adept farmers plummeted, and famine set in, not just for the farmers but for the industrial workers who relied on the collective farms for their foodstuffs. The government confiscated farmland, equipment, and seed in accordance with new laws and subjected the farmers to starvation and death. Compared to farm life, the wartime navy seemed a safe and pleasant place to send a boy.

Seaman Arkhipov rode minesweepers while older men fought and died in the Great Patriotic War. The navy replaced his family before his childhood departed, but the desperate plight of Russian farmers haunted him. His resentment simmered anew when he sent half of every meager paycheck to his parents to support their survival.

The old man came from Brest in Belorussia, near the Polish border, with a strong Jewish influence. The Germans attacked Brest in 1939, the year that Arkhipov joined the navy. After four days of bombardment and street battles, the citizens of Brest were forced to watch a Victory Parade that turned their region over to the Soviets under the prearranged Molotov-Ribbentrop non-aggression pact. Two years later, the Nazi's attacked again, driving out the Soviet army and seizing Brest. Thousands of civilians were swept into forced labor details to aid the occupation, but others joined the resistance, guerilla fighting from the forests, inflicting damage to supply lines, railroad tracks, bridges, communications and fuel dumps. They fought alongside the Jews and Russians, and the young Savitsky steeped himself in pessimism as Jews and Russians do. Short for his weight, his underbite evoked the image of a junkyard bulldog.

German army reprisals against the resistance killed civilians by public hangings, mass shootings, and unimaginable massacres in their attempts to establish law and order and prevent sabotage and terrorism. As a boy, Savitsky saw the Jewish population of Brest herded into ghettos, whipped, pillaged, enslaved, deported, and murdered, reduced from thirty thousand souls to only ten hollow survivors by 1944 when the Soviets recaptured the city. Everyone lost everything, and Savitsky left the ruins of the front to join the Soviet navy. Childhood memories of the front lines of war instilled in him a perverse indifference to human suffering. Nothing he could have done would have save them. The sea provided him a sense of freedom and escape, and he embraced the navy as his allegiance and lifelong commitment.

Starpom loved the navy. The captain loved the sea. Both men received naval training and education as they worked through the ranks to meet as unlikely and uneasy shipmates in Murmansk, but Murmansk was over. Months of ball-breaking, hurry-up-and-wait endeavours converged on this moment. Yard birds had closed out the last work orders, and the final loading operations wrapped up with the transfer of dry stores, fresh produce, eggs, milk, bread, and one hundred sixty tropical uniforms. The long hours of preparation for sea distracted them from the most disturbing elements of their mission.

As the days grew short, winter clouds surrounded the peninsula, anxious to close in. It had been a good refit in the Rosta shipyard of Polyarny. The crew had primped and preened the ship for the brass, but time had come to put to sea. September 30, 1962 was the B-59's last Arctic day, a fine day of warm sunshine except for the obfuscation of truth with deception and information deprivation enforced upon the men by their superiors.

While sentries with Kalashnikov rifles stood at parade rest on the dark pier, sailors clamored to their assigned stations amid the icy fog, their clouding breaths hovering like steam over hot tea. The veiled mission, a special ocean voyage to a secret destination, had been announced by the brass at the send-off ceremony, but the details remained hidden from the captains and crews. Noiseless, ghost-gray silhouettes traipsed to their deck assignments, forging a graveyard mirage, shrouded in stone-cold gloom. The anxious chill of an unknown sea gripped the air and the hearts of Captains Arkhipov and Savitsky. The nuke lay in its cradle, sealed orders rested in the safe, and the clock ticked.

The old man trusted no one and longed to slip below the waves, to steal away from the pre-sail turmoil of politics, planning, and redirection. He commanded a diesel submarine in a nuclear world, but nuclear-powered boats were new, unreliable and unsuitable for operational missions. Not knowing if the Admiralty intended to deploy him into combat or slough him off to some third-world country as an anachronistic asset to be abandoned on their beachfront, he hoped the security and secrecy surrounding the B-59's voyage to the unknown would neither endanger his crew nor impair their performance. When he addressed the crew, he had said:

"Tomorrow we embark on a bold adventure. I cannot tell you our destination yet, but our mission is momentous. The voyage may be arduous, but you are ready for any challenge. We carry a special weapon and special forces for the first time in naval history. This is no ordinary operation for ordinary men, but a monumental assignment. You will see." Their eyes radiated pride and intense dedication to the Motherland for they had been chosen.

Arkhipov understood that the special nuclear weapon payload on the four boats of the 69th Torpedo Submarine Brigade converted them into hunter-killer, doomsday machines. Some believed that the greatest tactical advantage emanated from overwhelming force. Others thought that tactical nukes created triggers for an all-out nuclear conflagration. Still others convinced themselves that the nuclear arsenal created the fastest path to lasting peace through the threat of mutual annihilation. It mattered not to Captain Arkhipov under his new title and name, Starpom of the B-59. Responsibility for initiating a massive war or maintaining a tenuous peace delegated itself to a handful of marauding, sea-roving sub captains.

The bilges were dry, sanitary tanks empty, fuel tanks full, batteries charged, and high-pressure air banks at capacity. The whale-sized stores load lay squirreled away, and the all-important ballast compensations were double checked and implemented, neutralizing weight and balancing equipment masses fore and aft by pumping seawater. Diesel engines had been warmed up and shut down, and brine buckets stood by to swash ice off the deck.

"Secure shore power. Shift to the batteries," Starpom ordered, preparing to sail away.

The crew sizzled with excitement, and the sailors shuddered with the lure of adventure, fifty-seven kilometers from the mouth of Kola Bay, where cruel maelstroms awaited them in the Norwegian Sea and beyond. Like beasts straining against their mooring lines, they yearned to venture forth and submerge beneath the surface. Fear of oceans faded, homesickness vanished, broken hearts healed, and all things ashore morphed into trinkets and baubles that distract landlubbers from their lackluster lives.

The sailors' money was gone, blown on women and *vodka*. The sea's spirit tugged at the large muscles in their backs as they hauled in spring lines, thrown into the water by lifeless line-handlers on the pier. Seamen sprang for bolo lines launched from tugs and bent on the tow lines.

"Take in the stern line… take in the bowline," Starpom's voice boomed. "Underway."

Grimy tugboats eased the boat away from the pier, careful not to bump the sensitive sonar sensors stamped into the ship's exterior, leading her out of Sayda Harbor into the open channel. The deck crew scurried to coil hawsers and stow stanchions into the boatswain's locker before the channel chop washed over their feet. Men donned life jackets, harnesses, and safety leashes, standing by to cast off the tow lines and fold cleats back into the superstructure as though they never existed.

Starpom's demons, blackish, formless ghouls, more fearsome than wild iron-toothed witches, evaporated under the onslaught of adrenaline in anticipation of getting underway. Squeezing his eyes shut to fend them off, he stood on the bridge next to the captain, wrapped in his *kanadka,* layered in wool and oilskin, an Arctic foul weather suit adopted from the Canadian merchant marine. Starpom manned the Officer on Deck (OOD) post, and he had the conn, operational control of the ship. All orders from the captain conveyed via him to watch stations, and incoming reports funneled through him to the captain.

"Cast off the tow lines. All-ahead dead slow." Starpom turned to verify that three bronze screws bit and churned the water aft of the boat, propelling the submarine away from the tug and up the deep-water channel of Kola Fjord, bound for open ocean under her own power.

"Right standard rudder. All-ahead one third. Steady on course 005." The B-59 eased up the channel without running lights at low speed. The remaining submarines performed the synchronized water ballet of getting underway. One by one, at thirty-minute intervals, they fell into a majestic procession: B-59, B-36, B-130, and B-4. The diesel engines fired up after Sayda Bay fell behind the promontory. They rolled over, rumbled, and belched trails of smoke that lingered over the fog abaft the boats like black fingers pointing into the stiff wind. Gusts blowing down the channel chopped the surface and teared the eyes with salt spray from wave slap on the bow.

The junior navigator, Victor, manned the navigation periscope on the sheltered deck below the bridge, swinging the reticle port and starboard, taking bearings to lights on shore while the navigator at the chart table plotted the bearing lines to fix the ship's position in the channel. It was time for Victor to take the conn for the first watch.

"Secure the sea detail. Set the underway watch." Starpom sniffed the cold night scent, light and airy, reminiscent of his Olga's Red Moscow perfume, the original bouquet of Chanel Number Five.

"Right standard rudder, steady on 073. All-ahead two thirds." The diesel plume trailing the snorkel mast veered left as the ship swung to starboard, belching greasy black soot on Arkhipov's *kanadka* as Poli, the watcher, climbed the ladder to the conning tower behind Victor.

They called him Poli aboard ship, neither a derogatory nor endearing moniker, but an abbreviation of his title, *zampolit*, deputy political *kommissar* — a mysterious man, rumored to be the bastard child of the infamous General Ivan Ivanovich Maslennikov, former deputy to the Supreme Soviet and member of the Central Committee. The decorated general had enforced Stalin's policies of forced labor *gulags*, mass executions and deportations of entire nationalities and *kulaks* to Siberia. Under investigation for *kompromat*, ugly compromising material, he was subjected to interrogation before his sudden death back in 1954. He committed suicide.

Poli's name was Ivan Semonovich Maslennikov, but he never admitted a connection with his namesake because of the questionable circumstances surrounding the general's death. However, his denials were faint enough to lend credence to the rumors. Poli was a true believer in communal ownership and the absence of class, the Utopian ideal of equality and abundance. "Take from each man in accordance with his ability and provide for each man in accordance with his need," as Marx prescribed. The illusion trumped the truth that he craved association with powerful men and enjoyed the privilege and access of elites in a classless society. His primary purpose aboard ship was to prevent the captain from turning its military might against the state, but the captain was all navy and more inclined to over-obey orders than to turn rogue. Poli did not stand watch. His duties of recruiting communists from the crew, providing indoctrination briefings, and writing performance logs on crew members comprised his daily activities, but he felt nauseous, and he needed fresh air to quell his queasy stomach. "Request permission to come up."

"Come up," he heard the response from the bridge. He uttered *Thank you* in his mind before he cursed aloud. Seasickness had gripped him at "underway."

With the old man, Poli, Victor, and two lookouts glued to their binoculars, the bridge grew crowded. Starpom labored through the watch turnover process with Victor, ticking off the status of the ship's equipment, identifying landmarks onshore, marking the other submarine positions, and reviewing the captain's standing orders. Poli, the ever-present, green-around-the gills, watcher of watchstanders, looked on with the captain.

"Anything else I should know?" Victor double checked, nodding in the direction of Poli and the old man.

"*Nyet.*" Starpom handed his duties and binoculars to Victor as OOD. "I stand relieved."

The captain, satisfied with the turnover, dropped down the ladder into the conning tower and then into the crowded control room below with surprising agility for the old man. The bustling commotion accelerated his heart rate. Starpom followed him to the periscope deck.

"This is Comrade Mikhailov," Victor announced. "I have the conn." He raised his glasses to survey the fjord ahead. The ship ran dark in the black night, punctuated by lighted landmarks along the coast to guide their way. Poli lingered on the bridge to breathe and to appear dignified.

Starpom stole one last look through the periscope at civilization's channel lights on the shores of Kola Bay, shrouded in fog halos, before sliding down into the control room where the old man pored over the channel chart on the navigation table crammed behind the periscope wells.

"Captain, I recommend course 052 on my mark," the navigator spoke out. "Mark."

"OOD, this is the captain," he spoke into the mic. "Come left to 052, full speed ahead, set diving stations."

The third leg of the passage included preparations to dive the boat under the cover of darkness. At dawn, an American U-2 spy plane would photograph empty Sayda Bay piers and alert the Brits and Norwegians to the four missing submarines. On the fourth leg, at the two-hundred-meter depth curve on the glacial-carved floor of Kola Fjord, they would submerge into the submarine underworld to avoid detection by antisubmarine seek-and-destroy forces.

Adversity followed Arkhipov like a loyal dog: the farm, the war, and his prior submarine experiences. He considered it a blessing that emboldened him to dig inside himself in search of strength and wisdom beyond his natural valor and sense of derring-do. He hadn't put to sea for over a year, recuperating from radiation sickness after his previous voyage. Nightmares hounded him with night sweats and debilitating headaches. He kept their secrets inside himself, battling them alone. They tormented him, but never demanded that he do something awful. He was on a submarine again, sailing into the unknown. Arkhipov had tried every trick to avoid the assignment, but when his brigade commander fell ill in response to the Kama briefing, his die was cast. The old man was right. It was a bad omen. When the new brigade commander arrived in Polyarny one day before sailing, there was no escape. As Starpom, he worried that life undersea might trigger more hallucinations, and he wondered how he would react as he wiggled out of his *kanadka* and hunkered next to Poli and the ship's diving officer in the dark, cramped space.

The *starshy michman,* the senior enlisted man and diving officer of the watch, entered the control room and positioned himself behind the helmsman, the bow planes man, and the stern planes man, all seated on a tiny bench, facing the faint control panel lights and gauges.

The speaker squawked, "Bridge, RIS, radio contact bearing 023, designated Echo One."

"Bridge, aye, determine bearing rate," Victor reported the contact to the captain who didn't expect an RIS contact report so early in the egress. Either the contact had penetrated Kola Bay, violating international law, or *Osnaz* had enhanced their electronic detection capability against the US antisubmarine monstrosity.

As Arkhipov had revealed, an *Osnaz* special ops group had boarded the B-59 prior to the voyage. Nine commandos with a suite of radio intercept system (RIS) equipment had piled into the petty officers' mess, the first time that Soviet special forces, organized as independent reconnaissance and sabotage companies tasked to eliminate American nuclear weapons systems, were deployed on submarines. Their officers, specialists, and petty officers were trained for infiltration behind enemy lines, assassination of government leaders and military officers, diving, hand-to-hand combat, use of elite weapons and explosives, underwater demolition, and ground warfare.

"Bridge, RIS, Echo One is drawing right at one degree per minute. Classify as a radio signal from an AGI." AGIs were Norwegian intelligence ships, modified sealers, stuffed with modern equipment, sponsored by the CIA and operated by American specialists.

It was only yesterday that the *Osnaz* commandos had roared up to the nested submarines in four two-and-a-half ton GAZ-52 trucks with white fluted grills, bookended by high-beam headlights under flashing, amber indicators.

Nine officers and men leaped from beneath the canvas covers behind the cabs of each vehicle and assembled at the gangway of each boat. Had they not passed through three layers of security, the captains might have thought they were under attack.

"Senior Lieutenant Vadim Pavlovich Orlov reporting for duty," said a child-faced officer, standing at attention and saluting. "Permission to come aboard."

As the old man strode down the gangway, approaching the formation like the shadow of a cloud passing the moon, Orlov extended his file folder of orders. He accepted the transfer package, inspecting the contents for omissions or errors that would allow him to reject the troupe from his boat, but these were not routine personnel assignments. The files of orders were vague and vacuous, but the paperwork was impeccable. He inspected the squad of nine young men, fit, confident, and determined, without a hint of intimidation. "These orders say that your team is required to maintain security on my submarine for the duration of the mission. How the hell will you ensure our security?"

"Radio intercepts, electronic surveillance, and intelligence," Orlov responded. "Our specialization. Your electronics mast was upgraded during the refit for our modern surveillance radio intercept system. We'll provide enhanced tactical and strategic information for the patrol."

"What have you got, secret ears?" The old man detested the never-ending flurry of surprises.

"Receivers and amplifiers in the truck. We need to set up in a secure operating space. Top Secret."

The old man grimaced. "Every damned thing about this voyage is Top Secret. With members of the brigade staff on board, we already suffer from overpopulation and severe space shortage. Ever sailed on a submarine?"

"*Nyet*, Comrade Captain," the youthful lieutenant said with a confident, no-problem enthusiasm.

The dubious old man had no choice but to welcome the mysterious, elite, special purpose commandos aboard the B-59 despite his loathing of spooks on his ship.

Eying Orlov with deep suspicion, he announced, "Submarine life stinks. You'll inhale horrible smells and produce a few yourself. Prior to boarding, lead your men to the toilet on the pier and conduct your business. Report to the *starpom* for orientation, assignment of watch and battle stations, and hot bunk rotations. Your team will spend the night installing your equipment. Leave non-essential gear on the truck. Your team will report to the *starshy michman*, who will qualify them to use the head on board."

"The *starshy michman*, Comrade Captain?"

"The *starshy michman* is the ship's chief petty officer. He'll train your commandos to crap on a sub. Your station name will be RIS for Radio Intercept System, and I will call you Oz, short for *Osnaz*. That is all." The captain wheeled around and stomped up the gangway, returning Starpom's salute and making his way to the next evolution, the special torpedo loadout.

Starpom welcomed the men aboard and summoned the *starshy michman* to the quarterdeck. He watched them disappear, one by one through the forward deck hatch like the fresh young faces from his previous ship, excited to get underway and inhaling the overpowering odor of diesel fuel that no one else noticed any longer. Starpom wondered how they would impact the voyage but knew that they would never see the world the same again. At Starpom's urging,

Oz's team confiscated the petty officers' mess, between the galley and medical room, for the B-59's RIS station.

The most experienced man on the boat, the *starshy michman,* viewed Oz's team as joy riders and sightseers. He issued each man a hefty qualification manual that required them to trace and memorize communications, electrical, mechanical, hydraulic, water, sewage, weapons, and pressurized air systems lodged within the pressure hull, the people tank. The chief toured them throughout the boat, demonstrating how to slide through watertight doors without damaging knees or skulls.

"Submarines do not fail safely," he said. "They fail catastrophically. Like a helicopter, a submarine is a flying rock, and when things go wrong, it will drop like a stone unless the humans on board take immediate actions to regain control of the craft." The chief gave his standard lecture for the newcomers, "If a solo man is trapped alone within a compartment, he must enact precise commands to close valves or secure power without any question about which device among the maze of choices is correct."

To emphasize his point, the chief led them through valve wheel alley, a narrow passageway lined with over thirty valve wheels, color coded blue, red, black and yellow, and stopped at the head, a grimy red toilet surrounded by a snake pile of pipes, valves, gauges, hoses, and wire bundles from deck to overhead and a small sink.

As the nine commandos peered over each other's shoulders at the ugly manhole, the chief announced, "Gentlemen, the procedure for operating the head begins by verifying that the ball valve is not tagged out. If the ball valve is tagged out, do not use the head because we are blowing sanitary tanks, or you will join the high-pressure air club and wear your shipmate's turds embedded in your hide for the duration of the patrol. Ensure the ball valve is closed; close the drainage gate valve; open the water valve and fill the bowl to five centimeters, no more; close the water valve; use the head; open the ball valve to drain the bowl; close the ball valve; open the water valve; fill the bowl to two centimeters; close the water valve; open the ball valve; close the ball valve; open the drainage head valve; wash your hands. Any questions?"

Perplexed and overwhelmed by the endless trivia required to defecate, the commandos stared at each other until Oz glanced at his senior petty officer, giving him an imperceptible nod to say, "Time to step in and save us all."

"Could you please repeat the protocol?" he said. Word for word, the chief ran through the procedure, only faster. Oz did not try to memorize the procedure, but he visualized the exact system and the precise purpose of each action in the sequence. He got it as he internalized the complexity and discipline required for submarine duty.

"Thank you, chief. Excellent presentation. Let's move on. We have a mission ahead."

The bearing rate of the AGI spy ship indicated that she had not yet detected the submarines' egress from Kola Bay, and the captain had to submerge before the intruder sensed a solid radar return off his sub's sail. He dared not communicate to the other subs for fear of detection by the AGI's high frequency, direction finding (HF/DF) gear.

"This is the captain, clear the bridge."

Reacting to the order, the *starshy michman* moved to his dive station, and the conning crew lowered the periscope and slid down the ladder into the belly of the boat. Victor, the last man down, grabbed the frozen chain on the hinged manhole cover, wiped the watery ice off the hatch seal, and dogged it tight before descending into the rigged-for-red lighting of the control room.

The *starshy michman* said to the helmsman and planes men seated before him, "Good morning my young buccaneers. I'll be your *ded*, your military grandfather, for our journey. Do as I say with precision, and we'll put our fighting ship through her paces. Ready to dive?"

"*Da*, comrade," they responded in unison, sitting shoulder-to-shoulder, knee-to-knee in the red glow.

"Prepare to dive," the captain spoke into the mic that broadcast his pronouncement throughout the boat.

Submarines glide in slow motion. They cross the threshold from the ocean surface into the depths of obscurity and revert to stealth, maintaining radio and sonar silence, in pursuit of dangerous duty assignments. National leaders, military advisors, and admirals suppress details of undersea operations while thirty-five-year-old commanding officers execute provocative missions. Submarine captains enforce absolute discipline as they roam beneath the sea, blind and incommunicado. Passive listening systems, called *Arktika*-M sonar suites, warn of other ships. Navigators, behind closed doors, provide own-ship's position to only a handful of men on the sub. Should they sink, no one would know when, where, or why, only that they never returned.

The old man itched to submerge, to guide his crew from their land lives into the insular submarine underworld where life hung in suspense and time no longer mattered. They existed only in their subsea hovel, in their collective mind, and in the memories of those they left behind. Diving safety protocol required two hundred meters of depth to allow reaction time in case of loss of depth control and the possibility of rescue for submarines that hit bottom.

"Switch to battery propulsion, secure the diesels," the captain commanded the OOD to initiate the dive sequence. "Extend the bow planes and lower all masts."

Diving the submarine involved performing complex executions, dangerous and difficult to recover if things went awry. Valves and hatches were rendered watertight, masts lowered and secured, propulsion shifted from diesel to electric, diesel engines shut down and secured, air vented from main ballast tanks to allow seawater into the tanks, bow planes depressed to press the bulbous nose into the sea and stern planes pointed up to lift the tail until the ship pointed downward in search of ordered depth. Starpom and Poli surveyed the closed confines, wrapped in low-hanging cable runs, valve wheels and ducting from under the red light between the periscope wells in the cramped control room with the ship's diving officer who had conducted the final ballast calculations. Starpom watched the gauges, and Poli watched the crew.

The OOD took charge. "Secure the radio watch. RIS, report the last bearing of Echo One."

"Echo One bearing zero three two, drawing right at two degrees per minute."

The Norwegians had already suspected submarine activity, and the captain marveled at the intercepted signals.

"Lower the electronics mast. Secure the RIS watch. Secure the diesels." The boat quieted as the throbbing diesels shut down and air circulation in the control room ceased to flow.

"Depth below the keel." The captain was impatient. The report came back, "192 meters."

Close enough. "Take her down to fifty meters." The old man could wait no longer.

Victor was ready, and he believed that the ship guaranteed safe passage for their precious cargo.

"Aye, aye. Sound the diving alarm. Make your depth fifty meters," he ordered.

The chief took charge, reaching for his mic and the diving alarm. The klaxon sounded. *Aah-ooh-gah. Aah-ooh-gah.* "Dive, dive. Bow planes ten degrees down. Open the flood valves. Open the forward vents. Open the aft vents."

On the empty deck of the B-59, awash in sea scud, twelve white spouts shot into the air like whale blows fore and aft, and the bow dipped into the water. "Ten degrees down angle." All noises ceased as the boat responded to commands and dived into the oppressive subsea silence. Starpom focused on the depth gauge as the stern planes man reported the keel depth, "Twenty meters…thirty meters." The B-59 immersed with noticeable ease and grace, unlike Starpom's previous boat that wallowed like a pig in a mud puddle.

The chief sensed the problem before anyone else. The dive was too smooth, too accommodating to be normal. His instincts screamed that the B-59 was heavy and threatened, and he needed to make her neutrally buoyant, or she might sink. He closed the vents and raised his voice.

"Emergency procedures. All-ahead full. Blow the forward group. Zero the stern planes. Bow planes full up." He tugged the high-pressure air valve and initiated the emergency blow. *Chee-ta-kah.* Air rushed into the forward ballast tanks, pushing seawater out the bottom flood grates it had just entered. The screws cavitated, generating noisy bubbles that shook the boat from the stern as it accelerated toward the bottom.

"Forty meters…fifty meters," the stern planes man reported. "Ten degrees down angle."

The captain moved behind the chief, eyes agog, watching the maestro conduct his operatic performance to snatch the boat from harm's way. The chief was far ahead of him, and he knew not to interrupt his chain of vigorous actions to lift the bow, to arrest the plunge into the fjord floor, and to save his ship. His heart pounded in his head as they fell through fifty meters.

"Sixty meters…seventy meters. Fifteen degrees down angle."

The chief engaged the trim pumps to drain the forward trim tanks into the sea. His mouth dried out. With increasing velocity, the boat slid downhill while the bow planes strained to hoist the nose, gaining power with the additional flow over their surfaces. The air bubble in the forward ballast tanks added lift. "Stern planes full up."

"Eighty meters…ninety meters. Fourteen degrees down angle."

No one other than the chief, not Starpom, a man of resolute courage, and not the captain, a man of absolute action, had detected the danger. Their minds raced to fathom the unforeseen condition as their hearts pumped adrenaline through their mortified bodies. Poli's ashen face stared open-mouthed at the animated execution of the emergency procedures. He was the last to comprehend the peril that enveloped the boat, but the first to imagine drowning in a watery grave. Victor trembled. The chief focused on solving the problem, saving his ship and his shipmates, ignoring everyone except his planes men.

"One hundred meters…one hundred ten meters. Ten degrees down angle," the bow planes man reported. The hull groaned and popped as it compressed under the pressure of rapid descent.

"One hundred twenty meters. Zero angle." The chief saw that the protocol was working, but it was too early to ease back.

"Thirty degrees up angle," the chief ordered the boat to its maximum stable parameters.

"One hundred thirty meters. We have ten degrees up angle." Wiping his sweating nose with an arm swipe, the chief checked his gauges and turned to glimpse the old man's black brow overhanging his dark eyes and jutting chin. Everyone glistened with perspiration, except Poli whose blanched face mimicked spinal shock. "One hundred forty meters, twenty degrees up angle." The chief worried that he might exceed thirty degrees and sink by the stern.

"Zero the stern planes. Maintain thirty degrees up angle," he ordered. Everyone simultaneously leaned forward and took hold of a cable or pipe in the overhead. The *Osnaz* crew slid into the aft bulkhead on the RIS bench seat, tangling arms, legs and torsos. Resounding crashes rang out within the people tank; objects not bolted or strapped down rolled off no-longer-horizontal surfaces and hit the deck like severed heads.

Starpom's breaths came in spurts. His head ached, and his ghouls ganged up on him, swimming in the engine room, calling his name, begging with bubbled sounds for release. Starpom saw them coming, as they did day and night. He hated that he couldn't prevent their onslaught and that he couldn't speak of it to anyone. Ignoring their ghastly incantations, he had taught himself to squeeze his eyes shut and will them back into his repository for unspeakable things. Starpom forced himself to concentrate on the impending catastrophe.

"Come on, beautiful girl," the chief spoke directly to the boat. "I give you everything you need. Don't let me down. Work for me." The ship moaned as opposing forces stressed her back.

The old man clenched is teeth, watching the gauges and madly calculating the rate of descent, the acceleration, and the ship's angle. "Brace for impact."

Poli sputtered, "I soiled myself."

"One hundred fifty meters. Twenty-five degrees up angle," the stern planes man reported. His hand cramped as he jiggered the plane's stick, easing off the maximum plane angle, seeking the right setting to hold the thirty degrees up angle. He applied both hands to steady the stick.

"Don't lose the bubble son, make small changes," the chief cautioned.

Employing trial and error, undershooting and then adding more planes angle, the young sailor figured it out. "One hundred sixty meters." The boat's up angle slowed the ship's speed and rate of descent as the hull provided lift. "Thirty degrees up angle," came the report.

"One hundred seventy meters. Steady at thirty degrees up angle," the planes man gasped.

The chief stared at the depth gauge as it slowed and settled at 178. He paused, breathing deep breaths for a long moment before he looked back at the old man and gave him a wink.

"Captain, steady at 178 meters, proceeding to one hundred meters," the chief announced.

"Very well. As you were," the captain whispered, breathing an audible sigh, repeated by every man in the control room. Pumping water and easing the ship's angle, the chief made minute adjustments as the B-59 began to rise. When the planes man pushed the bow planes to full down to maintain the boat's up angle, he opened the ballast tank vents momentarily to leak some air and take in water.

After thirty minutes of coaxing the ship away from the sea floor, he reported to the captain and all who heard his voice, "Holding steady at one hundred meters. I need another hour to trim the ship, recommend all-ahead two-thirds." He needed to balance the waterborne teeter-totter.

"Good work," said the captain. He turned to the OOD. "Reduce speed to two-thirds and follow the *starshy michman's* speed recommendations as he trims the boat."

Victor's voice broke like a poltergeist suspended in the death moment, "All-ahead two-thirds." Slowing the speed reduced the planes' effective lift. Victor feared another loss of depth control, but the chief needed to sense the ballast condition to achieve absolute neutral buoyancy by distributing weight and fine-tuning the ballast placement for safety's sake.

"Knock your balls together so we can hear you." The old man needed a punching bag.

"Aye, aye, Comrade Captain," Victor repeated the command in a stronger voice.

Grinning and unaware of the severe jeopardy, Oz burst into the control room. "We nailed that AGI. I told you we'd enhance your classification capabilities."

His yes bulging, the captain pivoted to face him and jabbed his index finger into Oz's forehead. In his command voice, he said, "You tell me nothing, sailor. Dismissed."

"Aye, aye, captain." The words tasted bitter on Oz's tongue as he turned to leave, surprised at how the captain's command presence cowed him into submission. He and his men were stealthy, tough and lethal. They knew their strengths, and they had proven themselves, despite their flaws, mastering their emotions and pushing themselves to the limit. Yet, the sheer force of the captain's aggressive will intimidated him.

The captain turned to Victor, "When the chief finishes trimming the ship, set the submerged underway watch and rig ship for regime quiet. Starpom, huddle with the diving officer and figure out what damn near killed us."

The old man stumped to his private stateroom, halfway between the control room and the torpedo room, and his mind bolted before him as the weight of command responsibility slammed him into his chair. Near-death experiences accompanied submarine service. *We train, we focus, and we survive, but near misses expose the truth.* He considered the consequences. *We could have jammed ninety men, a submarine, and a nuclear weapon into the · mud.* His fists tightened into knots for he had handed a heroic moment to his *starshy michman* who would become a savior to the crew. Rumors would sweep the ship: the captain choked, and the chief saved the day. He needed to deal with the aftermath. Spies surrounded him. Poli would start a file, *Osnaz* eyes peered around every corner, and the brigade commander had installed Starpom, his chief of staff, because he didn't trust the new captain in the brigade. The old man needed a diversion, another opportunity for heroism. It was time to open the sealed orders.

Victor finished his watch. Poli rushed to his stateroom to cleanse himself, and the crew recovered and changed into middies, pullover jerseys and blue lightweight cotton trousers akin to heavy-duty pajamas, suitable for life in a climate-controlled shell with limited space. Starpom labored with the diving officer who insisted that his calculations were correct and verified by the captain. After investigating for an hour, they solved the mystery and set out to make their report to the captain, wedging themselves into the old man's cozy, wood-trimmed stateroom with space for only two men to stand next to his bunk.

"Captain, we verified the ballast calculations, as you did, but the baseline data seem to be flawed. Tank levels were forty thousand kilograms heavier than any previous tank levels in the log. The tank level indicators failed. We checked with the chief, and he saw the problem as he emptied the trim tanks." Starpom handed the ballast log to the old man for inspection. He studied the book for several minutes, flipping back and forth among the pages.

The old man looked up. "The depth indicator is located amidships. By my calculations, at a thirty-degree up angle, our screws were kicking up silt at two hundred meters. Had we hit a rock, we could have broken one of our shafts and ripped it out of the back of the boat, a nonsurvivable condition. The little things will kill us at sea — doing the wrong thing, thinking it's right. You never know who will save your life on a submarine."

"I recommend that we mask over the tank level indicators so that only the flow meters are available for measuring ballast. The diving officer can make the changes," Starpom suggested.

"Make it so. We will discuss the incident later when we prepare the report. Dismissed."

The old man waited until the diving officer stepped out before saying, "Starpom, please stay. Close the door." Starpom complied with his request. As the door shut, the captain said, "Poli cracked under pressure."

"He was too close to disaster and gave in to his fears. Perhaps the trauma will transform him, give him some pride and courage," Starpom offered, rethinking his own internal weakness. "No one will fear him now."

"We could use a better man. Can't expect him to sprout attributes he doesn't possess. Can't hand him more crisis than he can manage." The captain had no use for weakness. "Keep your eye on him when things get rough."

Starpom thought for a moment before saying, "The Prophet says, 'Trust in Allah, but tie your camel.'"

"Ha. That's a good one. You believe in the Prophet?" the captain queried.

"The Prophet is historical fact. Whether he is the Prophet of Truth or the Prophet of rumor, I cannot say."

The captain mused, "I thought we were sunk. A few seconds' delay and we'd be with the Prophet. It was like plummeting with ninety dead men in an iron coffin, and the chief was the only living man on board. I felt like a specter hovering over our demise. Sounds crazy. I've seen death first hand during the Great War, but not my own death. This was personal, internal yet remote."

Starpom searched the old man's eyes, rethinking how his own revenants distorted the reality of the near catastrophe at the most crucial moment. He said, "A glimpse of the nothingness of non-existence is never crazy, but it drives some men insane. In that moment we lived more than we ever lived before, but control is your illusion. Sure, you exert your will, but other forces act against you."

The captain leaned forward and looked at his shoes. "You seemed to have your specters under control."

Starpom responded a little too quickly, "I don't believe in ghosts."

"No?" asked the captain. "You think I don't know how it is with you, that I have no experiences in my past? Call them what you will, but I know."

Taken aback by the turn of the conversation, Starpom stuttered, "This is different."

"Yes, of course, you're so special, so unaffected," the captain said, looking up from his shoes. "Be honest with me and with yourself. It's always different except when it's the same."

"I don't discuss all of my thoughts, but I will tell you that I don't fear death any longer."

"Really? You're at peace with your life's purpose, nothing left to change, nothing more to do? You're prepared to die for your country?"

"The exact opposite. Let others die for their country. The meaninglessness of death fills me with life and the will to struggle through the last moment with hope and faith. I've met the monster that'll drag me to my grave, but the thing I've learned is that the best way to know another man is to see death with him."

The captain pointed at the deck and said, "It wasn't hope and faith that kept us from slamming the bottom."

"True, but hope and faith prevented every man from giving up, except maybe Poli. The room was thick with it."

"So, you think we saw death?" The captain's eyes rose. "You think we all saw death together?"

Starpom paused before responding, "Some did. Others will be skeptical, unable to imagine mortality. You said yourself, 'ninety dead men in an iron coffin,' but the chief saw only a dangerous condition needing corrective action. More crazy situations will arise. They always do."

"*Da,*" the captain shook his burly head. "The chief's heroics and the men he saved can never be revealed. There will be no report on our loss of depth control." He looked up and added, "We'll never discuss it."

"The chief did his duty. There are no heroes, only men of purpose who arise when they are called to action," said Starpom. "It's your choice what to report. You decide what's important, what's mission critical. I'll congratulate the chief on a nice piece of seamanship."

The old man ground his heel into the deck. "Good. Fetch Poli. Meet me in the wardroom," he said, raising his eyes to meet Starpom's determined expression. There was nothing more to discuss, "It's time to open our orders."

An aurora borealis bloomed over Kola Bay and rolled across the water, flashing fiery flecks on white-capped waves. The B-59 veered west into the Norwegian Sea, into its assigned sector and depth band to avoid collisions with other subs in the brigade. She was blind in the baffles, deafened by her own-ship's noise in the aft quadrant. The AGI pressed her search, but her radars and HF/DF screens showed no contacts. The brigade had disappeared like Beluga *vodka*.

Side View of Project 641 Attack Submarine (NATO Designation: "Foxtrot")

(By Mike1979 Russia - Own work, CC BY-SA 3.0,
https://commons.wikimedia.org/w/index.php?curid=9880063)

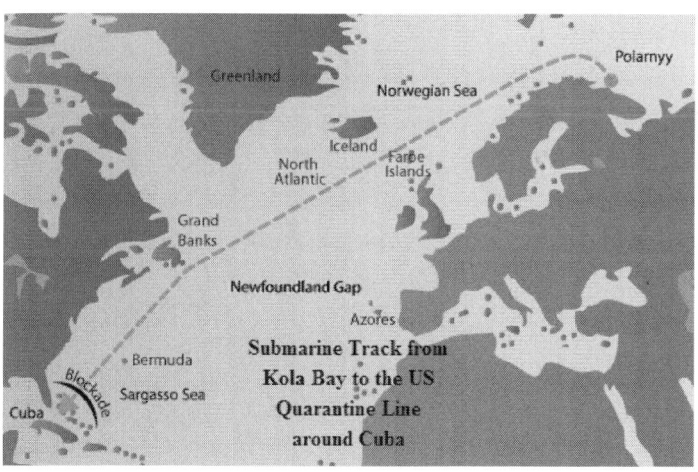

Soviet 69th Torpedo Brigade Track from Kola Bay to

the US Quarantine (Blockade) Line

Chapter Three – Cuba

Commander in Chief, US Atlantic Fleet, (CINCLANTFLT) directs increased readiness to execute an invasion of Cuba. On October 1, CINCLANT orders military units to increase their readiness posture to execute Oplan 312, the airstrike on Cuba. With the new orders, the pre-positioning of troops, aircraft, ships, and other equipment and supplies are directed to increase readiness to follow an airstrike with a full invasion of the island using one of two US invasion plans... **CINCLANT Historical Account of Cuban Crisis, 4/29/63, p. 40.**

"Cuba?" The captain slammed his fist on the wardroom table. "Should've figured. Cuban rumors ran wild like an unleashed lie. I never believed it, even when they loaded those tropical girly pants on board. I was sure that it was Africa. What the hell do we know about Cuba?"

Not knowing infuriated him, leaving him no basis for decision-making, and the old man bellowed when he got angry. An iron man and star hockey player, he approached life as he approached the game, with training, preparation, and on-the-fly tactics. He knew each player's position on the ice, their strengths, their weaknesses, and how they moved. He knew where the puck was going, and that's where he was heading. As a natural leader who accepted responsibility, he sweated the details, and his shibboleth was "Keep Attacking." Always wanting to be on the front line, he researched his missions in relentless detail, gathering intelligence, studying charts, and assessing recon data.

Captain Savitsky was rough on his men for their own good. If anyone suggested that he was too tough, he would retort, "No, I've been too soft." Still, he had a big heart and protected his flock as though they were his children. He knew with certainty that his way was best.

Still jittery over his encounter with death and accustomed to the extreme quiet of the silent service, Poli jumped at the fist noise. Starpom leaned back in the wooden bench seat and sat with his hands folded on his lap. They had opened the communications safe together and extracted the double-wrapped, sealed packet that bore wide red stripes to signify the secrecy of its contents. Starved for information, the captain opened the inner package to take the first look at the orders in the bound booklet labeled "Kama" in large black letters.

"A playground for American gangsters under Batista," Poli spoke. Funny looking by any standard, his crooked teeth exaggerated his smirk, and one of his ears, lower than the other, folded over like a shepherd puppy. One eye wandered, so he squinted to focus. He had no feel for the truth, but he smiled when everyone got along. "Fidel Castro led a glorious revolution two years ago to throw them out. Thousands died for Cuba. Castro said, 'History will absolve me.'"

The captain scrutinized Poli and asked, "What are their industries? What's their source of national pride?"

"None that I know of," replied Poli.

"No industry, no laborers, no pride? Where are the Communists? Not much of a revolution. Sounds to me like the whores took over the whorehouses." The old man waved him off. "Starpom, what do you know about Cuba?" Poli slumped, feeling the ridicule as his destiny.

Arkhipov leaned forward. A quiet man with piercing eyes, hazel with gold flecks that sparkled in the light, his intelligence and instant recall of vast knowledge made him a fierce competitor. As a voracious reader with a keen memory, he handled difficult challenges with an aplomb that other men envied. He never angered, remaining calm and cheerful in the face of danger or treachery, and carried himself with confidence, certainty, and able-bodied farm strength. Arkhipov was a masterful chess player whose style incorporated analysis of his adversary, observing every move and building a mental profile of the man across the table. Never underestimating his competition, he allowed his opponent to reveal himself before moving in for the kill when the beleaguered man faltered. A consummate professional, interesting and easy to like, his only desires were to exorcize his voracious demons, survive the mission, and return home someday.

"Never studied Cuba. Never important," said Starpom, thinking, but not saying, *sounds like they swapped an unequal distribution of wealth for an equal distribution of misery.*

The captain continued, "We sail to Mariel Bay to establish a new submarine home base on a backwater island full of whores and peasants with zero situational awareness. It's madness. Why the secrecy? Why *Osnaz*? Why that damned nuke? What the hell is happening in Cuba?"

Starpom knew the scenario. Prior to embarking on the B-59, he had been briefed by the admirals and sworn to secrecy with the new brigade commander in the classified conference room with the long green table aboard the *Dmitry Galkin*. He had found himself staring at the lineup of his chain of command, grizzled, steely-eyed, and bleak in black dress blue uniforms, red shoulder boards, and gold stars as if he were standing before a murder board.

"Please sit next to our new brigade commander." Admiral Fokin took charge of the meeting, "This is a top-secret briefing. No notes and you are not authorized to divulge any knowledge of the contents to anyone. Do you understand?" The admiral leaned and farted.

"*Da*, Comrade Admiral," both captains responded together, suppressing their laughter.

When the flatulent admiral completed his briefing, he stood, and the officers shot out of their chairs. The admiral extended his hand, "Good luck comrades and smooth sailing. *Do svidaniya*." The admiral departed with his entourage, but the brigade commander, Captain First Rank Vasili Naumovich Agafonov, remained behind and closed the door for a private talk.

"Vasya," he called Arkhipov by his nickname for they shared the same given name Vasili, meaning protector or guardian. "It's a pleasure to meet you and to serve with you. We have a great responsibility and high honor to lead this mission. Few men have your experience with nuclear power at sea. Your wisdom will serve the Motherland well in this delicate and dangerous enterprise." He studied Arkhipov's expression. "I once sailed a burning sub out of Polyarny to prevent it from exploding the town. I know crisis, and I know how you feel. You'll be fine." He let the words sink in before he continued.

"Our ghastly memories guide us through new catastrophes. Resist launching the nuclear torpedo. You must be certain that you have verifiable orders, or if war breaks out, that there is no option. Captain Savitsky is a hard man and an exceptional leader. I'd want no other man in a shooting war, but we are not in a shooting war, so defer to him in all things except for using the special torpedo. His *zampolit* will crumble under pressure, so you must be certain." Arkhipov understood that Agafonov wanted to keep control of the nukes in his own hands when he added, "A bad peace is better than a good quarrel."

"*Yest,* Comrade Commander."

"Good, someone will finish packing your office. The brigade is moving from Polyarny to the piers on Sayda Bay for the special weapons loadout. I am required to escort you to the B-59 as I board the B-4, and we are restricted to the subs until we get underway. You understand we must take every precaution to maintain *maskirovka.*" Captain Agafonov, the brigade commander, reached out and shook Arkhipov's hand. "You'll be fine. Just keep seven meters below the keel."

Arkhipov pulled his thoughts back to Savitsky's query and his slight against peasants, saying "Like the peasants, we don't know what to expect." Searching for the words to avoid revealing what he had sworn to secrecy, he dodged the old man's question, "It seems that the life before us is not the one we planned. We should check with Oz. Those *Osnaz* guys are plugged in and must know something to help us understand what we're up against."

"Can't trust those spooks. They're not us," the captain said, reluctant to rely on *Osnaz.* "They're all rules, no mercy, living on lies and *maskirovka.*"

"True, but what choice do we have? They need a vast reserve of truth to live on lies, and rules can be bent. Why else are they here? Spies can work for you and help us. We can hear what they have to say before we decide what we believe. No harm in listening like submariners."

The old man glared at Starpom and said, "As long as we don't become their useful idiots, we'll listen."

Starpom turned to Poli and said, "Please break Lieutenant Oz out of his rack and ask him to join us." Poli rose and left to fetch the spy, happy to escape the tension.

"Can't trust Poli," the captain fumed and tapped his forefinger on the table for emphasis. "He's hollow in his core. Acts like a socialist, but he'd sell his sister for a stolen mule. Oz is a professional liar, real trouble, and I can't even trust you, an agent of our brigade commander."

"You need an assistant that you can trust," Starpom reacted in calm, flat tones. "You're the reason I'm here and not at home with my wife. You're the newest captain in the brigade, on your first mission as commanding officer. The others are proven, trusted *chempiony*. Captain Ketov is on his second command, so the brigade commander, rides with him. Captain Dubivko is an engineering standout, so the brigade weapons officer rides with him. Captain Shumkov is a weapons expert. He fired two nuclear torpedo tests from his boat. The brigade engineer rides with him. You're the new guy, a *chempion* in your own right, on the fast track to admiral. One of the first men on Earth to carry a nuclear torpedo to an operational mission. They could have chosen me, but they chose you. Take pride in your rise to command, but nobody wants to ride with the new guy. With all due respect, comrade, my job is to help you get to our new home alive. I am your *starpom* and the chief of staff for your brigade commander. We're a *troika*. My job is to help you succeed, and you will trust me in time."

Starpom considered his remarks. It was true that he intended to help the old man succeed, but what he needed was to vanquish his inner demons and make his way back home to Olga. He had put the *kulak* specters behind him by throwing himself into his naval career, but he prayed for their tortured souls every time he sat down to a meal. The dead young sailors of his prior submarine were different. They were dead before they died, and he knew they knew it. A man was never meant to stare into the void of his own death before his own appointed hour.

"They've ordered us to arrive in twenty days, covert and undetected," the captain lowered his voice. "It's too fast. We won't be able to snorkel. We'll have to run all day submerged at full speed, draining the batteries only to risk full exposure on the surface every night using three noisy diesels for propulsion and to recharge the batteries; we'll be sonar and radar pigeons for American submarine hunters. I can't understand why the Admiralty would jeopardize the mission by keeping their commanding officers in the dark. We're on the front line. We don't need a damned blindfold. We need sound information to make proper decisions."

"We just need to evade Norwegian search parties and get to the North Atlantic," whispered Starpom.

"Don't be fooled." The captain worked the muscles in his jaw and said, "I've seen these devils before, and it's not that easy. Their mothers are Viking whores, and their uncle's name is Sam. I want you to stand watch. I need someone to trust when I sleep. We must report our secret codes to Moscow at our assigned waypoints, so they can monitor our progress. They need solid information, too."

"As I said, your success is my job." Starpom passed his first test. "Whatever you need."

Oz entered the wardroom, admiring Arkhipov's perfect spit curl above his forehead as he rubbed his hand over his own batch of bedhead. Oz resembled a weasel with beady eyes, a pencil-thin mustache, and a pointed nose. His youthful mannerisms betrayed his tendency to lock his jaws onto a mission and not let go. "Good evening, comrades. How can I help?"

"We've just opened the sealed orders for our mission," the captain said.

"So, we're discussing Cuba?" Oz stopped, taken aback by the snapping heads and shocked expressions. "They didn't brief you? *Osnaz* read us into Operation Anadyr so we could train for our mission." The Kama packet hadn't mentioned Operation Anadyr.

"What is your mission, Lieutenant Oz?" The captain's tone hardened.

"I'll disembark in Mariel Bay with my team and report to General Pliyev, commander of all Soviet Forces in Cuba, to establish electronic listening posts that can feed intelligence to him during the invasion."

"Invasion?" The old man hated his own ignorance. "Who do we invade during Operation Anadyr?"

"*Nyet, nyet*. The American invasion of Cuba. It's no secret. Ambassador Gromyko confronted them two weeks ago at the United Nations. Of course, they denied it, but there's a boatload of naval activity in south Florida to prove they're lying. The Americans are planning to invade Cuba."

"So, how will your electronic intelligence help to repel an invasion?" the captain pressed him.

"We'll support troop movements, anti-aircraft missiles, tactical nuclear weapons, and even nuclear ballistic missile launches." Oz worked hard to be helpful, but his audience sank deeper into confusion and dismay as he spoke. They needed to know what he knew. "Let me explain Operation Anadyr to you. The Kremlin inserted sixty ballistic missiles with megaton warheads into Cuba, a third of which could reach Los Angeles. Can you imagine? It changes everything."

"That's six thousand Hiroshima bombs of firepower sitting ninety miles from Miami." Starpom made a mental calculation, "Or one hundred Hiroshima bombs per city for sixty cities."

"There's more," Oz continued. "They've also sent tens of thousands of combat troops, anti-aircraft batteries, fighter planes and bombers, and almost one hundred tactical nuclear weapons. Everything will be operational by the end of the month. We'll meet their invasion of Cuba with overwhelming force and a crippling, knock-out punch that could bring the destruction of America. Admiral Fokin and General Zakharov dreamed up Operation Kama for naval support to Operation Anadyr with Khrushchev's approval." Oz paused, searching the old man's face for understanding. "The plan is so much larger than the deployment of the 69th Torpedo Submarine Brigade. Operation Kama, the naval deployment to Mariel Bay, is just a small piece of Anadyr. Rumor has it that when Premier Khrushchev learned that American Jupiter missiles were manned and ready in Italy and Turkey, he exclaimed, 'Why not throw a hedgehog into Uncle Sam's pants?' That's how he left it for his military planners to take this fight to the Americans."

"How do submarines join that fight?" The old man wondered how he fit into this plan.

"There are submarines, and there are targets. You shoot the targets carrying the invading American soldiers. Cuba is under our protection. You keep the invaders away from their shores."

"What do the Americans know about this Soviet incursion into Cuba?" the captain asked.

"War is deception. Our blankets of information denial and deceit are more brilliant and complex than Anadyr itself. We're spreading so much fake information, we're annihilating the US analysis capabilities to see the truth before their eyes. We lie, and lie about the lies, and lie about the lies we're lying about, an artful science to weave the lies with enough truth so they're indistinguishable. It's *maskirovka*, and our enemy knows nothing. Operation Anadyr sent a hundred ships with missiles and soldiers in checkered farm shirts into Cuba under the pretense of embargo-busting with shipments disguised as humanitarian deliveries of food and farm equipment. Our adversaries have nothing to confirm any suspicions they may have. Nothing. It's the greatest conquest in Soviet history."

The old man sensed in Oz an overenthusiasm for the mission. "Why did you join *Osnaz*?"

"I like to know what other men don't." The old man's eyes widened at the insolent implication. Oz sought to smooth it over, "Why did you become a sub captain?"

"I like to decide when other men can't. What good is information if you can't act upon it?"

Starpom motioned to Oz and said, "We need your help, but how do we know when we can trust you?"

"I report everything I know to you. You decide what to believe." Oz smiled and said, "Remember this, comrades. Until we get to Cuba, we're all in the same boat, and the Norwegian sea-rovers are searching for all of us."

The captain accepted his answer and brought the discussion to a close, "Thank you. You've given us plenty to think about. Not a word to the crew. Tomorrow you'll prepare a detailed briefing for us. Get some sleep. We'll need your team when we surface tonight. One more thing, tell them they did an excellent job detecting and classifying that AGI this morning. The Norwegians want our balls in a vice. They were not alerted this morning, but they are by now, like sharks in a feeding frenzy, and we're the chum."

"Thank you, captain. Goodnight." Oz stepped out of the wardroom. It was noon.

The three men searched each other's faces as the intelligence information registered in their military minds. The old man read aloud from the orders he held in his hand.

"Weapons will be made combat ready for use during transit. Conventional weapons may be used at the discretion of the commanding officer in case of an attack against the submarine. Torpedoes with atomic weapons may be used only as directed by the Ministry of Defense or the Main Navy Staff." The captain looked up. "That's not what the admirals told us in Polyarny."

They had been briefed on the special weapons by the brass before they left Polyarny. Captain Shumkov of the B-130 had asked a direct question regarding when to use the nuclear torpedoes, but the answer left different impressions in each of their minds.

Northern Fleet Vice Admiral Rassokha had said, "Write down when you should use these. ... In three cases. First, if you get a hole in your hull while under the water…Second, a hole above the water. If you must come to the surface, and they shoot at you, and you get a hole in your hull. And the third case — when Moscow orders you to use these weapons." He added, "I suggest to you, commanders, that you use the nuclear weapons first, and then you will figure out what to do after that." Admiral

Fokin had nodded in approval and added, "If they slap you on the left cheek, do not let them slap you on the right one." The admiral's face-slapping metaphor made more sense now, and the admonition to use the nuclear torpedo first, and then figure out what to do next, had new meaning.

The captain spoke first, "They've sent us to a real shooting war."

Starpom looked up. "The mother of all wars. Repelling an invasion is just the beginning. We lost twenty-six million Soviets in the Great Patriotic War, but a nuclear war would take five times that in one day. We don't need that again. American losses were what? Three hundred thousand? It's nothing. Are they ready for a war on their homeland? Are they prepared to sacrifice a hundred million people over a steamy Caribbean playground? I doubt it."

"They're planning an invasion." The captain stuck to the obvious information.

"They don't know that we're prepared to defend against it," said Starpom. "That's the whole problem."

"What will they do when they figure it out?" asked Poli, hoping not to stumble into the biggest war ever.

Starpom responded, "They could do nothing. Let's hope for that, but it's unlikely. They could blockade the island and prevent us from completing our mission. That's piracy and violates international law, risking war. They could bomb the missile sites or launch a full-scale invasion to take over the island, also illegal and would guarantee a war. Cuba's in real trouble, ground zero if war breaks out."

"Who do we shoot with our nuke?" the captain asked. "We have one chance to make a big splash."

"Let's hope it doesn't come to that," Starpom revealed his aversion to nuclear attack.

"We shoot the carrier, take out the whole carrier group with one punch." The old man slammed his fist into the palm of his left hand. "We have one elephant gun and twenty-one pea shooters. We use the purple-nosed nuke to rip the ass out of the elephant, then go with our gut."

"There's a carrier group?" Poli's eyes squinted to focus. "No one mentioned a carrier group."

"There will be. Invasions need air cover, so there will be a carrier if they plan to invade," Starpom explained. He was not shocked that the *Osnaz* crew had been read into Operation Anadyr, but not the captains. He wondered if it was a deliberate part of the *maskirovka* or a dangerous bureaucratic symptom of the right hand losing track of the left. With *Osnaz* involved, he suspected both.

Poli wrung his hands. He approved of Castro's Communist toehold on the threshold of the Americas, but earnest discussion of nuclear war was above his pay grade, and he couldn't add to the solution. He didn't ponder geo-political decisions; that was for national leaders, and he was their mouthpiece. He didn't contemplate strategic thinking; that was for admirals, and he was their cheerleader. He didn't participate in operational planning; that was for brigade leaders, and he was a follower. He didn't determine tactical actions; that was the captain's job, and he was the scorekeeper. He had zero inclination to hurt anyone and less to hurt himself. The three-man discussion in an underwater wardroom assessed international problems, and he had nothing. He uttered a silent plea in his mind. *Please, don't embroil me in altering human history.*

"Poli, where's your mind?" He lurched as the captain addressed him, "You're quiet as a pregnant nun.

Make up some notes for me to address the crew, what to say and what to withhold."

"Aye, aye, captain," he said. However, his mind screamed, "No, no, no."

"I want Oz to join us for evening meal before we surface tonight. I may have underestimated his value to our mission," the old man said, seeking any advantage over his American pursuers.

"*Da*, he's bursting with surprises and anxious to share his intelligence with us. We should attempt to trust him." Starpom added, "There's a good chance that the B-59 would not survive the blast wave from our own special weapon. Captain Shumkov says that his B-130 was tossed about like a toy when they tested the nuclear torpedoes, even at maximum standoff range."

"Bullshit. He's on this mission, on the B-130, is he not? We have three weeks to reach Mariel Bay. Nightfall is fast approaching. Tomorrow we'll milk Oz for all he knows. Tonight, well evade the Norwegian freebooters and their villainous American cousins."

Starpom agreed, "Good. The Prophet said, 'Conduct yourself in this world as if you are here to stay forever and prepare for eternity as if you will die tomorrow.'"

"Again, with the Prophet," the captain stood and glanced at Poli. "The Jews say, 'Ask not for a lighter burden, but for broader shoulders.' Goodnight, gentlemen. Sleep well." After the old man left the wardroom, everyone else shuffled out in silence.

Starpom could not sleep well, not for over a year. His specters appeared to him as cherubic seamen lying naked on the beaches of Key West wearing gas masks and raincoats flung open in the sunshine. Their reddening bodies swelled as they rose and waded into the water to attack the shores of Mariel Bay, Havana, and Guantanamo Bay. Their flesh fell into the sea in chunks under the sun's radiation, leaving charcoal clouds with mouths, but no eyes, storming the beaches to capture Russians. They advanced ever closer, calling his name. "Captain Second Rank Vasili Aleksandrovich Arkhipov, stand down. You couldn't save us. We begged you for a bullet in the brain, but you refused to take away our pain. Leave us now. You're no good to us. You never were." It was true. They had cried out for death, but he couldn't shoot them to relieve their ghastly suffering. No one could. Only their nuclear torrent could terminate their nuclear torment.

In horrific moments, he focused on breathing in, breathing out, as he thought of Olga, Old Norse for light and holy, but in Russian, the name of his beloved wife. Her steadfast hope and purity formed Starpom's foundation. Generous in prosperity and thankful in adversity, her compassion infused him with zeal and happiness. She reflected truth and wisdom in her perseverance through difficult times and claimed that she would have been a great and honorable man. He heard her voice, clear as birdsong, in things she always said, "Stand on your hind legs. Strive to serve, and never yield." She jerked him from his trance, and he focused on the silent noises in the night.

Poli munched on a piece of fruit he had bought from the stores boat that tied up to the nest in port when the sailors knocked off. They had yacked in the excitement of a far-off port, flocking to the floating commissary to purchase sundries, apples, and *zakuski*, special treats available in Murmansk: favorite smoked meats, fruit, pickled fish and other snacks to complement vodka.

Submarine life is ninety percent boredom and ten percent sheer terror. *Zakuski* conveyed a man from the lonely depths of tedium and desolation within the iron bubble, vanished from the face of the Earth. Poli relaxed and rode the *zakuski* transport to sharpen his memories of home and to intensify his hopes that everything would remain unchanged until his return.

The old man sat in his stateroom, ruminating on the day's events. He needed a moment with the special weapon and soon found himself shuffling under the nightlights, rigged for red during periods of darkness, a few steps forward in the shoulder-width passageway past the sonar shack toward compartment one. Opposite the wardroom, his stateroom lay halfway between the control room and the torpedo room while Starpom's and Poli's staterooms rested aft, between his berth and the control room. The circular watertight hatch, the width of his body, yawned open, inviting him to peer inside where the explosive fish and the special weapon officer beckoned him. Wearing coveralls and a black *pilotka* or garrison cap called a piss cutter, the officer wore the uniform that distinguished submariners from other navy men, but he was no submariner. On his belt hung a Makarov pistol in a brown leather holster.

He saluted. "Good evening, Comrade Captain."

Stepping through the round steel door, the captain folded his body to pass through the porthole into the cave. Shuddering as he returned the salute, he surveyed the cavernous space, stacked with racked layers of counter-rotating, twin-propeller torpedo cylinders reclining abreast and atop of each other for the length of the room. Twenty-one regular torpedoes had been loaded, one by one, through the angled hull hole deck hatch — seventeen forward, four aft, ten stuffed into torpedo tubes, and eleven lying on racks before the captain. His eyes searched the eleven gray-nosed weapons for his purple-nosed treasure, the special weapon from the T-5 project, a torpedo with a fifteen-kiloton nuclear warhead. Interchangeable with conventional, gray-nosed warheads, the purple nose lay strapped to its rostrum on the starboard side, positioned for loading into one of the six forward torpedo tubes. The weapons security officer accompanied the device for the voyage, sleeping in a curtained bunk, slung from chains above the warhead. He conducted torpedo maintenance and carried special keys for assembling the warhead onto the torpedo for combat use. He alone provided nuclear safety and security for the weapon. Descending the ladder to the grated deck above the bilge, the old man slid past the center row toward the purple nosed monstrosity. His future lay on rollers before him in its sea cradle, identical to others except for shades of purple that appeared to sharpen its tip.

"Doesn't look ten thousand times larger than its gray-nosed comrades." Starpom's voice broke the trance.

"No, but we know her secret." The startled captain blurted out his unwelcome thought, "They've placed the national will into my hands. We could attack Miami."

"Too much firepower?" said Starpom.

"Not for me. Greatness derives from power. In any fight, we want the biggest bomb. Could have used something like this in Belarus. Our objective to sail four submarines into Mariel Bay, sight unseen, to establish a magic base overnight is irrational. The plan is too small to succeed and too big to hide. Those ignorant Americans will discover us without knowing that we've already invaded Cuba or that we have enough firepower to terminate their bid for world domination. They'll attack, mistaken in their belief that they have nothing to fear. Their might and arrogance will destroy them because their reasoning is fallible. We'll fight back with a vengeance they'll regret. Our brigade commander agreed that if one of our subs releases a special weapon, we all shoot. That's the thing about nukes. We shoot one, we shoot them all. I'm ready."

"Little wonder we can't sleep," said Starpom. "This weapon will force us to discover who we are. Our only escape from our nuclear secrecy is the secret passage of our purple-nosed passenger, and the only way to rid ourselves of these nuclear weapons is to shoot them. The US Navy will never knowingly allow our atomic bombs in their hemisphere. They'd rather die."

The captain reached out to place his hand on the purple nose as if for luck, but Starpom stopped him. "That's not a good idea. You don't want what I have. You can't feel it, but that radiation is poison."

The old man jerked his hand back and pivoted to peer into Arkhipov's eyes. He didn't appear to be sick or crazy, but he was too young to be this old. "Tell me something," he said. "What do you think is so damned important about Cuba?"

Starpom put his hands into his pockets and shivered with cold. "Only two things. It's on America's doorstep, and it's expendable."

Chapter Four – Norwegian Sea

I have taken steps to insure our contingency plans for Cuba are kept up to date. The Navy plans to attack SA-2 (surface to air missile) targets at low level using 4 divisions of A-4D's (4 attack bomber aircraft per division) armed with 250#, 500#, and 2000# low drag bombs and napalm…the Air Force plans primary use of napalm and 20 mm cannon delivered at low level, and crews are proficient…As new missile sites are located, they are picked up in the target and attack plans within a few hours of receipt of photographs. **Memorandum from Secretary of Defense McNamara to President Kennedy, October 4, 1962.**

Cuba had never been important, not worthy of consideration, not worth dying for, not even worth killing for. The old man folded his arms across his chest and stood in utter silence. Starpom was right. As the newest captain in the brigade, he was surrounded by seasoned *chempiony*. The burning-submarine-packed-with-high-explosives hero of Polyarny, Captain First Rank Agafonov, had been hand selected by Fleet Admiral Gorshkov and was renowned throughout the Northern Fleet. Arkhipov's legendary status spread from rumors, even folk songs, about his courageous role in a disastrous nuclear submarine incident.

The old man craved to conn his ship into Mariel Bay, to see his enemies agog with fear and wonder, unable to comprehend how checkmate appeared in paradise from the emerald seas surrounding their own beaches. His black submarine plied the deep water, listening hard, collecting data and confounding North Atlantic Treaty Organization

(NATO) efforts to discover its hidden existence. The keys to mission success, *maskirovka* and covert passage, stressed the importance of avoiding detection by the sophisticated Norwegian Navy.

The American antisubmarine warfare (ASW) campaign had foreseen and prepared for this day with technology. To monitor Kola Bay, U-2 spy planes photographed Polyarny and Sayda Bay, and advanced threat notifications shot out to NATO North Atlantic naval forces, trained to find and destroy them, if necessary.

Between the stark coasts of Norway and Greenland from the North Cape to the North Atlantic, the Norwegian Sea remained ice-free year-round due to the warm Norway Current. Separated from the Atlantic Ocean by an undersea ridge between Iceland and the Faroe Islands, the sea floor drops two kilometers into the abyss off the continental shelf where the US Navy had installed sensors for the Sound Surveillance System (SOSUS) in the deepest shallow spots, choke-point ridges on the sea floor. Even spies marveled that the Americans had worked subsea miracles on the seabed. SOSUS cued Norwegian maritime patrol aircraft, hunter-killer submarines, and AGIs to locate Soviet submarines that were as expendable as Cuba.

Trusting his ship to Starpom after midnight, the old man tried to sleep. They had grown to trust the *Osnaz* radio intercept data for finding and evading enemy ships and aircraft that buzzed about them like flies, and they dunked the boat several times each night.

Stepping into the Birch-wood-paneled wardroom the next morning after his watch, Oz found Starpom sitting at the table, reviewing a stack of personnel files. The Spartan gathering place for officers contained a book rack, a small refrigerator, a credenza with a wall-mounted curio for dishes, and a four-man, café-style booth with a table that doubled as an emergency operating room.

"May I join you? I'm preparing the captain's briefing. They say he has a murderous temper," said Oz.

Starpom's eyes flickered at the thought, and he said, "A captain must maintain appearances."

Oz smiled under his moustache and replied, "Rumor is that he's a bloodthirsty fighter, killed lots of Germans."

Starpom smiled and said, "They also say he's half man, half machine, but anyone can see that he's three quarters machine. By all means, come in and sit down. As I review our personnel records, I see that we could staff a small university with our nuclear weapon expert and your crew." Project 641 submarines carried eleven officers, fifteen petty officers, and fifty-four sailors, an elite array of educated experts, skilled in thermodynamics, sonar, Doppler analysis, radio communications, navigation, meteorology, oceanography, and medicine. "We're not all Communists down here, but we share certain human traits that keep our crew functioning down here without panic. The psychological exam that tests whether a man is crazy enough to live under the water with a chance of drowning is the toughest in the world."

As *starpom*, Arkhipov managed the administrative functions of the sub, including personnel assignments, watch bills, daily schedules, training fore and aft, logistics and hundreds of reports and logs of the ship's activities. As second in command, he would assume command should the captain become incapacitated.

Oz liked Starpom who had extended a welcome and devised an ingenious plan to cram his gear into the petty officers' mess with a minimum of additional cable runs, despite the grumbling from the displaced *michmany*. Oz responded, "My team's electronic surveillance and intelligence provide real tactical value, and special forces men pass a crazy test as well. How did you become an underwater man?"

"Easy transition for a farm peasant with dust on his shoulders — long hours and mind-numbing monotony sprinkled with horrific accidents, working for a man you'll never know. Ever ridden a sub?"

"*Nyet*, prior to this assignment, I had only a vague notion of the submarine service. I assumed that we'd be riding nuclear powered boats." Oz's nose twitched as he sat across the confined booth. "But, here we are on a diesel."

Starpom watched him, searching for some hidden indication of his real purpose. "The nuke boats aren't ready for missions, and nobody cares about diesel subs until we disappear into the abyss. When we vanish below the layer our silence becomes deadly, and our foes take notice."

"Disappearing is normal for *Osnaz,* too. We never exist until we show up, and we learn to live with danger, but I'm not an underwater man. You think that we're monolithic, but the lens of our world changes with every assignment. We adapt to changing conditions, seeking each new enemy's weakness and searching for some advantage we can use against them."

Sitting back in his booth bench, Starpom said, "You got a taste of the terror that visits our quiet subsea world."

Oz laughed, replying, "That's not normal? My first ride on a sinking a ship. How was I to know what's normal? I figured you were measuring the layer."

"Oh? What do you know about the layer?" Starpom asked with a mocking smile, surprised at Oz's casual use of common submarine terminology.

"I'll tell you a story. After a destroyer operation off the coast of Turkey, we anchored near Canakkale, and the anchor buoy fouled in the chain, dragging it underwater. I had my scuba gear, so I volunteered to dive in and unravel the problem. I followed the anchor chain, hand over hand, until my right hand disappeared after reaching through the layer where the light no longer penetrated. My missing hand gripped the icy chill below the layer that felt like cold meat. I panicked, hyperventilated into my regulator, and almost fell off the anchor chain before I could collect my senses. Again, I'm not an underwater man, but below that below the layer is where submarines hide."

Amused and impressed, Starpom said, "A fine story, but you experienced an anomaly." The horizontal layers vary gradually with changes in salinity, temperature, and pressure because variations in sound speed bend sonic waves, creating zones of silence where a sub can hide. "The layer is deeper and subtler than you describe, but your analogy provides a sound working model."

Starpom changed the subject, "On another topic, I apologize for the limited accommodations aboard the B-59. Our crew hot bunks in twenty-seven racks, and your men must triple up with them. The at-sea routine is eight hours of watch, eight hours of work, and eight hours in the rack. Since your RIS watch stations will be manned at night when we conduct surfaced operations, your rack hours will be during daylight hours while we run submerged. Your non-commissioned officers will hot bunk in the petty officers' bunkroom, and you'll hot bunk with Victor, the junior navigator. It's the best I can offer."

As dusk descended on the first polar night at sea, ASW flights activated from the North Cape to Bear Island, and the Norwegian Navy flexed its muscles with AGI's and hydroplanes chasing the missing submarines they knew were sneaking past their defenses, but the Soviet Project 641 subs had all the advantages with quiet propulsion under a large sea. At low speeds, the submarines could remain submerged for four days, but at high speeds, they burned through the batteries in twelve hours. The subs had the acoustic edge over the surface ships because they could hear the enemy long before the search craft could detect their presence, allowing the subs to maneuver away from danger. The primary submarine vulnerability was their eventual return to the surface to ventilate the boat, recharge batteries and check for messages. On the surface, the submarine radar systems watched for low-flying aircraft searching for boats making way toward the Atlantic Ocean for nefarious purposes. By day, the brigade shunned the surface, but after dark, they only ducked below the waves when threatened. To maximize their speed of advance, stealth strategies were left to the discretion of the individual sea captains.

According to his plan, the old man initiated his process to transform his crew because he knew that when the hatches clang shut like prison doors, and a man breathes another man's exhalation, the pipes and valves close in, and the labyrinth within the ear sloshes like brains in a bucket. The discontent of submarine incarceration, tinged with terror, leaves each man abandoned by everyone except his brethren aboard ship, so they worked together as one, or they perished.

The old man encouraged camaraderie after the dive but gave his crew no rest after the refit because only two days of auspicious weather lay between them and the wild North Atlantic. The B-59 became their village, their *mir*, their world, where the primary objective was survival with no guarantees. Fire and flooding drills, torpedo loading drills, and watchstanders qualification drills combined with multiple surface and dive maneuvers day and night.

After the extended port visit, one-third of the crew had changed over, and the new members needed to requalify before joining the watch rotation. Prowling the B-59 to trace and memorize her innards and to regain their sea legs after months ashore, the crew had no idle moments until everyone requalified by performing repetitive drills to demonstrate proficiency. The calm weather provided a stable platform for them to race around imaginary disasters in soft-soled shoes, making as little noise as possible.

Poli contemplated a utopian ocean with warm, circular currents, a gyre sitting on the Tropic of Cancer, absorbing tropical sunshine, growing islands of olive-brown Sargassum and circulating about Bermuda. The Sargasso Sea was the final open ocean to navigate before they could slip through the Bermuda Triangle en route to Mariel Bay, twenty kilometers west of Havana. He tried to think of anything he knew about Cuba: hot sunshine, white sand beaches, palm trees, fine cigars and dusky women. He was certain those five things awaited them in Cuba.

In addition to his standard forms for reporting the activities of his shipmates, Poli had procured entertaining propaganda films for the crew. Showing movies of the

Great Patriotic War and parades in Moscow demonstrating Soviet military prowess with cheering masses egging on the soldiers' display of zeal, he preferred the velvet glove to a jackboot approach for Communist indoctrination and recruiting. He employed engaging videos of Martin Luther King's arrest and sentencing to four months at hard labor in Georgia, fiery attacks on Freedom Riders, savage beatings by Alabama and Carolina Ku Klux Klan mobs, and state troopers quelling Mississippi riots. By stressing the significance of their submarine missions to project the people's will beyond their borders, he befriended the crewmen, telling them how exceptional they were to have been selected for submarine duty. Like other men, they never tired of hearing praise and appreciation for their enduring sacrifice. Poli's smooth interactions kept the crew coming back for more, making him the most popular man on the boat, despite his penchant to start a file on the slightest push-back against his propaganda. Except for the old man, everyone on board enjoyed his company.

Sitting in his stateroom with his new typewriter, Poli scrutinized the personnel files, focusing on the *Osnaz* rider files that told him nothing. *Osnaz* shock troops were rumored to spy on *zampolit* officers for the party, a rumor that Poli believed without question, and his mind imagined their watchers watching his watchers.

A young seaman knocked on his open door and spoke as he looked up. "Comrade, the captain requests that you join him for dinner in the wardroom at 17:00."

Detecting the worried look behind the young man's stoic effort to hide his emotion, Poli asked, "What's bothering you, son?"

"I tried to call my mother this morning to say goodbye, but the phone lines were dead."

Squinting and searching the infantile face of a boy trying to be manly, Poli replied, "*Da*, they secured telephones during the sendoff ceremony. We can't have young sailors jeopardizing their mothers or our ship's movements with loose lips, can we?"

"No, comrade."

"When did you last speak to your parents?"

"Last week. They know I'm assigned to a sub."

"Then they understand that a sub puts to sea in secret to avoid detection on its mission. That will be enough for them. They must be very proud." The boy's face screwed tight again after Poli's best attempt to make him feel better. "Now what?"

"I'm delinquent on my qualifications, and the chief told me that he would trade me to the B-4 for a sour mop and a bent trash can."

Poli smiled at the sailor. "Do you want a transfer to the B-4 so you can ride with the brigade commander?"

"*Nyet*, comrade."

"Do you think you are worth more than a sour mop and a bent trash can?"

"*Da*, comrade."

"Well then sailor, I suggest you square yourself away, get yourself off the dink list, and show your chief some guts and initiative. That is all."

The youth sped off, chopping down the passageway and spouting, "Aye, aye comrade."

When Poli walked into the wardroom, the old man, seated at the table with Starpom, extended his arms and hailed to him with a nod and a wink, "Come in and join us. I've asked Starpom to tell us the story of Hiroshima."

"On August 6, 1945, America announced to the world, 'If you fight us, we'll annihilate your cities,'" Starpom began his story as Poli sat down next to him. "A continuation of the firebombing against Japanese civilians, a strategy to intimidate Stalin and to prevent him from invading Hokkaido. Eight square kilometers of babies and buildings, children and churches, women and warehouses, blasted up to fourteen thousand meters of purple-gray smoke. Ten thousand tons of explosive power, much like our special torpedo, introduced the nuclear age."

"Magnificent command of history, but I was asking about the K-19," Captain Savitsky needled Arkhipov. "Don't they call her 'Hiroshima' now? Isn't that why you are designated as a hero and why they call you a legend?"

"*Da*, they do, but I don't talk about it," Starpom said in a gentle, but defiant voice.

"Why not? Because it is classified?" The captain leveled a wicked eye at Poli, the snitch.

Fifteen months earlier, on the fourth of July 1961, Arkhipov had quelled a near mutiny aboard the K-19, the first Soviet nuclear-powered, ballistic missile submarine. He had the conn when a reactor coolant pipe burst and fire broke out in the reactor compartment. The two pressurized water reactors overheated, threatening to melt through the hull or explode the nuclear weapons. The engineering crew averted catastrophe from runaway reactors by jury-rigging the ship's fresh water into the primary cooling system. The shipyard rush to complete the submarine had cut corners by limiting essential testing, and the K-19 was launched and certified for sea duty with a microfracture in the main coolant pipe. Installation of the backup coolant system had been scratched to maintain the launch schedule.

Captain First Rank Nikolai Zateyev, commanding officer of the K-19, sacrificed his engineers by sending them into the reactor compartment, the viper's mouth, where they faced intense heat and radiation, wearing only useless chemical protection suits and oxygen breathing apparatuses while implementing emergency repairs. When the men emerged, irradiated and vomiting white-yellow foam, struggling to speak or see with swollen tongues and eyes, the captain ordered the ship's small arms inventory thrown into the sea, except for five pistols. Radiation levels bloomed throughout the ship, communications equipment failed and prevented calls for assistance, and the crew panicked, edging toward a mutiny aimed at beaching the sub on a nearby island to abandon the ship. Arkhipov stood his ground with a contingent of loyal officers and the five pistols, defended the captain, saved the sailors from themselves, and maintained discipline until the entire crew was evacuated onto a passing submarine. After returning to Polyarny, the survivors were plagued by nightmares, panic attacks, hallucinations and behavioral dysfunction.

When the ghost ship was towed back to Kola Bay, the details of the incident remained classified to bury the truth, but rumors swirled of eight men with bloated crimson faces, unrecognizable and sweating blood. They died within days after their return, and their radioactive remains were encased in lead coffins and buried in unmarked graves, and their sacrifices papered over their leaders' ineptitude. The brass had sent them on a mission without the necessary resources to deal with the inevitable calamities of the seafaring life. A military commission declared the crew to be heroes, medical records were falsified, and the sailors were sworn to secrecy. The survivors were left to deal with the physical aftermath of radiation poisoning and the psychological symptoms of severe traumatic stress for the rest of their lives. They were banned from talking about the incident with their doctors.

"There are things men don't discuss, like the loss of depth control or the loss of a reactor, but if you need a better answer, *da*, it's classified." Starpom's eyes narrowed as he stared at the old man's face who returned an edgy bulldog expression.

"You supported your captain?" The old man brought home his point.

"I did my duty." Starpom squeezed his eyes shut for a moment, battling his sea devils and ending the discussion.

Starpom looked up, face calcified, and his eyes bored into the captain. The wardroom compressed under the awkward silence until the steward walked in to serve salads and laid them one-by-one before the silent officers. They sat untouched until the captain relaxed, ready to eat.

Poli grasped the opportunity to change the subject, "Were you able to say goodbye to your wives before they shut down the phones?"

Breaking his trance, the old man said, "I sent my wife home when they accelerated the refit. This past month was hectic, but we're ready now, a week early."

"I sent Olga back to Moscow last week," Starpom chimed in. "We said our goodbyes."

Poli glanced at Starpom, "Did she leave you letters to take on the trip?"

"Yes, they were lovely." Starpom smiled. "I read them and burned them for luck."

"So?" the old man asked, trying to understand his enigmatic *starpom.* "You are a suspicious man?"

"I don't believe 'Hiroshima' happened because her bow couldn't break a champagne bottle at the launch ceremony if that is what you are asking."

"Do you think of those men often?" The captain probed with another question.

"*Da*, every day, and they visit my dreams at night." Their youthful faces filled his mind, and his eyes welled with tears at the thought of their anguish and sorrow. "We did all we could, but we had almost nothing to ward off catastrophe. I felt so guilty that I wrote letters to each of their families, but I still remember the faces of the men who put them to sea, in harm's way like mice in an experiment."

"Pardon me, Comrade Captain." Oz stepped into the wardroom, interrupting, "Are you ready for your briefing?"

"Come in and sit down next to our *zampolit*," the old man tore himself away from Arkhipov and took charge of the meeting. "Top secret briefing. No notes. Proceed."

Oz handed his notes to the captain and began to speak from memory in a deliberate voice, "On August 29, 1949, we detonated our first nuclear bomb named First Lightning. Only then did the Americans treat us with respect, as equals. Without nuclear weapons, we were nothing in this world. For that reason, Premier Khrushchev reacted to the installation of American Jupiter nuclear missiles in Turkey and Italy, aimed at us, with Operation Anadyr." Oz paused, searching the faces around the table for understanding before he continued, "Under Anadyr, we deployed to Cuba thirty-six medium range R-12 ballistic missile batteries with two-megaton warheads that can strike every city from Dallas to Washington D.C. Twenty-four intermediate range R-14 missile batteries with half the explosive power, but twice the strike distance, are ready for deployment and probably on their way by now."

The captain raised his hand and said, "You said that Anadyr was to repel an invasion."

"*Yest*. That's the other reason," Oz responded. "The Americans attacked Castro last year at the Bay of Pigs, but Kennedy lost his nerve and left over fifteen hundred men abandoned on the beach to be captured and thrown into Cuban prisons. The CIA attempted to assassinate Castro many times, but they failed. President Kennedy is preparing a full-scale naval invasion. We have fourteen surface-to-air missile sites operational today, capable of shooting down fighters, bombers, and U-2 spy planes. We've secretly inserted over forty thousand combat troops with ninety-eight tactical nuclear warheads. The combat troops and tactical nukes are for repelling the invasion. The missiles provide a strategic balance to nuclear military might. The short and medium-range ballistic missiles are useless when they sit in Russia, but in Cuba, they balance the American strategic threat because they're within reach of American soil. Once the Americans realize what we have achieved, they will never feel safe to attack us."

Starpom sat riveted and composed, Poli squirmed next to him, and the old man folded his arms on his chest under his jutted jaw. Oz cocked his head and added, "*Maskirovka* cannot last forever. We can't masquerade a missile as a coconut tree. The camel's nose is under the tent, and soon the camel will live inside. You may not know that another submarine, the B-75 carrying two special weapons, reconnoiters somewhere in the Bermuda Triangle awaiting our arrival. They will join us to spearhead the new submarine base. That's all I have."

The captain uttered, "With a new and special torpedo on the rack, we have instructions to deter American aggression against Cuba." After a long pause, he glanced at his orders, "We're directed to arrive in Mariel Bay in three weeks. Whatever happens, we must have verifiable orders to use it or, if war breaks out, and there's no alternative. We don't want the cork popped before the champagne party starts." He looked up at other officers. "The admiral wishes us happy sailing and great success in our mission."

"I know Captain Nantenkov on the B-75, but who knew he's already out there with two nukes." Arkhipov wondered how much more he did not know. "It's like a ghost ship on the vanguard of this assault, another riddle. Too many things remain unknown."

Oz blanched and said, "We need more intelligence."

The captain held out the orders out for all to see and said, "Agreed. This enigma can't unravel and the precious little information we have, and I don't like it. I don't like one damned thing about it."

After dinner and sunset, it was time to surface the B-59. Like graceful zeppelins, submarines fly at depths of fifty meters or more to guard against accidental sinking or broaching. The dangers of surfacing a sub stem from the blindness of the event. Because submarines do not surface during daylight hours, the nighttime evolution doubles the danger of being slammed to the bottom by a deep-draft merchantman running on Iron Mike, the autopilot. The big air bubble in the hold of a merchant ship masks the engine and screw noise from a submarine surfacing in its path.

When preparing to surface, the captain and the OOD entered the watertight conning tower above the control room, slowed the ship's speed and raised the periscope for those nerve-racking moments before the optics break the surface and they could swirl 360 degrees to check for ships appearing close aboard. Once the sub was safe to raise the masts, snorkel, ventilate, charge batteries, and monitor message traffic, all efforts focused on collecting everything they needed until they were forced to dive to avoid discovery. Diesel exhaust blew seawater out of the main ballast tanks to conserve the high-pressure air for emergencies. Diesel intakes took suction from the boat's interior and pulled any built-up, explosive, hydrogen gas from the battery compartments and methane from vented sanitary tanks, replacing the stale atmosphere in the sub with fresh sea air. The captain ordered the auxiliary gang to charge his high-pressure air banks, depleted by the emergency blow, by gulping night air.

In RIS, Oz discovered Norwegian hydroplanes patrolling the sea lanes with an aggressive vengeance, but his gear allowed the B-59's to disappear before detection. Despite the dead-serious game of cat and mouse, avoiding maritime patrol craft amused the OODs by frustrating Norwegian pilots with deft precision. By day, the B-59 followed the Norwegian Coastal Express while submerged but maneuvered away from the sea lane for safety's sake on the surface by night.

Without exposing the sail at periscope depth, they could snorkel with one diesel to charge the battery and one to propel the ship at low speeds to limit the stress forces of water flowing past the snorkel mast. Two periscopes poked above the waves, the navigation periscope with a large wide-angle optical head and the tactical periscope with a narrow high-powered objective lens. However, snorkeling was too slow compared to surface operations that employed two diesel engines to drive the screws for higher speeds and to provide uniform water flow over the rudder and screws, minimizing the detectable acoustic signature levels by reducing propeller blade cavitation noise.

During subsea operations, Oz's team tackled the qualification program as a group, splitting the book into eight sections and assigning one section per man to trace out the ship's systems. They preferred the warmth and headroom of the engine spaces and hated ducking through the control room, banging their heads on valves or cable hangers with the officer corps looking on. After spending off-duty hours sharing data, they completed their books and passed their qualification tests in record time.

The complex systems were simple enough. Aft of the forward torpedo room lay the first battery compartment where half of the ship's batteries occupied the bottom two levels below the officers living quarters and the control room on the top level. The periscope wells and vertical mast shafts stood behind the forward battery compartment. The aft battery compartment mimicked the forward version with the *michmany* living quarters and galley on the top level over two layers of batteries. The aft third of the boat carried three Kolomna diesel engines, three electric motors, and three drive shafts passing through the aft torpedo room that doubled as the crew's berthing compartment.

An incident from Oz's first day on the boat taught him a vital lesson outside the formal training. After the *starshy michman* had completed the orientation tour and led his commandos up the escape hatch, he took leave with some urgency to post the internal security watch for the special weapon loadout. Oz had sent his team to unload the trucks, carrying their sensitive gear onto the afterdeck because the forecastle was secured for loading the special torpedo. They passed the gear down the aft deck hatch and carried each component through the engine spaces, forward to the petty officer's mess, their assigned operating space. The specialized communications equipment was as highly classified as the special weapon, but the commandos understood that secretiveness trumped security, and they squirreled the gear into its new quarters without arousing notice from the scurrying crew members rushing about to complete their pre-sail checklists. Oz estimated the weights of each piece of gear and each man with sea bag and set out to find the diving officer to make his report.

Unsure of where to find the diving officer, he moved down the passageway toward the torpedo room where he saw the *starshy michman* standing at parade rest, blocking the watertight door. He knew the chief would help, so he approached, glancing down to verify his figures.

"Halt," the chief commanded. Oz looked up to find himself staring down the barrel of a 9mm, eight-round Makarov semi-automatic pistol. Hands raised, he stopped short, caught off guard. Aiming the weapon between Oz's eyes, the *starshy michman* held the weapon steady and said, "You are not authorized to enter this space." Oz focused on the weapon like a peregrine falcon in a predatory dive, so he was not seeing the chief's determined facial expression.

"I assure you my security clearance is much higher than yours," Oz explained.

"You do not have the need to know. You are not authorized. You could be a wrecker," the chief said.

"Fair enough," said Oz. "I need to make a report to the diving officer."

"Proceed to the wardroom, and I will request that the diving officer join you there."

"Very well." Slowly, Oz turned so as not to trigger a knee-jerk reaction from the chief as he forced his eyes away from the weapon, hoping the chief would holster his pistol. He did. In security matters, Oz reminded himself, military protocol is abandoned.

"He wasn't planning to shoot you tonight," said Arkhipov, standing directly behind Oz. "The captain invites you to join us each night for evening meal before night ops." Oz shook his head and melted into the wardroom.

One night at dinner, the old man, attempting once again to understand the mind of his senior assistant, turned to Starpom and said, "Tell me something I don't know."

Starpom searched his mind for a compelling topic before he spoke, "The universe is filled with powerful surprises. Do you know of Tunguska?"

"Sure, an attack by aliens on Siberia," the old man grinned. "Let 'em have it, I say."

"*Nyet*, those are peasant fairy stories. The truth is that on June 30, 1908, near the Stony Tunguska River in Siberia, a one-hundred-million-kilogram space rock detonated in the sky. The scientific theory is that a comet or meteorite, about fifty meters across, entered the atmosphere traveling at fifty-five thousand kilometers per hour, heating itself to twenty-five thousand degrees Kelvin, hotter than the sun. At an altitude of nine thousand meters, the heat and pressure caused the super-bolide to annihilate itself, producing a fireball equal to one hundred eighty-five Hiroshima bombs."

"I knew that I could count on you to entertain us. How do you know these things?"

"I had time to read in the hospital last year." The captain went to his special cabinet and pulled four cans of beer as Starpom continued, "Our scientists conducted multiple expeditions, and I read their reports."

"Olivaria, my favorite beer from Minsk, dark and masculine," the old man said as he passed a beer bottle to each man. "What happened? Give us details. Tell us everything you know."

"Two thousand square kilometers of Siberian forest were leveled in an instant. Poleaxed into a tree and charred by the flames, one hunter became the only human casualty, but many reindeer herds were struck dead by the blast. If the meteor had struck three hours earlier, it would have exploded over Moscow. Five hours earlier, St. Petersburg."

"What did our scientists report?" Oz interjected.

"Leonid Kulik led the first Tunguska expedition. He estimated that eighty million trees were knocked down, flattened like hair combed away from the ground zero, the epicenter of the blast, with their bark and limbs stripped away like a forest of fallen telephone poles. Hiroshima had branchless trees."

Intrigued, Poli erupted, "Did anybody see it?"

"Of course, observers reported deafening explosions and fiery clouds from five hundred kilometers away, appearing as a brilliant fireball with thunderous noises that shattered windows and crockery. Burning trees shrouded the countryside in smoke and soot, and reindeer herders sleeping in tents were blown sky high and knocked unconscious thirty kilometers away. The night skies grew bright across Europe and Asia, and folks read books and newspapers and played golf past midnight."

"Did the papers report it?" the old man asked.

"They did. The Irkutsk newspaper reported that the peasants saw a shooting star with a fiery tail that split the sky in two, and fire poured out brighter than the sun. When the fireball touched the ground, it pulverized the forest and covered it with pillars of fire and clouds of ash and smoke. In their *mir*, buildings shook the panicked inhabitants into the street. Everyone thought that the end of the world was near. Eyewitnesses reported that one-thousand reindeer owned by the Evenki people were killed and burned in the wildfire. It was the Evenki people who led Kulik's team of scientists to the impact site."

"Fascinating, what can we make of it?" The old man enjoyed learning new information in the story form.

"Rocks that large strike the planet every thousand years or so. The bigger the rock, the less often it strikes, but when such an explosion happens it brings millions of megatons of destruction, choking the atmosphere with dust, cloaking the earth in blackness and stifling plant growth for years, no sun, no photosynthesis, no crops."

"No wonder people don't believe in God," the atheist in Poli couldn't resist. "Who could worship a god that throws rocks at us?"

"God or no God, rocks are on their way," Starpom smiled. "The Earth hurtles through a universe cluttered with stone debris, relying on nothing but blind luck for salvation. The Prophet says, 'Everyone will taste death.'"

The old man mused, "Starpom quotes the Prophet, Poli claims to be an atheist, Oz professes no philosophical affiliation, and I am cynical. What if Allah throws a huge rock? Could be a civilization-ender, and yet, here we are."

"Nature doesn't comprehend extinction," Starpom reflected. "It rolls forward, adapting and evolving to fill in the holes of angry gods and evil men. The difference between Tunguska and Hiroshima is that the rock thrown at Japan was smaller but well-aimed with horrible efficiency. Now we have a rock to hurl, but only one unless we engage our brigade brothers because the brigade commander has agreed that if one rock is thrown, all is permitted, all rocks will be released, all hell will be unleashed over the globe."

The cook entered with four steaming plates of pork chops covered with guinea-fowl eggs, serving the captain, then Starpom, then Poli, then Oz.

"Gentlemen, we celebrate a run of great luck, and we've become accustomed to a smooth ride. For two days we kept those Norwegians under our belt and avoided their antisubmarine tricks, thanks in large measure to *Osnaz* RIS gear," the old man made his pre-dinner pronouncement.

Starpom added, "Our philosophical differences aside, we are bound by the confines of our vessel and united by our commitment to mission. The Norwegian Sea is our realm, but none of us has ventured beyond the Faroe-Icelandic Gap. Like other voyages, we never know what to expect when exploring new realms, and realms beyond those realms. We prepare for the worst and accept our lot together, so let's enjoy our dinner tonight and drink some wine. We need a full battery charge tonight before we shoot the gap tomorrow. After that, it's going to get rough in the North Atlantic."

Chapter Five – North Atlantic

From "Song of the Stormy Petrel" by Maxim Gorky

High above the silvery ocean winds are gathering the storm-clouds, and between the clouds and ocean proudly wheels the Stormy Petrel, like a streak of sable lightning.

Now his wing the wave caresses, now he rises like an arrow, cleaving clouds and crying fiercely, while the clouds detect a rapture in the bird's courageous crying.

In that crying sounds a craving for the tempest" Sounds the flaming of his passion, of his anger, of his confidence in triumph...

Ever lower, ever blacker, sink the storm clouds to the sea, and the singing waves are mounting in their yearning toward the thunder.

Strikes the thunder. Now the waters fiercely battle with the winds. And the winds in fury seize them in unbreakable embrace, hurtling down the emerald masses to be shattered on the cliffs...

In the crashing of the thunder the wise Demon hears a murmur of exhaustion. And he knows the storm will die and the sun will be triumphant; the sun will always be triumphant"

It's the storm" The storm is breaking"   ***The battle anthem of the revolution.***

"This is the captain. Rig ship for heavy weather."

Fighting the sea required a worthy ship, a well-trained crew, and some luck. Using rough weather to his advantage, the old man made his own luck to confound his adversaries and to toughen his crew, including Starpom. In October, North Atlantic weather increases its activity and intensity as polar air wrestles with subtropical moisture for control of the sea along the northern extension of the Gulf Stream. Tracking from the Canadian Maritimes to the British Isles, storms grow in frequency, duration, and strength. Cold fronts sweeping the US coast from Maine to Florida, guarantee a rough ride from Iceland to Bermuda, with gale-force winds and eight-meter seas as atmospheric currents rush northward over the vast fetch of ocean.

The deep-water exodus from the Norwegian Sea through the Faroe-Icelandic gap prevented the crews of the 69th Submarine Torpedo Brigade from viewing the angry black clouds on the horizon or hearing the wind rip over the rolling waves building above them, but Arkhipov sensed the maelstrom. Storms accompany life at sea, and ships in the North Atlantic are bound for heavy weather, which the old man preferred to a point. Planes, ships, and radars could spot submarine sails and diesel plumes in fair weather, but in rough seas, white-capped waves present a random patchwork to the naked eye or the radar screen, cluttering the senses with ghosting objects that disappear as they emerge in a kaleidoscope of sparkles. Diesel exhaust blows away, and a submarine sail appears as a smudge of flotsam or jetsam. However dangerous for the crew, heavy weather supported the mission as an ally until it became the enemy.

As a submersible ship, a diesel submarine is designed to operate on or below the surface of the water, but is not ideal for either. A destroyer hull is optimized for surface warfare, and the modern teardrop hulls of nuclear submarines are optimized for submerged operations. The bastardized Project 641 hull wallowed like a hog on the surface where it was hoisted by the rising crests of waves surging below the keel.

As the B-59 ran through the heavily instrumented gap, Starpom ordered the ship rigged for regime quiet to prevent objects from clanging. American SOSUS stations strove for deep-water, long-range discovery of submerged submarines by monitoring the deep sound channel for faint, man-made, acoustic noises. SOSUS employed long, high-gain arrays of low-frequency hydrophones bored into deep-ocean ridges near Iceland, Greenland, the Faroe Islands, Newfoundland, and the Azores, natural choke points where submarines transit to the North Atlantic. British Shackleton Maritime ASW aircraft patrolled the Greenland-Iceland-United Kingdom (GIUK) gap like palace guards, lingering on station along the gap and dropping sonobuoys on potential contacts suspected by the SOSUS array.

To evade the Brits, the B-59 snorkeled on the surface among hundreds of fishing boats by night and submerged deep below the nets of their noisy fishermen friends on fresh-charged batteries and air supplies to prevent propeller cavitation and flow noise. While the antisubmarine ogre roamed and terrorized the airspace, the sea surface and the subsea realm of the B-59, American Neptune airplanes joined the search as the brigade passed unnoticed through the sensor-laden ridge between Iceland and the Faroe Islands into the blustery North Atlantic.

"I want the OOD, the lookout, and the helmsman in protective clothing this evening," Starpom explained as he relieved Victor in the control room for the evening watch. The relieving helmsman fetched three rubber suits, and they struggled to pull them on, assisting each other the way *cosmonauts* dress one another into their spacesuits. "It's going to be wet up there," he added with a grin.

"This is the captain, set the surface watch. Beware of British and American search planes."

Starpom brought the boat, rolling and heaving under his feet, to periscope depth and poked the electronics mast up for a sniff. Oz's crew could find patrol craft threats and provide bearings and bearing rates that allowed the B-59 to remain surfaced longer than normal, only to emergency dive to avoid detection just in time when necessary.

"Conn, RIS, all clear," Oz reported.

The conning tower housed the submarine's torpedo attack center in the squat, compact chamber above the control room with three watchstanders on the helm, radar, and sonar. It contained the search periscope manned by the OOD and the attack scope reserved for the captain. The hatch to the protected enclosure of the open bridge above the conning tower was high enough above the waterline to remain open while the submarine was underway on the surface, allowing the ship to breathe deeply, except in heavy weather. The search periscope's large-barrel lens gathered light in dim conditions, but it made a noticeable wake, even at low speeds. The captain's attack periscope had a small diameter that allowed for higher speeds without bending and leaving only a minimal wake during an attack. The forward end of the conning tower hosted the helm displays and indicators, including engine order telegraphs, rudder position indicators, a gyrocompass repeater and a magnetic compass. Behind the helm lay a plotting table, navigation gear, a sonar console and an electro-mechanical torpedo fire control calculator that received target and own-ship information to determine the torpedo solution. The torpedo firing control panel had four red switches on the left to select the aft torpedo tubes, and the six switches on the right for the forward tubes, plus two red firing buttons.

Starpom started up the ladder with the helmsman behind him but stopped to spin the hefty wheel to undog the deck hatch. When he lifted the heavy hatch to open it, salt water rushed down the ladder, splashing on the deck. He scrambled through the hatch, held it for the others and shut and dogged it from above. Poli stood on the bridge above the protected deck where the helmsman sat strapped into his chair, happy to view the horizon to stabilize his inner ear, warding off the seasick feeling swamping over him. After dusk, colors washed out of the seascape leaving a spectral swipe from white to gray to black. The waves formed rows of water piled high before the bow, stretching port and starboard, rank after rank, as far as he could see. Coated with foam and froth, the water cascaded up the sail as it lifted the bow, spraying up and aft over the afterdeck.

"Raise the snorkel mast," Starpom ordered.

The roiling wake aft of the screws phosphoresced and flowed with luminescent sparkles into the night. The bow glowed as it dipped and split the waves, and water rolled off Starpom and Poli in shining rivulets, splattering on the open bridge deck. Resembling an open cask pressed into the top of the sail, the bridge lurched in response to the lifting, pitching, and slamming of the ship into the water, forcing the watchstanders to hang on to the inner safety rails. With every roll, they swayed port or starboard within the exposed capsule of the protective bulwark. Wind-driven salt water raked their faces like icy talons, but the rubber suits felt like their own private *dachas* as Poli leaned over the side and hurled his dinner into the wind. Starpom got the diesels online, and the warm exhaust provided some small comfort if he stood in just the right spot and protected his face with his hood. The spectacular, powerful waves formed long canyons with high edges and crests breaking into spindrift and streaks of blown scud. Darkness descended, beauty vanished, and the ocean menaced the terrified watch crew in the dismal blackness.

The sea's wicked tricks played out inside the people tank where objects got tossed about, flying, tumbling, and sliding until secured. Starpom and Poli caught salt spray every twenty seconds, and with every seventh wave, a rush of bottle-green water forced them to duck behind the shoulder-high bridge bulwark surrounding them. The salt water closed the electrical contacts on the head valve atop the snorkel mast, slamming the mushroom cap shut to prevent flooding.

Below decks, in RIS, Oz felt the rush of a cold salt breeze as the diesel engines fired up and inhaled stagnant sewage odors from the ship. Fresh air flowed through the battery compartment, flushing out explosive hydrogen and cooling the space before breezing through the rest of the ship's compartments. Refreshing airflow helped quell the uneasiness in his stomach, and he breathed deeply to maximize the effect. When the head valve slammed shut, the diesels pulled air from the cabin areas without replacement, pulling a severe vacuum within the hull and creating a suction that pulled the inner ear toward the tracheas and the eyeballs toward the eyelids. Everyone hated the feeling but understood it would self-correct just before it became unbearable. Sitting in stoic concentration, plastic bag between his knees, Oz could relieve his stomach at will, without taking his eyes off his RIS screens.

In the aft torpedo room berthing compartment, sailors spread their legs to prevent rolling out of their bunks and occasionally leaned over the edge of the bunk and vomited on the men vomiting below them. Others cleaned up the mess as shipmates had done for them in the past. The old man joined Starpom on the bridge with the *starshy michman*, well-seasoned, having made peace with heavy weather long ago, observing how his watch crew coped with the ship's motion.

"The school of hard knocks. Just the way I like it," said the *starshy michman*. "Whitecaps on my coffee." He gingerly lifted his mug while holding three points of contact with both his feet and another hand. "Our boys become sailors today, and it's only going to get worse."

"Chief, have the *michmany* make the rounds to check on their sailors and to secure any loose items," Starpom glanced at the chief, who was enjoying the moment. "Don't need any injuries or equipment breakage."

"Aye, aye." The chief dropped down the conning tower ladder into the control room with agile movements cultivated over years of tossing about in rough weather.

The captain turned to Starpom and said, "You still think we're on a pleasure cruise without consequences?"

Starpom hung his head and replied, "*Nyet,* you were right, and I was dead wrong. Our mission could go horribly wrong, escalate out of control, maybe explode."

"I thought hearing you say you were wrong would make me feel better, but you've made me feel worse. How bad could it get?" the old man queried, tugging at his ear.

Stapom lifted his gray eyes and said, "A dead ocean, or worse. Too many unknowns are like poison that drives our minds go to the worst places. We're alone out here, cut off, isolated, and deprived of the one thing we need as the pressure builds. Too many secrets for safety."

"Secrets work both ways. We're the secret and the poison and the pressure. We keep attacking, don't you think?" the captain stated flatly, without conviction.

"I'm not so sure. It depends on what changes. No, it depends on what we're fighting for. Hear that?"

Listening for something else, Starpom heard a faint, pounding noise forward of the control room, coinciding with the heaves of the boat. Sliding down the ladder at the end of his watch, he followed his ears to Poli's stateroom and opened the door. Poli's prized typewriter slammed between the deck and the overhead, systematically dismantling itself as the boat tossed it up and down until the miniature keys and type hammers tinkled down like coins and stir sticks amongst the inky ribbon unraveling itself about the berth. Grabbing a belt with a pair of pants still attached, he pounced on the machine as it hit the deck, hog-tying it to a low hanging drawer handle. As he got back to his feet, he thought, *Damn sloppy. He won't be happy when he comes inside, sick as a dog and soaked to the bone.*

** Living at Sea in Heavy Weather **

As the pounding intensified, shooting little shocks through the knees and hips, accumulating damage and fatigue little by never-ending little, everybody anchored themselves with three points of contact while eating, sleeping or watch-standing. Making his rounds, Starpom discovered that a pail of dish soap had broken open in the galley, and a container of wax had burst in the main passageway, spilling the slimy ooze to slosh about until a sailor slid into the friction-free sluice, almost breaking bones, trying to hang onto slippery railings or stanchions. The old man had the navigator sacrifice his Indian Ocean charts by throwing them on the deck to absorb the slimy goo. Starpom ordered the cook to shut down the galley and quarter-fill the deep, hot sink so officers and crew could toss a can of mystery meat from their sea rations into the water to heat it before eating.

After his watch, Oz went down to the aft torpedo room with a cup of tea to rinse the acidic vomit from his mouth and settle his stomach. He almost completed the act of sitting down, with one arm extended to rig the hot tea away from his body, when the bench rose fast and slammed his ass into the air. Still in the sitting position, tea rigged and all, he smashed into the bulkhead on the far side of the compartment that was trying to lie down on its side. He slid down the bulkhead, wearing the tea, and tumbled across the deck to his original seat selection, holding only the tiny handle of the shattered teacup.

Sleep came in spurts for the next ten days. The intense rolling of forty-five degrees and more battered the crew, but the worst thing for a ship is the repeated impact of the hull pitch-slamming into the troughs between waves that had grown to thirteen meters. During the day, the constant heaving subsided while the ship ran submerged, and the men found makeshift places for cat naps. Poli lay without pants in his bunk for days, paralyzed by nausea, groaning and unable to eat, drink or sleep. The captain set the watch rotations to four hours and adjusted the clocks to promote better sleep cycles for the crew, four hours to sleep submerged and four hours to ride the rack like a bucking bull on the surface. If he timed it just right, Oz found that he could stride up or down a ladder to the next level in one step. The trick was to hug the ladder as he sensed the ship about to drop or rise, then reach up or down and shoot himself through the hatch the way he had been shot across the aft torpedo room.

The topside watchstanders on the bridge donned safety lines to prevent themselves from being washed overboard, and they got soaked every minute. Waves whipped their faces, burned their eyes, and filled their mouths and noses with salt water until they couldn't rid themselves of the acrid taste between watches. The protective clothing stank of vulcanized rubber, mildew, and other men's sweat. The head valve slammed mercilessly, invoking pressure-induced headaches and toothaches beneath dental fillings for those within the hull. Because the crew had wasted so much water scrubbing soap, wax, and vomit off their gear and their bodies, the captain forbade the use of fresh water for washing or cleaning.

When his demons withdrew during the night watch antics, Starpom thought of Cuba and wondered how he would live in a tropical climate. He couldn't bring his family to such a God forsaken strip of nothing. Plowing into the bowels of a black ocean, Leningrad and Stalingrad, Kola Bay and Murmansk, Moscow and Olga all seemed like another world, a world that knew him as Vasili Arkhipov. In moments of ennui, he thought of Olga and home and the joy they bestowed, wondering why they couldn't always be enjoyable. He had been sleepwalking through life until the day he met her and their ballet opened. The dull ache and pining for the woman he took for granted, the love of his life, and the desire of his loins engulfed him in a restless, love-sick nostalgia and *toska*, the deepest shade of Russian melancholy. When Olga's face appeared in his mind's eye, her eyes flashed chards of delight, hoodwinking him over to her side of every argument. Brilliant, beautiful, and unapologetic, her pastry skin beckoned, and she offered happiness, hope, and light in his submarine world of disappearance and darkness, and she believed him to be perfectible.

He recalled his last days in Polyarny. As snowy owls nested on the shore and tuxedoed guillemots marched on the rocks to open water, he caught wild salmon in the sound and foraged for red king crabs in the icy water. He reveled in the tulip fields of floral fuchsia and stared into the spectacle of blazing northern lights.

After Olga's departure for Moscow, he lived in Severomorsk, a closed city of dirty streets winding among ramshackle buildings on a defunct naval base. He walked among the residents who wore tattered clothing, despite their employment on his boat during the refit in Polyarny. In a blustery summer blizzard, he paid his respects to those who went before him at the grim submarine graveyard in Nezametnaya Cove. With reluctance, he had replaced the prior *starpom* who disappeared just days before the voyage.

Alone in his stateroom, the old man bounced in isolation and brooded about his crew, his ship, and his mission. The gale sprung from ocean surge across the wild runs of squalls and frontal systems in the open sea, and the sea-induced suffering toughened his men into submariners. He chose to run on the surface at full speed to sustain the proposed schedule, to eavesdrop on radio signals in the air, and to keep attacking, although he understood that speed exacerbated the punishment on his crew. They sustained bloodied lips, blackened eyes, sprained wrists and multiple hematomas from being thrown into immovable objects. The pounding continued and intensified until it wove itself into the fabric of the crew's existence, becoming second nature, expected and anticipated. One day they would enter Mariel Bay as seasoned sailors. The crew would go ashore, unable to walk in a straight line, unable to stand without leaning, until their sea legs became land legs once again.

The old man reflected on his surprising orders to Cuba, terrified by what he didn't know and unable to satisfy his need for intelligence and situational awareness. With the whole world chasing him down, he struggled to visualize the ever-morphing, maniacal ASW menace aligned against him, and he wondered if the other captains knew something more or if they were even less informed.

One night, Oz brought a message to the captain and Starpom from Captain Dubivko on the B-36. After passage through the Norwegian Sea, the B-36 encountered the vicious seas of the North Atlantic while exiting the Iceland-Faroes gap, and she suffered the series of sea beatings experienced by all the boats of the brigade, but Captain Dubivko faced a more serious problem. His senior sonarman, Petty Officer Pankov, developed acute appendicitis that antibiotics could not suppress. Feeling a special kinship with the young sailor who reminded him of his own son, Captain Dubivko could not bear the thought of stuffing the deceased youth into the freezer for the duration of the voyage, so he called on the ship's Doctor Buinevich to swab the wardroom table with rubbing alcohol and prepare for emergency surgery, despite the throws of gale-force-eight weather conditions. Dubivko took his ship to the surface that night, braving the violent seas and the painful suction of the head valve slamming as waves overtook the snorkel mast above the sail, attempting to drown the diesel engines. While risking detection, he found solace in the visual and acoustic camouflage of the rough surface; he risked a greater medical emergency should the appendix burst before he could go deep enough, long enough to smooth the ride for a successful surgery on the wardroom table, but he risked injury to his officers and crew as they tossed within the people tank and on the bridge. One of his officers slammed into the bridge bulwark and suffered three broken ribs during his watch after being thrown about the cockpit. The sonarman and the injured watch officer were recuperating and planning to rejoin the watch rotation.

"I understand Dubivko," the old man said to Oz. "He's fallen behind our waypoints, but we never leave a man behind or let him die." Oz nodded. He did not either.

Captain Shumkov joined the discussion from the B-130. Only two years old, his ship sustained mechanical problems that included hairline fractures in the large, auxiliary drive gears for two of the three main diesel engines. In addition, the ship's batteries were nearing end-of-life and needed replacement, a major shipyard repair. The flaws were discovered after a shipyard visit, so the unscheduled repairs were deferred until the next major overhaul. The batteries and the diesel engines ran hotter than normal, but within operational parameters, so Shumkov worried about the B-130's readiness for the prolonged and critical mission.

"This is exactly what's wrong with our navy, shoddy shipyards and drunken yard birds. They'll send young boys to die at sea, but they'll never miss a shift break. They're lazy, sloppy, and halfhearted, and their managers are worse. They would certify a turd for sea duty if it made them look good." Starpom unleashed his feelings about his shipyard experiences while the others sat silent. If Shumkov runs into trouble with his diesel's, there will be hell to pay in the shipyard. I see to that, and I guarantee it."

The old man's thirst for intelligence would not be quenched by two of the three sea captains who had battled their immediate troubles in lieu of considering the broader strategic scenario. He hoped to hear from the brigade commander on the B-4 or from Admiral Fokin in Moscow.

The radiomen searched the short and medium wave channels for Moscow communications, but, except for fishermen chatter, only long-wave channels provided even marginal reception of the nightly broadcasts. Starpom and Captain Savitsky, familiar with radio blackouts in the Arctic Ocean due to northern lights and magnetic storms, expected the anomalies to clear, but the farther west they traveled, the more garbled were the Moscow midnight broadcasts that arrived earlier each evening as the B-59 traversed time zones toward the deep unknown. The dearth of data left a blind spot, an infuriating void, a hollow, quiet death trap.

Slow, silent, and deep, the brigade sneaked past the next choke point, the Newfoundland — Azores Gap, ever farther from the Motherland, evading detection at the hands of Americans.

Chapter Six – Grand Banks

October 14, 1962. Early morning: A U-2 aircraft flies over western Cuba from south to north. The reconnaissance mission, piloted by Major Richard Heyser, is the first US Strategic Air Command (SAC) mission after authority for the flights is transferred from the CIA to the Air Force. The photographs obtained by the mission provide the first hard evidence of MRBM (medium-range ballistic missile) sites in Cuba. **McGeorge Bundy, Danger and Survival: choices about the bomb in the first fifty years. New York, NY: Vintage, 1990., p. 301.**

Listening to his stomach groan, Oz forced himself to eat a little, hoping against hope that it would stay down. With his hunger gnawing at him since the day they sailed, he no longer thought about it unless he was taking another notch from his belt to keep his pants around his diminished waist. The old man hungered for dinner, Starpom seemed distracted, and Poli no longer attend the evening meal. The captain took his favorite tack to stimulate conversation, "Lieutenant Oz, tell me something I don't know."

Wanting to impress the old man, Oz said, "Cuban President Dorticós is raising hell at the United Nations. He called on the UN General Assembly to condemn American trade embargos against Cuba."

"I thought Castro was the president," the old man said, not understanding what Oz was talking about.

"Castro's the kingpin," Oz explained. "He installed Dorticós as president under his control who says: 'If attacked, they will defend themselves...with sufficient means and inevitable weapons they would have preferred not to acquire and do not wish to employ.'"

Captain Savitsky exchanged ominous glances with Starpom and Oz. The seaborne beatings had pushed the thought of a shooting war to the back of everyone's mind. He said what they were thinking, "Everyone talks around the nuclear threat, but it sounds like the Anadyr bear is out of the cave. How can you know this?"

"We picked up a news discussion on Newfoundland radio," Oz said. "The speech was on October 7, but last night they were speculating on what he was talking about."

"They were speaking Russian on Canadian Radio?" Starpom questioned, knowing it could not be true.

"No, English. They broadcast from St. John's to the fishing fleets in the Grand Banks."

"You speak English?" The incredulous captain licked his lips, and his brain jolted at the astonishing implications of the consequential reveal.

"*Da.* I'm third generation Naval Intelligence. My father was stationed in America during the Great War, so I lived there for years. I wanted to follow in his footsteps, so I learned the American English and culture."

The old man sputtered, "How long were you there?"

"Too long, I know how they think. That's why I was selected for this mission."

"I'll be damned," the captain gasped and slapped his knee, grasping the opportunity to fill his need for up-to-date information. "You can listen in on Canadian radio broadcasts and translate what you hear for us? Is that true?"

"*Da*, I can listen in on any broadcast in English and report the information to you." The captain's eyes widened.

"Starpom, this is the break we need, so take Oz off the watch bill. His guys can handle the watch. I want him to spend his time building situational awareness." He turned to Oz, bursting with excitement. "I want daily briefings at dinner until further notice. Be concise. We have zero from Moscow. We'll find a way to figure this out or make one."

"No question," Starpom pumped his fist. "This is the break we needed to break the information logjam."

The captain continued, "I want everything. No detail is too small. Do you have anything else?"

"The Yankees lead the Giants three games to two in the World Series."

"I thought they were all Yankees," the old man said with a grin. He loved banter and stimulating new ideas.

"It's an athletic team from New York. The Giants are from San Francisco. Baseball is the American national pastime, an ingenious competition where they play to the last out. Time exists, but it doesn't matter."

"Like on submarines?" The captain had a new window for viewing a confounding world.

"*Da*. Just like on submarines," Oz chuckled. "Baseball is the national sport in Cuba as well. You'll get to see some games there after we arrive."

"What is it like in America?"

"It's nice. The lights are always on, supermarket shelves are stocked every night, and they don't work two days of every week. Americans derive their scruples from movies and hold simple beliefs with fanatical certitude."

"What do they do?"

"They love their cars and go wherever they want, no restrictions. They go to church and to Las Vegas, lusting after life and all its joys, despairs, loves and hatreds. They like to fight each other or a common foe, it doesn't matter. They've known peace too long and are bored sick with it."

"What do they think of us?"

"They fail to understand us, so they blame us for deceiving them. They think we are barbaric thugs, and they hate us. Khrushchev told them, 'We will bury you.' They say, 'Better dead than red.' Some cities issued dog tags to their children for identification in case of war."

"Ominous. You must brief me on this baseball before we get to Cuba, but only after we have situational awareness. Do they play baseball when they go to war?"

"*Da*, but it's not as good. Excuse me, but I have to get back to work." Everyone stood and shuffled out of the wardroom, thinking about a peculiar part of the world with Cuba, nukes, and baseball.

Preparing for the evening watch, Starpom struggled into his disgusting, protective stink suit. He climbed the ladder and opened the hatch to the periscope deck. Because it was too dangerous to stand on the open bridge deck without being strapped in, the OOD offered him the safety line clasp. The rest of the watchstanders looked out the bridge windows below them and used the periscope to search the horizon for planes and ships. Starpom relieved the watch and scanned the sky through his binoculars to identify the stars of Orion, arranged like diamonds on black velvet on the celestial equator, three stars for the belt, three for the sword and five others for hands, feet, and head. Like sailors since the dawn of time, he mused on his lover, Olga, hoping she was star gazing at the same moment, thinking of him. He felt her love and zest as sure as he felt the wind. She was his great love, his playmate, and his distraction from a ruthless world. She provided his source of courage, his sense of justice and his reason for patrolling the planet. He pivoted to find Sirius to ensure he did not mistake her brilliance for a search plane as the watch wore on.

Running at full speed on the surface through the darkness, hounded by American ASW assets as they moved ever closer to the coast, the B-59 blended into the blips and noises of the Grand Banks commercial fishing fleet. Black backs and herring gulls flocked above the sub, wondering why it wasn't tossing fish remnants over the fantail like the other boats in the water. Enjoying the motion of the ocean, a giant tuna leaped out of the sea, and a school of tunas accompanied the boat for hours, keeping pace with the ship, diving and then surfacing with powerful splashes.

"Conn, sonar, biologic noises in the water."

"Roger that, sonar. We're surrounded by fish. They don't seem to mind if Soviet sailors swim in their ocean."

The fearsome wind and waves conspired as if plotting to stir up the perfect storm. A large wave piled over the top of the sail and drilled Starpom into the deck grates, giving him instant overpressure ear aches. The day-after-day punishment grew worse as the voyage wore on.

Working his magic, Oz reconfigured his gear to receive and interpret broadcast signals, and he discovered an accidental find while searching for St. John's news and weather. A shore-based NATO radio message, bouncing off the Kennelly-Heaviside Layer in the ionosphere to the US Fleet, came in loud and clear. The communication revealed minor logistical details of a military exercise under the code name Operation ORTSAC in which more than forty US warships were headed to Vieques, an island off the coast of Puerto Rico, to train for an amphibious assault on Cuba. Broadcasting military information in the clear had to be a mistake. He didn't think a training exercise was time critical, so he determined to gather all the data he could get while the atmospherics supported his spy efforts and while the enemy operators didn't realize they were broadcasting wide open.

The rocking, rolling, heaving, and pitching that pulverized Starpom and made Poli fear that he would not die in his bunk, dissipated for Oz as he locked onto real intelligence. His powers of concentration transported him into his spy world all night long, until the signals faded as the dawn emerged from the beneath the angry sea, and he grew hungry for breakfast in the wardroom.

"May I join you?" Oz said to the old man and Arkhipov who sat wrapped in towels and blankets, his face white as sea foam as he sipped hot tea and watched the captain wolf down eggs and sausage. "I have news. Those eggs smell good." Oz turned to the cook, motioning toward the old man's plate, and said, "I'll have what he's having."

"It's good to see that your appetite has returned. What have you got?" The captain checked on Starpom's shivering condition. "You all right? Your eyes look like two pee holes in the snow."

"I'm learning to enjoy the pleasures of the sea," Starpom replied. "What's the news?"

Oz relayed the story of his nocturnal activities and discoveries about Operation ORTSAC. His eggs arrived as he finished the tale, and the captain said, "It's free cheese, pure and simple. Your giant Yankees can't be so foolish as to broadcast in the clear for that long without realizing it. Free cheese is always found in a rat trap. Trouble is, it sounds so true. They're skilled at *maskirovka*."

Oz added, "Not particularly subtle, either."

"How so?"

"ORTSAC is Castro spelled backward in English."

"It's the invasion?" Starpom gazed up through red, salt-fired eyes. "We're going to war?"

"*Nyet*, not yet," Oz replied. "They're calling it an exercise for training and positioning their invasion assets."

Starpom acknowledged the response and evaluated his adversaries, saying "Planning's over, and the plan's in play." He excelled at synthesizing intelligence data to paint a complete picture in simple terms. "They're running a full-blown simulation to prepare for the invasion. It's coming."

The captain grew jovial with fresh news and a belly full of eggs. "Great work. You're a wizard and a hell of a spy, like you can see around corners to collect intelligence and tactical info. Have your men search for more American voice comms while you sleep. They know what English sounds like. Have them wake you if they stumble into a clear channel." The captain paused until everyone turned to face him. "No schemes or tricks of translation. If we're about to be vaporized, I want to know when and why."

At 5:15 pm local time, October 15, 1962, just after midnight in Moscow, the radiomen received an encoded message from the Soviet defense minister. Encrypted for the captain's eyes only, the old man was summoned to the conn. He read the message, scratched his bulldog beard and muttered, "What the hell? Fetch the navigator."

"Navigator to the conn," boomed over the general announcing system.

Everyone remained silent in anticipation of the first significant communication from Moscow since they left port. The navigator burst into the control room.

"What is it, captain?" They disappeared into the nav shack and shut the sliding door.

"The brigade is assigned to form a barrier north of the Turks Island Passage and take up combat positions in the Sargasso Sea. Something changed."

"May I see the coordinates?" The navigator reached for the paper message.

"*Da*, when you finish plotting, chop the data through Starpom, Poli, and Oz. I want to know if they see anything in it that I don't see. I need to know what the hell is going on." Behind the sliding door, they puzzled over the unexpected changes in private at the navigator's chart table, plotting their position southeast of Newfoundland and the new course to the assigned sector. The crew started new rumors based on zero understanding of the report. Oz quivered with excitement in the control room where he waited for the old man to emerge.

"I have more excellent news. Every American broadcast is in the clear: shore-based, ships, submarines and patrol craft. We can listen to their voice chatter, and we can read their message traffic. I can't say how long this will last, so I want to reorganize my team to focus on the intelligence effort, to collect situational awareness, and to determine the status of the invasion. They're sending subs, destroyers, and patrol craft to secure the Newfoundland-Azores Gap. Based on intel, I'd say they don't realize our brigade is here, but they seem to know that we're coming. If they discover us, they'll launch the fleet against us."

"Like hawks on rabbits," the captain contemplated the situation, weighing the orders against his intelligence. He decided, "I want to run at full speed on the surface toward the Grand Banks tonight, collecting intel as we go.

We'll hide among the fishermen again. *Osnaz* will watch for overflights and intelligence opportunities. The radiomen will monitor our broadcast frequencies for Moscow message traffic." He turned to Oz. "Anything else?"

"Bad news. October is hurricane season, and a big one is coming straight at us. A tropical cyclone formed southwest of Bermuda. It stalled, but it's expected to turn north as it develops into a full-blown hurricane over the warm water." Oz pointed at the Bermuda Triangle on the navigation chart. "It's impossible to know when it will hit."

"A hurricane will throw a wrench into the American practice invasion," Arkhipov said. "Flat-bottomed amphibs will be full of troops swimming in their own puke."

From radio weather reports, the navigator plotted the cyclone's positions, due south of the B-59, wobbling north, intensifying by sucking up warm seawater to fuel its ferocity. Reluctant to approach the US east coast for fear of detection and afraid to approach Bermuda in the dangerous northeast quadrant of the meteorological monster, the old man said, "I want to proceed through the Grand Banks to remain within radio range of St. John's. Update hurricane position data when we receive new information and record any shore-based developments. Everything will clarify with time, but hurricanes are unpredictable. We'll follow our orders for as long as possible."

Anxious to share their universal lack of knowledge or understanding of the situation, the crew vibrated with excitement as the rumors of a new assignment swept through the boat. They had been too busy qualifying and riding the North Atlantic's bull ride to enjoy other forms of entertainment, including Poli's movies because he was sick in his rack and out of commission. Stories of a shortcut to their new port, an American sea battle, and a hurricane circulated for hours. Because sailors didn't experience hurricanes in northern operating areas, gossip swirled as they huddled around the dinner table in the aft torpedo room, sitting on racks that served as mealtime bench seats. In heavy weather, the last compartment in the boat carved vertical figure eights in space, taking the crewmen for the wildest of rides. They laid wet towels on the table to prevent plates from sliding and held their food on the plates with their hands to prevent it from flying to the overhead. Legs locked onto bunk stanchions to keep their bodies from doing the same.

"Scuttlebutt says hurricanes make women horny."

"*Nyet*, you idiot, hurricanes fill women with fear."

"That's what makes them horny. They're afraid the hurricane will swallow us, and they won't get laid. They love to get hammered and sickled." Everybody snickered.

"*Nyet*, you're nothing but an ignorant turd chaser. They're afraid the hurricane will swallow us, and they won't get paid."

Everybody roared with laughter, and they put the mysterious hurricane out of their minds.

Chapter Seven – Hurricane

On October 14, a tropical depression developed…and intensified into Tropical Storm Ella. On October 17, Ella strengthened into a hurricane…Ella attained its peak intensity of 111 miles per hour; the strongest hurricane of the season…and its eye grew to an unusually large diameter of ninety-six miles. Ella is historically notable for its role in the Cuban Missile Crisis. The storm greatly complicated naval operations relating to the 'quarantine' blockade of Cuba and badly damaged several Soviet nuclear-armed submarines en route to the island, contributing to the escalation of the B-59 Incident. **Gary E. Weir and Walter J. Boyne.**

Hurricane wrath is unimaginable to the uninitiated.

Always beginning his briefings with the valid date of his information, Oz updated the captain and Starpom on the news and weather. "October 17, 1962. President John F. Kennedy held a foreign policy press conference yesterday. He said his major challenge is to ensure survival without starting a third and final world war. Something changed. Just a month ago he stated that he had no evidence of a Soviet military buildup in Cuba."

"A strange statement if he's planning an invasion. What's he talking about? Did he discover our nukes?" Starpom wondered aloud as he prepared for his watch. "We've heard nothing from Moscow for two days."

"Hurricane Ella's barreling north, raising hell with the US fleet as Starpom predicted." Oz continued, "We're in a brief period of calm before the storm slams our sector.

The forty ships heading for Puerto Rico were diverted, and ASW ships are heading toward us, racing to beat the storm, hoping it blows itself out before it reaches Newfoundland."

The captain glanced at the chart and said, "The US Navy has no idea where we are, they'll fly by us like Slavic wild witches. We'll dive and reduce speed to maintain the acoustic advantage against their nuke boats. Is that all?"

"The Yankees won the World Series. Baseball season is over."

Rolling out of his rack, Poli limped into the passageway and joined the solemn parade of other seasick sailors exploring the steady deck below their feet. Their faces wore funeral-mask expressions with hollow cheeks furrowed like rain-washed gullies.

Unlike the refreshing relief of dry, crisp air, the diesels pulled humid sea air, tepid, thick and smelling of decaying seaweed, through the ship. As he made his way to the control room where the old man was leaning over the chart table, Poli began to sweat.

The captain scorned him by saying, "Look at you. Your hair looks like moldy hay. You've done nothing for almost two weeks. Get yourself cleaned up and square away, sailor. The sea is calm, but the world simmers."

"Aye, aye, Comrade Captain." The metaphor was lost on Poli, but the urgency was clear.

"You'll brief the crew tonight, so make sure you're ready. Remind them how Admiral Fart Fokin arrived on the pier just to come on board and shake every man's hand. That's how much the brass supports our mission."

Captain Savitsky remembered how the brass had arrived on the pier in a gleaming black, GAZ M21 Volga executive sedan, slow-rolling with shiny bumpers and grills resembling chromium teeth. The two senior admirals had conducted surprise afternoon tours of the four submarines, shaking hands with everyone and wishing all, "*C' bogom,*" an old Russian farewell meaning "Go with God."

"*Da*, Comrade Captain." Poli's twisted expression divulged his disapproval of the old man's sarcasm and casual conflation of the Admiral with his flatulence, but the captain was ready for him.

"What? You never farted?"

"*Da*, I did."

"I farted myself. The admiral farts too, but he overachieves in everything he does. That's all I'm saying."

"*Da*, Comrade Captain. I understand."

"Great. So, quit farting around like a bunghole. You have a speech to write."

Poli slumped and limped off, feeling like a rejected guest, an unwanted orphan.

Back on the bridge watch without the stinky rubber suit and safety line, Starpom watched tiny flying fish, the size of his hand, skimming over the glass surface and flying across the bow. The sea was quiet between New York and Bermuda, but the air hung heavy as the storm approached. The setting sun blazed the red sky like an angry viper on the horizon, itching to release its venom on the crew.

"My first hurricane," he thought inside his Arctic sailor's mind, not sure what to expect from the warming air dripping sticky off the metalwork.

The sea's personality split — moonless calm, gentle and serene on the surface, but violent lightning forked the sky, flashing unrepentant on the horizon, bellowing like bulls in the awful grip of some unseen power. Hurricanes at sea are harrowing experiences that sailors seek to avoid, with powerful winds and walls of water towering skyward, battering the sturdiest vessels with swells of salt water that smash the ship sideways, snap rolling her from port to starboard and back. In the jaws of a storm, survival depends on steering way and sea room.

Steering way is the energetic forward motion required to steer a ship through wind and waves. Sea room is the safe distance from coastlines, ships, and other obstacles required for harmless passage during periods of limited control. If the OOD keeps the ship's bow pointed into the waves, safely plowing through them, he can prevent capsizing from a massive wave side-striking abeam and sinking the boat. Hurricane winds chop up the water, blowing the tops off waves that lift the boat, causing the screw to leave the water, shuddering a rolling growl throughout the boat. Forceful wave action will uncover suction ports and disrupt the natural flow of seawater coolant. Diving deeper, the water becomes less choppy, forming a rhythmic ebb and flow, eliminating the punishing pounding of the bow crashing down a cresting wave into the foaming sea, but still so rough it feels like being on the surface in the North Atlantic. Starpom worked to pack in maximum battery charge so they could ride out the hurricane in deep submergence without having to surface to recharge the batteries in the middle of the storm.

Poli stopped at the doctor's office to requisition an alcohol-dipped gauze swab to wipe his face, neck, armpits, groin, and buttocks. Feeling alive again, he broke out his clean uniform and dropped by the wardroom for crackers and tea. Like Starpom, he climbed the ladder to the bridge without protective gear to view the spectacular seascape and to catch up on all that happened since he had fallen ill.

He thanked Starpom for his understanding and for backing him up, and Starpom accepted his appreciation with dignity and grace. After surveying the night sky with binoculars, he handed the glasses to Poli, pointed toward the storm, and said, "Hurricane dead ahead. The rains will begin soon." It wasn't clear that Poli understood. He was not a mariner.

The captain planned to use his ship to protect his men from Hurricane Ella by using a simple dunk and cover maneuver. With Oz's data, he tracked the storm plowing north, filling the ocean between Charleston and Bermuda and scattering the US fleet away from the B-59's position and her intended course. Radars and sonars swamped with reflections from distant rain squalls and waves, so he determined that he could use Ella to mask the last leg of their journey to the Sargasso Sea. The key was an optimal combination of course, speed, and depth to dive below the storm and ride it out as the tempest passed over the top. Gale force winds extended five hundred kilometers north of the eye and three hundred kilometers south. The eye was moving north at ten kilometers per hour, so if he continued south, the B-59 would be under the hurricane for forty hours, with no ability to surface, no matter what.

"Control, bridge, the rains have begun. Please inform the captain."

Shortly thereafter, the old man showed up with his salt-laden clothes and shimmied up the ladder. He soaked his clothes in the rain as he washed his hair, his eyes, and his body in the fresh water. Starpom followed suit and informed Poli that he should provide each crewman with two-minute opportunities to clean themselves. He ordered the mate to pass the word and to organize the line of men anxious cleanse their bodies and clothes before the dive.

Starpom arranged for a special evening meal to be served, with choices of beef, pork, and sausage until every man was full, with the leftovers served at midnight.

The old man instructed the cook to create his favorite Belorussian *borscht* and provided the recipe: pork, carrots, onions, cabbage and red beets, greens and all. Simmering all afternoon in aromatic spices, the blood-red concoction made the captain happier than any day so far.

Enjoying the hours of smooth sailing, the crew played cards, whittled blocks of wood and whalebone into figurines, and weaved strips of leather into lanyards. Good-natured abuse, nautical salty language, and stories of grandiose exploits of women, storms, and emergencies at sea accompanied their activities. Youthful beards, two weeks in the making, grew from their faces and necks, itching as the stiff hairs curled back into the skin. Resembling bullies in the schoolyard, their actions grew sinister, and some of the young toughs captured a scrawny seaman in the torpedo room by tricking him into placing his fingers in the vice. Once he was rendered defenseless by a twist of the handle to lock his hands in place, they dropped his pants and threatened to lubricate his orifice with a grease gun until he begged for mercy. His penalty for clemency required him to kiss the hairy belly of the senior torpedo man. The boredom-driven antics continued until the word was passed to line up for bridge showers in the rain. They cleansed and refreshed in three-minute intervals for several hours until the weather drove them below decks.

On the bridge, reading the wind and sea, converging from different directions as the storm approached, became difficult because the waves attacked in chaotic confusion before they resolved into recognizable patterns. The wind screamed. A thundering wave caught the B-59, slamming her off her southern course. The sea moved in a random fashion with no distinguishable order as wave crests blew away and spumed into the air. The submarine got punished, shoved, lifted, and dropped by black waves bashing the bow face and the beam simultaneously. The deck bucked beneath the crew's feet as they hung on like punched-out boxers, pummeled by a relentless foe. Nobody was seasick; they were too afraid. The sounds of storm waves slugging the superstructure carried through the boat like cannon shots. There was no quiet as gale noises reverberated throughout the nickel-steel pressure hull. Eighteen hundred metric tons of B-59 lifted on pewter waves, whose foamy white tops exploded into the sky, where she hung for a terrifying moment before she dropped into the drink with the shock-noise of a heavy bomb detonation, driving the crew to their knees. A rogue wave accumulated the power of piling swells and consolidated them into a freakish palisade, ascending from the trough with no backside, no water behind this towering monster, only air. The diesels raced, the hull vibrated, and all three screws lifted out of the water. The B-59 pitched downward and plunged bow-down into the void to crash into the unyielding sea, flinging sailors forward through the air like a head-on collision until their momentum was abruptly terminated by some immovable object. Thousands of gallons of seawater swallowed the bridge as they surged over the sail, slamming the head valve shut.

"Clear the bridge, prepare to dive, check for damage. Make your depth 175 meters."

The bridge watch and shower seekers descended the ladder, hanging onto slippery wet rungs, closing and dogging the hatch. The OOD moved the conn below decks as the last man down. The control room filled with smoke as the wind blew the diesel exhaust directly into the head valve. Damage reports came in negative from all stations.

"Lower all masts." The OOD checked the green board. "Bow planes ten degrees down. Open all vents. Dive to 175 meters." Oz stepped into the control room as the B-59 submerged.

"Do you have operational updates?" the captain inquired, hungry to know everything.

"I do. They're moving fighters, bombers and patrol craft to Florida and Guantanamo Bay on the southeastern tip of Cuba. The attack carrier *Enterprise* put to sea out of Norfolk. The vaunted American Navy is no match for this tempest. It's difficult to distinguish a hurricane reaction from the invasion and war preparation. They're scattering everywhere," Oz stated. "There's more. Radio reports that the B-4 rode out the North Atlantic on the surface. That was ballsy, but the brigade commander discovered seams in the American's jamming sequence that may help us push radiograms to Moscow." Oz produced a timing diagram and smoothed it out on the navigation table. He continued, "The brigade commander found flaws and weaknesses that we can exploit in the enemy's tactics. We've lost ultra-shortwave, shortwave, and medium wave comms with Moscow, and our longwave channels are erratic. Captain Agafonov discovered patterns in the American jamming schema and identified the clearest frequencies at certain times of day. Cracks in the jamming wall leave brief windows of clear airways for secure comms with a low-power radio transmitter, but radiograms may still require twenty to thirty attempts to complete for sending and receiving. The brigade commander wishes us good fortune as we approach the hurricane."

"What kind of enemy jams our signals from Moscow and lets us listen to everything they say?" The old man mused, "It's a *Potemkin maskirovka*, an elaborate ruse, nothing more. Does it strike you as strange that Americans would broadcast their intentions to the world?"

"Civilian news broadcasts, no, but I never expected open military frequencies," Oz replied.

The captain asked, "Isn't it possible that it's a charade to feed us fake information?"

"*Nyet,* I don't believe it. It's all true and real. There are no other communications on other frequencies. We'd see encrypted traffic but wouldn't be able to break their codes. There is no other traffic. It's all open."

The old man rubbed his chin. "I'll be damned. We're heading into the Bermuda Triangle relying on the enemy as our guide."

Chapter Eight – The Bermuda Triangle

*Jack Kennedy had a keen appreciation for the vagaries of history. His experiences commanding a patrol boat in the Pacific during World War II, reinforced by the lessons from the Bay of Pigs, had taught him to mistrust the assurances of military leaders. He knew that there can be a huge gulf between the orders…of the man in the Oval Office and how that policy is actually implemented on the ground. One of his lasting impressions from the war was that "the military…screws up everything" The events of the (Cuban Missile Crisis) would confirm JFK's view of history as a chaotic process, replete with accidental figures whose role in history is often overlooked…***Michael Dobbs.***

Creaking and groaning, the ship pitched downward and rolled as she descended, but the explosive pounding and snap rolls ceased as soon as she was fully submerged. As the slow-motion cycles soothed their fears, the crew gradually relaxed their white-knuckled grips. Exhibiting hurricane chaos, wind-driven wave motion generated from the fetch, the distance, the time, and the velocity of the wind over the deep ocean. Energy rolled and amplified in the direction of the wind, transmitting itself, molecule to molecule, to move water up and down. The submerged submarine pitched, escalated up and down, and rolled port and starboard, making it difficult for the helmsman and the planes men to control the ship's course, depth, and attitude. Captain Savitsky instructed the OOD to allow course and pitch variations of plus or minus ten degrees and depth variations of up to five meters. He explained that a ship flailing in the underwater wave structure, trying to fight the weather could defeat itself. The control surfaces should be used to keep the boat upright and generally pointed in the right direction for the duration of the storm. He had the OODs provide damage reports after every four-hour watch.

The captain ordered the cooks to throw a party with beer and wine in addition to every type of meat in the cold room. When he informed the crew that Cuba was their destination and that they were below a hurricane, the horrifying news caused no panic because most Arctic sailors had never heard of a hurricane and none had ever experienced Cuba. Poli's half-hearted speech about beaches and palm trees, warm sun, Cuban women, and cigars lifted their hopes. Having lost weight during the North Atlantic excursion, the crew gobbled their unlimited multi-meat dinner. Clean and refreshed by the rain, they entered the hurricane with high spirits, but the onset of the violent weather had unnerved them. They heard the cannon-like reports of crashing waves above them, and they secretly bargained away the bad things they enjoyed in life if only the B-59 could hold together and transport them to the safe side of the weather front. They mistook their profuse perspiration for stress-induced sweat and thought it would pass when the hurricane passed.

The sonar system's sensitive sensors overloaded and clipped hard, overcome by the noisy ruckus above, painting swaths of bright chartreuse across the screen as the circuits drove into the stops from overpressure, pumping heat into the sonar shack. They were flying blind, but other than the four submarines of the brigade they expected no maritime activity. Any ship or aircraft in the storm above would be blinded with zero visibility, blind sensors, water in the waveguides, and mighty struggles to avoid death at sea. Before diving, the captain received a message from Moscow, the first in four days since the reassignment of the sortie on October fifteenth, but it was only a useless farm harvest report. He had risked his ship, his crew and his life to for a damned crop report. He would receive no situational awareness while submerged for two more days. Having made his decisions, he was left to monitor damage reports, sweat the small things, and hope for the best.

Starpom slept like a baby rock. Full-bellied and fatigued, his body longed for recuperative rest. He agreed with the old man's choices to handle the hurricane and to avoid the pack of enemy bloodhounds, and within the stability of deep submergence, he could grab seven straight hours of uninterrupted sleep. After being away so long, his demons visited him, swimming in the leviathan waves above, screaming, capsizing, covered in and crushed by the maelstrom, but they could not rouse him from exhaustion. The Prophet also visited him with the reminder, "Happy is the man who avoids hardship, but how fine is the man who is afflicted and shows endurance."

Huddling with his crew, Oz developed intelligence summaries, because, as far as he was concerned, they were winning the war. With two days to analyze their data, they wrote reports, conducted preventive maintenance on their equipment, and prepared for the next their anticipated covert activities in Cuba. Poli should have asked him about Cuba because he had studied Cuba while training for their mission, but Poli feared his *Osnaz* affiliation.

Collecting the many pieces of his typewriter, Poli decided they could not be reassembled and arranged for them to be tossed overboard when they surfaced in two days. The air inside the boat was too humid to dry out his wet clothes, one set soaked in rainwater and the other soused in salty seawater. They hung before him, dripping on the deck as he sat in soggy skivvies, wondering where he had gone wrong. He hated discomfort, he feared war, he could not imagine nuclear conflagration, he added no value to his shipmates, and he was a coward, the laughing stock of the wardroom. He hadn't held a single indoctrination briefing since the Norwegian Sea, and he was two weeks behind on personnel reports, but what could he report? That he was too sick and too weak to observe anything, that stronger men had carried his load while he cowered in his bunk? His Cuba speech to the crew was shit, *govno*, and he was *govno*. If he survived the wicked passage to Cuba, he would need all his cunning to create a good cover story.

Captain Savitsky stood alone at the chart table and closed the sliding door before he rummaged through the chart packet for Mariel Bay and the Straits of Florida. The approach through the straits would be tricky, hiding under a noisy transport ship, but it was the shallow, lung shaped Mariel Bay with a city, a pier, and a narrow opening to the sea that disturbed his mind. An obvious choice for some Red Army general seeking to repel an invasion with no appreciation for submarine safety or security, but inside Mariel Bay his ship would be a fish in a bucket the moment he passed through the choke point. Moreover, he cringed at the thought of reporting to another command, another boot on his face, as he returned the chart to its place in the file.

The sea had befriended him as had his comrades Arkhipov and Orlov, and despite his cynical tendencies, he trusted both men as they supported his mission with no indication that they intended to undermine his authority. Oz provided critical strategic and tactical information, and the old man couldn't imagine wrestling with the ignorance he endured before *Osnaz* reported aboard. He also appreciated Starpom's assumption of responsibility for the crew's daily activities and the evasion tactics he used against the ASW beast. If joy existed in a sea captain's life, this was it.

The old man wondered how it would end in the Bermuda Triangle. The hurricane wouldn't get them, he'd see to that, and the Sargasso lay ahead with designated combat positions. However, plans only lasted until the first shot was fired, and already the plans had changed. Perhaps it was the Kremlin's attempt to forestall a shooting war, or to prevent a shooting war from escalating to a nuclear war.

Arms and legs stretched out against slow-motion gyrations, the old man, Starpom, Oz, and Poli found themselves together in the wardroom again. Even though the B-59 remained completely incommunicado, the captain longed for his daily intelligence briefing. "What do you think is happening up there?"

Reading the captain's mind, Oz stated, "Same, no shooting yet. Moving assets, preparing for the invasion, reacting to the hurricane, and a little *maskirovka*."

"What do you know about Cuba?" The old man had never asked Oz this question.

"Cuba was a strip of nothing, a Spanish plantation colony with African slaves producing coffee and sugar. They threw out the Spanish in 1898 with American help and became a corrupt satellite nation of the USA until Castro's revolution three years ago. Cubans love Castro; Americans hate him. They hate that he's a Communist, and they hate that he swore allegiance to Moscow and is under our protection. Now he's a nuclear powerhouse, as they will soon discover. We've sent a powerful message: Don't invade Cuba. We need to get there in time to back it up."

"When they discover the deception, what will they do?" the captain asked Starpom.

"They'll fight. Our nukes are death on their doorstep." Arkhipov had given the question considerable thought. "They've been isolated throughout history, watching the rest of us die on their television sets and movie screens. When the American people realize that they will bear the brunt of death in the next war, they'll panic, and Kennedy will follow them because he's their leader."

"You think they know we're here?" he turned the discussion back to Oz.

"*Nyet*. They've deployed no sonobuoys," Oz observed. "The admirals haven't demanded submarine detections yet, but if they get a good SOSUS sniff, they'll send a patrol craft with Jezebel sonobuoys and Julie echo ranging explosives to investigate." Jezebel sonobuoys were mass produced, compact, expendable electronics packages dropped into the water like underwater ears that relay acoustic signals to the aircraft via surface-to-air RF radio transmitters, where the information is processed to locate submarines under the sea. Julie was an echo-ranging explosive depth charge, set to detonate at specified depths with a forceful impact noise that would reflect off the submarine back to the Jezebel listening devices, providing accurate ranges and bearings. "They know we disappeared, and they probably estimate that we are moving at covert speeds, so they think we're only halfway here. Those waypoints were a burden, but our burden has become our strength. That's why they're racing north to intercept us when we're already here."

"He's right, they're looking for us in the wrong places. We could still make Cuba, but…" Starpom looked up. "We'll get hammered once they're alerted."

Poli remembered the vicious pounding they endured while rushing through the North Atlantic and jumped into the conversation, "You think our beating we was worth it?"

A knowing moment of silence preceded the captain's fatherly voice, "The sea will beat us for no reason other than we are here. It doesn't care if we're strong or weak, courageous or cowardly. It battles our existence and tries to swallow us. We stand in the breach, execute our mission, and fight back together, shoulder to shoulder, arm in arm like a chain. The sea will never respect us. We must respect ourselves. We have our ship and our shipmates and nothing else, but it's all we need. We keep attacking."

"*Da*, Comrade Captain, like comrades." Poli looked up, as if to the heavens, and everybody felt it. Inexplicably, the motion stopped while thousands of meters above them, the vertical eyewall of fierce storms passed overhead; the eye, the focal point of the storm around which the violence rages, was calm, clear, and breezy as the Coriolis effect pulled the air and evaporated the clouds away from the quiet, vacuous centroid. They couldn't know that the merchantman, Iron Cavalier, sailing under the British flag, was also passing overhead, near the eyewall, but outside the eye, and battling to survive. The submariners ate their dinners in eerie silence as though they were in a chamber hall during the muted moment between the clashing cymbals and roaring timpani of an overture, as though the gods had gone on break.

"The special weapon lies on its rostrum," the old man raised himself to his feet. "Do you think we should load it into tube number two for operational readiness as instructed by our Kama orders?"

"Too risky," Starpom relaxed and pushed back on the suggestion. "We're still trapped below a hurricane, and it will get rough again within the hour. The worst thing we could do is break the warhead. The Kremlin might consider playing with a nuke in the middle of a hurricane to be a deliberate act of wrecking. It's safer to wait for calm water. Besides, who would we shoot, each other? Nobody else would dare to enter the Bermuda Triangle now."

Everyone stared at Starpom, calmly enjoying his evening meal in the warm cradle beneath the sea. He nodded and said, "The Prophet says, 'Show mercy to those on Earth, and God will show mercy to you.'"

The captain smiled at Starpom's incessant quotations from the Prophet and retorted, "And the Jews say, 'only one eye for one eye.' The Law of Retaliation."

Breaking out a bottle of wine, the old man capitulated without another thought, and with ceremonious gestures, he poured a glass for each man. They toasted the ship, they toasted the journey, and they toasted the Prophet. Even Poli, who considered himself an atheist, joined the life-affirming celebration of men against the sea. The warmth of camaraderie glowed within him, steeling him against the onslaught of the second half of the hurricane and bolstering him against the remainder of the voyage. When they rose from dinner, the storm tossing began anew, but with less vigor than before.

As the captain turned to face them, the corners of his bulldog mouth formed a devious grin and said, "This is not how our mission played out in my mind." He grimaced and continued, "Relying on an unreliable enemy. Who does that? It's time for the latest damage report."

As the night wore on, the noise and the churning subsided. Consequently, the sonar screens recovered, and after clearing baffles, the sonarmen reported that no motorized vessels trailed the hurricane. Although the sailors returned to their boredom-induced forms of entertainment, something had changed. As they approached the Sargasso Sea and Bermuda Triangle, the seawater temperature rose to three times the temperature in the Norwegian Sea. The heat off the electronics, the engines, and the cooking surfaces began to build within the compartments throughout the ship, above thirty-seven degrees Celsius, the normal body temperature, and the cold-water crew perspired until they soaked their socks.

Nothing about the B-59, insulated for Arctic operations, was designed for subtropical climates, not the equipment, not the refrigeration and cooling systems, and not the crew. Calm seas and high temperatures replaced the North Atlantic storms. For a few brief hours, the change was pleasing in transition, but the compartments within the ship began to swelter. To no avail, the captain ordered the ship to a depth of 280 meters to seek relief in cooler water. The delight of calm seas and warm climate faded as the suffocating environment intensified to blistering air temperatures creating a new threat and an additional source of exhaustion for the crew. One of the men, who had suffered most in the heavy weather, who had lost too much weight and strength, fainted from heat stroke and needed medical attention. The increased temperature and humidity overheated many pieces of mission-critical equipment, bringing them to the dangerous redline, and the operators couldn't service the gear without burning their hands.

The air temperature rose to 113 degrees Fahrenheit in the forward compartments, and 149 degrees in the engine compartment. Refrigeration systems for the freezers, stocked with meat not eaten due to the storms, began to fail, and the crew had no experience operating, servicing, or cooling equipment under such high temperatures. The cooling side of the desalinization plant failed with the rising heat, and fresh water was in short supply. When the time approached for the evening broadcast, the old man prepared to reach the surface, ventilate the boat, charge the battery, and listen for new messages. He wondered if the Admiralty knew about the hurricane, how the brigade had fared, and what the Americans had accomplished while he was hiding under Ella's skirts.

"Make your depth fifty meters. Chart the sound velocity profile," Captain Savitsky ordered a search for the layer, the physical foundation for antisubmarine chess matches. Every time they dived the ship, they measured the sound velocity profile to calculate the perfect hiding place among the horizontal layers and sound channels in the stratified ocean.

"Sonar, control, standby to clear baffles." He was certain that no vessel had sneaked between B-59 and the hurricane, but he needed to check his baffles to verify. As the OOD swung the ship about, sonar reported a faint contact behind them, designated Sierra One, classified as a merchantman. He was shocked that some crazy merchant captain had sailed his ship through hell, but even more shocking was the sound velocity profile. It was vertical; the sound velocity was constant from the surface to test depth, and the layer had vanished, leaving nowhere to hide. He hadn't anticipated that the hurricane would physically emulsify the water column, converting the calm ocean into a crystal-clear, sonic fishbowl. The submarines sampled the sound velocity as part of their normal progressions through the water column, but surface ships and airborne sub chasers dropped bathythermographic devices into the water to make the measurements. They would know soon enough that conditions were perfect for finding submerged subs. "Control, Sonar, no other sonar contacts."

The captain said, "Take her to periscope depth."

As the OOD brought the ship up, the startled voice of Oz came over the announcing system, "Control, RIS, dive, dive." The OOD dunked the ship and lowered the mast. Oz burst into the control room wearing a mask of fear. "We can't surface. Our screens lit up like Victory Day. Americans are everywhere, more than we can count. Carriers, destroyers, and aircraft. We need to skip the broadcast and make a plan for surfacing after dark."

"Fetch the junior navigator to plot contacts on the navigation chart." Captain Savitsky knew this moment would arrive, but today it surprised him that he had made it to the front line. "This will be our combat center."

Poli's jaw dropped, and his eyes widened before he said, "What happens now?"

"You know damned well what happens." The captain glowered before he continued, "We're a Soviet fighting ship heading for the Battle of the Sargasso Sea. We follow orders. We keep attacking."

Chapter Nine – Sargasso Sea

*. **October 20, 1962.** "Gentlemen, today we're going to earn our pay. You should all hope that your plan isn't the one that will be accepted." "We are very, very close to war… there is not room in the White House shelter for all of us."* **John F. Kennedy.**

"Can't surface the ship and risk detection, but we desperately need situational awareness." Captain Savitsky briefed his team in the overheated control room, "We'll snorkel to ventilate the ship and use radar, RIS, and sonar to divine the scenario by plotting all contacts on the chart after poking the masts above the waterline for one minute. Then we lower the masts and take four minutes to plot the data. Repeat the process until we see the complete tactical picture. Turn to." He twisted two fingers in the air.

Swamped in heat and humidity, the watch teams departed for their stations, and the OOD raised masts, as prescribed, for only a minute. To promote communications, he threw open the sliding door to the nav shack, and Oz and Victor plotted bearings to each contact from the B-59's position with updates from the navigator. Over the next hour, the process repeated a dozen times, interrupted only by the sweat dripping from the noses of the men hovering over the navigation table until the mate was dispatched to fetch towels. With time, the scenario clarified. Dozens of naval ships blasted radar sweeps to search the ocean for other ships, and three ships blared air search, track-while-scan radars unique to aircraft carriers conducting flight ops. Supporting the analysis was the presence of both surface and airborne radars clustered near the carriers, confirming the presence of the carrier groups with ASW destroyers.

With Oz's assistance, the old man determined that the signal strengths of the radar contacts were too weak to provide a reflected return to the search vessels, but sonar detected a contact not visible through the periscope. He realized that sonar could pick up the engine noise of surface ships in the sonic fishbowl before they reached visual ranges, a distinct acoustic and tactical advantage. His decision was informed by his need to ventilate, charge batteries, and collect intelligence.

"Let's surface and run all three diesels. We'll cool down the ship while we collect more intel. Keep alert for contacts with a steady bearing and decreasing range. Oz, turn the radio intercept tasks over to your team and focus on eavesdropping on radio broadcasts."

"Aye, aye, captain. I didn't have time to record any intel but noticed they are still broadcasting in the clear."

"All of them?"

"*Da*. Every word I picked up was in the clear."

"That's no way to run a *maskirovka*. Let's go up and hear what they have to say."

The OOD climbed the ladder to the periscope deck, took the ship to the surface, and raised the snorkel mast and the electronics mast. The diesels rolled over and fired up, pulling in the external air and the warm, sulfurous, rotten egg stench of Sargassum seaweed. The long-awaited fresh air was slightly cooler than the air inside the ship but laden with humidity and a nose-slamming stink never experienced above the Arctic Circle.

The OOD panicked and screeched, "Captain to the bridge." Flying up the ladder, the old man expected a collision at sea, but neither man could comprehend the thing they faced. The bridge above the periscope deck was blanketed in layers of olive-brown weed, dripping with little beige berries, shining under a brilliant half-moon and fouling the air as tiny sea creatures wiggled out of the soggy nest and flopped on the deck, wriggling underfoot. Reaching his hand up the back bulkhead and shoving the pile of sodden flora and fauna forward enough to poke his head through the opening, the captain inspected the mast configuration. Gulf seaweed dangled from everything, and the B-59 was surrounded by a floating island of algae for which the Sargasso Sea was named.

He explained to the OOD, "Sargassum. Get the mate into a rubber suit and a safety line. Send him up to clear the muck off the masts but leave the rest in place. We've caught a piece of luck. No enemy eyes could spot us in this camouflaged cover, and the wet weeds will absorb and scatter radar beams. The sea's calm, so let's drift in this. Only magnetic detectors can find us, so watch for maritime patrol craft. We'll have a full night to spy on the American fleet. Meanwhile, we hide, use the diesels to cool the ship, and lay out the tactical situation." The old man slid down the ladder into the control room after the mate in the rubber suit and the safety line climbed up.

Noisy diesel engines charged the battery, pumping sea funk throughout the ship and filling the dark night sky with smoky exhaust while the watch crew tracked incoming signals and monitored the sonar all night. Swamped by voluminous open communication, Oz listened to the chatter on multiple frequencies for items of greatest interest. He read message traffic from the carriers to their escort ships and airborne units and correlated call signs with senders and recipients, struggling to pull together the big picture from the slurry of bits and scraps. The old man was anxious for info, but too early is bad data and too late is too late.

"How much time do you need, Oz?" the captain asked, clapping his hands for emphasis.

"Maybe another hour, captain," Oz asked for all he thought he could get.

The old man couldn't wait that long, "You've got thirty minutes. I need a briefing."

Oz hated to break away from his source of information, but the captain demanded his intelligence. He collected his notes and made his way to the wardroom where he always briefed the senior officers who waited impatiently for him to unveil the full tactical scenario.

"20 October 1962," Oz began. "American operational aircraft squadrons capable of air defense, reconnaissance, and ASW patrols are moving into Florida. Other units are moving north, but I don't understand why. The nuclear carrier *USS Enterprise* left Norfolk yesterday, following the hurricane north and conducting air ops. Another attack carrier, the *USS Independence*, is also heading north. There are at least forty other ships in the Sargasso Sea, including the ASW carrier *USS Randolph*, her destroyer escorts and several amphibious squadrons."

"Formidable. Sounds like the invasion's imminent." The captain asked, "Anything from Moscow?"

"*Nyet*, nothing from Moscow and no talk of invasion, just exercises. I'd say they're posturing for an invasion, or just practicing. With all communications in the open, it's as if they are flexing their muscles in the mirror. They seem to want us to know where they are and what they're doing, roaming like packs of wild dogs with no mention of a plan."

"Maybe they don't have one," said Arkhipov. "Washington might be keeping them in the dark."

The old man snapped, "They may not need a plan, but we do with only four days to get to the South Sargasso through forty ships and a carrier group. Moscow's missing in action except for that useless crop report, we don't know where our brigade went, and the B-75 is still missing. The hurricane stirred the seawater, so the layer is gone. There's nowhere to hide, and it is too damned hot to submerge. The desalination plant is crapped up, pumping out brine, and even on the surface, our temperatures have only dropped a few degrees. The meat is melting, and the sun hasn't even come up yet. Any suggestions?"

Starpom's ideas gushed out of him at the, "This rancid weed pile is no good for hiding after dawn. With no wind, the planes will spot our diesel plume, but at night it's a good ploy if we can find it again, but maybe we got lucky last night. We'll need to ration the water and augment the freshwater with fruits, juices, beer, wine, and whatever else we have. We should eat that meat before it goes bad. We could issue the tropical uniforms to the men. They are clean and cool compared to their dirty middies. We should dump trash under the Sargassum to avoid alerting the Americans. The torpedo room is cooler than anywhere on the boat, so we might consider relaxing nuclear security to allow the crew to rest there between watches."

"You've given some thought to our situation, and these are excellent suggestions," the old man nodded. "Magnetic anomaly detection concerns me. Those aircraft are equipped with MAD gear for finding lumps in the

Earth's magnetic field caused by steel hulls, even when hidden. To avoid inbound planes, go deep to avoid MAD detection. Oz, have you found Bermuda radio?"

"*Da*, but I need time to listen for political news tonight," Oz yawned.

"Good, brief me in the morning. In fact, brief me every morning. You can sleep after we dive. Starpom, issue that goofy tropical clothing to the crew and authorize them to wear cotton shorts, light shirts, and sandals. Only the OODs will wear the Soviet uniform when we surface. We're cut off from the rest of the world, and we must adapt. With no thermocline, the layer is below crush depth and conditions are harsh, even hellish. Ration the remaining fresh water to one cup per man per day plus whatever is needed for cooking. I want two-hour watch rotations to limit the time the enginemen spend in the broiler."

Oz discovered two additional ASW groups led by the hunter-killer aircraft carriers, *USS Essex* and *USS Wasp,* operating south of the B-59 plus increased shore-based ASW aircraft activity, indicating a systematic search of the region. When he was ready, the captain took the conn, lowered all masts, opened the main ballast tank vents and let his ship sink below the surface to avoid fouling his screws or superstructure with Sargassum before engaging the electric drive motors to propel the B-59 southward once again. The dual demons of heat and humidity rose in the sonar shack, the radio shack, the RIS room, the battery compartment, the engine room and the electric motor room. After turning the conn over to Victor, the old man walked to the navigation table to review the latest positions of the three carrier groups conducting ASW sweeps in the sea of weeds. Concerned about the communications rendezvous with the other submarines of the brigade, he reviewed his decisions since the communications séance, estimating the most opportune position for the evening broadcast. Pointing at the map, he said to the navigator, "Here, this is where we surface for the evening broadcast at 16:00."

Both cooks busied themselves in the galley, cooking thawed meat while dripping sweat as the oven heat flowed into the passageway. Off-watch sailors normally loitered in the aft torpedo room to play cards or discuss the status of various equipment under their purview, but not today. Each space aft of the galley stifled them, driving them forward to escape the fevered areas. One whiff the smells of roasting pork from the overheated galley forced them through the control room to the forward torpedo room, already crowded with men from every part of the ship.

The torpedo compartment, where the pressure hull tapered toward the pointy end of the boat, had no levels, just deck grates over the bilge under twelve torpedo racks. Stepping through the vertical watertight hatch into a grotto-like space resembled crawling into a cave. A temporary berthing tent hung suspended from the overhead for the special weapons officer, his pistol, and his nuke. The place smelled like a locker room with men sweating through their clothes, having no way to clean or dry their skin for three days running. Noisome aromas of dried eggs and beans mingled with trench foot, like Russian army sweat socks and French cheese, combined with the pungent stench of armpits. The room filled with sallow faces sagging like molten wax with hollow and darkened eyes, ravaged by hunger, dehydration, heat exhaustion, and uncertainty about their destiny. While they endured this hell on Earth, but not quite on Earth, they itched, scratched, and stared at the special weapon, wondering what was special about it. They didn't speak or acknowledge the arrival of others, no banter, no humor, no *vranyo*, the far-fetched tales of Russian sailors.

By noon, the heat grew insufferable, the humidity approached one hundred percent, and intense thirst plagued every man. "Take us up to periscope depth," the old man said, knowing that he needed to snorkel and ventilate.

"Aye, aye, captain." Victor had the conn as OOD. "Make your depth eleven meters." As the ship rose in the water column, he climbed to the conning tower and raised the navigation periscope, executing a swing search to scan the forward sector first for ships close aboard, then port, then starboard, and finally aft. Oz searched for radios and radars blasting the airwaves to find enemy subs.

Following Victor up to the conning tower, the captain manned his attack scope. "Up periscope two." With the powerful optics and of his tactical scope, designed for aiming torpedoes at targets, he searched the airspace with expertise and familiarity. "Plane. Dive, dive."

"It's busy up there," Oz spoke to the captain at the nav table to update the tactical situation. "Same units on the surface and a sky full of aircraft. You saw a patrol craft."

"Sonar didn't pick it up," Victor said as he took the ship to one hundred meters. "They weren't close enough for their MAD gear to find us."

"They're not dropping Jezebels or Julies," the old man responded, talking to himself. He caught a quizzical look from Victor and lost his temper. "Think like an adult. In a big ocean, they search every sector with equal intensity, flitting over the surface like flying fish, heedless of the dangers in the depths, traveling erratic paths to pointless ends until something dark and unknown reaches up to grab their attention. They don't think we're here, so they're less alert in their efforts. When they start dropping Jezebels, we'll know they've been alerted. When they start dropping Julie noise bombs, we'll know they're on to us. The last thing we need is to alert them, but we must snorkel for at least an hour. One of those planes will spot our diesel plume soon enough. Stay alert, and if there's any question, there's no question. Dive."

Stationed in the conning tower, Victor took the boat to periscope depth multiple times in the next three hours, ventilating and battery charging until a long-range, land-based P2V Neptune ASW patrol drove them below the surface to avoid detection. Even a full hour of ventilation provided minimal, temporary relief from heat and humidity under the midday sun, and the battery overheated so charging ceased. Finding it difficult to focus, he thought only of his thirst, drifting into trances before slamming back to confusion and chaos in his conscious world. Try as he might to clear his mind, Victor found himself staring at the simplest task, mulling over multiple options without forming a decision. Feeling goofy in his aching head, he longed to lie down in his own sweat. Tiny pink pustules formed in the folds of skin behind his knees and elbows, and his crotch grew inflamed, but his tenacity surged, so he hung on in silence until Starpom relieved him.

Before 16:00 local time, they prepared to receive the broadcast at periscope depth. The brigade commander's communication séance protocol was for each submarine to rebroadcast received messages to maximize the distribution of information. Due to equipment limitations and a dearth of available frequencies, communication from the western

Atlantic to Moscow proved tenuous and intermittent, making it difficult for the submarines to report into Russia. Shore-based US installations blasted radio interference to defeat Moscow's command and control capability by energizing interference transmitters at the start of Russian broadcasts, resulting in sporadic communications. At times, it took up to forty-eight painful attempts to successfully clear one radio report while languishing on the surface. The brigade commander requested, without success, that the broadcast time be changed to match darkness in the western Atlantic, but Moscow maintained their inflexible submarine broadcast schedule, despite their knowledge that receiving messages on the submarines involved coming to periscope depth to expose the antenna above the waterline before sunset. As much as the captain longed to hear from the other subs, he dreaded the approach of the broadcast time as they encountered increasing levels of surveillance.

As messages began to flow, Oz brought the initial reports to the old man and Starpom in the wardroom, where they learned that all the brigade subs had all survived the hurricane, but the B-4 and the B-130 had sustained storm damage. Captain Ketov on the B-4 had received a Russian distress call while on the surface during the storm and decided to pass by the merchantman who had lost power and foundered in seventeen-meter seas.

The old man expressed his views, "Captain Ketov had no choice so there was no moral dilemma. We're under strict orders to remain covert, and a merchantman always reports a sub sighting. He has the brigade commander on board, plus a submarine is no good for rescues in heavy seas. There's nothing he could have done to save those sailors from drowning."

"He might have relayed the distress call," Arkhipov countered after considering the dilemma. "No ship could execute a rescue in six-story waves, but he could have relayed their cry for help, so others could search for the merchantman when things calmed down."

The captain shot to his feet, angered by Starpom's insolence, but the man was so clever. He had agreed with the captain's assessment while offering an alternate and reasonable point of view. The old man sat and said, "Perhaps he did. Certain things that help commanding officers sleep can't be revealed."

"Just remaining on the surface was rough enough," Oz broke through the tussle. "The B-4's aft deck hatch bent on the twisting hull and requires packing to reduce leaking. That's not all. The B-130's in bad shape with all three of her diesel engines damaged, and on the B-36 the vertical countermeasures decoy launcher is leaking. It's a tough situation. Everybody's damaged, but us."

"The B-4's flooding into the crew's berthing space in the aft torpedo room," Starpom analyzed the situation. "The B-130's batteries and diesels are running super-hot in this cauldron. The B-4 has no significant depth capability, the B-36 is restricted to about seventy meters, and the B-130 is speed restricted which also means they, too, are depth-deprived for reasons of safety. Poor bastards are in real trouble. Thankfully, our old man brought us through unscathed, so far."

The captain accepted Starpom's praise and said, "The damaged boats will have no choice but to struggle on toward the Sargasso. Except for some banged up sailors, we're in good shape. We can't look back, and we don't know what will happen next."

"The brigade commander is calling for a picket formation to run southeast toward the Greater Antilles Islands," Oz added.

After nightfall and Oz's assurances that there was no immediate threat from US forces near the boat, the old man began cycling his suffering sailors, scratching at their itching flesh, up to the bridge for a few minutes of fresh air in the relatively cool environs. Oz had been up most of the day and had a full night ahead of him, listening to the radio and American naval chatter with his perspiration soaking his shirt to the elbows and his pants to the knees. From time to time, they were forced to submerge by a flyover as the searches intensified, but it seemed random, scattered, and chaotic, bereft of direction or purpose for their presence.

Having difficulty describing the opposing forces to the captain at the morning briefing, Oz reported, "There's no sense of urgency. They're milling about in a great show of force, maybe posturing themselves for an operation. It's like the whole fleet got dumped into this ocean. I say let's get to Cuba before they figure out what's going on."

The captain acknowledged his frustration, "We need to get to Cuba before they get serious, but the B-130's damaged diesels will slow our progress. The Americans endure endless hours of staring at scopes that stare back. A disappearing blip will be assumed to be a false positive. That'll change when they're alerted. Even in these horrid temperatures, we must remain hidden." He scratched his chest and groin and surveyed his men. "Is that clear? It's going to get worse, and we can't be the first one detected."

It was Oz's turn in the rack that was still wet from the junior navigator, Victor, his hot-bunkmate. Too exhausted to deal with it, he flipped the mattress over to his side of the fart sack. He'd had his morning tea ration and a biscuit, and for just one moment before he passed out, he felt satisfied. His men were holding up as well as could be expected, accustomed to hardship and priding themselves in out-toughing tough guys, but these submarine sailors were surprising, no strangers to misery. Like the baby in a *Matryoshka* doll, he slept hard in his tiny bunk as the temperature shot up when the B-59 submerged. Dreaming that he was frying to death on a sandy beach, he crawled toward a palm tree that moved away faster than he could approach it. His clothes tore at his flesh, twisting into soggy knots that held him back from the shade as he felt his life creeping out of his body, burying itself in white-hot sand.

The door opened, then closed, and his nose slammed shut under olfactory assault from the man who had entered. What was that beefy odor? A man's urine and body stench and rotting meat, coated in mildew. There was more to it: distilled sweat and goat acid with a touch of decaying sewage. It reminded Oz of Millionka, the once Chinese sector of his hometown of Vladivostok before Stalin had it liquidated. After enduring thousands of miles of punishment from the ocean, the crew perspired from exertion in searing heat until their bodies formed a membrane, exuding the byproducts of fat decomposition through their pores to mingle with salt stains and grime. Their skin reddened in reaction to the putrid moisture and dirt, and Oz admired their Spartan tenacity and animal gumption. If only until Cuba, he was proud to share their personal ammonia, and he rolled over and slept again, but when he awoke, he was still exhausted.

"All that meat is stinking up this place," he heard Starpom say to Poli in the wardroom.

"We have to dump it overboard tonight. The freezers are failing with this heat. They weren't designed for it. The old man secured all stoves and ovens, and nobody is eating hot food anyway. The cooks broke out the sea rations." Starpom watched Poli open a small tin of red meat with a tiny curl in the center as though it had been squirted from a tube. "What the hell is that?"

Oz leaned over to inspect. "That's corned beef, but it looks like baboon ass."

Poli dipped his fork and placed a taste in his mouth. "It tastes like baboon ass." He spat it back into the can. "Thank God for *zakuski*." They made their way to the control room to prepare for the evening broadcast.

Chapter Ten – Ashes in Their Mouth

They both lied. *Nikita Khrushchev claimed that the USSR was making nuclear missiles like sausages. JFK campaigned on claims that the Republicans had allowed the Soviet Union to surpass US nuclear capability, creating a huge "missile gap." The truth was that United States had amassed nearly 7,000 nuclear warheads, while the Soviet Union had only 500 by 1962. The US had conducted over 1,000 nuclear weapons tests, totaling 298 megatons of yield, including 140 nuclear tests totaling 229 megatons of yield in 1961-1962. The Soviet Union also conducted tests with nearly 1000 devices, totaling 197 megatons of yield, including 135 nuclear weapon tests totaling 38 megatons of yield in 1961-1962. Together they exploded nukes three times per week in 1962.* ***Douglas Gilbert.***

US Navy search activities went dead, as though the search planes had knocked off between shifts, and the sea mellowed into absolute calm while everyone took a breather. Gentle breezes crossing the bridge belied the cruel torment inside the hull, horribly hot in the coolest places, driving every man crazy as they struggled to breathe. The crewmen fought to execute their normal work, maintaining equipment, operating the boat, monitoring intercepts of US radio broadcasts, diving to avoid detection, and surfacing for communication séance sessions with Moscow.

The crew preferred frost and snowstorms. Their skin rashes deepened and became infected due to profuse sweating and dehydration. Crew members had lost weight, some as much as a third of their body mass, appearing emaciated. The sun seared the seawater by day, refracting shades of purple and navy blue, and warmed it to steam bath temperatures. Tiny flying fish, dark and shimmering, flitted about, gliding on their greenish wings, beautifully translucent in the sun. Two satellites loomed in the sky, one Soviet and one American, like brilliant stars flickering overhead in separate orbits.

Both confusing and disturbing, the American broadcast news reported that Soviet military troops had moved to full alert in anticipation of a full-scale American invasion of Cuba. The brigade received new orders to proceed to a one hundred square kilometer combat sector of the South Sargasso Sea and to loiter on station in secret, awaiting additional orders. The brigade commander ordered the picket formation to alter course away from Cuba in a southeast direction, but the B-36, experienced and undamaged except for her decoy ejector, received separate orders to proceed through the Caicos Straights on a dangerous solo excursion.

Crowding around the navigation desk with Starpom, Poli, and the navigator, the captain asked, "What the hell is going on up there? It's spooky."

Starpom responded, "The only change is the threat of Soviet nukes in the Western Hemisphere. Seems like we're crawling toward...or maybe away from war. It's too quiet, like the day before the hurricane. Feels explosive."

After losing Bermuda radio, Oz picked up a new station out of Miami, and he couldn't believe his ears. He rushed out to the control room to inform the old man, who pored over charts with the navigator, laying out the new course, the other submarine positions and the sector boundaries of their destination. Noticing Oz enter the compartment, he held up his hand to say, "Not now." Oz's insistent look indicated that he had essential information that the captain needed to hear, but he knew not to interrupt the man who had grown to trust his intelligence.

"All right, Oz, what is it that you need to report?"

"The Americans elevated their military readiness to Defense Condition Three. President Kennedy will address the nation by radio tonight to discuss the Cuban situation."

"Son of a bitch." The captain froze, and his mind raced through the implications. The American president would address his people about Cuba. *What could it mean? Would he launch the invasion? Would he declare war on Cuba? Had he discovered the missiles? What could he say? The missiles were perfectly legal according to a bilateral agreement between two legitimate governments. What would he tell his people?* The Americans continued to mystify the captain.

"Keep monitoring that radio. I'll join you in RIS with Starpom and Poli for the President's speech." He kicked the navigation table. "What the hell?"

Oz returned to his lair and listened to American stories about President Kennedy meeting with the Ugandan premier, the Pacific Science Center opening a Seattle facility, and the USSR performing yet another nuclear test at the Semipalatinsk test site in northeast Kazakhstan. Piled high with classified radio intelligence equipment, the Birch-wood-paneled *michmany* mess, converted into the RIS operating center, left ample room for the old man, Arkhipov, and Poli to sit on bench seats as they did in the wardroom. When they entered the cramped space, the radio news anchor announced that they were switching to the

White House, where the president of the United States would address the nation. Oz gave a nod, and Starpom produced a notepad.

"Are they ready? Tell me everything he says, exactly as he says it," said the captain, leaning toward Oz.

As though President Kennedy wanted everyone in the world to write down his words, he spoke with a deliberate voice, "Good evening, my fellow citizens."

The captain cocked his head and said, "Is that him?"

"*Da,* listen." Writing notes in Cyrillic shorthand, Oz struggled to grasp the significance of the words as he translated from English. "He says the US government has unmistakable evidence of Soviet missile sites with nuclear strike capability against the Western Hemisphere."

The old man shook his head. "*Maskirovka* is over."

"He says the new missile sites include medium-range ballistic missiles with nuclear warheads and a range of over a thousand miles. Each of these missiles is capable of striking Washington, D. C., the Panama Canal, Cape Canaveral, and Mexico City. More sites were observed for intermediate range ballistic missiles, capable of striking most of the major cities in the Western Hemisphere, from Hudson Bay, Canada, to California, to Lima, Peru. In addition, jet bombers capable of carrying nuclear weapons are being uncrated and assembled in Cuba."

"I didn't know about the bombers," said Starpom, inadvertently revealing his knowledge of Anadyr. Nobody noticed. They focused their attention on Oz's rendition of Kennedy's speech.

"He says we are liars and have been planning the offensive for months. They cannot tolerate deception and offensive threats. Nuclear weapons are so destructive and ballistic missiles are so swift that any possibility of their use or deployment is regarded as a definite threat to peace. The missiles in Cuba add to an already clear and present danger."

"It is a clear and present danger and a thumb in their eye. That's the whole point," the old man observed.

"He says the secret, swift, extraordinary, clandestine buildup of Communist missiles is deliberately provocative and unjustified. Further action is underway, and these actions are only the beginning. They will not risk the cost of a worldwide nuclear war in which the fruits of victory would be ashes in their mouth, but they will not shrink from a risk if it must be faced."

"There it is. If we hear this, they're broadcasting to Havana and Mariel Bay. 'Ashes in their mouth.' That's a vivid image." Starpom spoke aloud and began writing.

Captain Savitsky shifted on his bench. "It won't stop until it's all over, and it will be over in a heartbeat. Nothing left but dead silence."

Oz interrupted, "He directs the following initial steps be taken immediately:

"First: A strict quarantine on offensive military equipment shipments to Cuba. All ships of any kind bound for Cuba, containing cargoes of offensive weapons, will be turned back, effective at 10:00 on 24 October.

"Second: He has directed increased surveillance of Cuba and its military buildup.

"Third: He regards any nuclear missile launched from Cuba against any nation in the Western Hemisphere as an attack by the Soviet Union on the United States, requiring a full retaliatory response upon the Soviet Union.

"Fourth: He has reinforced the base at Guantanamo with additional military units on alert.

"Fifth: He calls for an immediate meeting of the Organization of American States.

"Sixth: Under the Charter of the United Nations, he requests an emergency meeting of the Security Council to act against this latest Soviet threat to world peace and call for the dismantling and withdrawal of all offensive weapons in Cuba.

"Seventh: He calls upon Chairman Khrushchev to halt and eliminate this reckless and provocative threat to world peace. He calls upon him to abandon his course of world domination and to join the historic effort to end the perilous arms race and to transform the history of man. He says that Khrushchev has an opportunity to move the world back from the abyss of destruction by returning to his government's own words that it had no need to station missiles outside its own territory. He calls on us to withdraw these weapons from Cuba, to refrain from any action which will widen or deepen the present crisis, and to search for peaceful and permanent solutions."

"He sounds serious, and we're in the vice, squeezed between the Kremlin and the White House," said Poli.

"Now he is speaking to Cuba. He says he is a friend of Cuba. He knows their deep attachment to their fatherland and shares their aspirations for liberty and justice. He says their nationalist revolution betrayed their fatherland and fell under foreign domination. Their leaders are puppets and agents of an international conspiracy that turned Cuba against its friends and neighbors in the Americas and turned Cuba into a target for nuclear war — the first Latin American country to have these weapons on its soil. He says the new weapons are not in their interest, and the US has no wish to cause them to suffer. The Cuban people have risen to throw out past tyrants who destroyed their liberty, and he has no doubt that Cubans look forward to the time when they will be truly free from foreign domination, free to choose their own leaders, free to select their own system, free to own their own land, free to speak, write and worship without fear or degradation. Cuba will be welcomed back to societies of free nations and associations of the hemisphere.

"He says the path is hazardous, but consistent with the character and the courage of their nation and their commitments around the world. The cost of freedom is high, but Americans have always paid it. The one path they shall never choose is the path of surrender or submission. Their goal is not the victory of might, but the vindication of right; not peace at the expense of freedom, but both peace and freedom, here in this hemisphere and around the world. God willing, that goal will be achieved."

"God willing," Starpom looked up. "He's ready for war. His troops are on a war footing. He's willing to sacrifice Cuba, his country and ours."

"That's why the Kremlin changed our orders and why everything went quiet." Oz figured it out, "They got advanced warning of this speech, and they both needed time to figure out how to deal with the quarantine without tripping any wires."

The captain closed his mouth, but he needed more, "It's a wall in the ocean, like Guantanamo or Berlin. Switch to the military frequencies to get a sense for their reaction. Kennedy can say anything he likes to America, but our future hinges on what the US fleet hears. We've no choice but to attack that wall, to blow a hole the size of Russia."

He asked Oz to transcribe his notes into longhand and have the mate deliver them to the wardroom before he walked out and summoned Starpom and Poli to join him. Starpom, though thin, appeared to be whole, but Poli looked rough. He had lost too much weight; his face and arms were covered with a red prickly rash from blocked and swollen sweat ducts producing incessantly itching discomfort. When Oz's transcript arrived, the old man read the notes aloud, so they could hear it once again. When he finished, he said, "So it's a blockade."

"Not exactly a blockade; he's only turning military weapons away from Cuba," Starpom said, believing the distinction to be significant. "He's protecting his invasion."

"We carry offensive weapons," Poli added. "They won't allow us to reach Mariel Bay."

"We're not even heading for Cuba. Admiral Fokin Flatus gave us stand-down orders to some backwater combat sector in the southwestern Sargasso, probably because Moscow's reconsidering Operation Kama. We could've made Mariel Bay before the blockade starts. A carrier hunter-killer group can search a swath twice as wide as our sector, so we'll be unable to maneuver away from them. It's such a kick in the balls. If the general staff in Moscow can't protect their own submarines, how can they protect the Motherland? We'll be hanging around, waiting for instructions until we are captured or sunk." The captain gave Poli an askance glance, "You need to see the doctor for that rash."

"It'll take two days to reach our sector," Starpom estimated. "Moscow's afraid we'll be detected passing between the Caribbean island choke points. They don't want us to provoke a war, so they have us loitering on station until they figure out their next move."

"If our discovery provokes a war, we'll be ready," the old man said as he scratched his chest under his sweat-soaked shirt. "Perhaps they want us to monitor the blockade or intervene."

Hoping for a rejoinder, Poli looked at Starpom who locked onto his eyes, "The captain's right. It's our duty to protect the Motherland." Poli felt trapped. He was supposed to be a leader, a motivator and an inspiration to the officers, and they had him trapped like a wharf rat.

"When I'm prepared to launch our special weapon," the captain paused to consider the moment, the threshold, the palpable Rubicon he was crossing. "I will summon you both by title to the conn." He nodded to Poli, "*Zampolit.*" Then to Arkhipov, "*Starpom.*"

Poli lowered his eyes and leaned forward. "Aye, captain."

Starpom stood tall, looking directly into the old man's eyes. "Aye, captain."

Oz walked in. "Pardon me. US naval activity has intensified again. Airborne and surface ship radars are lighting up our *Nakat* screens. The chatter's gone wild, and they're chasing merchant ships to determine which ones are bound for Cuba. It's chaotic, but I'll keep scanning."

The captain slapped his thigh. "Good. For the first time, I know what we're up against. Now I can think."

Starpom spoke up, "We didn't expect such a blow, such a fatal assignment. With this announcement, the ASW pressure will intensify as we approach our sector, and we won't have another opportunity to relieve the crew from these hellish conditions. ASW carrier groups are covering the sea with a web of surveillance. The battery is charging slowly in this heat, and we need to complete a full battery charge while their ASW ships and aircraft get organized. It is calm tonight. We could slow and open the fore and aft deck hatches to suck the cool night air into the engine room and the torpedo room for direct ventilation. It's against protocol at sea, but it could give a few hours of relief. We should also empty sanitary tanks to give us a fresh start before we reach the blockade."

The old man shook his head, sweat flying in all directions. "Screw protocol. Make it so. Nobody on deck. Post a two-man watch on each hatch in case we need an immediate closure. Blow the sanitary tanks. Continue south by southeast to our combat sector."

Reducing the ship's speed to dead slow, the OOD ordered the deck hatches to be opened, and the evening air rushed into the engine room from the aft torpedo room, feeling cool only because the ambient air rushing through the diesel engines was so overheated. The sailors lifted their faces, gulping air through their open mouths. The sonar system remained clear of close-in contacts, but the *Nakat* and RIS sensors picked up the redirected motions of ships and planes to block merchant vessels bound for Cuba with hulls filled with contraband.

Chapter Eleven – Blockade

[Americans always] exaggerate the outside threat because they've never experienced that threat before. The Soviet Union had a 20th century with three major wars that fully destroyed their country… Americans never had enemies on their borders, so they exaggerate this threat like the Cuban Missile Crisis and 9/11. On 9/11, some caveman terrorist was lucky to have destroyed buildings in the United States. It doesn't mean that they can destroy the United States. But if you look in Washington, D.C., you see fortification around every governmental building, around the Congress, on the different agencies. It looks like people believed bin Laden controlled the streets of Washington, D.C. It was the same psychological reaction in the Cuban Missile Crisis. **Sergei Khrushchev.**

The warm sea air wafted cooler than Murmansk breezes compared to the sweltering days and nights since the hurricane. After a full night of soothing but illegal ventilation, Starpom ordered the deck hatches closed. Once he verified the pressure hull hatches were watertight, he slid down the ladder from the bridge into the conning tower and dogged the bridge hatch. Before dawn, he brought the ship down to periscope depth to give Oz the opportunity to evaluate the tactical situation prior to the morning briefing.

Oz's voice boomed over the announcing system, "Conn, RIS, dive, dive. They're using SOSUS to vector those damn planes at our diesel rumble. We're showing them where we are."

Executing the all-too-common, well-practiced, emergency dive procedures, including sliding down the ladder into the control room and dogging down the pressure hull hatch, Starpom settled the ship at one hundred meters before he received another report.

"Conn, sonar, fly over contact." He ordered the ship to her maximum safe depth of two hundred eighty meters, to avoid magnetic anomaly detection (MAD). The ASW aircraft carried a super-sensitive ohmmeter that hiccupped when it found a bump in the smooth magnetic field of the Earth, indicating a large mass of steel; the deeper the sub, the less pronounced the bump. After fifteen minutes without a second flyover, Starpom deduced that the plane failed to detect the B-59's presence, and they were safe to proceed toward their assigned sector, submerged and silent.

Covered in neon green ink as though he had been painted by a child and wearing his khaki shorts and a formal navy blue uniform tunic, Poli arrived to survey the watch transition looking both frightening and hilarious. The doctor had prescribed a chartreuse tincture that soothed his infected rash and knocked back the discomfort. Poli summoned the most dignified expression he could muster. "It looks ridiculous, but it doesn't itch."

Scratching his own rash that was still a few days behind Poli's symptoms, Arkhipov smiled and said, "That's excellent. Temporary escape from our brotherhood of suffering." They sent the mate to find the helmsman, who was late for his watch.

"He is crapped up, but..." the mate returned with his report. "He's getting cleaned up."

"What, in precise terms, do you mean by crapped up?" Starpom quizzed the mate.

"Comrade Arkhipov, he filled his pants with *govno* waiting for the head. Then he puked," the mate responded.

Victor took the conn, and Starpom rushed off to investigate. He visited the ship's doctor who informed him that the crew was in the grip of dysentery, probably caused by rotting meat and unsanitary conditions. He prescribed bowel medication for the afflicted, but all three heads serving ninety men on board were in constant use. The doctor also reported that dozens of sailors had received green paint for dermatitis, and he requested permission to break out the rubbing alcohol for use as a disinfectant to combat both illnesses. Starpom agreed and left for the wardroom and the tactical debrief in the rising heat.

He described for the captain the illnesses sweeping through the crew and steps to solve the problem, "The doc says the thermometers are reading off the scale, and he can no longer measure a man's temperature because the boat is so much hotter than the normal human body temperature."

The old man exploded, "You think that I don't see the threats to my crew? The men are the weakest link on a submarine. I eat the same food and the same water ration. I knew they were sick before they did. I shit myself three times this morning, but what choices do we have? We gave our crew a reprieve last night, but now we're submerged at the mercy of our submarine design in a tropical climate. Our water plant output is down to ten liters per day, one-eighth of a liter of warm water per man. The only thing we can offer them is leadership. It's rough, but they are tough submariners. When the time comes to fight, they'll fight."

Oz's post-dive briefing was fascinating as he delivered the news from behind his green war paint. "October 23, 1962. The enemy's chaos has self-organized.

Somebody ordered them to find submarines. There's so much chatter, I recognize their voices before I hear their call signs. They're flying S2F Trackers off the carriers and P3 Orions and P5M Marlins out of Florida to scour the Sargasso Sea. They're searching for subs, merchant ships bound for Cuba, and subs under merchant ships bound for Cuba. There's no *maskirovka*. The people hear everything. The National Broadcasting Corporation broadcasts the news every hour on the hour with news correspondents at the Pentagon. The entire situation unfolds in full view through radio news on military events that are astonishing, accurate, and truthful. The fleet thinks it's hilarious that Kennedy called the blockade a quarantine, as though we were diseased. They worry that we'll attack their carriers. They're determined not to allow our subs to operate in US coastal waters and will use any means necessary to drive us away. Our days are numbered. How much truth do you want? They're coming after us, and they're coming hard."

"Every damned bit of it. We'll go deep, avoid their MAD gear, and hope for cooler water." The sick feeling in his gut told him all he needed to know. He closed the meeting with orders to the OOD, "Take her down to two hundred eighty meters. There's no layer, nowhere to hide. It's hotter than hell up and down the water column. We'll remain silent to avoid detection. Rig ship for regime quiet."

The relative coolness of the night air, sucked into the ship through the deck hatches, vanished with ascending heat, humidity, and torment. Temperatures soared when the B-59 submerged, and the oppressive heat drove them back to the surface for ventilation, but every time the boat ventured toward the surface, the US Navy threatened their utter existence.

The world's largest navy projected its will over the Caribbean with the greatest ASW force ever assembled. Strike aircraft and carrier fleets dominated the Soviet assets. US surface ships could be defeated in one-on-one battles with Soviet submarines, but the two hundred US ships and hundreds of aircraft ganged together to improve their kill ratios. Fixed wing maritime patrol aircraft provided wide-area coverage of ocean areas to detect and engage submarines at great distances, vectoring ASW destroyers to pursue enemy submarines far outside torpedo range of the carrier. The overwhelming forces arrayed against the four submarines and twenty-five unarmed merchant vessels were hungry for a real enemy.

Starpom slept in fits of horror and hallucination with his revenants dancing salsa on the water, swinging nukes at destroyers and carriers and swearing like Slavic sailors, hissing, spitting, and gnashing sharpened teeth. A Siberian shaman appeared above the fray and spoke in the *Tungusic* tongue of the Evenki people, "I cannot alleviate your spirit's torment. There are obstacles for you to grapple and mysteries to unravel among your malevolent brothers. If you fail, your demons will snatch your world. Life is menacing and cruel while you live before it all goes quiet."

The days dragged on in stifling fever, exacerbating itching, painful scratching, raging thirst and severe headaches due to prolonged, deep-body dehydration at the cellular level. The emaciated crew, dizzy, sluggish and weak with swollen tongues that stuck to their pallets like parched leather, gravitated to the torpedo room. They stared into space, wide-eyed and shiftless, or at the purple-nosed leviathan within the compartment. The watch changed every two hours to prevent men from passing out at their posts. As the hour approached for the communications séance, the captain took the conn and ordered the ship to eleven meters after clearing baffles and convincing himself that no surface contacts were in the vicinity. He did not engage the diesels. He worried that the noisy diesel engines would attract attention and force him under the surface before the broadcast was complete. He shared his concerns with the other captains in the brigade during the previous broadcast and was anxious to hear their thoughts.

Captain Dubivko led the discussion regarding the blockade of Cuba, the threat of a thermonuclear conflict, American preparations for a decisive invasion to remove Soviet missiles from Cuba, and the construction of special camps in Florida for captured Soviet prisoners of war. The commanding officers expressed extreme surprise, tension, and confusion as they faced the threat of impending war without communication from Moscow, as though Admiral Gorshkov forgot that his submarines needed orders and direction. They only received Moscow's order to maintain constant communications with exposed periscopes for the remainder of the voyage, making detection unavoidable in their tiny combat sectors. No explanations, no context, no additional information, and no sign of the mysterious B-75.

Distant explosions indicated that ASW aircraft had intensified their pursuit of submarine targets with Julies and Jezebels. With darkness descending after the broadcast was complete, the old man had all the situational awareness he could glean, so he surfaced the ship and fired up all three diesels. Keeping the conn while the OOD shadowed his every action, he felt the enemy taking up battle positions, and he wanted to experience the moment first hand, to feel it in his gut where he made his decisions to punch and counterpunch. In less than thirty minutes, he spotted a Neptune flying directly toward him.

"Secure the diesels. Clear the bridge. This is the captain. Comrade Mikhailov has the conn. Take her down to two hundred meters. Stay on course. Have Comrades Arkhipov, Oz and Poli meet me in the wardroom." The mate ran to fetch the officers who entered the wardroom and slid into the tabled enclave. The old man, animated and still standing, leaned forward and placed his outstretched fingers on the table.

"Gentlemen, it's menacing. Every time we light off the diesels, there's a maritime patrol craft crawling up our ass in less than an hour, and thirty minutes is not enough time to charge the battery or ventilate the ship. It's that damned SOSUS picking up our diesel noise and vectoring in ASW planes. Of course, they don't know where we are, but they have a line of bearing, so they send out a plane. Starpom, rig ship for reduced electrical to save battery power and keep the heat generation to a minimum. Those fans aren't helping. Shut them down. Proceed ahead slow on the creeper motor. We'll reach our sector by tomorrow, but we need to sweat it out and conserve batteries. We're in for a miserable day. Oz, what did you pick up?"

"Same situation. Several destroyers are heading toward the blockade line. We'll close them by tomorrow when the blockade goes into effect. You're right. it's menacing beyond hope."

The captain frowned and shot back, "We can't lose hope. You know we could be at war at any moment. When that plane has been gone for thirty minutes, we'll go back to periscope depth. We'll use the blower to cool things down as best we can while we listen for instructions. Every damn thing is stacked up against us. Exercise extreme caution as we approach the blockade."

After thirty minutes, they returned to periscope depth with the prescribed masts, running the blower to ventilate the ship, consuming energy, not charging batteries and barely cooling the reeking, stifling hell-hole hull while waiting all night for instructions that never came. They energized the diesels around midnight, but the noise in the water attracted the attention of another Neptune aircraft, and they had to dive once again. After another thirty minutes, they returned to periscope depth to reestablish communications channels. At 04:45, shortly after energizing the diesels for the second time, another plane swept through the area with an initially high bearing rate. It changed course to close the range at a steady bearing. They secured the diesels, dropped the masts and dived to two hundred meters when sonar reported, "Flyover, flyover, buoys in the water, bearing 090, fifteen, maybe sixteen."

Bang. An explosion in the water.

"Damn," Victor blurted. Every man aboard reacted with a simultaneous and involuntary duck and cover, lifting palms to their ears after weeks of ultra-quiet submarine life, but there was nowhere to escape. The captain heard it as he headed to the control room when he felt the ship diving, and the shock wave stabbed at his chest.

"They found us, probably on radar and dropped sonobuoys and an echo ranging explosive on our heads. This is the captain. Right full rudder. Make your depth two hundred eighty meters. Steady on course 270. All-ahead one-third. They think we'll run, but we'll sit below their buoys. The echoes off the bottom will mask our presence."

Another explosion. No one on board had witnessed the business end of explosive echo ranging detonations, but sound travels through water with intense efficiency, and the ensonified steel hull resonated under sonic impact, trapping and amplifying the energy, thwacking the eardrums with convincing evidence of attack. Even the captain was rocked by the explosive impact of the percussive force.

The crew cowered at their watch stations, on their bunks, or in repose. Feeling little concern for their own lives, they didn't know nuclear, but their weapon was special, and it instilled in them a Soviet sense of pride, but now they were under attack. With Americans dropping bombs on them, they hated not fighting back and called for smashing the Americans. They demanded battle stations.

Their old man spoke so everyone could hear him convince himself to linger below the surface until it was safe to emerge. "They've lost us already. They search. We wait. They leave. We wait until we're certain before we proceed. The waiting is the hardest part."

At 10:00, Thursday, October 24, the captain was ready for his first look at the blockade. As his periscope broke the surface, he spotted two ships on the horizon near the blockade line with their radars blasting the *Nakat* screen. He swung forward, then port, then starboard and aft. All clear. Swinging forward again, he watched the destroyer approach alongside a merchantman for photo documentation. The merchantman hove to, dipped her colors, and proceeded on her way. He couldn't read hull numbers, but it was clear that the blockade was operational. A helicopter dipped its variable depth, pinging sonar to look below the merchant for a submarine.

Chapter Twelve – The Chase

You just can't have this kind of war. There aren't enough bulldozers to scrape the bodies off the streets. **Dwight D. Eisenhower.**

With his blood pounding in his head, the captain peered through the attack periscope at the active blockade. The *Nakat* lit up with another maritime patrol craft on a steady bearing, and he was forced to drop the masts and submerge the B-59, disappearing into silent calescence, mystery, and forced patience. On the first blockade day every hour saw aircraft and surface ship radars jamming the *Nakat* frequency spectrum. The pressure to stay submerged in insufferable heat under the thumb of ASW overflights mounted, but the old man ignored his personal discomfort as he labored to update the brigade submarine positions. Maintaining tactical coordination via encrypted messages between overflights, including data retransmission for any boat that missed the broadcast, his contemptuous attitude toward the brass faded as his need for concrete direction burgeoned. He expected war at any moment.

Captain Shumkov reported that the B-130's damaged diesel engines needed repairs that could only be completed on the surface. Captain Ketov communicated that the B-4's damaged aft deck hatch was still leaking, severely limiting her depth capability. Captain Dubivko's decoy ejector damage on the B-36 limited his depth to seventy meters. The B-59 diesel cooling system was contaminated by salt water, packing glands were leaking, and the electric air compressors had broken down. The old man felt as though everything they touched turned into *govno*. He transmitted Oz's horrifying report that a US aircraft sighted a Project 641 snorkel mast and periscope south of Bermuda. Three attack carriers, the *USS Essex* (CVS 9), the *USS Randolph* (CVS 15), and the *USS Wasp* (CVS 18), swept the Sargasso in reaction to the new submarine contact. Their visual sighting of a Soviet submarine set the US Navy airways abuzz and ignited the launch of more ASW aircraft to loiter on station.

The brigade remained submerged to evade waves of maritime patrol craft vectored to their positions by SOSUS, but the underwater environment grew treacherous for the crew within the B-59. The OODs abandoned the navy-blue jacket, worn for propriety's sake, and replaced it with a blue and white armband. Twisting the periscope for two-hour sessions in the white-hot sunlight and placid sea whenever they could poke a mast through the ocean surface, their nerves began to fray because American aircraft on high alert would not let them show their snorkels, even at night, to get a whiff of fresh air or a battery charge. Captain Savitsky took the conn and held it for long hours, multiple watches, denying himself rest as he attempted to figure out the unknowns on the surface of the sea above. He was hunted while his crew suffered. The submarine-turned-steam-bath gave everyone multiple problems, especially with their feet. Trench foot ran rampant, inflaming the soles of their feet, rendering them swollen, supersensitive, and evil-smelling. The desperate situation left most men feeling ill, weak, and unable to sleep in the monstrous heat and suffocating air. Everyone's skin erupted in rashes with no ability to wash off dirt and sweat, and the doctor expended the last of his green antiseptic tincture to control infections.

The men went directly to their bunks in exhaustion after standing watch without drink or nourishment. Limited reserves of fresh water permitted only one cup of water per person per day during prolonged periods of heavy sweating and dehydration. They ate one cup of compote, a dairy meal, two cups of tea and a glass of red wine each day. Freshwater was rationed for cooking, so the crewmen's thirst intensified while they steeped in their own perspiration, their fingertips growing white and wrinkled.

On the following day, Friday, October 26, Oz reported more submarine sightings by the American flotilla, spawning chatter like chum in the water, speculating as to the total number of enemy subs to produce so many observations. Sixty miles south of Cape Hatteras, a Coast Guard R5D plane had sighted a snorkel mast, maybe the long-lost B-75. A gull-winged, T-tailed, P5M ASW flying airboat reported a confirmed a Project 641 sighting northeast of the quarantine line. The B-59 had sailed into the enemy's lair.

Grousing that the US naval armada was fifty times greater than the Soviet submarine combat capabilities in a confined expanse of ocean, the old man knew they would be found again, but he had emergency stealth tactics to escape. Submarine B-130 had been detected while repairing a failed diesel engine. The B-36 was seen by a destroyer, the *USS Charles P. Cecil*. The B-4 was discovered by ASW aviation, but hey had evaded pursuit by submerging with charged batteries. Hoping that his comrades would not be captured, the captain heard the echoes of distant explosions. He feared being forced to the surface, and he feared incarceration for his crew in a Florida prison camp.

His diesels were his solution and his problem. While bringing fresh air into the ship and slowly charging batteries, their extreme noise drew fresh attacks from SOSUS-directed aircraft, exposing the B-59 to discovery of their snorkel mast and diesel plume. When submerged on ultra-quiet battery power, they vanished into the safety of silence and the suffering of sweltering distress.

As American destroyers exercised brazen piracy by forcing transport ships to heave to for inspection, the old man stared through the periscope, knowing that he was in the right, but he had never imagined being hunted like a criminal in international waters and unable to fight back. Small amounts of damp air flowed through the snorkel mast in short bursts from the blower to mitigate the choking conditions and expel toxic battery vapors. The ASW aircraft forced them to dive again and again, and the inexorable battery drain could not be remedied underwater. Shaking in claustrophobic fear, the men breathed with mouths wide open. The captain's anger swelled into a rage that boiled inside him, and he began tormenting his men when they needed to conserve strength.

"Where is the engineer?" His frustrations exploded. "Can't we fix that distiller and get these men more water? Release some high-pressure air into the ship so they can breathe. Where's the medico? Can't he help these sickened sailors? I want to see assholes and elbows. Square this damn ship away." His indignation bloomed into paranoid defiance.

"Radio, this is the captain. What do you have from Moscow?"

"Conn, radio, no information, just a synch tone to let us know they are transmitting."

"A synch-tone? Moscow's trying to get us killed. Why do I have to rely on the damn enemy for information? If I kill them, I'll have no info at all."

The captain feared discovery. His standing orders prohibited loss of secrecy and utter humiliation at the hands of the enemy. Such flagrant violations would bring severe consequences from the brass in the Soviet Union. As the situation degraded, Moscow refused to inform the brigade of developing geopolitical or tactical situations to maintain the security of classified data. Suspecting misleading falsehoods in the information gathered from US radio broadcasts and fleet communications, his reports from Oz provided his one insight for tactical and strategic scenarios.

Practicing patience after being driven down by a P5M with a thirteen-hour loitering capability, the old man received the first good news in over two days since the blockade began, "Conn, sonar, we are picking up rain overhead." Cool, fresh, and life-sustaining rain could mask his submarine from visual, sonar, and radar detection, and he brought the ship to the surface at dusk. Calling for Poli and Starpom, he charged them with organizing the crew for two-minute trips to the bridge for a navy shower and to gather and drink as much rainwater as their cupped hands could capture. Stormy and wet, a vast cooling veil swept over the boat in a flurry of clouds, rain, and wind. Furious gusts and delicious blasts of violent rain assailed their grateful, tortured torsos. The old man's preoccupation with caring for his haggard crew prevented him from noticing the P5M still on station. Circling the B-59 before darkness fell, the plane identified the Project 641 submarine, cataloging her as contact C-19 on the surface 350 miles south-southwest of Bermuda, northeast of the blockade line. Oz intercepted the US contact report in RIS, but it was buried in a blizzard of message traffic that masked its importance. When the carrier reacted by launching waves of patrol aircraft in their direction, Oz panicked and rushed to the navigation plotting station to fix the C-19 contact position. The old man continued to resuscitate and cleanse his crew, ventilating the ship and charging batteries when the P5Ms arrived to drive him below the surface.

Oz met the captain as he slid down the ladder from the conning tower into the control room and blurted, "They found us. They call us C-19. Hunter-killer Task Group Alpha on the *USS Randolph* has changed its course to close our position. They have a squadron of shore-based patrol aircraft, two nuclear submarines, and a half-dozen destroyers on the attack."

"Damn it all." The captain took off his soaking wet piss cutter and threw it on the deck. "Right full rudder, make your depth 275 meters. We'll go straight at them. Steady on 090. This squall is churning up the surface, so they'll have a hell of a time tracking us in this weather. We'll wait them out. Those waves are too large to permit snorkeling or ventilating at periscope depth, so we'll sacrifice the communications session to escape. Fetch Poli and Starpom and meet me in the nav shack."

When Oz arrived with Poli and Starpom they found the old man hunched over the nav table, water dripping off his nose onto the C-19 position on the chart. He looked up as he wiped off the moisture with his sleeve. "Shut the damn door. This is all my fault. I was trying to relieve the crew's suffering, and I've condemned them to a Florida prison camp. I underestimated the enemy."

"We can break away," Starpom offered. Poli shuddered and stepped backward.

"*Da.* We've already escaped," the old man shook with anger. "They couldn't find their own asses with both hands in this weather, but I've drawn them into our sector. We have nowhere to go. The carrier will stand off, outside torpedo range, and send destroyers and planes to find us. I should have been more cautious. There'll be hell to pay."

The oppressive heat bloomed within the boat. After dark, the captain brought the ship to periscope depth with the electronics mast exposed and the snorkel mast stowed. Powerful aircraft search-radar sweeps overwhelmed the *Nakat* scope and surfacing the boat for temporary relief was too risky. He knew that he was compromised. The B-59 heaved and pitched and slammed into the waves, rolling and tossing the crew all night long, expending energy and preventing sleep. The crew had been beaten by the sea and roasted inside the boat, but this night they roasted while they were beaten, and it continued into the next day.

Oz verified that the B-59 had attracted the pursuit of the *USS Randolph's* attack group of destroyers, *Berry, Lowry, Beale, Bache, Bill, Eaton, Cony, Conway*, and *Murray*, and fixed-wing aircraft and helicopters. The storm raged through the night and the next day, creating a standoff in which the American assets could not maintain submarine contact due to blinding weather, but the B-59 could not escape due to Moscow's sector restrictions and their staunch insistence on maintaining continuous comms that required dangerous exposure at periscope depth.

Hanging with the old man during the snorkeling evolution, Oz searched the UHF and VHF bands for revealing utterances from US Navy voice transmissions, and HF and shortwave bands for commercial radio broadcasts. He reported that one of the *Randolph's* Trackers, delayed until midnight by the limited visibility in the storm's extreme blackness, had laid sonobuoys in their sector despite the squally weather. In the wee hours of 27 October, it detected C-19.

"They got us," Oz passed the word to Starpom, who stopped into RIS before the 04:00 watch. He climbed the ladder to the conning tower to inform the old man.

"Just a matter of time," said the captain. "They can't do *govno* in this weather. We must get a battery charge, and it's too rough to snorkel. One of our electronic intelligence trawlers, the *Shkval* (squall) is bobbing around out here. I'll surface the boat near the *Shkval* and rotate the crew through nature's shower. It's the best we can do."

"Agreed," said Starpom, practicing stoic tolerance as he gave orders to surface the boat, raise the snorkel mast, and engage the diesels one last time. "We can escape, but we need fresh, charged batteries before we dive again."

"I've always resented the brass for meddling in our operations, but now with war brewing over our heads they remain silent," the old man said with his face pressed against the periscope. "They starve us for information, and we choke on the foulest air. Nobody cares."

Starpom patiently rushed the men through shower rotations, aware of the threat of aerial scrutiny. The captain battled the stormy seas until he sighted the *Randolph's* airborne Tracker at 09:00. A jolt of adrenaline left a metal taste on his teeth as he sent his men below.

The chase was on.

Chapter Thirteen – Black Saturday

On Black Saturday — October 27, 1962 — the leaders of the US, Russia, and Cuba came close to blowing up the world. They and we escaped, in large measure, because of luck. **Dark beyond Darkness, Blight and Lang.**

We knew, one mistake and we would invite disaster onto humanity...so we were careful.
Captain Second Rank Nikolai Shumkov, Commanding Officer, Soviet Submarine, B-130.

October 27, 1962 – later designated as Black Saturday by the White House – emerged as a dangerous and horrifying day in terms of a nuclear apocalypse. The fear of impending disaster encircled the globe, intensifying as the doomsday moment crept forward. Elevated defense conditions prevailed, one step shy of war. One provocation could tip the fragile balance beyond the point of no return, and the US Strategic Air Command targeted fifty-five hundred bundles of nuclear wrath against the Red Menace, with three thousand nuclear warheads aimed at targets in the Soviet Union, awaiting the launch command. The Pentagon's nuclear order of battle called for launching the complete inventory against a thousand sites.

The US tested two nuclear weapons that day: a ground explosion at the Nevada Test Site, viewed by thousands of tourists quaffing "atomic cocktails" at blast parties along the Las Vegas Strip, and a lesser-known atmospheric detonation over the remote Johnston Atoll, in the Pacific west of Hawaii. Across the globe, the Soviets air-dropped 262 kilotons on Novaya Zemlya.

The *USS Randolph's* sonobuoys bobbed in the stormy Sargasso, prosecuting C-19 while a US U-2 spy plane, over the North Pole, monitored the nuclear tests at Novaya Zemlya with high-altitude air samples and high-resolution photography. Flying blind into the northern lights at twenty thousand meters, the American pilot's magnetic compass spun in frantic circles, contorting itself, attempting to point straight down at the North Pole. The U-2 penetrated three hundred miles into Soviet airspace and scrambled six MiG fighter planes intent on shooting it down. Having spent time in North Korean prison camps during the Korean War, the pilot had no interest in going down over enemy territory again. He escaped death and avoided capture by racing toward an alternate landing strip at a remote Alaskan radar station. As he crossed back into American territory, the MiGs peeled off, but his fuel tanks emptied, and his engines flamed out. Averting disaster and military escalation, he glided to an emergency landing.

At 06:00, the CIA reported that five Soviet R-12 nuclear ballistic missile sites in Cuba appeared to be fully operational. Around noon, U-2 pilot, US Air Force Major Rudolf Anderson Jr., flew at 70,500 feet to photograph missile sites near Guantánamo Bay. Two Russian surface-to-air missiles, fired from Cuba, detonated, and shrapnel punctured his cockpit canopy and pressure suit. Under violent decompression, his lungs exploded and vaporized into a pink cloud that shot through the windshield of his disintegrating Dragon Lady at half the speed of sound. The remains of his body, strapped to the remnants of his plane, crashed on Cuban soil. His top secret mission did not exist except as a lost radar contact.

Pravda, the Soviet newspaper, hit the street with an announcement that Khrushchev had confirmed the presence of Soviet nuclear missiles in Cuba, but he would remove them if Kennedy removed US nuclear weapons from Italy and Turkey. Moscow radio broadcast his offer around the world, but not to the Soviet 69th Submarine Brigade.

Captain Savitsky operated the B-59, in his assigned combat sector in international waters on depleted electrical reserves and a limited air supply, unwilling to raise the snorkel mast to ventilate. While keeping the periscope and electronics mast exposed to communicate and to maintain situational awareness, his every attempt to rejuvenate the overheated batteries attracted ASW planes before the slow charging process could add energy. Making his rounds after the watch, Starpom found much of the crew gathered in the forward torpedo room where temperatures were a bit cooler. His breathing grew labored due to excess carbon dioxide, the human trigger to exhale, and his head felt ready to burst from oxygen starvation and the bullpen stench of the crowded room. With dwindling medical supplies, the doctor tended to men who lost consciousness and struggled to resuscitate the fallen sailors.

Starpom coughed. His limbs tingled and trembled as his blue-tinged fingertips pressed against a torpedo to steady himself. Fighting his tunnel vision, he called the control room, "Request permission to release some high-pressure air into the boat to improve the oxygen supply and reduce the carbon dioxide concentration."

"Permission granted," the old man responded in halted snorts. "Just a little."

Starpom sent the chief torpedo man to execute the order, adding, "Release all you can."

As the captain drew his first deep breath of the day when the audible rush of air increased the pressure in the boat, Oz reported that the *USS Randolph* positioned herself near the quarantine line to intercept C-19, the B-59, twenty kilometers away. Poking the attack scope above the water, the captain observed the *Randolph* conducting flight ops with S2F Trackers flying concentric circles around the carrier to examine the ocean inside the eleven-kilometer T-5 torpedo radius before widening the search. He sensed the aircraft on *Nakat* radar and heard the flyovers on sonar, although Jezebels were not deployed. The standoff dragged on until late morning when the aircraft reported a visual periscope swirl on a disappearing contact designated C-19. When the captain decided they had escaped, he took his ship deep to avoid MAD detection on a second flyover.

Three of the fast, maneuverable, long-endurance Fletcher-class destroyers peeled off the carrier screen and set course for the last-known C-19 position with their rakish bows slicing through the waves. The *USS Cony*, *USS Beale,* and *USS Murray* established a search formation to investigate C-19 with sonars pinging 235 decibels of ultra-high power into the non-layered ocean. Sonar-blind with flow noise over their bow domes at thirty-five knots, two destroyers raced toward C-19 at all-ahead flank, while one hung back at ten knots, pinging and hunting. After ten minutes, one of the fast ships slowed to search, as the other dashed to the site. The original slow ship lurched to flank speed while broadcasting its last contact information. The B-59 sonarman reported distant pings and cavitating screw noise from high-speed ships, calculating the destroyers would be on top of them in twenty minutes.

The old man viewed the destroyers' leapfrog, sprint-and-drift tactics in his mind's eye, and he knew the destroyer captains would expect him to run from their cavalry style charge at his position. His fevered soul felt the boundaries of peaceful coexistence dissolve under the onslaught of the ticking clock. Moscow had him penned in like a hog. Opening his mouth wide to stretch the muscles of his aching jaw, he inhaled to stave off waves of nausea. A dam within him collapsed, a flood of cold sweat poured out of him, and he veered the B-59 at the charging ships, increasing speed to all-ahead full while diving. Ringing pain into every man's ears, the destroyer pings hit the submarine hull like a ball peen hammer. The captain took the boat to max depth, got a bearing and bearing rate to the destroyers, and set course to evade.

"To hell with Moscow," he thought. As he fled the sector, he jettisoned noise-making rattle cans to jam passive sonars and ejected magnesium, gas bubble generators that reflected active sonar transmissions to simulate a contact.

"Welcome to our combat sector," he said to the destroyers, loud enough for the men to hear. "You search for us here while we keep attacking." Listening as the formation passed by, still chasing their original target solution, he had maneuvered into their baffles and to follow their search pattern. He bent down and placed his hands on his knees, fighting off the strangling surges of panic. He could breathe for a moment with their now-faint pings and sweeps aimed away from his ship.

All Captain Savitsky had ever wanted was to command a fighting ship in the teeth of battle on the front line, and he had dreamed of this moment all his life. *Keep attacking*, he thought. As he had always done in his dreams, he adjusted his ship's course to close the carrier.

The Tracker aircraft stationed over their sector received the destroyers' lost contact notifications and made a wing-over turn to approach the last known posit, releasing a full load of sixteen Jezebels in a search line. As the buoys came online, the pilot executed a box turn and dropped a Julie in the vicinity. The echo-ranging explosive sank like a dead weight to its appointed depth. *Bang.*

The B-59 sonar operator ripped off his headphones to rub his aching ears. Climbing the ladder to the conning tower, the old man heard the report in his baffles without the aid of sonar. The sonarman recovered and reported the destroyers had reversed course. Their deafening pings again clipped the sonar electronics, turning the screen bright green and impairing the sonarman's ability to hear or see anything else. Another Julie exploded.

On the sub, Julie blasts could not be distinguished from tactical depth bomb explosions. Wondering what his attackers had in mind, the captain evaluated his options. He knew the sonarmen on the Tracker had seen the B-59 echo return on their sonar screen and reported the contact to the destroyers were on their way to his position, with torpedoes and depth bombs.

"Main battery at ten percent. We need a charge," a voice reported from the engine room. He had four, maybe five hours left, but low-battery reports were notoriously inaccurate. Losing power at test depth could kill his ship by the loss of depth control, so going deeper was no longer an option with no backup for dead batteries.

"Make your depth eleven meters." He was taking her to periscope depth, the sub's attack depth, no longer able to hide. The desperate, low-power scenario prevented him from employing speed, except for short bursts, and from going deep, even momentarily. The Americans had chased him for four days, but he had foiled their onslaught, but now he was trapped with nowhere to run. His own Admiralty had boxed him in, limiting his maneuverability, forcing him to expose his position at the surface while waiting for signals that never came. *The ignorant bastards deliberately placed us in the claws of destroyers, and the destroyers are closing in to destroy us.*

As the old man surveyed the room, his sweat glands in his hairline pulsed perspiration droplets into his hair, and the sweat coursed down his face to dribble off his nose. His beleaguered crew squatted in dirty undershirts, emaciated, rash-infected, dehydrated, and out of fight. Their swollen tongues lolled from dry mouths and sunken cheeks. Hollow eyes followed his movements, striving to comprehend his activities, to string them together in their confused brains, deprived of nutrients, water, oxygen, and information.

The captain grabbed the mic, "Battle stations." The Americans left him only one escape option, and he was ready for a fight.

The crew rose from their prone positions and moved to their battle stations as though a second wind had blown through their embattled souls, finding energy where none existed. Oz rushed to RIS, knocking down larger men scurrying to their assigned positions. Experienced men stood at the significant fighting positions, ready to deliver battery power for ship's maneuvers and firepower to the enemy until nothing was left to deliver. Secondary and tertiary waves of men formed backup teams in case of casualties during the fight, damage control teams to inspect and defend battle wreckage from flooding or fires, and runners to relay information or fetch sundry items during the engagement. Phone talkers manned sound-powered phones that continued functioning like sophisticated soup cans on taut strings when ship's power was lost.

"Battle stations manned and ready," Poli, the phone talker, reported to the old man about to fight the battle. He used the crosshairs in the reticle of his attack scope to shoot bearings to the bull noses of the *Cony*, the *Beale,* and the *Murray*. The destroyers had been released from the carrier screen formation to chase the C-19, but they had lost contact again, floundering in temporary confusion until the Tracker vectored them back onto their prey.

Starpom stood over the nav chart, plotting destroyer and carrier track lines overlaid on own ship's position. He broke the silence, "What's the tactical situation?"

"We're in extremis," the captain said in a quiet voice. "Every time we show ourselves, they drive us down. The American commanders understand our limitations better than our own brass. They mean to suffocate us into surrender, but we will not surrender. We keep attacking."

The destroyer captains, pesky and persistent, pursued the submarine-like attack dogs. As expendable platforms in the battle order, they posed as tempting targets to lure a submarine into shooting one of them, so the others could pounce with ASROCs and depth bombs while the expended target strove to remain afloat.

"I'm not falling for that ploy. I want the carrier," said the old man. "We take out the entire hunter-killer group, and our problems go away. We terminate their plans for a Cuban invasion."

He swung the periscope west toward the blockade line. The *Randolph's* magnificent hurricane bow turned into the wind, conducting flight operations, launching a fresh wave of ASW Trackers to coordinate with land-based aircraft and the destroyers. "Stand by for a radar burst on my mark, ready mark. Carrier bearing 295."

"Carrier range — thirteen thousand meters."

"They think they have us. *Nyet*. Don't let the bastards wear you down. It's the wolf they can't see that they must fear. We keep attacking."

Secrecy had prevented his freedom to maneuver, but he was sick of skulking about, hiding from the giant Yankees. Now, at long last, he was stalking a carrier, clashing in a remote sector of black, empty ocean, holding fast to his naval instincts, mission objectives, and standing orders. His operational and tactical execution pitted his submarine against the full carrier group. He knew he could not attack, but neither could he compromise. He resolved to offer to the task force commander and the aircraft carrier commanding officer the torturous pain of unrelenting tension and fear. He wanted them to feel the crippling agony of uncertainty and frustration. He was determined to become the face of their death on the high seas.

Arkhipov commanded the combat information center at the nav table, plotting enemy contacts to calculate fire control solutions prior to the attack. His malevolent fiends danced in his head, black-hearted devils trying to leap the chasm to his side, no longer addicted to impulsive death, but seeking to submit to sanity. He had kept them secret from his doctors and his superiors since the K-19 disaster, but they threatened to expose him. When he turned to face them, he questioned why he let them dominate his considered view of life, his commitment to preservation, and his dedication to service. They begged him to satisfy their cravings, to feed their perverted memory of brave sailors who offered their lives at the altar of nuclear power to save their shipmates. The time had come to take up the scepter of fallen submariners in defiance of their ghosts and to fight alone, to offer his life at the temple of nuclear war to save his ship, his Motherland, and his Olga. Turning away, he left the *dybbuks* on the far side of the chasm.

"Carrier range, 12,498 meters." Starpom announced, "Course to close, 255."

The old man had risked detection with a radar burst, but with all the *Nakat* activity, a passing pulse might go unnoticed. Running toward the carrier at full speed chewed through his remaining battery, but he needed to position his boat on the edge of attack range to maximize his kill ratio and minimize his chances of being sunk by his own blast. In fifteen minutes, he would slow and go up for another carrier posit to improve his target motion analysis for calculating a torpedo solution. Oz entered the control room, breathing easier after oxygen-rich air drifted down from the conning tower, and reported that the *Randolph* had fanned out four destroyers in a forward screen and a fifth as plane guard in the wake of the carrier. Three other destroyers chased C-19, and the airwaves buzzed with chatter about submarine sightings and aggressive contact pursuit.

Back on the attack scope, the captain took the B-59 to periscope depth, preparing to snort oxygen into the watery hellhole, when he sighted an aircraft bearing down on his position. The Tracker sighted his periscope and reported a disappearing radar contact with a visual swirl.

"Emergency dive." He dived with only five percent battery charge remaining — maybe two hours left. "Make your depth fifty meters."

"Rig ship for emergency power." Except for shadowy red glimmers that shrank the conning tower into a grouping of rose-faced phantoms, the lights went out. Oz counted fourteen RIS contacts — they were bringing in reinforcements. The Tracker set its track for a Jezebel drop and deployment of explosive echo ranging grenades.

An ear-shattering explosion reverberated through the boat. With almost no reserve power, they could neither run nor hide to evade the successive groups of Trackers launched at them from the *Randolph* with more sonobuoys and MAD gear to pin them down. Joining the fray with dipping sonars, three Sea King helicopters pinged at maximum decibels to reestablish contact. The destroyers zeroed in on the helicopter hovering overhead and presided over the ear-splitting ping party with Doppler sweeps to measure the submerged speed of an escaping sub. After five hours of catch and release, the *USS Beale* and *USS Cony* regained solid sonar contact on C-19 and needed no further assistance from the airborne contingent, but the

Trackers continued to swarm and drop echo-ranging depth bombs. The *USS Murray* maintained contact with constant pinging for four straight hours throughout the chase.

Chaos ensued. The multi-headed US antisubmarine beast wielded enormous firepower with overwhelming enthusiasm against one struggling, but deadly, submarine. Mimicking clowns at a crime scene, the helter-skelter antics ignored any clues of danger or even death lurking below the surface and kicked up mist into their own faces. Low-flying Trackers threatened to collide with sonar-dipping helicopters, who blocked strafing runs by destroyers prepared to launch practice depth charges, signaling grenades designed to beckon a submarine to the surface. The constant over-pinging rendered life inside the hull of the B-59 excruciatingly painful. Men reached for greasy rags to stuff into their tender ears, accustomed to submarine silence. The incessant pings and doppler sweeps felt like nails being driven into each man's skull, and the implacable explosions were reminiscent of freight trains roaring in their ears. Internal communications became impossible amid the pandemonium because the crewmen blocked their ears against the deafening assault.

Documenting political concurrence with official orders as the command phone talker, Poli could not protect his ears. Panting and leaning against the railing near the ladder to the control room, his bones and skin covered in oozing, ulcerous blotches, surrounded by faded green war paint, his humanity had left him long ago. He surrendered to circumstance, no longer caring that they were under attack or how they would respond. He only wanted it to end. The object of the mission was the mission. The purpose of the nuclear weapon was the nuclear weapon. The singular possible reason for a nuclear war was the damned nuclear war, and nothing would be solved by all the deaths. He didn't care. He just wanted it to stop.

The US antisubmarine force regrouped, yielding operational control to destroyers at the scene. The *USS Beale* conducted a strafing run on the submarine's position, dropping five practice depth charges as prescribed for signaling submarines to surface. Each depth bomb, *Bang,* descended until, *Bang,* it reached its designated, *Bang,* depth pressure to detonate, *Bang,* in order of launch, *Bang,* with much greater intensity than echo-ranging grenades.

Saturated with carbon dioxide, hydrogen, and methane, air aboard the B-59 ran low on oxygen, driving the crew into hypoxia, lethargy, and confusion. High temperatures caused dehydration, starvation, and heat exhaustion. The choking men, lying about the boat in grimy underwear, quivered with cramps, and some fainted under the emergency lighting as carbon dioxide concentrations exceeded danger levels. The eighteen endless hours of agonizing submergence, under constant attack in a steel tank, culminated in an ominous hail of subaquatic grenades that brought visions of walls of fire or walls of water. The old man checked his watch — one hour of battery left, maybe. The remaining time to fight drained away like an hourglass, and oxygen deprivation closed in.

"Torpedo room, control. Assemble the special torpedo, prepare it for launch."

"Control, torpedo room, this is the special weapon expert. Aye, aye, captain." Subjected to the explosions and the high-powered pings, he knew they were at war.

The *USS Cony* pounded the submarine with five more depth bombs, while all three destroyers banged away with their bow sonars. "This is the captain," he spoke into the general announcing system microphone. "*Starpom* and *Zampolit* report to the conning tower." The signal for initiating the nuclear weapon protocol was his calling for Poli and Starpom by their official position titles, even though they were both in the conning tower. The *USS Beale* closed the last known C-19 position, ejecting jackhammer depth charges that exploded with spectacular power and proximity to the diving hull like a hundred-knuckled fist, damaging radio antennae two meters above the old man's head. "Damage reports, damage reports," he screamed into the announcing system mic. He screamed from shock, from his red curtain of rage, and from the loss of ability to modulate his voice with his deafened ears. Damage reports were negative despite undetected damage in the sail. More hunter-killer destroyers joined the *Beale* to pummel B-59 with more explosives.

"Control, torpedo room, the special weapon is assembled and battle ready."

"Torpedo room, control, load the special torpedo into tube number two." The captain turned to the navigator, "Prepare the carrier fire control solution for transmission to tube number two." He wheeled around to face Starpom and Poli, who supported himself on an overhead strap.

"We're surrounded by ten American ships trying to sink us." His wild eyes reflected his words, "We suffer lack of breathable air and insufferable heat. Our battery charge is down to water, and we need to surface. They're hitting us hard, but it's how hard we hit back that shows that we are

Russians. These illegal attacks prove that war rages above us. The only way out of this is to punch straight through it."

"We're surrounded by chaos that makes no sense." Arkhipov spoke up, "If the Americans wanted war, they would have it. There can be no war above us, not even an attack. Our boat may not be doomed if we stand down."

"No, you stand down, sailor." The captain shoved his finger into Starpom's forehead. "We're under attack in international waters. They're dropping bombs on our heads." As if on cue, the OOD shadowing the captain, passed out and collapsed in a pile of naval exhaustion.

"Perhaps they ask us to surface, dropping depth bombs port and starboard, noisy, not lethal." Arkhipov could not be intimidated, saying, "These explosions are mouse nuts, not elephant balls. They're saying, 'We know you're there. Identify yourselves. Come up. We intend no harm.'" He looked at the fallen man and said, "Somebody fetch the doctor to revive the OOD." The mate hauled ass.

"Control, torpedo room, torpedo tube two is loaded with the special weapon."

"This is the captain. Flood tube number two."

"Control, torpedo room, flood tube two, aye."

Arkhipov experienced a moment of clarity rarely known by Russians whose government's lies wove threads of truth to stitch deceptions into credible disinformation. He saw that there was no war. The Americans wouldn't waste their substantial resources dinking with a diesel submarine if a full-blown war had broken out, and there was no other kind of war. They would either kill the sub or abandon it without a second thought. He saw that a nuclear attack on a US carrier would unleash immediate, all-out nuclear insanity across the globe. He saw that he would battle Captain Savitsky, but the conflict would be short-lived without ship's power, oxygen or water. He saw that the only solution was to surface the ship and proceed with saving the crew. He needed to remain conscious, keep his distance, and prepare for the fight of his life. He would hold his own and tell the truth. There would be consequences, but he would stand behind his word.

"Control, torpedo room, torpedo tube two is flooded and equalized."

"There's no evidence of war," Arkhipov pressed his case. "They have us nailed. If they wanted us dead, we'd be dead. You start this war, you condemn us all to death." The doctor rushed in with a stretcher and laid it next to the OOD. Gently rolled the man onto the canvas between the rails, he and the mate lifted him, transporting him in silence out of the room. Everyone faced the old man, needing someone to follow to their fate. Another explosion detonated, surprising, infuriating, but not deadly.

"Damage reports," the captain winced as Oz entered the room, but his calm voice reflected Starpom's remarks that had foreshadowed the recent concussion. "Torpedo room, open the torpedo tube door."

"All damage reports are negative." Before Poli could finish his report, five explosions, close aboard, thundered through the boat, knocking him to his knees.

"The war has already started up there, and we are down here doing somersaults," Captain Savitsky lost his composure in the asphyxiating madness. He glared at Starpom, raised his voice, and screamed, "We're going to blast them now. We'll die, but we will sink them all. We won't disgrace our Navy or shame the fleet. Navigator, update the carrier solution and download it to the number two torpedo tube."

"Aye, aye, captain." The navigator worked the fire control station.

"We cannot do this," Arkhipov said. "May we speak in private?"

"What the hell is wrong with you?" Savitsky grabbed his shoulder and shoved him into a corner of the control room. He sputtered, "We agreed to use the nuke when attacked. By God, I'll cut your head off and impale it on my periscope if you defy me. This is my choice, not yours." He wiped the spit from his purple face.

Starpom lowered his shoulder into a defensive physical position and released a tense breath in the red shadows of the darkened control room.

"*Yest*, it's your choice when you are certain with no trace of doubt, but look at the facts. Check your damage reports. No damage. No hole in our hull. The admirals said to use the nuke if war breaks out and you have a hole in the hull. You think this chicken shit tease is war?" Starpom pulled away. "You said with your own words, 'only one eye for one eye.' They have nuclear depth bombs, and we have no damage. There's no war unless you launch it. You command this ship, and you cannot send us into the viper's mouth. We hold human history here, in our sub. You can't unleash *Tunguska* on our enemies, on our Admiralty, and on our Motherland. You'll loathe yourself for all eternity. Yes, they harass us, but we can't respond with anger. It's a time for certainty, not for guessing. Get yourself under control and find another way. You never want to start this fight. You'll become the most reviled man in history."

The words struck the old man like a fist to the face, snapping his head back and shocking his senses. "We can't trust this enemy," Captain Savitsky said as he dropped his hands. "They give us no alternative."

"Don't trust them, test them. Release a single sonar ping in response to their depth bombs to indicate that you seek a peaceful resolution. Then we listen." Arkhipov dropped his hands as well. "If the bombardment ceases, we know they don't intend to kill us. We'll turn east, surface, and save our crew. If I'm wrong, if they shoot us, I'll join you and use your fire control solution. We kill everything."

Chapter Fourteen – Surface

It seems that what determines the choices a man makes in critical, life-threatening situations is still his inner conviction, his sense of responsibility for the events around him, his personal conscience. **Nikolai Zateyev, Commanding Officer of the Soviet Submarine K-19.**

A man does what he must—despite personal consequences, in spite of obstacles and dangers and pressures—and that is the basis of all human morality. **John F. Kennedy, Profiles in Courage.**

Placing the back of his hand against his fevered forehead, the old man struggled to think through his ice pick headache, the profound ringing in his ears, and his blurring vision from insufficient oxygen in his capillaries. A single ping could signal only one of two things: the intension to surface in peacetime or a final range check prior to a wartime attack. He found no harm in Starpom's solution, a clever ploy that demonstrated wisdom, honor, and courage and still left him with the tactical options to resolve the crisis. He remembered the dead soldiers he had known in Brest and felt their agony as he surveyed his crew. The batteries and the oxygen would give out at any moment, and his crewmen needed to surface even if a battle ensued. He was leading them to certain slaughter on his current course, but one ping, one small risk, could reveal the enemy's intentions as well as their positions and give him that final kernel of situational awareness he needed to trust his fire control solution.

Reaching his trembling hand for the mic, he said, "Sonar, conn. This is the captain. Transmit one full power ping, only one." He stared at the ravaged souls assembled before him. "Record ranges and bearings to all contacts." *Ping.* Their own ping rang through the hull with the same intensity as the destroyer pings. When the ringing died away, they listened. Thunderous, ear-splitting, wondrous silence. After a few quiet moments, sonar reported ranges and bearings to the carrier and the three destroyers and indicated that they had simultaneously come to a full stop.

The old man stood for a long minute in the absence of violence before he uttered, "Right standard rudder." As he looked across the control room once again at the ghostly red-shadowed faces, mouths and eyes wide open, his limbs tingled from adrenaline flooded hypoxia. With his heart pounded in his head, he said, "Steady on course 090."

Starpom remained crouched in a defensive posture, and Poli clung to the ladder, headphones perched at an odd angle on his head. Oz knelt in supplication near the aft hatch, ready to spring for RIS. Starpom nodded. Poli quivered. Oz raised one thumb straight up. No one spoke.

Bringing the B-59 from the violent underworld to the precarious and unknown conditions of periscope depth, the captain raised the attack scope and peered into the Stygian darkness, swinging port and starboard until he spotted the running lights of the destroyers. Peaceful and quiet, the cross-haired view confounded his military mind.

"Torpedo room, conn. Close the torpedo tube door. Planes man, make your depth seven meters. Raise the snorkel mast. Engage the diesels." The post-gale evening air rushed through the boat, energizing the panting crew as the diesel rumble rolled over their grateful souls. Shaking his burly head, the old man breathed deeply to clear his mind and to make sense of the sudden reversal of every thought he had believed to be true.

When the B-59 broached the surface, a blue-white light blared from the *USS Cony*, flooding her decks and making it impossible to see in the night. Ascending to the bridge, wearing a pugnacious scowl and shading his eyes, the old man stomped his feet with fury. Starpom followed, inhaling oxygen-rich night air, and Oz climbed into the conning tower, eager to breathe in cool temperatures. Wild jazz music and floodlights blaring in the blackness from the *USS Murray* reminded him of Mardi Gras and dissipated his tensions of impending war that gripped his guts.

Flummoxed by the flagrant display of buffoonery and reckless horseplay, the old man alternated between bare eyes and binoculars to ogle the spectacle before him. "It's a dog's breakfast, an absurd farce. What the hell do we see before our eyes, *pizdetz*?"

The captain's question was directed to Oz, the expert on all things American. "Oh, my Lord, Starpom was right. The idiots never intended to sink us. God Almighty, it looks as though they've thrown us a party." Oz's serious assessment sounded silly when he said it aloud.

The captain scowled. "Or a public execution. They both start out the same way. These imbeciles tried to kill us and dared us to kill them, sons of bitches."

"The Americans should not be allowed to play with nuclear weapons," Oz thought out loud. "If they can't take nuclear devastation seriously, what do they hold sacred?"

"It's not how we fight," the captain said and slowed the ship in the serene water. He ordered his crew to stand down from battle stations, "Open the both deck hatches for the crew. Let them escape their steel coffin."

The hatches slammed open, and the crew streamed onto the main deck, stripping off sweat-soaked clothes, howling expressions of joy and relief, ignoring the *USS Cony*, steaming off the starboard beam, inside the dead zone of submarine torpedoes. A red flashing light blinked out a message from the *Cony's* communications officer.

"Oz, do you read Morse code?" the captain stared at the red sparks. "What's he saying?"

"It's not Morse code. They're signaling in Cyrillic. He says, 'Identify yourself.'"

"Send the signal lamp to the bridge." Having no use for games, the old man was free to operate his ship without interference. He reverted to his deep sense of *vranyo*, his dry Russian sense of humor. "Send in Russian, '*korabl*.'"

"Ship?" Oz grinned and set the signal light on its stanchion. "You want to say 'ship?'"

"*Da*, we have to explain everything to your giant Yankees," the captain felt comforted yet aggravated to communicate with his foe, a common man like himself. "We are a Soviet ship steaming in international water."

Oz used flashing light signals to pass the message, and they waited for the Americans to decipher the code. The old man struggled to reconcile his feelings of relief and defeat, of escape and capture, and of release and revulsion. He had stared into the seventh circle of hell, the circle of the violent. He stood fast, never blinked. He emerged to meet them face-to-face in some lurid circus.

The red light winked out, "What ship?" The captain read the signal himself and responded, "X. Tell 'em '*korabl* X.' They can find us in their recognition manuals."

As Oz flashed the message, the captain continued to reflect on his disorienting angst. With no sense of bravery, he took pride in his resolute strength and discipline, but he had been the worst kind of wrong, and the implications petrified his mind. He was mistaken, as humans have always been, in his essential notions of right and wrong.

"What is your status?" the flashing light inquired.

"The bastard wants to know how much damage he inflicted," the old man scoffed. "Tell him we're conducting normal operations on the surface."

Oz flipped his wrist to activate the signal shutter in reply, but the captain wondered what normal meant now. With moral certainty under pressure, Arkhipov's approach was brilliant, right and just. Leaders need solid information, sound reasoning, and good advice to make good decisions. American bombs still echoed inside his head, but despite the attack and the heat of battle, in the end he had made the correct call. He was right, and that was all that mattered.

"Do you require assistance?" the *Cony* questioned.

The captain nudged Oz away from the signal lamp and sent his personal reply, "*Nyet.*"

"Do you hear aircraft?" Starpom broke the silence.

They spun around to see a formation of low-altitude S2F Trackers flying at them. The jazz music yielded to the roar of twin-engine aircraft jettisoning white phosphorous. Without warning, fifty-million-candlepower incendiary devices exploded above their heads producing blazes of brilliant white light designed to activate photoelectric camera lenses. As their eyes slammed shut, they bent down and could not see each other. They grasped for familiar objects, a rail or gunwale, to orient themselves in blindness. Above the plane engine roar and diesel rumble, they heard reports of aviation cannons as hundreds of rounds sliced into the roiling wake abaft the boat.

"Order the chief to break out the small arms and prepare to repel boarders," the old man reverted to his rage against being under attack. "Torpedo room. Open torpedo tube two door." It was a bluff. Submarines have no antiaircraft weaponry. They sink ships.

"Oz, send this message in Morse code, in English, 'This ship belongs to the Union of Soviet Socialist Republics. Halt your provocative actions.' Then go below and broadcast the same message in an English radiogram on their frequencies. Damn Yankees."

The *Cony* viewed the open torpedo door above the waterline under the floodlights and got the B-59's message. They ripped out flashing light regrets for aggressive actions. "Apologies. Smooth sailing." Acknowledging the apology, the old man closed his torpedo tube door.

The *USS Cony* escorted the B-59 so closely that the officers on both ships could read each other's faces. The big gun, manned on the *Cony*'s forecastle aimed straight ahead, not at the B-59. The *Randolph's* aircraft and helicopters flew over the sub a dozen times at altitudes of twenty to one-hundred meters, searchlights aimed at the B-59's bridge, blinding the officers and lookouts.

Standing between Oz and the captain as he scrutinized the chaos on the decks below the bridge, Starpom said, "They're having a good look at us like we're the freaks in this carnival." All hands, on deck in shirt sleeves or less, breathing normally and cooling their tormented bodies while distracted by the midway light show surrounding their emergence from the depths of hell.

"Message sent and received," said Oz when he returned to the bridge and extended his hand. Starpom clasped it. Oz turned to shake the old man's hand, "They say that Americans will do the right thing after they've tried everything else. They don't know how close they came to a fight, and they feel victorious when we hold their lives and their country in one torpedo tube."

"The Prophet says, 'To overcome evil with good is good, to resist evil by evil is evil,'" Starpom shrugged. "God willing, Americans are done trying everything else."

"I am sick to death of hearing the quotes from the Prophet. Not all evil leads to harm. Nobody died, but life changed, and we're bound by what happened." The old man became more reticent, "No choice now but to live. They're planning some sort of trickery, but I will not let them board this boat."

"My apologies," said Starpom. "We must inform the brigade commander and Moscow that we've been discovered, but not attacked." Starpom thought about the attack and added, "Not attacked with intent to destroy."

"*Da*, we'll report that we surfaced to charge batteries and that we have American escorts. We'll request further orders." Nodding in agreement, the captain turned to Oz, "Help the comms officer draft a report and monitor the radio to see what transpired while we were away."

They watched other destroyers converge on the B-59 with cameras at the ready while the *USS Beale* pulled alongside and bathed the sub with blue-white floodlights. Seabat helicopters and fixed-wing aircraft harassed them with repetitive photo runs to document their role in the successful hunt for big game. Feeling humiliated, the old man knew that his ragged crew came under scrutiny at their worst moment. They had been magnificent under the cruelest circumstances and deserved better, but they were satisfied to breathe oxygen and soothe themselves outside their iron sarcophagus.

Back in RIS, Oz heard celebratory chatter on the airwaves and a *USS Randolph* report that she was departing for Norfolk with a boiler problem. He smirked and said, "Good, we'll add that to our sitrep. We broke the carrier."

Poli climbed the ladder to the bridge for a whiff of fresh air and a peek at the party outside that held no joy for him. He gulped so much sea air that he swooned and almost fell overboard, but nobody noticed his prostrated body, face down on the deck grates. It was over, all of it. The threat of nuclear conflagration, the incessant pounding, and a Cuban future. What was not over was facing the Soviet brass to explain their failure to remain covert, failure to evade the Americans, and failure to complete the mission. Heads would roll, and Captain Savitsky had failed in his first mission. His career was over, and Poli could no longer follow his leadership. He would start a new file.

Oz reappeared on the bridge to report urgent news to Starpom and the captain. "American radio reports that Kennedy and Khrushchev are talking. Khrushchev publicly requested an American pledge to never invade Cuba and to remove the American nukes from Turkey in exchange for the withdrawal of our nukes from Cuba. He is trying to save face. Kennedy's thinking it over."

"They're just weighing each other's balls, but it's about damned time. Any word from our brigade comrades or the missing B-75?" asked the old man.

"*Nyet*. They're all submerged, probably under attack, living our nightmare." Oz wished he had more.

"Any one of them could start a fight at any time," the captain said. "Monitor the tactical networks and be prepared to dive within minutes. We need to survive until morning to give our batteries a chance to rejuvenate."

"Aye, aye." Before Oz left, he stole another look at the aircraft carrier *USS Randolph* conducting night flight ops. He remembered their voices and the call signs he had come to know so well. He almost never had the opportunity to see his marks in person. Oz noticed Poli rising to his feet and helped him down the ladder to the safety of the boat.

The old man observed the empathetic and generous gesture and said to Starpom, "You think you know me after all we've been through, but you're wrong. You're not the only man carrying ghosts from your past. Every man who survived the Great War with limbs intact hauls his ghosts behind him. We bear their suffering, trying to make sense of the senseless. They speak an unspeakable truth to us. Still, I get red-assed every time somebody drops bombs on my head," the old man spoke to Starpom. "It's been that way since I was a kid. It's like the Germans attacking all over again. I had to rise up, fight back, keep attacking. There's an animal inside me that won't be cornered."

"I know," said Starpom. He turned to face the old man and reached out to clasp his shoulder. "I was there, and you fight well for the most junior captain in the navy."

They stood for a moment, smiling with tears welling in their eyes, before the captain said, "*Da*, so you understand. You're a submariner. If they had sent subs to chase us, they wouldn't have dropped bombs on us. They comprehend subsea warfare. They know how we think."

"It's true. These undisciplined Americans broadcast in the clear with no *maskirovka*," Starpom remarked as he released his grip. "They don't study warfare, so they trip over themselves, and their music is painfully primal. They're angry villains, and anger is an evil counselor."

"They're overflowing with villains, and I tried to stand up to them," the old man searched for answers that could give him resolution. "It was not heroic to give in. There were no heroic choices. I needed a dose of reason. I thank you for that. I'm nothing if not a reasonable man."

"You did the right thing and killed your anger while it was small. You saved your crew."

"If we had launched that torpedo…," the captain shuddered. "Washington wouldn't know what to think, a nuclear explosion out of nowhere. They would have figured that we had a new secret delivery system that they could not detect. Can you imagine the panicked response?"

"The carrier would have had about ten minutes to identify a torpedo in the water."

"Right, but after a nuclear blast, the carrier's gone. The Americans couldn't be sure of the cause. We'd be dead. We couldn't surface into radioactive fallout. We couldn't stay down. The destroyers would've had ten minutes to attack us with real depth charges." The captain pointed at the *Cony*. "See those boxy mortar launchers? They're called Hedgehogs. They launch the whole box in less than a minute. Our only salvation was that everybody held their fire, and it's not over yet. Our comrades are out there, under attack, deciding for themselves how to deal with these crazy Americans, and we can't contact them." The old man kicked a deck grate. "We're held hostage on the surface by our dead batteries Lord knows how long they'll take to recharge in this damned heat. Get a tech up here to fix that damaged antenna."

"Aye." Starpom considered their predicament, "What is your plan from here?"

"Look at the facts," the captain rubbed his bulldog chin. "We need to snorkel all night to vent the ship and charge batteries. We'll use the time to collect intelligence and communicate with Moscow. Things are changing fast, so we expect the Admiralty to react with a new directive. No rush to escape, and the crew will enjoy the sunshine. We can escape tomorrow night. Work with the chief and the doc to tend to the crew. I'll hold the conn."

"An element of kindness lurks inside you," Starpom smiled. "It's a sign of faith."

"I'm no believer, but you've taught me something about your famous Prophet."

"Pardon me for saying so, but the Prophet says, 'When Allah wishes good for someone, he bestows upon him the understanding of Islam.'" The captain laughed out loud, and Starpom left him embroiled in thoughts of what he might have done. He had no real choices. His decisions were just his recognition of the tactical situation, but he imagined how he might have made an error. His comrades were below the surface even now, under duress and starved for information, trying to catch a breath inside the pressure cooker. He wanted to pray for them, but what good would it do. He would try to inform them that there was no war on the surface, but his tactical antenna was damaged. His only hope was for Moscow to relay the vital situational awareness and avoid a mistaken Armageddon.

After midnight, Oz appeared with a message from Moscow directing them to escape their American escorts, throw off their pursuers and move to a combat holding position near Bermuda.

The old man stewed, "Don't those bastards understand what it means to surface and charge batteries? They act like they're directing nuclear submarines that can remain submerged for months. We told them that we surfaced to charge batteries, right?"

"*Da*, we did." Oz also reported that the US tactical radio chatter buzzed with the tactical prosecution of three Foxtrot-class diesel submarines, two inside the circular five-hundred-mile quarantine line, and President Kennedy's message of congratulations on raising a Soviet sub.

"Raised us hell. They didn't raise us. I hate those damn Yankees. We raised ourselves so we could breathe. Am I the only one who knows what's going on? Moscow's still putting us in the penalty box, and your giant Yankees are declaring victory." The captain stomped his feet on the deck grates and slammed his fist into the signal lamp. "It's not over yet, and war could break out any moment. Have Starpom clear the decks in preparation for an emergency dive. Leave the deck hatches open to cool the ship, but post a quick reaction watch to shut them when ordered. Have the mate break out a flag," the captain added as Oz turned to leave. "Not the Soviet flag, the big red Russian flag."

The destroyers' lights flooded the B-59 as they plowed through the calm sea, and the old man viewed the US efforts to collect photographic and acoustic intelligence on their captive foreign prey. His crew did the same. The sonarmen, radiomen, and the *Osnaz* commandos actively recorded acoustic and electronic data from US ships. Intelligence is a 24/7 operation with both sides collecting signals for post-operational analysis.

The mate poked his head through the hatch. "Request permission to come up."

"Come up. Raise our flag for all to see. The Americans want Russians in their photos."

The mate climbed atop the sail and secured the red flag in the black night with a quick release knot. The *USS Murray* inquired for the B-59 to identify itself via flashing light. This time the old man, with a comic chuckle of his own, had the signalman send "*Prinavlyet,*" essentially Cyrillic gibberish equating to "I understand in a hurry." Two more destroyers, *USS Bache* and *USS Barry*, steamed within signaling distance, blazing away with their flashing lights to demand, "Identify yourself." The captain replied, "*Prosnavlast,*" or "Wake up power," leaving the American skippers to scratch their heads over the communique. To the captain, Americans were strange creatures.

After the mate returned to the control room, Oz popped up from the hatch like a weasel, "Good evening. News from Captain Shumkov. Not good. May I come up?"

"Come up, brief me," the old man needed company.

"I brought coffee," Oz said as he hoisted himself onto the bridge deck. Captain Shumkov's B-130 is under attack, and he's in bad shape. He had surfaced to repair one diesel engine by cannibalizing the other two. The US Navy designated him as contact C-18. We were C-19, so he was detected before us. Shumkov is trying to evade, but he can barely move or charge with damaged diesels."

"Thanks for the caffeine. I haven't slept in two days, but Shumkov's situation is much worse than ours."

"Exactly. The *Essex* carrier group is hounding them. He's limping along on one semi-functional diesel engine." With the hunter-killer group all over them, the B-130 had the same problems as the B-59's tropical operations plus leaking hermetic hull orifices and cable openings.

"Does he have fresh water?"

"No more than us. He's near the end, out of air, out of power, and out of options with damaged bow planes from the attacks. Surrounded by destroyers, he's probably deciding whether to surface or to shoot his way out."

"Same nightmare, but worse for the broken diesels and the damaged bow planes. We'll try to communicate with him when he surfaces and ask if he needs assistance."

Captain Savitsky dismissed Oz and hoisted his binoculars to survey the *USS Cony*. He spotted the ship's skipper's face peering back at him from his bridge window. No giant Yankee, he saw a common man in naval garb, taking long, glowing drags on his cigarette before tossing it out the window into the sea. The old man pondered what thoughts ran through his mind as he addressed his foe across the water, "I don't display my weapons on deck for you to see, so you crave to come aboard to search my boat, but if you did, your balls would shrivel, and you would shit your pants." His voice vanished in the diesel rumble.

"We've cleared the decks and posted the hatch watch. The doc recommends that we cycle the men into the sunshine for thirty minutes each," Starpom said as he climbed the bridge ladder. "He says it will help their skin and their morale. He also says that bridge watchstanders should be cycled every thirty minutes to minimize sunburn. That sun will fry your skin like bacon. He reminds you that enduring hours in the sun will sacrifice your health."

The old man wagged his head. "The crew needs a good breakfast before dawn. If we bring them up five at a time for twenty minutes, they cycle twice in twelve hours. Cycle the bridge watch every twenty minutes, too."

Starpom reported, "Talks between Khrushchev and Kennedy have progressed with Khrushchev agreeing to remove our nuclear missiles from Cuba if Kennedy pulls his nuclear missiles from Italy and Turkey. They say tensions are still on the rise."

"Still on the rise?" The captain was incredulous. "We almost blew them into oblivion twice last night. How do tensions rise from there?"

Oz returned and said from his espionage-centric point of view, "They don't know that they don't know."

The *USS Murray* maneuvered alongside playing "Yankee Doodle," but its significance was lost on the Russians. "What's this horrible music?" the captain asked.

Oz replied, "It's nothing. Something stupid about a pony and macaroni. Makes no sense."

"So, it's *vranyo*?"

"*Da*, it's *vranyo* and more spectacle," Oz's quip left the captain perplexed by his strange American enemies waging a deadly comic form of war on the high seas.

"Thank God we didn't shoot our nuke into this nonsense," he mused. "There are still three, maybe four submarines armed with nukes out there. We must inform them that it's all a cruel joke."

Dog tired from days without sleep, the old man remained on the bridge, while Starpom tended to the crew with the chief and the ship's doctor. When the menacing orange sun bloomed above the horizon, the crew rotated through their sunshine baths, nature's disinfectant, in small doses to protect their unaccustomed eyes and pale skin from sunburn. The captain relinquished the conn to Victor as the sun's heat fired the morning, and he huddled with the navigator to plan their next move while the crew recovered.

Flying out of RIS, Oz announce for all to hear, "Premier Khrushchev announced he'll disassemble and remove nuclear missiles from Cuba. It's over. They all came to their senses."

"We can't believe the American news. It's another farce, more absurd tricks. We must remain alert."

"Khrushchev's pronouncement was announced on Moscow radio this morning," said Oz in response.

The old man tilted his head, raised his eyebrows, widened his eyes and exclaimed, "*Bychit*." The old man stood. "What did he say about the hundred tactical nukes?"

"Not a word," Oz replied. "Kennedy probably didn't know enough to ask for their removal."

"The train station whores of Havana will party tonight if Khrushchev leaves those nukes behind."

"It's true, but I can't believe he wants to make Cuba a nuclear power," Starpom spoke up. "He could leave the troops and the warheads to protect Cuba from invasion."

The captain's face screwed tight as he said, "He doesn't give a damn about protecting Cuba. If his missiles come back, everything comes back. We just received a message from Moscow directing that we only use nuclear weaponry on specific orders from Moscow. The message also went to our ground forces in Cuba."

"Finally, some clarity. How will Americans view Kennedy when this is over?" Starpom wondered aloud.

"There is no telling with Americans," Oz replied. "He created the crisis, then solved it. They could make him out to be a hero or shoot him down in the street like a dog."

"That's why Americans are so dangerous. They're unpredictable, untrustworthy, and unfathomable," the captain growled. "Torpedo room, this is the captain.

Remove the special weapon from torpedo tube two." He gazed at the lazy destroyers crawling like flies over the blue enamel sea. "Replace it with a conventional torpedo. Change out the purple nose for a gray nose device. Secure the purple nose device in its designated rostrum. It's over."

"Conn, engine room, the battery is only at twenty-five percent. We halt charging to cool the batteries when they overheat. We need at least thirty more hours."

"I'll be damned if I'll dive this boat without a full battery. That's how we got trapped on the surface like a rusty scow. I've never spent so many days at sea in the sunlight, but we can't escape until tomorrow night. My head aches from my eyes focusing past five meters." He turned to Starpom. "The situation seems to have stabilized. You ready to take the conn for a few hours?"

"*Da*, I am, and I agree with your assessment. These Americans were never ready for a war. They're all bluster." Starpom paused and added, "I said it before. You did the right thing."

"Doesn't matter. I failed in my mission, and they'll classify this day. They'll bury all evidence of our voyage, swear us to secrecy under penalty, and only the brass will ever know. There'll be an inquiry. What's that like?"

"It's bad. A thousand questions, a few surprises, and a boatload of blaming and shaming to no end."

The captain looked into the blue sky and said, "I heard a story during the war of a young officer who failed his mission. They took him out back, stripped off his uniform, shot him, and buried him in a ditch. By some miracle, he showed up back at his unit later that night in his underwear, covered in mud and dried blood. They shot him again. That was the Red Army under Khrushchev and

Stalin. You think the Red Navy under Admiral Gorshkov and Premier Khrushchev today is any different?"

Starpom could only say, "They don't shoot people much anymore, but they have other ways and means. Looks like the *Cony's* on the move."

The USS *Cony* closed in for daylight photography. Her sailors flocked to the port rail for a close-up look at real Russians. They jumped up and down, giving them the finger, throwing Coke cans and packs of cigarettes and shouting, "Russians go home."

"Screw them," Starpom blurted. "Look at those damned Americans, so brash and ignorant, waving fists and fingers at us. They're civilization-enders, technological titans, but moral miscreants, narcissistic, belligerent, and recalcitrant." His nostrils flared as he ran out of insults, and he shook with rage. His neck veins bulged like purple trails. "Give us your homeland, or you get our nukes. America first. To hell with everyone living in the real world. Money grubbing bastards."

"Such nautical language," the old man had never seen him like this, even in extremis.

"My apologies, but they piss me off. We've been trained to fear and hate these people who dance around like monkeys. You can't hate monkeys, but they have bombs and guns." Starpom paused to look at the *Cony*. *What a soft life they lead in crisp uniforms and air conditioning. Their future reflects their kind, an inhuman form of humanity.* "My faith is shaken. No matter what the Kremlin does with these war monkeys, the die is cast, there's no going back."

"Sadly, what you say is true, and it's not over. It'll never be over. More captains, more subs, and more nukes, lurking in their ocean holes where no one can find them like the B-75, ever ready to destroy. If the world was ever safe, it can never be safe again, even after they send us home. What'll you do when you get there?"

Starpom looked down shuffling with acute embarrassment. "I'll give my Olga a Sargasso kiss, so hot, so sweaty, and so explosive that she will bear a child. To think I counted her among the dead in our worst moment. We'll live in happiness. One day that child will bring a child into the world because we did the right thing."

"How many children are there in this world?"

"Hard to say, maybe a quarter of all people. Millions and millions, almost a billion. Mostly peasant boys and girls with big dreams. Like me, all they want is the chance to be somebody."

"We saved those children, didn't we? We left the world intact for them…and for their children. That will be our secret legacy. Whenever you see a child, you'll see the Sargasso sun reflected in their eyes and haphazard hope emanating from their playful laughter. They'll carry their blissful ignorance into adulthood until some future threat arises to destroy their fantasy. It's a sorrowful legacy."

Starpom shrugged. "The world always disappoints, but it's a fine legacy. What'll you do when you get home?"

"All I ever wanted was to command a submarine. If we make it home, I'll be relieved of command, and I'll go the way of all things, maybe home to Brest if they allow it, or to a gulag in Siberia. Captain Shumkov had a broken boat, but I have no excuse for my failure. I will disappear like the 69th Torpedo Submarine Brigade at the mouth of Kola Bay, like the Jews of Belarus."

Chapter Fifteen – Homeward Bound

Our commanding officer, Captain Savitsky, had a shadow aboard who was the brigade chief of staff, Captain Arkhipov. For the crew, it was like having two commanders. But we were good and gave the Americans the slip after being forced up only once in a month of hiding. **Senior Lieutenant Vadim P. Orlov, Radio Intercept Officer, Project 641 submarine, B-59.**

Opening the door to his Birch-wood-paneled stateroom, the old man stepped inside. *How ironic. I have the most luxurious berth aboard ship and no time to use it,* he thought his last thought that day as he sat on his bunk. Exhaustion swept over him and pulled him under.

In his absence, Starpom worked with the doctor and Poli to rotate crewmen through the sunshine and arrange a hearty breakfast and a tasty lunch. Monitoring the start-and-stop battery charge and taking news and weather reports from Oz, he yearned to hear from the other submarines, but like Moscow, they remained silent.

Rumors ran rampant with stories of the old man's balls to start a war, the *starpom's* wisdom to prevent one, and the crew's impressions of the Americans that they had seen for the first time. The sailors speculated about the American's fighting ability and their sexual prowess or lack thereof. They decided Russian girls would be disappointed if they had to settle for the Yankee boys and expressed their regret for not meeting Cuban girls. No matter how dire the situation, the sailors always brought the conversation back to girls in the most indelicate manner.

"The best solution for marriage is *vodka*." The banter continued.

"What's fun about being sober?" They loved the same old, worn out jokes.

"Not a damned thing," they sang out in a chorus.

"Here's to the nights we'll never remember," they waxed nostalgic.

"And a crew we'll never forget," another chorus.

"How often do submarines sink?" They joked about their deepest fear.

In a chorus, "Just one time."

Late in the day, the ruckus roused the old man. "What the hell?" He opened his stateroom door and heard the commotion from all the way back in the aft torpedo room. He donned his piss cutter and strode through the control room, past RIS, across the engine room, and into the berthing compartment wearing his well-practiced growling bulldog scowl.

"Captain on deck," someone shouted. All hands snapped to attention.

"As you were. Carry on," he announced in his stern voice, looking them over hard. His mouth burst into a broad grin, "Break out the *vodka* for dinner." He shook every sailor's hand and thanked them for their steadfast service.

"Another day in paradise," said the old man, on the bridge in time to watch the sun dip its orange ball into the sea. "Poli, where have you been, working on my file?"

"*Nyet*," Poli glanced at Starpom, happy to see the old man in a playful mood. "I was thinking about last night. It was chaotic, another beating at sea, out of control."

"Starpom says that control is my illusion. Do you remember saying that?"

"I say a lot of things," Starpom winked. "It was *vranyo*. Sometimes my alligator mouth overrides my hummingbird ass. I don't recall, but the biggest lie we tell ourselves is that we're in control."

"You were cornered by noisy diesels, unbreathable air, and weak-ass batteries," Poli said gravely. "You had balls once the battle line was drawn. The *starshy michman* told the men it was a nice piece of seamanship."

"High praise." The old man was skeptical, "Your flattery smells like a political trick."

"No tricks, and it's not political. I flatter because you deserve flattery. I've spoken with the crew, and they respect you as their *chempion*. If you face the *Bolshevik's* blade back home, it won't be mine."

The old man's broad smile irradiated Poli. "I'll be damned. This voyage has been good for you. You think like a submariner." He turned to Starpom. "The crew is in fine spirits. Any news from our comrades?"

"Not a whisper. Nothing from Moscow or our American friends. All quiet."

"I want a briefing at dinner. Stand the crew down tonight, but tomorrow we'll have a field day, all hands. When you feel like *govno*, clean your house to feel better. My mother said that. Everything gets scrubbed, including the men. Use salt water. When it dries, wipe down the salt. When they cycle through the sunshine, have them take their fart sacks to air them out and wash their stinking clothes. Square this ship away for inspection. I have a plan."

"Aye, aye." It was good to have the captain back, thinking ahead, saving the day.

After a hot day of cleaning and drying, the sunset and darkness brought cooler air. The destroyers peeled away one by one until only one remained while the *starshy michman* and the torpedo men concocted a radar dummy out of wooden crates with reflective edges, crafted from empty tins and foil. After Starpom brought the last of the crew inside the boat at dusk, the *starshy michman* kicked the dummy overboard and dogged down the deck hatch. With no warning, under cover of darkness, the B-59 pulled the plug, disappearing in the hell-hole of the Sargasso Sea, knowing with certainty that war was not an option. The US hunter-killer group lit up their high-power sonars and dropped echo ranging depth bombs, but nobody cared.

The old man dived the B-59 to test depth, reversing course to confuse his tormentors by heading toward Cuba at maximum speed. After a half hour, he jettisoned noise-making rattle cans to attract attention and jam passive sonars. After ejecting two magnesium gas bubble generators to reflect active transmissions like a bona fide sonar contact, he reversed course toward Bermuda and cut his speed for silent running. The Americans had only detected the B-59 when she was on the surface, but never while she was submerged. With a full battery charge and a ship filled with fresh air, the captain's confidence returned as he led his men below the waves to escape the ASW ogre.

"My respect for American ASW started low and tapered off. They can't find *govno* served on a *zakuski* platter," he said. He had suffered defeat and loss of face, but his ship and crew remained intact. His trick to distract destroyers with a radar dummy gave him time to vanish and escape. He was back, hungering for news of his comrades.

The next day, Moscow radioed orders to all merchant ships bound for Cuba to reverse course outside the blockade line and return to Russia. The B-130 had surfaced. Forward sections of her damaged diesels had sheared and fractured the massive drive gears, blowing off the engines' gear boxes. Moscow was sending the sea-rescue tug boat *Pamir* to tow her home.

Captain Dubivko on the B-36 had broached to snorkel in broad daylight, less than eight kilometers from *USS Charles P. Cecil* (DDR-835). The old man knew the story. It was his story, but with the *USS Wasp's* hunter-killer destroyers. He compiled the B-36 story during her time on the surface with American escorts, verifying his theory that the Kremlin had set them up for failure by limiting their information and restricting their tactical agility for avoiding detection. The B-4 was a different story, one that both pleased and vexed the old man.

Captain Second Rank Ryurik A. Ketov commanded the B-4 with the 69th Brigade Commander, Captain First Rank Agafonov riding on board. To support information-gathering for situational awareness, the B-4 had tackled the turbulent Atlantic on the surface, prioritizing mission over the health and welfare of the crew. Spartan discipline allowed the B-4 to function while enduring the brutality of the savage weather. The brigade commander focused on communication with Moscow and the other submarines, and his decision to ride out Hurricane Ella on the surface subjected Captain Ketov's crew to another brutish beating, sufficiently violent to bend the aft deck hatch, which began to leak and prevented excursions to significant depths. Despite the handicap, they realized that Sargasso storms appeared often enough for the B-4 to maintain a full battery charge, fresh air, and a clean crew every twenty-four to forty-eight hours, so whenever they came under attack, they escaped. They alone had the new RG-10 passive sonar that gave them a distinct acoustic advantage over their foes, so they could detect approaching vessels with advanced warning to find an escape route to avoid an encounter. By November 1, only the B-4 remained on station.

Captain Savitsky reconnoitered the B-59 in his Bermuda combat sector for a full week, listening in on the episodic adventures of his brethren commanding officers and monitoring the American radio broadcasts for news of the continuing crisis. With each passing day, he felt the threat of nuclear war subside. He adopted the B-4 tactics for ventilating at periscope depth at slow speeds while monitoring communications, and he, too, recognized that regular afternoon microbursts of rain often coincided with his communications séance, providing both cover and fresh water while the B-59 steamed on the surface. Snorkeling on diesels at night maximized his charge time, waiting until airborne radar beacons boomed before diving because radar detection of a periscope was impossible among the waves.

On November 3, Oz picked up a discussion of *The New York Times'* summary of the Cuban Missile Crisis. It filled in the gray areas of their knowledge and highlighted the American's dangerous lack of understanding of realities in theater. He prepared a comprehensive briefing for their traditional evening meal discussion.

"November 3, 1962. Summary briefing of Operation Anadyr from the American perspective: The crisis began when an air force U-2 reconnaissance plane photographed San Cristobal on October 14. It revealed Soviet, medium-range missiles one hundred miles west of Havana. That ended our *maskirovka*, and the Americans became convinced that Premier Khrushchev planned to present the United States with a nasty set of alternatives."

"*Da*. Nasty alternatives," said the captain.

"Hurricane Ella's cloud cover delayed U-2 flights for a week and blocked high-altitude surveillance. Kennedy intensified air surveillance of Cuba and disclosed the existence of Russian bases and considered an invasion, a surgical strike to take out the missile sites, or a blockade. Kennedy met with our Ambassador Gromyko, who lied to his face about our missiles. They chose a blockade, called it a quarantine, and sent advanced letters to sixty embassies. Forty-six ambassadors in Washington, D.C. received direct briefings, and Premier Khrushchev received his personal letter with an advanced copy of the speech."

"Aha. I knew it," the old man slapped his knee to celebrate his Pyrrhic victory. "I smelled it in the Kremlin's tepid instructions to lay off Cuba at the last minute."

"The next day *Tass* released a statement accusing the Americans of violating international law, piracy on the high seas and international provocation. The Organization of American States unanimously supported the quarantine with solid support of their NATO allies. The sudden reality that missiles that could reach Latin-American countries caused their national leaders to defy Khrushchev."

"Spineless bastards of Havana whores," the old man never spoke well of Cuba or Cubans.

"*The Times* reports that the quarantine began at 10:00, November 24, as we know. The Soviet government rejected Kennedy's proclamation as unacceptable, and Khrushchev proposed a summit meeting. American officials viewed it as a delaying tactic, but U Thant, the Acting Secretary General of the United Nations, acted largely on his own to draw the nuclear powers together. He sent letters to Kennedy and Khrushchev urging suspension of both the blockade and the arms shipments to Cuba to allow for negotiations to be held. Khrushchev agreed, but Kennedy did not. The oil tanker *Bucharest* was stopped but allowed to proceed to Cuba without a search because it carried only petroleum. Twelve other Soviet vessels sailing to Cuba turned back, probably with offensive cargoes. Work to bring missile sites to full operational condition continued. The Pentagon threatened 'pinpoint bombing.' On October 26, Khrushchev ordered Soviet vessels away from the blockade line, and Kennedy commanded the Navy to avoid direct confrontation with Soviet ships. That night Khrushchev sent a letter to Kennedy that included a veiled offer to withdraw the offensive weapons under United Nations supervision in return for lifting the blockade and assurances that the Americans would not invade Cuba."

"Neither one of them knew the American navy was pounding us with depth bombs," Starpom observed. "Politicians can't be bothered with tactical details."

"The Times reports that Premier Khrushchev offered, in a second letter the next day, to trade his bases in Cuba for the NATO missile base in Turkey. The Americans replied that Cuba was a special problem that had to be settled first. Castro screamed defiance on Cuban television, vowing to shoot down intruders, and a U-2 went missing over Cuba, presumed lost after drawing antiaircraft fire."

"No mention of submarines?" The old man led with sarcasm. No one ever mentioned subs.

"*Nyet*. The Americans sent a letter to Moscow, offering to end the blockade and promising not to invade Cuba in return for removal of Soviet offensive weapons. This letter was delivered two hours before we surfaced." Oz stopped. His voice cracked as he recalled the fearsome pounding and suffocation they had endured at that moment. He wiped his eyes. "None of the officials expected the Cuban showdown to 'turn nuclear.' That's what they said."

"Ignorant asses don't understand human nature." The captain replayed the crucial moment in his mind's eye.

"Kennedy remarked that it that it could have gone either way. He thinks he made the war/no war decision."

"Moscow radio didn't broadcast its stand down until 09:00 the next morning. I don't see how the Admiralty can blame us for what happened, but they'll have time to figure that out." The old man's mind drifted back to Moscow, still a world away.

"Kennedy welcomed Khrushchev's decision to dismantle Cuban bases and return offensive weapons to the Soviet Union under strict verification as statesmanlike, a 'welcome and constructive contribution to peace,' he said in an announcement on Voice of America radio."

"No mention of the remaining tactical nukes or submarines?" He knew the answer.

"No, but *The New York Times* noted that there may be missing details in its early reporting of events."

"How American of them." Starpom remained pissed off at the Americans. "Not a word about principles. They don't understand that principled ideas undergird a great nation. They have no strategy for the ages."

On November 5, the Soviet ship *Aleksandrovsk* departed Cuba with the thirty-six short-range nuclear warheads, reloaded for transport, and the twenty-four medium-range warheads that had never been unloaded.

On November 7, the B-36 damaged two of her three diesel engines due to human error and were directed back to Polyarny, limping on one diesel in stormy conditions.

The next day, the B-130 contacted the tugboat *Pamir*, but had to wait another day for a break in the weather. No need to send men on deck in safety lines to secure the towline, risking what the Americans called a Nantucket sleigh ride, dragging through the water in a safety harness.

The B-4 and B-59 remained in separate combat positions, unaware that the warheads had been removed from Cuba, operating with caution near ASW aircraft carrier groups. On November 12, they received orders to proceed five hundred miles north to a new area near the Newfoundland-Azores Gap. They were homeward bound.

Living conditions improved when water rations were lifted as temperatures subsided. Spirits soared, hope emerged, and sailors longed for home.

Multiple pairs of low-altitude Neptune spy planes and solo high-altitude long-range reconnaissance aircraft streaked across the sky, so the subs operated with caution in separate quadrangles to evade them until they received orders to return to Polyarny, recalled with no explanation. The subs continued to glean intelligence about the political situation from radio broadcasts, Russian and American.

Suffering in silence, part of him remained a dutiful commanding officer of a *bolshoi* Soviet torpedo submarine, returning home intact after a protracted and demanding operation halfway around the world. Part of him remained horrified at the cataclysm he nearly perpetuated against all living things on Earth. Part of him was feared banishment to a Siberian gulag for failure to complete his mission, but what tortured his soul was the irrefutable conclusion that life at home, or anywhere, could never be the same as it had been only a month ago. He couldn't let it go. It blurted out of him one evening in the wardroom.

"The world has changed forever. Our most brilliant scientists created monsters to end civilization and turned them over to common men, soldiers, sailors and politicians like Castro, Khrushchev and Kennedy. What the hell were they thinking? Where's the brilliance in that?"

"You could blame Hitler for initiating a nuclear program," Starpom added his thoughts. "The irony is that he didn't have the heavy water to pull it off. You could say it's Truman's fault for nuking Hiroshima and Nagasaki. He didn't see nuclear weapons as a civilization ender, just a bigger bomb to intimidate Hirohito into unplugging his kamikazes from their dugouts across the Pacific. They were wrong. We can no longer fight without killing everybody, every damned thing. We can never go back. We can't return to Cuba to unscrew this thing, and when we get home nothing, will be recognizable. A single snowflake could spark an avalanche."

"Murmansk will never change," Poli took the bait. "If you don't think about it, it won't bother you. Our sailors don't even comprehend what they've been through."

"Not entirely true. *Pravda* published articles about American bandits and warmongers," Oz corrected the misperception. "*Izvestia* ran headlines: 'The Planet Faces Conflagration.' Khrushchev's been bragging up his nuclear arms. The *proletariat* knows about Cuba, the blockade, and the crisis. The captain is right. Things will never be the same." The old man poured *vodka*.

"Praise be to Allah that Olga doesn't know we went to Cuba," Starpom muttered.

"It's true that nobody knows about the submarines," said Oz. "No one ever does."

"What bothers me is that the world receded from the edge of annihilation because men like Arkhipov and Kennedy and Khrushchev chose life on the same day, at the same time. They embraced humanity," the old man had become obsessed with one thing. "What if one of them didn't care, or worse, sought mass destruction. What if they elect an idiot with no common sense? Where will we be?"

"You don't have to worry about that," Oz reassured him. "Their founding fathers were wealthy men, and they built their country for wealthy men. Like every country, they fell victim to organized greed. It's all rigged; big money buys everything. They would never trust an idiot with crucial decisions. They let their best and brightest men make the big mistakes."

The old man smiled, relaxing for the first time since the incident. "If all it takes is money, we could unite our citizens and buy a clown and a whole damned election."

Everybody laughed. It felt good to laugh again. They loved *vranyo*.

Poli couldn't resist, "A big fat clown with a yellow helmet or a pig."

They roared and toasted the clown and the pig with a fake pig nose over his real pig nose.

Once the laughter subsided, Oz had a request, "My team is of little further use, and the petty officers want their mess back. Request permission to disassemble our radio intercept equipment and move it to compartment one for offload. *Osnaz* will extract us for our next mission when we return to port. One more thing. Could you refer to me as Lieutenant Orlov?"

"Permission granted, Lieutenant Orlov. You are released from watch standing," the Captain rubbed his chin. "Anybody else have a request?"

Starpom spoke up, "I'd like to prepare a request to billet the crew in shore-based housing or on the *Dmitry Galkin* to get them off this stinking boat."

"Permission granted. Poli?"

"I'd like to tell you something you don't know. You never asked me."

"Go on," the old man was dubious, unwilling to endure some arcane political lecture.

"You want to know if General Maslennikov was my father. Fact is, I don't know. Abandoned as a baby on the doorstep of an orphanage with nothing but a name pinned on my blanket, I was labeled as a 'child of an enemy of the people.' They said apples fall near the tree, and I had no choice but to prove my extreme loyalty to the Party. Beyond the shame and class guilt, my allegiance kept me off the train to the *gulag*, but that fundamental choice surrounded itself with a witches' brew of lesser lies of who I am and how I came to join the navy. That's how I became your *zampolit*." Poli hung his head and wiped his nose on his sleeve. "No escape for me, no chance to be better man."

Silence. Not one word. Oz clapped Poli on the back. Starpom squeezed his shoulder. They left. The captain jostled Poli's hair and smoothed it off his forehead. Poli lifted his sad face and looked at him with hopeful eyes like a faithful shepherd seated before his master.

The old man smiled again, "You know what family feels like? It feels like the navy, just like the navy." Then he turned and walked out of the wardroom, leaving Poli to compose himself.

The captain pulled Starpom off the watch bill and left the conn to the junior officers for experience and training. The return passage mimicked the initial route with stormy waters in the North Atlantic and maneuvering among the fishing boats. It was rough, but not terrifying. The water distiller output returned to normal, allowing the crew to hydrate their bodies and cleanse their skin. The crew subsisted on canned stores. Seasickness subsided, even in heavy weather, and the sailors knew to hang on and move with the ship's motion. Same crew, more experience.

The B-59 slipped into the Norwegian Sea amid a severe snowstorm that persisted for the duration of the voyage. Their *mir* converted from hell-hole into icebox. Torpedo men, wearing tropical uniforms under their middies, became hypothermic. They sought warmth in the engine spaces where the diesels and electric motors threw off heat like a furnace.

The *Pamir* towing the B-130 made landfall on the North Cape on December 3, and two days later, they turned into the channel that led to Kola Bay. Captain Shumkov had charged his batteries with his semi-operational diesel during the long ride home, and he sailed into Kola Bay without the tug and docked at the same pier he had left in the middle of the night across from the B-75 which had returned on November 10. There was no roast pig, no brass band, and no parade drums for a Russian sub returning from an arduous mission. Only *Kontr* Admiral Rybalko, sitting in his black Volga sedan, awaited them. Captain Shumkov and his crew were confined to the boat, pending a full investigation of how they disobeyed orders to remain covert and undetected, in accordance with the Communist custom that "every outstanding nail gets the hammer." It mattered not. They made it home, and the *Kontr* Admiral and his wife had personally parlayed enough green salad, sardines, pickled herring and cow's tongue into a platter of *zakuski* to fill their shrunken bellies. Best *zakuski* ever.

The investigation could not start without the brigade commander, and guards were posted to enforce restriction orders. On December 16, the B-4 steamed into Sayda Bay and moored at the pier abaft the B-130. She was the second boat to arrive and the second crew to be restricted to the ship. They were not allowed to mingle with or speak to the crew of the B-130.

It was December in Polyarny, the days of darkness when the light is mostly night. The investigation could begin.

Chapter Sixteen – Polyarny

"The man who prevented a nuclear war was a Russian submariner. His name was Vasili Arkhipov. I was proud, and I am proud of my husband, always." **Olga Arkhipov.**

The crisis was not over. US forces remained at Defense Condition Two and gradually wound down to normal readiness condition on November 22, and Soviet strategic missile troops shifted from full combat readiness to routine training activities. The ballistic missile nuclear warheads left Cuba on November 5, but the Americans suspected a great hoax, questioning whether the Soviets could be trusted to remove the weapons or if they plotted some ingenious trick prior to the midterm elections. The Americans had not requested the removal of the ninety-eight tactical nuclear weapons because they did not know that the Soviets had turned Cuba into the first Latin American nuclear power. The nukes were introduced into Cuba as part of a planned, long-term Soviet presence in the region, but without Soviet oversight, Castro might do anything with the nuclear weapons. Khrushchev faced his second Cuban crisis, so he dispatched Soviet Deputy Prime Minister, Anastas Mikoyan to Havana to wrestle the weapons away from Castro, who was furious that he had been left out of the negotiations and decisions to end the standoff. Mikoyan did his job, and on November 30, the tactical nuclear weapons were loaded aboard the ship *Arkangel'sk* that sailed for the USSR, arriving on December 20th.

The B-59 and B-36 made their way back to
Polyarny the same way the B-4 had plowed through the
heavy weather of the North Atlantic, the ASW choke points
and the Norwegian Sea snow squalls. The B-36 was speed
limited by her diesel engine problems, but on the B-59,
Captain Savitsky opted to proceed at slow, covert speeds to
minimize detection and further loss of face. The B-59 made
port in the pre-dawn hours of Christmas Eve and received
notification that the B-36 had rounded North Cape,
scheduled to arrive late on Christmas Day. The B-36 had
discovered in the Norwegian Sea that they had lost
thousands of gallons of diesel oil and lacked sufficient fuel
to complete the voyage. Bulk diesel fuel was stored in the
midships ballast tanks, and a mistaken opening of the vent
had allowed the lighter-than-water fuel to escape. They
limped home in the frigid weather by mixing the remaining
diesel oil with low-energy lubricating oil for fuel. Once
they arrived, they emerged from the boat exhausted,
emaciated, hypothermic, infected, and smelling like
buzzards on a dung heap, only to find themselves under
security restriction in a raging blizzard. The only man to
meet them with Christmas wishes was Starpom, the brigade
chief of staff, Vasili Arkhipov.

Security became their worst nightmare, and military
guards cordoned off the pier, holding them prisoner on their
boats as the Christmas blizzard buried them in the snow.
They ate dinner and slept under fresh blankets provided by
the admiral. The next day, *Kontr* Admiral Rybalko arrived
to meet with the brigade commander Vasili Agafonov, his
chief of staff, Vasili Arkhipov, and the four submarine
captains. He bore another platter of *zakuski*, prepared by his
wife for the men. He gave the captains the Kremlin's view

of how Operations Anadyr and Kama had been compromised and how the brigade had sailed into the largest ASW armada ever assembled.

After the meeting, *Kontr* Admiral Rybalko left for the headquarters of the Northern Fleet in Severomorsk where he was relieved of his command, forced into retirement, and never seen again. Fidel Castro visited Polyarny, but he never visited the diesel subs. Brigade Commander Agafonov was promoted to *Kontr* Admiral and assigned to the nuclear submarine fleet, the future of the Soviet Navy. Captain Ketov was promoted to command a nuclear submarine. They had both sailed on the B-4 and were never forced to surface.

The investigations examined disobedience and mission failure. No awards were presented, except for the sonarman who had survived appendicitis. Even the doctor received no praise. Captains Agafonov, Ketov, Shumkov, and Dubivko and Lieutenants Orlov and Mikhailov lived to tell their tales of the journey. Lost as a legend in the official cover up, Captain Second Rank Vasili Arkhipov, never spoke of the voyage prior to his death from kidney cancer like so many of the K-19 survivors. He said it was classified.

Captain Savitsky disappeared. Poli too. These things happen in Russia.

Glossary of Acronyms and Russian Words

Anadyr – Russian town, river, gulf, and estuary. Also, the Soviet operation to place nuclear weapons in Cuba in 1962.

ASW – Antisubmarine warfare, includes the use of submarines, ships, aircraft, and shore-based installations to detect, track, localize and destroy enemy submarines.

Beluga Vodka – A classic Russian vodka, clean and crisp with a little bit of grain flavor. Perfect for drinking straight, as is the Russian way.

Bolshoi – Large.

Bychit – To act like a bull.

C'bogom – Go with God.

Chempion – Russian for champion. Plural – *chempiony*.

Clear Baffles – Submarine maneuver to reverse course to search for an enemy submarine trailing behind the ship

Dacha – A Russian cottage or country house typically used for vacation getaways.

Ded – Grandfather, the experienced military enlisted man who looks after young recruits.

Dybbuk – A malicious, wandering, possessing spirit that invades the bodies of living souls with the dislocated soul of a dead person until exorcized or once it has accomplished its goal.

Fart sack – Slipcover for bunk mattress to allow flipping for hot bunking, one side per man.

Golosh boots – Wet weather boots.

Govno – Shit.

Gulag – Main Administration of Corrective Labor Camps, a system of forced labor detention camps and prisons within the Soviet Union.

HF/DF – High-frequency direction finding gear for detecting/calculating a line of bearing to a radio transmitter.

Irkutsk – A large city located on the banks of the Angara River in Eastern Siberia.

Izvestia – A daily broadsheet newspaper in Russia.

Izba – Russian peasant farmhouse

Kalashnikov – A Russian rifle or submachine gun originally designed by Mikhail Kalashnikov. The most popular version is the AK-47.

Kama – The sickle, without the hammer, sharpened for use as a weapon or a sensuous desire for sexual satisfaction. Also, the naval contingent of Operation *Anadyr* involving permanently placing an attack submarine squadron (20th Operative Submarine Squadron) consisting of seven missile boats and four torpedo boats with nuclear torpedoes and the submarine tender *Dmitry Galkin* in Mariel Bay, Cuba.

Kanadka – Arctic foul weather suit adopted from the Canadian merchant marine.

Kommissar – Commissar, Communist Party official.

Kompromat – Compromising material, often used to instill loyalty with blackmail.

Kontr Admiral – Russian Navy equivalent of rear admiral

Kulak – Fist or tight fist. A term used in the Soviet Union to indicate a peasant farmer wealthy enough to hire labors and to sell their outputs for money. *Kulaks* resisted Stalin's farm collectivization program and suffered persecutions that included death or deportation to Siberia.

MAD – (1) Mutually Assured Destruction. The Cold War notion that no one would release nuclear weapons if both sides would suffer mass destruction.

MAD – (2) Magnetic Anomaly Detector, a three-axis magnetometer for detecting blips in the Earth's natural magnetic field due to large lumps of ferromagnetic material like submarine hulls below the water.

Makarov – Standard issue Soviet military side arm.

Maskirovka – The Soviet military doctrine of information denial and deception.

Matryoshka doll – Russian nesting doll, a set of wooden dolls of decreasing size placed one inside another.

Michman – Soviet Navy warrant officer or noncommissioned officer.

Michmany – Plural for *michman*.

Mir – A Russian self-governing community where local people lived near one another to share limited resources. Other meanings include "world" and "peace."

Nakat – 1-10 GHz search radar (NATO designator Stop Light) with a cathode ray tube display. The active/passive antenna carries four frequency bands of direction finding antennas.

Nezametnaya – Imperceptible.

Ni figa sebe – Vulgar Russian exclamation of surprise.

Nyet – No.

Oblast – Province.

Olivaria – State-owned beer company in Minsk, Belarus.

OOD – Officer on deck. The officer with operational control of the ship while underway as a rotating watch station in the control room or the conning tower or on the bridge.

Osnaz – Soviet era special forces, not military, but political. Syllabic compression of *osobogo naznacheniya*, interpreted as "special purpose." As syllabic abbreviations, they are not acronyms and are not normally capitalized.

Pilotka – Garrison cap. Slang, piss cutter.

Pizdetz – Russian slang derived from the word pizda (vagina) meaning complete wreck with sexual overtones.

Pravda – Official Newspaper of the Communist Party in the Soviet Union.

Red Menace – American expression for the Communist threat.

Rodina – Motherland. Refers to Russia or Motherland – National Patriotic Union political party.

Rodina-mat' zavyot – Homeland Mother is Calling.

Sargassum – Brown macroalgae or seaweed known for its planktonic or free-floating species.

Sitrep – Situation report.

Shkval – Squall, also the name of the Soviet electronics intelligence trawler in the Sargasso Sea.

SOSUS – US Navy Sound Surveillance System of low-frequency seismic sensors mounted in the deep sound channel to listen for submarine-generated noise, monitored by shore stations.

Starpom – Executive officer, senior assistant to the captain and second in command.

S*tarshy michman* – Senior chief petty officer or warrant officer equivalent aboard ship and the most experienced man on the boat. Plural form – S*tarshy michmany.*

Svin'i – Swine, hogs or pigs.

Tass – Largest news agency in the Soviet Union, government-owned and operated.

Toska – Deep, painful shades of spiritual anguish, sadness and melancholia, with no single English word equivalent.

Turn to – Navy slang meaning "Get to work."

Vranyo – Lie, but a little white lie, exaggeration or hyperbole, often for humor or storytelling.

Yest – It is.

Zakuski – Something to bite, Slavic term for hot or cold bite-sized snacks, often eaten after a shot of vodka. Singular form – *Zakuska.*

Zampolit – Political *kommissar* of a military unit.

Bibliography

Archives

Declassified US, USSR and Cuban documentation from NSA Archives include charts, photographs, transcripts and government documents translated into English:

1. Agafonov, Vasili Naumovich, Captain First Rank, 69th Submarine Brigade Commander
    Report [undated, circa December 1962, prepared by the USSR Northern Fleet Headquarters] About participation of submarines "B-4," "B-36," "B-59," "B-130" of the 69th submarine brigade of the Northern Fleet in the Operation "Anadyr" during the period of October - December 1962, CARIBBEAN CRISIS, Translated by Svetlana Savranskaya for the National Security Archive.
2. Codi von Richthofen (2015-02-21), Missile Crisis: The Man Who Saved the World, PBS Documentary, retrieved 2017-02-26
3. Fokin, Vitaly Alexeyevich and Zakharov, Matvei Vasilevich, Report on Progress of Operation Anadyr, 25 September 1962, Top Secret of Special Importance for Premier Khrushchev, only copy, translated by Gary Goldberg.
4. Fokin, Vitaly Alexeyevich and Zakharov, Matvei Vasilevich, Initial Report of Soviet Naval Activities in Support of Operation Anadyr, 18 September 1962, Top Secret of Special Importance for Premier Khrushchev, only copy, translated by Gary Goldberg.
5. Lansdale, Edward, Brig. Gen. "Review of OPERATION MONGOOSE," Phase One, July 25, 1962.

6. McNamara, Robert. Secretary of Defense Robert military briefing, "Notes on October 21, 1962 Meeting with the President."

7. Mozgovoi, Alexander. The Cuban Samba of the Quartet of Foxtrots; interviews with Alexander Mozgovoi and Vadim Orlov by Svetlana Savranskaya, National Security Archive, 16 and 17 October 2002, Moscow.

8. Smith, Bromley. "Summary Record of NSC Executive Committee Meeting," November 2, 1962.

9. Smith, Bromley. "Summary Record of NSC Executive Committee Meeting," November 5, 1962.

10. Yurkin, Anatoly. "Book on actions of Soviet subs during 1962 Caribbean crisis," Tass, 19 June 2002.

11. Cable received from U.S. Ambassador to Turkey Raymond Hare to State Department regarding Turkish missiles, October 26, 1962.

12. CIA, Minutes, SECRET, "Meeting with the Attorney General of the United States Concerning Cuba," 19 January 1962 (Richard Helms)

13. CIA, Minutes, TOP SECRET, "Minutes of Meeting of the Special Group (Augmented) on Operation Mongoose," 4 October 1962.

14. CIA daily report, "The Crisis USSR/Cuba," October 27, 1962.

15. CIA Special National Intelligence Estimate, "Major Consequences of Certain U.S. Courses of Action on Cuba," October 20, 1962.

16. Chronology Compiled for The President's Foreign Intelligence Advisory Board (PFIAB), "Chronology of Specific Events Relating to the Military Buildup in Cuba," Undated [Excerpt].

17. Cuba, Letter, from Prime Minister Castro to Chairman Khrushchev, October 28, 1962.

18. Cuba, Letter, from Prime Minister Castro to Chairman Khrushchev, October 31, 1962.

19. Dillon group discussion paper, "Scenario for Airstrike Against Offensive Missile Bases and Bombers in Cuba," October 25, 1962.

20. DOD Memorandum from Secretary of Defense McNamara to President Kennedy, TOP SECRET, Washington D.C., October 4, 1962.: Kennedy Library, National Security Files, Countries Series, Cuba, General, 10/1-10/14/62.

21. DOD, Memorandum, TOP SECRET, "Cover and Deception Plans for Caribbean Survey Group," 19 February 1962 (Operation Northwoods).

22. DOD, Transcripts, SECRET, "Notes taken from Transcripts of Meetings of the Joint Chiefs of Staff, October-November 1962: Dealing with the Cuban Missile Crisis."

23. DOJ, Memorandum, TOP SECRET, "Memorandum for the Secretary of State from the Attorney General," on Robert Kennedy's October 27 Meeting with Dobrynin, October 30, 1962.

24. Interview with Vadim Orlov by Svetlana Savranskaya, National Security Archive, 17 October 2002, Moscow; Captain Joseph Bouchard, communication with archive editor, 16 September 2002.

25. National Security Action Memorandum No. 181, Presidential Directive on actions and studies in response to new Soviet Bloc Activity in Cuba, August 23, 1962.

26. National Security Archives Briefing Book #606, Edited by William Burr and Peter Kornbluh, Published: Oct 16, 2017. Based on CINCLANT message to Joint Chiefs of Staff, "Military Government Proclamation No. 1," 20 October 1962, Top Secret, released on June 8, 2017 under Mandatory Declassification Review.

27. President Kennedy's letter to Premier Khrushchev, November 6, 1962.

28. Prime Minister Fidel Castro's letter to Premier Khrushchev, October 26, 1962.

29. Radio-TV Address of the President to the Nation from the White House, October 22, 1962.

30. Report from General Zakharov and Admiral Fokin to the Defense Council and Premier Khrushchev on Initial Plans for Soviet Navy Activities in Support of Operation Anadry, 18 September 1962, describing arrangements to send to Cuba a squadron of submarines, including a brigade of torpedo submarines and a division of missile submarines, with two submarine tenders. Source: Volkogonoff Collection, Library of Congress, Manuscript Division, Reel 17, Container 26. Translated by Gary Goldberg for the Cold War International History Project and the National Security Archive.

31. Report from General Zakharov and Admiral Fokin to the Presidium, Central Committee, Communist Party of the Soviet Union, on the Progress of Operation Anadyr, 25 September 1962, indicating plans to equip the submarine brigade with one nuclear torpedo on each submarine and to send a

nuclear attack submarine to protect the transport ship Aleksandrovsk.

32. Recollections of Vadim Orlov (USSR Submarine B-59), "We Will Sink Them All, But We Will Not Disgrace Our Navy," Orlov's account includes the controversial depiction of an order by Captain Valentin Savitsky to assemble the nuclear torpedo. Source: Alexander Mozgovoi, The Cuban Samba of the Quartet of Foxtrots: Soviet Submarines in the Caribbean Crisis of 1962 (Moscow, Military Parade, 2002). Translated by Svetlana Savranskaya, National Security Archive.

33. Soviet Plans to Deploy Submarines. Source of reference 57: Volkogonoff Collection, Library of Congress, Manuscript Division, Reel 17, Container 26. Translated by Gary Goldberg for the Cold War International History Project and the National Security Archive.

34. Soviet Submarine Warfare Trends, Special National Intelligence Estimate, Director of Central Intelligence, SNIE 11-20-84/D, March 1985, SECRET, Declassified October 1999.

35. Special National Intelligence Estimate (SNIE) 85-3-62, Document 13, CIA National Intelligence Estimate, The Military Buildup in Cuba, 9/19/62.

36. Special National Intelligence Estimate (SNIE) 85-3-62, Document 433, CIA National Intelligence Estimate, The Military Buildup in Cuba, 9/19/62.

37. The Submarines of October, U.S. and Soviet Naval Encounters During the Cuban Missile Crisis, National Security Archive Electronic Briefing Book

No. 75, William Burr and Thomas S. Blanton, editors. October 31, 2002.

38. USSR, Cable, TOP SECRET, Dobrynin Report of Meeting with Robert Kennedy on Worsening Threat, October 27, 1962.

39. USSR, directive, TOP SECRET, Malinovsky's Order to Pliyev, October 22, 1962.

40. USSR, Directive, TOP SECRET, Prohibition on Use of Nuclear Weapons without Orders from Moscow, October 27, 1962, 16:30. USSR, Directive, TOP SECRET, CC CPSU Presidium Instructions to Pliyev in Response to His Telegram, October 27, 1962.

41. USSR, draft directive, Directive to the Commander of Soviet Forces in Cuba on transfer of Il-28s and Luna Missiles, Authority on Use of Tactical Nuclear Weapons, September 8, 1962.

42. USSR, Letter, from Chairman Khrushchev to Prime Minister Castro, October 28, 1962.

43. USSR, Letter, from Chairman Khrushchev to Prime Minister Castro, October 30, 1962.

44. USSR, Memoir, "Recollections of Vadim Orlov (USSR Submarine B-59): We will Sink Them All, But We will Not Disgrace Our Navy," (2002).

45. USSR, Memorandum of Conversation between Mikoyan and Cuban Leaders, TOP SECRET, November 5, 1962 (Evening).

46. USSR, Telegrams from Malinovsky to Pliyev, TOP SECRET, Early November (circa 5 November) 1962.

47. USSR, Ciphered Telegram from Mikoyan to CC CPSU, TOP SECRET, November 6, 1962.

48. USSR, Instructions from CC CPSU Presidium to Mikoyan, TOP SECRET, November 22, 1962.
49. U.S. Navy, TOP SECRET/SECRET/FOR OFFICIAL USE ONLY, Charts/deck logs of anti-submarine warfare operations related to USSR submarine B-59, October 1962.
50. White House, "Post Mortem on Cuba," October 29, 1962.
51. Nikolai Zateyev's memorial @ https://www.findagrave.com/cgi/bin/fg.cgi?page=gr&GRid=11756871
52. Cables, reports, deck logs, and after-action reports on U.S. ASW operations

1. Excerpt from meeting of the Executive Committee (Excom) of the National Security Council, 10:00 A.M.--11:15 A.M., 24 October 1962, during which President Kennedy and his advisers discussed the Soviet submarine problem and the Navy's procedures for signaling the submarines with practice depth charges.
Source: Philip Zelikow and Ernest R. May, editors. The Presidential Recordings John F. Kennedy, The Great Crises, Vol. III (New York, W.W. Norton, 2001), pp. 190-194; John F. Kennedy Library, Boston, MA.

2. COMASWFORLANT (Commander, Anti-Submarine Warfare Forces, Atlantic) cable to Task Group 81.5 (Bermuda ASW Task Group), 24 October 1962, noting task group report on "probable" submarine sighting (probably C-18) and requesting patrol flights to find the submarine.
Source: Washington Navy Yard, Naval Historical Center, Operational Archives Branch, Cuba History Files, Boxes

68-71, file: 21 (A) SS/ASW Contacts (Closed)-1
(hereinafter cited as CHF, with file name)

3. Commander TG 81.5 cable to task group
elements, 25 October 1962, assigning "highest priority" to
effort to track C-18, with a patrol squadron VP 45 assigned
the task on a "continuing basis."
Source: CHF, 21 (A) SS/ASW Contacts (Closed)-1

4. Commander TG 81.5 cable to
COMASWFORLANT, 25 October 1962, noting that ASW
squadron "Woodpecker Nine" made a visual sighting of a
Soviet Foxtrot submarine, probably C-18.
Source: CHF, 21 (A) SS/ASW Contacts (Closed)-1

5. CTG 81.5 cable to CTF 81 (Commander Task
Force 81) (COMASWFORLANT), 25 October 1962,
reporting on visual sighting of C-18 (Soviet submarine B-
130).
Source: CHF, 21 (A) SS/ASW Contacts (Closed)-1

6. "OpNav [Office of the Chief of Naval
Operations] 24 Hour Resume of Events 250000Q to
260000Q", 26 October 1962, recounting blockade and
ASW efforts as well as the preparation of forces for an
invasion of Cuba.
Source: Washington Navy Yard, Naval Historical Center,
Operational Archives, Flag Plot Cuba Missile Crisis 31-2,
file: Misc. Information

7. CTG 136.2 (Commander, Essex Task Group)
cable to COMASWFORLANT, 26 October 1962,
confirming that submarine C-18, identified with hull
number 945, dove after a sighting by ASW aircraft.
Source: CHF, 21 (A) SS/ASW Contacts (Closed)-1

8. CTG 81.5 cable to COMASWFORLANT, 26
October 1962, reporting sighting by "Woodpecker Five" of

submarine cataloged as C-19 (Soviet submarine B-59). Patrol aircraft maintaining "mad contact," that is, contact through magnetic anomaly detection (MAD).
Source: CHF, 21 (A) SS/ASW Contacts (Closed)-1

9. CINCLANT cable to AIG [Address Indicator Group?] 930, JCS, CINCARIB, et al., "Current ASW Status," 26 October 1962, showing visual sightings and SOSUS (sound surveillance system) (13) contacts with Soviet submarines--including C-18, C-19, and C-20--since 22 October. Source: CHF, 21 (A) SS/ASW Contacts (Closed)-1

10. CTU 81.7.9 (Element of Caribbean ASW Group/Roosevelt Roads Naval Station, Puerto Rico) cable to CTF 81 (COMASWFORLANT), 27 October 1962, summarizing "current ASW activity" in vicinity of Guantanamo Bay (GITMO).
Source: CHF, 21 (A) SS/ASW Contacts (Closed)-1

11. CTG 81.1 (element of COMSAWFORLANT?) cable to CTF 81 (COMASWFORLANT), "Appreciation of SOSUS Activity in Western Atlantic from 2300IZ to 273100Z," 27 October 1962, reports seven SOSUS contacts with conventional Soviet submarines, although noting difficulty of using SOSUS to track C-18 and C-19
Source: CHF, 21 (A) SS/ASW Contacts (Closed)-1

12. CINCLANT cable to JCS, "Summary of Soviet Submarine Activities in Western Atlantic to 271700Z," 27 October 1962, reporting various visual sightings and various technical intelligence contacts of Soviet submarines through radar, SOSUS, MAD, as well as Julie and Jezebel sonobuoys. (14) Source: CHF, 21 (A) SS/ASW Contacts (Closed)-1

13. Deck Log Book [Excerpts] for U.S.S. Beale, DD 471, showing tracking and signaling operations, with use of practice depth charges (PDCs), and surfacing of submarine C-19 on the evening of 27 October (local time). The Beale was part of the Randolph ASW task group 83.2. Source: National Archives, Record Group 24, Records of Bureau of Naval Personnel (hereinafter cited as RG 24), Deck Logs 1962, box 74

14. Deck Log Book [Excerpts] for U.S.S. Cony, DD 508, also part of TG 83.2, showing its role in tracking, signaling, and surfacing submarine C-19.
Source: RG 24, Deck Logs 1962, box 178

15. Deck Log Book [Excerpts] for U.S.S. Bache, DD 479, which tracked C-19 (identified as PROSNABLAVST) on 28 October. Source: RG 24, Deck Logs 1962, box 57.

16. CTG 81.1 cable to CTF, "Appreciation SOSUS Activity from 271201Z-2843000Z," 28 October 1962, reporting that SOSUS system "total remaining above normal", including 6 contacts of Soviet conventional submarines: C-18, C-19, C-20, and C-23.
Source: CHF, 21 (A) SS/ASW Contacts (Closed)-1.

17. Table showing deployment of non-nuclear components of nuclear depth charges at Guantanamo Bay, 1961-1963. Source: Assistant to the Secretary of Defense for Atomic Energy, "History of the Custody and Deployment of Nuclear Weapons (U), July 1945 - September 1977," February 1978, Department of Defense Freedom of Information Act Release.

18. Deck Log Book [Excerpts] for U.S.S. Barry, DD 933, which tracked C-19 (PROSNABLAVST) on 29 October. Source: RG 24.

19. COMASWFORLANT cable to AIG 43, 29 October 1962, describing C-19 as "raising and lowering masts and snorkel indicating hydraulic difficulties and/or repairs."
Source: CHF, 21 (A) SS/ASW Contacts (Closed)-1.

20. COMASWFORLANT cable to AIG 43, 30 October 1962, reporting that the Barry lost contact with C-19 after it "went deep."
Source: CHF, 21 (A) SS/ASW Contacts (Closed)-1

21. COMASWFORLANT cable to AIG 43, 30 October 1962, on surfacing of Foxtrot Submarine C-18 (B-130), side number 945, late in the evening of 29 October at 2310Z (Greenwich meridian time). Source: CHF, 21 (A) SS/ASW Contacts (Closed)-1

22. CTG 136.2 (Essex Task Group) cable to COMASWFORLANT, 30 October 1962, reports that C-18 "remaining on the surface."
Source: CHF, 21 (A) SS/ASW Contacts (Closed)-1

23. COMASWFORLANT cable to AIG 43, 30 October, reporting that C-18 [B-130] submerged early in the morning at 3000622Z, but that destroyers and aircraft were holding sonar (sound navigation and ranging) (15) and MAD contacts.
Source: CHF, 21 (A) SS/ASW Contacts (Closed)-1

24. U.S.S. Speed Cable to COMASWFORLANT, 30 October 1962, on MAD and sonar contacts with Soviet Submarine C-26 (B-36), although "have not attempted special surfacing signals viewed as part of lifted quarantine."
Source: CHF, 21.SS/ASW

25. U.S.S. C.P. Cecil cable to COMASWFORLANT, 30 October 1962, reporting B-36 [C-26]'s "strong attempt [to]

break contact ... in radical course changes and speeds to 15 [knots] and false echo cans."
Source: CHF, 21.SS/ASW
26. U.S.S. C.P. Cecil Cable to COMASWFORLANT, 30 October 1962, reports that contact was evaluated as "submarine" in light of 30 MAD contacts by patrol aircraft. "Maintaining continuous sonar contact" of C-26 [B-36]
Source: CHF, 21.SS/ASW
27. CTG 136.2 to COMASWFORLANT, 31 October 1962, reports surfacing of C-18 [B-130] after 14 hours of continuous contact by destroyers and patrol aircraft. "Sub was evasive using decoys, depth changes, backing down" but "sonar contact [was] never lost." After surfacing, submarine stated its number as 945 and stated that it needed no assistance.
Source: CHF, CHF, 21 (A) SS/ASW Contacts (Closed)-1
28. Deck Log Book [Excerpts] for U.S.S. Blandy, DD 943, which played a critical role in the surfacing of C-18 (B-130).
Source: RG 24, Deck Logs 1962, Box 91.
29. CTG 135.1 (element of invasion task group) cable to COMASWFORLANT, 31 October 1962, on radar and visual sighting of submarine cataloged as C-21 (possibly Soviet submarine B-4).(16)
Source: CHF, 21 (A) SS/ASW Contacts (Closed)-2
30. U.S.S. C.P. Cecil cable to COMASWFORLANT, 31 October, on efforts to hold contact with submarine C-26 [B-36] whose "evasive tactics" were increasing. "Submarine launched false target cans at least three occasions." Source: CHF, 21.SS/ASW
31. U.S.S. Aldebaran cable to COMASWFORLANT, 31 October 1962, reports on surfacing of C-26 [B-36] at

11054Z. The U.S.S. Cecil will monitor the submarine whose crew was "taking turns airing topside." The term "xmas" found in paragraph 4 stands for "unknown non-American submarine." Source: CHF, 21.SS/ASW.

32. Aleksei F. Dubivko, "In the Depths of the Sargasso Sea," Source: On the Edge of the Nuclear Precipice (Moscow: Gregory Page, 1998). Translated by Svetlana Savranskaya

33. CTG 81.1 cable to CTF 81, 31 October 1962, "Appreciation of SOSUS Activity from 301301Z to 311300Z," reports high detection visibility although a decrease in SOSUS contacts. Source: CHF, 21.SS/ASW

34. CINCLANT cable, to JCS, 1 November 1962, "Summary of Soviet Submarine Activities in Western Atlantic 271700Z to 311700Z," reviews previously reported and new submarine contacts through Jezebel, LOFAR (low frequency analysis and recording), and other detection systems. Source: CHF, 21.SS/ASW

35. U.S.S. C.P. Cecil cable to COMASWFORLANT, 2 November 1962, reports that the Cecil is keeping watch of C-26 [B-36], whose crew "worked on fittings under superstructure deck." C-26 submerged later in the day (see document 36). Source: CHF, 21.SS/ASW

36. Deck Log Book [Excerpts] for the U.S.S. Keppler, which monitored C-18 in early November. Source: RG 24, 1962 Deck Logs, box 467

37. CTG 135.1 cable to COMASWFORLANT, 3 November 1962, providing status report on contacts with C-21: "our attitude has changed from confidence to frustration to doubt as the nature of the contacts varied. My

present evaluation [is] that the original contact was a positive sub sighting." Source: CHF, 21 (A) SS/ASW Contacts (Closed)-2

38. COMASWFORLANT cable to AIG 43 et al., 3 November 1962, on the status of C-18, C-19, C-21, and C-26, among other contacts.
Source: CHF, 21.SS/ASW

39. U.S.S. Zellars cable to COMASWFORLANT, 4 November 1962, on unsuccessful efforts to track C-21.
Source: CHF, 21.SS/ASW

40. Special Report of the CNO Submarine Contact Evaluation Board As of 5 November 1962," 5 November 1962, showing confirmed sightings of Soviet submarines, but noting that contact C-21B is "tentative" because of a "lack of confirming evidence."
Source: Source: CHF, 21.SS/ASW 2

41. COMASWFORLANT cable to supporting elements, 5 November 1962, "Summary Soviet Submarine Activity in the Western Atlantic to 051700Z Third Report," reporting status of C-18, C-19, C-21, and C-26. Source: Source: CHF, 21.SS/ASW 2

42. CTU 81.7.9 (element of COMASWFORLANT) cable to COMASWFORLANT, 6 November 1962, on continuing efforts to track C-21 as well as the possible detection, through LOFAR and ECM (electronic countermeasures) of a nuclear submarine
Source: CHF, 21 (A) SS/ASW Contacts (Closed)

43. U.S.S. Keppler cable to COMASWFORLANT, 8 November 1962, on continued monitoring of C-18 (B-130), which appears to be experiencing "mechanical difficulty in separating fuel from water for diesel engines." Source: CHF, 21 (A) SS/ASW Contacts (Closed)

44. COMASWFORLANT cable to AIG 43, 9 November 1962, on rendezvous by C-18 (B-130) with an unidentified surface ship, probably Russian tugboat, Pamir.
Source: CHF, 21.SS/ASW

45. U.S.S. Keppler cable to COMASWLANT, 9 November 1962, on C-18's unsuccessful attempts to submerge.
Source: CHF, 21 (A) SS/ASW Contacts (Closed)

46. COMASWFORLANT cable to CTG 81.9, 9 November 1962, reporting that if Soviet tugboat Pamir is escorting and C-18 and both "are homeward bound", surveillance operation will soon end. As it turned out, the Pamir towed C-18 (B-130) back to port near Murmansk, a three-week voyage.
Source: CHF, 21 (A) SS/ASW Contacts

47. Carrier Division Sixteen, "Report of ASW Barrier Operations During the Cuban Missile Crisis by Group Built Around Randolph," 14 December 1962, describing aerial patrol efforts to track C-19. During one of the helicopter operations on 27 October, after PDC "surfacing signals exploded," sonar picked up noise caused by hatches slamming shut "leaving no doubt that we had a submarine contact."
Source: U.S. Navy Freedom of Information Act Release

48. Commanding Officer, Patrol Squadron Five, "Report of Support of Cuban Missile Crisis Operations," 15 December 1962, showing surveillance efforts against Soviet Submarine C-26, which surfaced because its "undersea capability ... had been evidently exhausted through continued restriction of its movement by air and surface units since the evening of 29 October 1962." Source: U.S. Navy Freedom of Information Act Release.

50. Charts

The following charts showing ship deployments and movements on each day of the Cuban missile crisis were the work of "Flag Plot" and "ASW plot," special components of the office of the Chief of Naval Operations. With these charts, formerly classified "Top Secret", one can track the massive buildup of blockade and invasion forces during the days after 22 October as well as the systematic effort to locate Soviet submarines and other Soviet ships. As the intensity of the crisis grew, the demands of senior officials for more timely information led Flag Plot to produce these charts four times daily; as the crisis ebbed, however, charts were produced only once a day. As the details of submarine sightings accumulated, by the end of October CNO staffers began to produce a daily "ASW Plot" chart that included brief summaries of encounters with Soviet submarines. Source for charts: Washington Navy Yard, U.S. Naval Historical Center, Operational Archives, "Flag Plot Cuban Missile Crisis" files: "Op-Sum Oct 62" and "Op-Sum Nov 62."

1. Carib As Of 22 Oct 1962 0800Q (17)
2. Carib As of 23 October 1962 0800Q
3. Carib As of 24 October 1962 0800Q
4. Carib As of 24 October 1962 1200Q
5. Carib As of 24 October 1962 2230Q
6. Carib As of 25 October 1962 0300Q
7. Carib As of 25 October 1962 0800Q
8. Carib As of 25 October 1962 1200Q
9. Caribbean As of 25 October 1962 2000Q
10. Caribbean As of 25 October 1962 2400Q
11. Caribbean As of 26 October 1962 0800Q
12. Caribbean As of 26 October 1962 1200Q
13. Caribbean As of 26 October 1962 1800Q

14. Caribbean As of 26 October 1962 2400Q
15. Caribbean As of 27 October 1962 0600Q
16. Caribbean As of 27 October 1962 1200Q
17. Caribbean As of 27 October 1962 1800Q
18. Caribbean As of 27 October 1962 2400Q
19. Caribbean As of 28 October 1962 0600R (18)
20. Caribbean As of 28 October 1962 1200R
21. Caribbean As of 28 October 1962 1800R
22. Caribbean As of 28 October 1962 2400R
23. Caribbean As of 29 October 1962 0600R
24. Caribbean As of 29 October 1962 1200R
25. Caribbean As of 29 October 1962 1800R
26. "Cuba ASW Plot," circa 29 October 1962
27. Caribbean As of 29 October 1962 2400R
28. "Cuba ASW Plot As of 300000R Oct 62"
29. Caribbean As of 30 October 1962 0600R
30. Caribbean As of 30 October 1962 1400R
31. Caribbean As of 30 October 1962 2400R
32. "Cuba ASW Plot As of 310000 R Oct 62"
33. Caribbean As of 31 October 1962 0600R
34. Caribbean As of 31 October 19621200R
35. Caribbean As of 31 October 1962 2400R
36. "Cuba ASW Plot As of 010000 R Nov 1962"
37. Caribbean As of 1 November 1962 0600R
38. Caribbean As of 1 November 1962 2400R
39. "Cuba ASW Plot as of 020000 R Nov 62"
40. Caribbean As of 2 Nov. 1962 0600R
41. Caribbean As of 2 Nov. 1962 0600R
42. "Cuba ASW Plot As of 030000 R Nov 1962"
43. Caribbean As of 3 Nov. 1962 0600R
44. "Cuba ASW Plot as of 040000R Nov 1962"
45. Caribbean As of 4 Nov. 1962 0600R

46. "Cuba ASW Plot As of 050000R Nov 1962
47. Caribbean As of 5 Nov. 1962 0600R48. "Cuba ASW
Plot As of 060000R Nov 1962"49. "Cuba ASW Plot As of
070000R Nov 1962"

---

51. Photographs
1. Photograph of Soviet Submarine B-59 taken by U.S.
Navy photographers, circa 28-29 October 1962. Source:
U.S. National Archives, Still Pictures Branch, Record
Group 428, Item 428-N-711201.
2. Photograph of Soviet Submarine B-59 taken by U.S.
Navy photographers, circa 28-29 October 1962.
Source: U.S. National Archives, Still Pictures Branch,
Record Group 428, Item 428-N-711199
3. Photograph of Soviet Submarine B-59 taken by U.S.
Navy photographers, circa 28-29 October 1962. Source:
U.S. National Archives, Still Pictures Branch, Record
Group 428, Item 428-N-711200.
4. Photograph of Soviet Submarine B-36 (conning tower
number 911), taken by U.S. Navy photographers, circa 31
October-2 November 1962. Source: U.S. National
Archives, Still Pictures Branch, Record Group 428, Item
428-N-711198.
5. Photograph of Soviet Submarine B-130 (conning tower
number 945), taken by U.S. Navy photographers, circa 30
October-8 November 1962. Source: collection of Dino
Brugioni, former senior officer, National Photographic
Intelligence Center (NPIC).
6. Photograph of Soviet Submarine B-130 (conning tower
number 945), taken by U.S. Navy photographers, circa 30

October-8 November 1962. Source: Dino Brugioni collection.

7. Photograph of Soviet Submarine B-130 (conning tower number 945), taken by U.S. Navy photographers, circa 30 October-8 November 1962. Source: Dino Brugioni collection.

52. Videos

1. Dorticos, Osvaldo. Video of the October 7, 1962 speech to the United Nations. http://www.criticalpast.com/video/65675026297 United-Nations-assembly name-plate sit-and-speaks.

2. Robert S. Norris, *The Cuban Missile Crisis: A Nuclear Order of Battle* (October/November 1962), A Presentation at the Woodrow Wilson Center, October 24, 2012.)

3. Orlov, Vadim. Video excerpt from the conference, "The Cuban Missile Crisis: A Political Perspective after 40 Years," Havana, Cuba, 11-13 October 2002.

Books and Journals

1.   Andreev, Captain Third Rank Anatoly. Diary, published in *Nikolai Cherkashin*, 'Povsednevnaya Zhizn' Rossiiskikh Podvodnikov' [Daily Life of Russian Submariners]. Moscow: Molodaya Gvardiya Publishing House 2000, p.111.

2.   Bouchard, Joseph. *Command in Crisis: Four Case Studies*, Columbia University Press, New York: 1992.

3.   Breyer, Siegfried. *Guide to the Soviet Navy*, United States Naval Institute, Annapolis: 1970.

4. Bundy, McGeorge. *Danger and Survival: Choices about the Bomb in the First Fifty Years*. New York, NY: Vintage, 1990., p. 301.

5. Dobbs, Michael. *One Minute to Midnight, Kennedy, Khrushchev and Castro on the Brink of Nuclear War*, First Vintage Books, New York: 2008.

6. Drent, Jan. "Confrontation in the Sargasso Sea: Soviet Submarines During the Cuban Missile Crisis," The Northern Mariner/Le Marin du Nord, vol. 13, no. 3 (July 2003): 1-19.

7. Dubivko, Aleksei F., "In the Depths of the Sargasso Sea," unpublished memoirs. Source: On the Edge of the Nuclear Precipice (Moscow: Gregory Page, 1998). Translated by Svetlana Savranskaya.

8. Evtuhov, Catherine, and Stites, Richard. *A History of Russia: peoples, legends, events, forces since 1800*. Boston: Wadsworth Cengage Learning, 2004.

9. Gribkov, A. I. and Smith, W. Y. *Operation ANADYR: US and Soviet Generals Recount the Cuban Missile Crisis*, (Chicago, Berlin, Tokyo, and Moscow: edition q, 1994).

10. 17. Huchthausen, Peter A. *K-19: the widowmaker: the secret story of the Soviet nuclear submarine*. Washington, D.C.: National Geographic Books, 2002.

11. Huchthausen, Peter A. *October Fury*, John Wiley & Sons, Hoboken: 2003.

12. Kennedy, John F. "Cuban Missile Crisis: Address to the Nation." *American Rhetoric: The*

Power of Oratory in the United States. 2 Dec. 2012.

13. Ketov, Ryurik A., Captain 1st Rank, Russian Navy (ret.). "The Cuban Missile Crisis as Seen Through a Periscope," *Journal of Strategic Studies* 28, No. 2, (2005): 217–31.

14. Krinov, E.L. *Giant meteorites.* Pergamon Press, Oxford, 1966.

15. Mikoiān, S. A., and Svetlana Savranskaya. *The Soviet Cuban Missile Crisis: Castro, Mikoyan, Kennedy, Khrushchev, and the Missiles of November.* Woodrow Wilson Center Press, Washington, D.C.: 2012.

16. Reznichanko, General Major V. G. *Taktika,* Moskva: Voyennoye Izdatel'stvo Ministerstva Oborony, SSSR, 1966, p. 148.)

17. Rubtsov, Vladimir. *The Tunguska Mystery,* Springer, New York: 2009.

18. Savranskaya, Svetlana. "New Sources on the Role of Soviet Submarines in the Cuban Missile Crisis." *Journal of Strategic Studies* 28, no. 2 (2005): 233–59.

19. Smith, Fredrick. *The Russians,* New York Times Book Company, New York: 1970.

20. Stern, Sheldon M. *The Cuban Missile Crisis in American memory: myths versus reality.* Stanford, CA: Stanford University Press, 2012.

21. Weir, Gary E. and Boyne, Walter J. *Rising Tide: The Untold Story of the Russian Submarines that Fought the Cold War.* Basic Books. New York: 2003, p. 75.

22. *Jane's Fighting Ships 1972-73*. Jane's Yearbooks, Sampson, Low, Marston and Co., London: 1972.

23. *The Great Soviet Encyclopedia*. The Gale Group Inc., Farmington Hills: 2010, 3rd Edition (1970-1979).

Newspaper and Magazine Articles

1. Bivens, Matt. "Horror of Soviet Nuclear Sub' '61 Tragedy Told." *Los Angeles Times*, January 3, 1994.

2. Knightley, Phillip and Pringle, Peter. "The Cuban Missile Crisis 1962: The world at death's door." *The Independent*, October 4, 1992.

3. Newhouse, John. "13 Days that Almost Shook the World." *New York Times*, July 27, 1997.

4. Schwarz, Benjamin. "The Real Cuban Missile Crisis, Everything you think you know about those 13 days is wrong," *The Atlantic*, December 20, 2012.

5. Serhan, Yasmin. "When the World Lucked Out of a Nuclear War," *The Atlantic*, October 31, 2017.

6. Special to the New York Times, "Cuban Crisis: A Step-by-Step Review," *New York Times*, November 3, 1962.

Notes

Chapter 1

Page 8. *"After a night of heavy drinking…"*: (Special National Intelligence Estimate (SNIE) 85-3-62, Document 13, CIA National Intelligence Estimate, The Military Buildup in Cuba, 9/19/62.)

Page 8. " The assignment's changed.": The operational plan for deploying nuclear weapons into Cuba was hand written and presented to the Chairman of the Soviet Defense Council and Nikita Khrushchev at an expanded meeting that included the Presidium on May 24, 1962. The approved operation, code named Operation Anadyr, was taken to Fidel Castro, who agreed by May 29. He was told the weapons would save the Cuban revolution, presumably from future American aggression. The date for completing the installations in Cuba was October 27, the last Saturday of October. (Anatoli Gribkov and William Smith, *Operation Anadyr, U.S. and Soviet Generals Recount the Cuban Missile Crisis*, Chicago, Berlin, Tokyo, and Moscow: edition q, 1994.)

Planning for the naval contingent of Anadyr was delegated to Vice Admiral Vitaly Alexeyevich Fokin, First Deputy Commander in Chief of the Soviet Navy, second in charge to the Navy's Supreme Commander, Fleet Admiral Sergei Gorshkov. He had less than five months to prepare and execute the deployment of the Twentieth Submarine Squadron of the Northern Fleet. His hand written, top secret, plan was delivered to the defense minister and to Nikita Khrushchev for approval on September 18, 1962. The plan included the permanent deployment of four torpedo submarines, seven missile submarines, two cruisers, two missile ships, two destroyers, two submarine tenders, and a battalion of auxiliary ships with a sail date of October 7. (Vitali A. Fokin and Matvei V. Zakharov, *Initial Report of Soviet Naval Activities in Support of Operation Anadyr*, 18 September 1962, Top Secret of Special Importance for Premier Khrushchev, only copy, translated by Gary Goldberg.)

One week later, Fokin revised the plan for Khrushchev's approval, reducing the force to four torpedo submarines with a new sail date of October 1. Fokin's plan included torpedo loads of twenty-one conventional warheads and one nuclear torpedo war head per submarine. The plan required briefing the brigade commander prior to departure. (Vitali A. Fokin and Matvei V. Zakharov, *Report on Progress of Operation Anadyr, 25 September 1962*, Top Secret of Special Importance for Premier Khrushchev, only copy, translated by Gary Goldberg.)

Page 9. "As the brigade chief of staff and second in command ...": Captain Second Rank Vasily Aleksandrovich Arkhipov from a province near Moscow, was the 69th Submarine Torpedo Brigade's Chief of Staff and second in command of B-59, previously a brigade rider on the ill-fated Soviet's first ballistic missile submarine K-19. (Ryurik A. Ketov, Captain First Rank, Russian Navy (ret.), "The Cuban Missile Crisis as Seen Through a Periscope," *Journal of Strategic Studies* 28, No. 2, 2005: 217–31.)

Page 9. "Captain of the B-59": Captain Second Rank Valentin Grigorievich Savitsky, Commanding Officer of the B-59, probably from Brest based on his surname. (*Ibid.*)

Page 10. "massive stores loadout": "The past week had been hectic. They had taken on a large quantity of fuel and stores, which took up almost every centimeter of free space in each of the subs." (Peter A. Huchthausen, *October Fury*, John Wiley & Sons, 2003. p. 52.)

Page 11. " He suffered a severe attack in Moscow…": Commander of the 69th Submarine Torpedo Brigade, Kontr (Rear) Admiral Yevseyev, suddenly took ill and was rushed to the hospital with an anxiety attack and soaring high blood pressure after his briefing in Moscow on Operation Anadyr. (Vasily N. Agafonov, Captain First Rank, *69th Submarine Brigade Commander Report*, [undated, circa December 1962, prepared by the USSR Northern Fleet Headquarters] about participation of submarines "B-4," "B-36," "B-59," "B-130" of the 69th submarine brigade of the Northern Fleet in the Operation "Anadyr" during the period of October - December 1962, CARIBBEAN CRISIS, Translated by Svetlana Savranskaya for the National Security Archive.)

Page 12. "Our mission is called Operation Kama.": "The Navy carried out preparations for operation 'Anadyr' under the codename operation 'Kama.'" (*Ibid.*)

Page 12. "Our new brigade commander arrives on Sunday, with the brass.": "Instructions to the commanders of the submarines and ceremony of launch were conducted by first deputy of the Supreme Commander of the Navy Admiral Fokin V. A. and Chief of Staff of the Northern Fleet Vice Admiral Rassokho A. I." (*Ibid.*)

Page 15. "Fleet Admiral Gorshkov": Fleet Admiral Sergey Georgiyevich Gorshkov was the Supreme Commander of the Soviet Navy, the highest ranking naval officer in the Soviet navy, equivalent to U.S. Chief of Naval Operations (CNO). (Peter A. Huchthausen, *October Fury*, John Wiley & Sons, 2003. p. 122-123.)

Page 13. "Premier Khrushchev": Nikita Sergeyevich Khrushchev was the General Secretary of the CCCP *(Союз Советских Социалистических Республик),* commonly referred to as the USSR (Union of Soviet Socialist Republics), equivalent to the President of the United States, John F. Kennedy. *(Ibid.* pp. 1-8.)

Page 13. "Deputy Fleet Admiral Fokin": Admiral Vitaly Alexeyevich Fokin was First Deputy to the Supreme Commander and second in command of the Soviet Navy, four-time recipient of the Order of the Red Banner and of the Order of Lenin, naval advisor to Khrushchev, coauthor of Operation Anadyr and senior officer at the brigade launch ceremony in Polyarny. (Vasily N. Agafonov, Captain First Rank, *69th Submarine Brigade Commander Report,* [undated, circa December 1962, prepared by the USSR Northern Fleet Headquarters] about participation of submarines "B-4," "B-36," "B-59," "B-130" of the 69th submarine brigade of the Northern Fleet in the Operation "Anadyr" during the period of October - December 1962, CARIBBEAN CRISIS, Translated by Svetlana Savranskaya for the National Security Archive.)

Page 13. "Agafonov?": Captain First Rank Agafonov, 69th Submarine Brigade Commander replaced Rear *(Kontr)* Admiral Yevseyev who fell ill after his briefing on Operation Anadyr. The new brigade commander reported, "Commander of the 69th submarine brigade Rear Admiral Yevseyev suddenly got ill after the briefing in Moscow, and Captain First Rank Vasily Naumovich Agafonov was appointed commander of the brigade the day before the start of the operation." *(Ibid.)*

Page 14. "nukes? ..."On diesel submarines?": "Preparations for the operation were completed on September 30, 1962 with loading 21 torpedoes with conventional load and one torpedo with nuclear load onto each of the submarines." (*Ibid.*)

Page 14. "There'll be riders, special forces.": "For the first time in Soviet naval practice, special OSNAZ groups were assigned to the boats…" (USSR, Memoir, "Recollections of Vadim Orlov (USSR Submarine B-59): We will Sink Them All, But We will Not Disgrace Our Navy," (2002). Source: Alexander Mozgovoi, "The Cuban Samba of the Quartet of Foxtrots: Soviet Submarines in the Caribbean Crisis of 1962," *Military Parade*, Moscow, 2002. Translated by Svetlana Savranskaya for the National Security Archive.)

Page 16. "I've assigned myself to replace your senior assistant as your second in command for this voyage": "The Brigade Commander, Captain Vitaly Agafonov, spent the mission aboard the B-4/Chelyabinskii komsomolets, while the Brigade Chief of Staff, Captain Vasily Arkhipov, was aboard the B-59." (Ryurik A. Ketov, Captain First Rank, Russian Navy (ret.). "The Cuban Missile Crisis as Seen Through a Periscope," *Journal of Strategic Studies* 28, No. 2, 2005: 217–31.)

Chapter 2

Page 18. "*Our voyage began…*": (Captain Third Rank Anatoly Andreev's diary, published in *Nikolai Cherkashin*, 'Povsednevnaya Zhizn' Rossiiskikh Podvodnikov' [Daily Life of Russian Submariners]. Moscow: Molodaya Gvardiya Publishing House 2000, p.111.)

Page 19. "…Soviet Premier Nikita Khrushchev deployed his submarines under a cloak of secrecy and deception to advance his political agenda, to project his profound commitment to advance the cause of international socialist revolution...": "Consequently we had to undertake something real. I must admit that I was very much pre-occupied with this problem. The loss of revolutionary Cuba...would undermine the will for revolution among the peoples of other countries. If ... revolutionary Cuba were preserved...and raised the living standards of the Cuban people to such an extent that it became a beacon of hope, a great light shining for all the insulted and injured...of Latin America, that would turn out to be in the interests of Marxist-Leninist doctrine." (Nikita S. Khrushchev, *Memoirs of Nikita Khrushchev: Volume 3, Statesman, 1953-1964*, Penn State Press, 2007, p. 314.). "At issue were how, and how forcefully, to advance Soviet strength and influence around the world without squandering forces on risky wars." (Catherine Evtuhov and Richard Stites, *A History of Russia: Peoples, Legends, Events, Forces since 1800*. Boston: Wadsworth Cengage Learning, 2004, p. 465.)

Page 20. "Prepare to get underway": The 69th Torpedo Submarine Brigade sailed from Polyarny under sealed orders at 04:00, October 1, 1962: The B-130 with Captain Nikolai Shumkov; the B-36 with Captain Aleksei Dubivko; the B-59 with Captain Valentin Savitsky; and the B-4 with Captain Ryurik Ketov. The Brigade Commander, Captain Vitaly Agafonov, sailed aboard B-4, and Brigade Chief of Staff, Captain Vasily Arkhipov, was aboard B-59. (Ryurik A. Ketov, Captain First Rank, Russian Navy (ret.), "The Cuban Missile Crisis as Seen Through a Periscope," *Journal of Strategic Studies* 28, No. 2, 2005: 217–31.)

Page 21. "to escape farm collectivization and the horrors of the Stalin's first social experiment": "By February 1930, 50 percent of the peasantry were collectivized in conditions producing utter chaos...by 1933, two thirds of the peasants were collectivized, and by 1939 virtually all. The horrors of this war were hidden from the Soviet people and from foreign eyes as well. Trucks bursting with volunteer agents of forced collectivization stormed the countryside… They occupied villages as in wartime, organized houses into blocks, shot resistors, confiscated animals, and burned churches. More than half the dekulakized peasants thrown off the land migrated to factory towns. Others ended in forced labor camps or settled far from home in the bleak wilderness of northern Russia, Siberia and Central Asia." (Catherine Evtuhov and Richard Stites, *A History of Russia: peoples, legends, events, forces since 1800.* Boston: Wadsworth Cengage Learning, 2004, p. 361.)

Page 22. "Starpom rode minesweepers": While attending Pacific Higher Naval School, Vasily Arkhipov was assigned to a minesweeper in the Soviet-Japanese War.

Page 22. "The Captain came from Brest in Belarussia…": Savitsky is the habitational name for someone from a place called Savichi, situated in Brest, Belarus. Its geographical coordinates are 53° 17' 0" North, 26° 17' 0" East.

Page 22. "…Victory Parade…": Victory Parade refers to an official joint military celebration in Brest-Litowsk held by German and Soviet troops on September 22, 1939 after the Polish invasion. German troops withdrew in accordance with the prearranged nonaggression pact that set lines of demarcation that handed the city and its fortress to the Red Army.

Page 23. "…Rosta shipyard in Polyarny…": (Peter A. Huchthausen, *October Fury*, John Wiley & Sons, 2003. p. 54.)

Page 23. "…nuclear-powered boats were new, unreliable and unsuitable for operational missions.": "The Soviet

Navy at the time did not have a sufficient number of nuclear missile submarines ready to be sent on this assignment, and consequently a decision was made to equip the Foxtrots with the warheads." (Svetlana Savranskaya, "New Sources on the Role of Soviet Submarines in the Cuban Missile Crisis." *Journal of Strategic Studies* 28:2, 2005: 233-59.)

Page 24. "The nuke lay in its cradle…": Each submarine carried one T-5 nuclear tipped torpedo, equivalent to a Hiroshima bomb. (*Ibid.*)

Page 24. "…sealed orders rested in the safe…": The captains received secret orders in sealed packets to be opened at sea and a set of charts for all oceans of the world. (*Ibid.*)

Page 25. "…hunter-killer, doomsday machines.": The brigade had four (designator B means bolshoi or large) diesel-electric Project 641 submarines, armed with 22 torpedoes, one with a nuclear warhead – totaling 88 torpedoes with a shooting range of nineteen kilometers of which four had nuclear warheads. (Ryurik A. Ketov, Captain First Rank, Russian Navy (ret.). "The Cuban Missile Crisis as Seen Through a Periscope," *Journal of Strategic Studies* 28:2, 2005: 217–31.)

Page 26. "Tugs eased the boat away from the pier…": Tugboats move submarines away from piers because the submarine bow is coated with mission critical sonar equipment that cannot be touched during the underway maneuvers. The delicate process takes the subs from the pier to the center of the channel, and aims them in the right direction, where they have the requisite steerage on their own power.

Page 27. "B-59, B-36, B-130 and B-4": Order and interval of departure. (Peter A. Huchthausen, October Fury, John Wiley & Sons, 2002. pp. 56-57.)

Page 27. "Victor, the junior navigator, manned the navigation periscope…" Lieutenant Victor Mikhailov - Junior Navigator, B-59.

Page 27. "…Olga's Red Moscow…": Russian expatriate, Ernest Beaux, claimed that his inspiration for Chanel No 5's distinctive bouquet was the fresh polar air from Kola Peninsula where he fought in 1920. He created its predecessor, Krasnaya Moskva (Red Moscow), a Soviet classic, packaged in a bottle resembling the Kremlin Towers.

Page 27. "They called him Poli…": Captain Third Rank Ivan Semonovich Maslennikov – B-59 Deputy Political Officer (Zampolit)

Page 28. "…infamous general…": General Ivan Ivanovich Maslennikov was a Deputy to the Supreme Soviet and a candidate member of the Central Committee. He was awarded four Orders of Lenin, four Orders of the Red Banner, the Order of Suvorov First Class, two Orders of Kutuzov First Class, the Order of the Red Star, and the Order of the Red Banner of the Mongolian People's Republic. (*The Great Soviet Encyclopedia*, 3rd Edition (1970-1979). © 2010 The Gale Group, Inc.)

Page 28. "Take from each man in accordance with his ability…": Karl Marx's popular slogan from his May 1875 Critique of the Gotha Program refers to free access and distribution of an abundance of goods, capital and services under the unfettered productive forces of communism.

Page 29. "…I recommend course 052…": Ship's course commands/readings derive from Russian navigation charts for Kola Bay.

Page 31. "An *Osnaz* special ops group…": Osnaz units were Special Forces units of the People's Commissariat for Internal Affairs (NKVD). They were Political Special Forces or secret police (not the military special forces called Spetznaz) executing Soviet directives including arrests, imprisonment and execution. Operation Kama was the first time that Osnaz units deployed on submarines, and each of the four diesel submarines carried an Osnaz group for the deployment. (USSR, Memoir, "Recollections of Vadim Orlov (USSR Submarine B-59): We will Sink Them All, But We will Not Disgrace Our Navy," (2002). Source: Alexander Mozgovoi, "The Cuban Samba of the Quartet of Foxtrots: Soviet Submarines in the Caribbean Crisis of 1962," *Military Parade*, Moscow, 2002. Translated by Svetlana Savranskaya for the National Security Archive.)

Page 32. "Senior Lieutenant Vadim Orlov reporting for duty.": Senior Lieutenant Vadim Pavlovich Orlov from Vladivostok, Leader of Osnaz radio intercept group assigned to B-59. (*Ibid.*)

Page 32. "How will you ensure our security?": A special radio intercept team sailed aboard each boat, in charge of communications with Moscow and conducting interception and decoding of US radio transmissions. Senior Lieutenant Orlov recalled that initially his men were greeted with suspicion and open hostility by Captain Savitsky and the officers because they were outsiders and NKVD representatives. (*Ibid.*)

Page 30. "Radio intercepts, electronic surveillance and intelligence": The Osnaz group brought specialized, classified, electronics equipment they integrated into the ship's masts and the petty officers' mess area. (*Ibid.*)

Page 32. "The Ship's Chief Petty Officer": Senior enlisted men in the navy rise to the rate of non-commissioned officer (NCO), also known as petty officer or michman in Russian. The senior enlisted man on a submarine holds a special, almost revered, position as the one man on the ship who knows everything through experience. On American submarines, the position is called Chief of the Boat (COB), and on Russian submarines, the position is called the Ship's Chief Petty Officer. He is the most experienced man on the ship, and he commands the respect of every member of the crew, including the captain.

Page 36 "Should they sink, no one would know": Emergency signal devices installed for locating downed submarines were routinely welded to the deck and rendered useless before deployment to avoid accidental release in heavy weather or during a depth charge attack.

Pages 38-42. "The chief sensed the problem before anyone.": Senior Lieutenant Orlov reported that the B-59 egress from Kola Bay proceeded without incident. The loss of depth control incident is my, the author's, personal experience that happened to another boat, at another time, entering another sea. The incident is included to demonstrate the omnipresent dangers prevalent in submarine life, how a single man is expected to save the ship from disaster, and how a crewman stepping up to control a dangerous situation when things go wrong, even with the captain and senior officers in the compartment, is not viewed as mutinous or insubordinate. The author was the ship's diving officer, who had calculated the ballast compensations, and who stood next to the brigade commander. After the incident, he worked with the executive officer to determine what went wrong and brief the captain. The captain noted that the screws were much closer to the bottom than depth sensor indicated, providing a false sense of security. After the briefing, the loss of depth control incident was never spoken of it again.

Page 47. "It's time to open our orders.": "Several hours before the departure commanders of the submarines received sealed, "top secret" envelopes, which they could open only after leaving the Kola Bay. They were instructed to inform the ship's personnel about the country of the new deployment only after the submarines reached the Atlantic Ocean." (Vasily N. Agafonov, Captain First Rank, *69th Submarine Brigade Commander Report*, [undated, circa December 1962, prepared by the USSR Northern Fleet Headquarters] about participation of submarines "B-4," "B-36," "B-59," "B-130" of the 69th submarine brigade of the Northern Fleet in the Operation "Anadyr" during the period of October - December 1962, CARIBBEAN CRISIS, Translated by Svetlana Savranskaya for the National Security Archive.)

Chapter 3

Page 49. "Commander in Chief, U.S. Navy Atlantic Fleet, (CINCLANTFLT) directs increased readiness to execute an invasion of Cuba.": (CINCLANT Historical Account of Cuban Crisis, 4/29/63, p. 40.)

Page 49. "Cuba?": The crews of the 69th Submarine Brigade and their families had been alerted to the possibility of a Cuban deployment before it became highly classified under Operation Anadyr. After the operation became classified, no information was provided. (Ryurik A. Ketov, Captain First Rank, Russian Navy (ret.), "The

Cuban Missile Crisis as Seen Through a Periscope,"
Journal of Strategic Studies 28:2, 2005: 217–31.)

Page 50. "…sealed packet bore wide red stripes…": (Peter
A. Huchthausen, *October Fury*, John Wiley & Sons, 2002.
p. 62.) "The captains received packets with secret orders,
which they could only open at sea, and a set of maps for all
regions of the world ocean. When the packets were opened,
the orders read that the boats were to go to Cuba and dock
at Mariel. The weapons on the boats were to be in a state of
full combat readiness." (Svetlana Savranskaya, "New
Sources on the Role of Soviet Submarines in the Cuban
Missile Crisis." *Journal of Strategic Studies* 28:2, 2005:
233-59.)

Page 50. "A playground for American gangsters under
Batista." Cuban dictator Fulgencio Batista fled the island
under urban and rural assault by Fidel Castro's 26th of July
Movement on January 1, 1959, amidst celebration in
Havana.

Page 51. "We're sailing to Mariel Bay to establish a
submarine home base for the Motherland, and we have zero
situational awareness?": "While it is one thing to move
ships openly – proceeding to a new permanent area for
subsequent duty while carrying out routine training
exercises at sea – it is quite another when one's boat is for
unknown reasons loaded with atomic weapons and sent
with vague objectives seemingly neither for a simple
transfer, nor for active duty in Cuba." (Ryurik A. Ketov,
Captain First Rank, Russian Navy (ret.). "The Cuban
Missile Crisis as Seen Through a Periscope," *Journal of
Strategic Studies* 28:2, 2005: 217–31.)

Page 52. "I once sailed a burning sub out of Polyarny…":
"…during a fire in the forward torpedo room of another ill-

fated Polyarny-based diesel submarine, B-139…Agafonov…piloted the burning submarine out of the crowded nest and into more isolated waters in case her remaining torpedoes exploded." (Peter A. Huchthausen, *October Fury*, John Wiley & Sons, 2002. p. 20.)

Page 54. "Captain Ketov…": Captain Second Rank Ryurik A. Ketov, Commanding officer of B-4. (*Ibid.*)

Page 54. "Captain Dubivko…": Captain Second Rank Aleksei Dubivko, Commanding officer of B-36. (*Ibid.*)

Page 54. "Captain Shumkov…": Captain Second Rank Nikolai Aleksandrovich Shumkov, Commanding officer of B-130. (*Ibid.*)

Page 54. "He fired two nuclear torpedo tests from his boat.": The B-130 under Captain Shumkov test fired two T-5 nuclear torpedoes at maximum range, one from a submerged position and one from the surface in NZ Area A, Chyornaya Guba, Novaya Zemlya, Russia on October 23 and October 27, 1961, respectively. (Vitaly I. Khalturin, Tatyana G. Rautian, Paul G. Richards, and William S. Leith, *"A Review of Nuclear Testing by the Soviet Union at Novaya Zemlya, 1955--1990"* . Science and Global Security, 10 April 2004.)

Page 55. "covert and undetected": "It is notable that the initial arrangements were for the boats to undergo the passage openly on a designated route, but the final operational orders called for the movement to be covert in nature." (Ryurik A. Ketov, Captain First Rank, Russian Navy (ret.), "The Cuban Missile Crisis as Seen Through a Periscope," *Journal of Strategic Studies* 28:2, 2005: 217–31.)

Page 56. "General Pliyev": Issa Alexandrovich Pliyev, General of the Army. During the Cuban Missile Crisis he commanded the Group of Soviet Forces, all Soviet forces, in Cuba under Operation Anadyr. (A. I. Gribkov and W. Y. Smith, *Operation ANADYR: US and Soviet Generals Recount the Cuban Missile Crisis*, Chicago, Berlin, Tokyo, and Moscow: edition q, 1994.)

Page 56. "Gromyko confronted them two weeks ago in front of the United Nations.": Andre Gromyko, Soviet ambassador to the United Nations, nicknamed "Mr. Nyet," accused the United States of whipping up "war hysteria" and seeking an excuse to invade Cuba on September 21, 1962. He also lied by saying "any sober-minded man knows that Cuba is not...building up her forces to such a degree that she can pose a threat to the United States or...to any state of the Western Hemisphere." (Statement by Andrei Gromyko before the U.N. General Assembly Including Comments on U.S. Policy toward Cuba, 9/21/62)

Page 57. "...Admiral Fokin and General Zakharov...": On 18 September, a detailed hand-written top-secret memorandum reporting status on Soviet Navy activities in support of Operation 'Anadyr' was sent personally to Premier Khrushchev, of special importance, signed by General Zakharov and Admiral Vitaly Fokin. (Vitali A. Fokin and Matvei V. Zakharov, *Initial Report of Soviet Naval Activities in Support of Operation Anadyr*, 18 September 1962, Top-Secret, of Special Importance for Premier Khrushchev, only copy, translated by Gary Goldberg.)

Page 57. "...Zakharov...": General Matvei Vasilevich Zakharov was the Marshal of the Soviet Union, Chief of the General Staff, Deputy Defense Minister. Coauthor of Operation Anadyr.

Page 57. "Kama, the naval deployment to Mariel Bay, is just a small piece of Anadyr.": "A Soviet submarine base in Cuba could be of considerable military value to the USSR. Submarines operating from a Cuban base could be maintained on station off the US coast for much longer periods than can now be sustained in operations from Northern Fleet bases. Such a forward base would permit Soviet missile and torpedo attack submarines, both conventional and nuclear-powered, more readily to conduct routine patrols off the US coast. It is possible that the Soviets might seek to establish such a base in connection with the provision of some submarines to the Cubans." (Special National Intelligence Estimate (SNIE) 85-3-62, Document 433, CIA National Intelligence Estimate, The Military Buildup in Cuba, 9/19/62.)

Page 57. "Why not throw a hedgehog into Uncle Sam's pants?": (John Newhouse, "13 Days that Almost Shook the World." *New York Times*, July 27, 1997.)

Page 57. "They've also sent tens of thousands of combat troops...": "Already 30,390 men are in Cuba with associated equipment." (Vitali A. Fokin and Matvei V. Zakharov, *Report on Progress of Operation Anadyr*, 25 September 1962, Top Secret of Special Importance for Premier Khrushchev, only copy, translated by Gary Goldberg.)

Nikita Khrushchev conceived the notion of placing nuclear ballistic missiles into Cuba at his Black Sea estate in the spring of 1962 after fifteen U.S Jupiter missiles became operational at Izmir Air Base. His Defense Minister, Rodion Malinovsky, pointed toward Turkey and noted that: "American rockets are pointing at us. They need only 10 minutes to reach our cities, but our rockets need 25 minutes to reach America." Khrushchev replied, "Why don't we install our rockets in Cuba and point them at the Americans? Then we'll need only 10 minutes, too." On May 14, 1962, Khrushchev proposed the idea with his Defense Council at the Kremlin. He directed a clandestine operation that would remain hidden until after the November U.S. mid-term elections. Alexander Alexeyev, Soviet ambassador to Cuba, reports that Khrushchev said, "Do it like they did to us in Turkey. Confront them with an established fact. The Americans are a pragmatic people. They'll accept it, like we had to in Turkey. Then we'll be able to negotiate with America on a basis of parity." The first of eighty-five Soviet merchant ships carrying offensive weaponry, the Maria Ulianov, arrived in Cuba on July 26. In the next three months, forty-three thousand Soviet military troops, sixty nuclear ballistic missiles and nearly one hundred tactical nuclear weapons were secretly deployed to Cuba. (Phillip Knightley and Peter Pringle, "The Cuban Missile Crisis 1962: The world at death's door." *The Independent*, October 4, 1992.)

Page 58. "It's *maskirovka*.": Moscow's surreptitious dispatch of nuclear weapons to Cuba employed information denial and deception, known as maskirovka in Russia. Russian military texts elevate maskirovka as the operational art of concealing the scope, timing, and details of maneuvers. The objective of maskirovka "is to conceal from the enemy the true position of our troops and to give him a false idea of it and thereby to lead him into error and force him to a conclusion which does not correspond to the situation." (General Major V. G. Reznichanko, *Taktika*, Moskva: Voyennoye Izdatel'stvo Ministerstva Oborony, SSSR, 1966, p. 148.)

Page 59. "Weapons will be made combat ready for use during transit.": (Peter A. Huchthausen, *October Fury*, John Wiley & Sons, 2002. p. 65.)

Page 59. "Write down when you should use…": (Svetlana Savranskaya, "New Sources on the Role of Soviet Submarines in the Cuban Missile Crisis." *Journal of Strategic Studies* 28:2, 2005: 233-59)

Page 60. "If they slap you on the left cheek, do not let them slap you on the right one.": "…on the day before their departure, the First Deputy Head of the USSR Navy, Admiral Vitaly A. Fokin and Chief of Staff of the Northern Fleet Vice-Admiral A.I. Rassokha spoke to the crews of the four submarines, and briefed them on their mission and the use of weapons. The only instructions concerning nuclear weapons that the captains remember receiving were given in that briefing. As Nikolai Shumkov recalls, he heard Admiral Fokin say 'if they slap you on the left cheek, do not let them slap you on the right one'." (*Ibid.*)

Page 62. "Captain Shumkov says that his B-130 was tossed about like a toy…": In 1962 Soviet Navy submarines were not equipped with nuclear-tipped torpedoes until they were sent to Cuba. The B-130 took part in test-firing two nuclear torpedoes in at Novaya Zemlya October 1961, from submerged and surfaced positions. The tests were successful, and Captain Shumkov became one of very few submarine captains, who had experience in using this type of weapon. (Peter A. Huchthausen, *October Fury*, John Wiley & Sons, 2002. p. 18.)

Page 63. "…a piece of fruit he bought from the stores boat…": "We even had a floating store docking with us. I bought two kilos of apples to take with me, which I finished today. Those were our last hours before leaving."

(Captain Third Rank Anatoly Andreev's diary, published in *Nikolai Cherkashin*, 'Povsednevnaya Zhizn' Rossiiskikh Podvodnikov' [Daily Life of Russian Submariners]. Moscow: Molodaya Gvardiya Publishing House 2000, p.111.)

Page 64. "…special weapon officer…": "Each nuclear torpedo had a special officer assigned to it, who stayed with it throughout the journey, and even slept next to it. (*Ibid.*) "He was in charge of maintaining the torpedo, and had one set of keys, which were necessary to load it. He was also the one responsible for assembling the torpedo for combat use if such an order had been received from Moscow." (Svetlana Savranskaya, "New Sources on the Role of Soviet Submarines in the Cuban Missile Crisis." *Journal of Strategic Studies* 28:2, 2005: 233-59)

Page 64. "…Makarov 9mm pistol in a brown leather holster…": "…along with the new torpedo came a single weapons security officer…accompanying the special weapon wore a small pistol in a brown leather holster…" (Peter A. Huchthausen, October Fury, John Wiley & Sons, 2002. p. 48.)

Page 65. "His eyes searched the eleven gray-nosed weapons for his purple-nosed treasure.": "These 533-millimeter torpedoes were marked with purple-painted noses to stand apart in the forward torpedo room from the twenty-one regular-war shot torpedoes with gray-painted noses." (*Ibid.* p. 47.)

Chapter 4

Page 67. "**Memorandum from Secretary of Defense McNamara to President Kennedy…**": (Memorandum from Secretary of Defense McNamara to President

Kennedy, Washington D.C., October 4, 1962." TOP
SECRET: (Kennedy Library, National Security Files,
Countries Series, Cuba, General, 10/1-10/14/62.)

Page 67. "…even folk songs…": "For years, Russians
knew the story of the K-19 only through underground
songs. But the Soviet Union, the nation those sailors swore
to defend, collapsed, and today the doomed vessel's crew
members are ready to flesh out those sad, romantic verses."
(Matt Bivens, "Horror of Soviet Nuclear Sub' '61 Tragedy
Told." *Los Angeles Times*, January 3, 1994.)

Page 68. "American anti-submarine warfare (ASW)
campaign": "We naturally assumed that our departure
would not go unnoticed by NATO forces, an assumption
that became justified as soon as we crossed the first barrier
between Norway's North Cape (Nordkapp) and Medvezhy
Island. Norwegian and British antisubmarine warfare
(ASW) forces tracked our speed of ten knots with enviable
precision, and began to 'close' the choke points. However,
we had by that time enough leeway to evade these efforts."
(Ryurik A. Ketov, Captain First Rank, Russian Navy (ret.),
"The Cuban Missile Crisis as Seen Through a Periscope,"
Journal of Strategic Studies 28:2, 2005: 217–31.)

Page 68. "U.S. Sound Surveillance System (SOSUS)":
SOSUS is an underwater sonar system of listening posts
mounted on the Atlantic Ocean floor in areas near
Greenland, Iceland, and the United Kingdom, as well as the
U.S. coastline for monitoring the deep sound channel.

Page 71. "I'll tell you a story.": The disappearing hand
story is a true story experienced by me, the author, one
summer, anchored off the coast of Turkey on a patrol
gunboat.

Page 72. "horizontal layers are due to various factors…":
"The ocean is divided into horizontal layers of sound speed
due to various factors, primarily temperature and water
pressure. Sound travels slower in lower temperatures and
pressures. The layers are measured to provide data to
support stealth tactics in the Sargasso Sea." (Ryurik A.
Ketov, Captain First Rank, Russian Navy (ret.), "The
Cuban Missile Crisis as Seen Through a Periscope,"
Journal of Strategic Studies 28:2, 2005: 217–31).

Page 72. "…I apologize for the limited accommodations on
board B-59.": "The presence of 'special weapons' required
separate berthing, special-pass access to the pier, and
inspections of supplies brought aboard ship. Fresh tests of
loyalty and staff reviews posed new tests for sailors
exhibiting their best work to enlist support from above."
(*Ibid.*)

Page 72. "ASW flights activated from the North Cape to
Bear Island…": "The antisubmarine forces of the opponent,
especially the aviation, were ready for an encounter with us
from the very beginning of our sail to the Cuban shores."
(USSR, Memoir, "Recollections of Vadim Orlov (USSR
Submarine B-59): We will Sink Them All, But We will Not
Disgrace Our Navy," (2002). Source: Alexander Mozgovoi,
"The Cuban Samba of the Quartet of Foxtrots: Soviet
Submarines in the Caribbean Crisis of 1962," *Military
Parade*, Moscow, 2002. Translated by Svetlana
Savranskaya for the National Security Archive.)

Page 72. "…stealth strategies left to the discretion of the
individual sea captains.": "After an oral briefing, the four
captains met and developed tactical schemes for the
voyage. Speed and stealth tactics were left to each
submarine commanders' discretion. They maintained
communications for tactical cooperation to allow for course

adjustments." (Ryurik A. Ketov, Captain First Rank, Russian Navy (ret.). "The Cuban Missile Crisis as Seen Through a Periscope," *Journal of Strategic Studies* 28:2, 2005: 217–31).

Page 74. "…films of entertaining propaganda…": "Soviet broadcasting on the current US racial crisis has recently attained a level seven times that of the Mississippi crisis last autumn. Recurrent themes have been: That racism is inevitable in the capitalist system and can only be eradicated along with capitalism itself; that the Federal Government is supporting the racists by its general inertia and because of unwillingness to antagonize Southern Democrats…The volume of Soviet broadcasting on the current US racial crisis has been enormous. The 1,420 Soviet commentaries beamed worldwide in the period May 14-26, for example, was more than seven times the amount broadcast at the two-week peak of the Meredith case last autumn, it was nine times greater than during the two-week high of May 1961 (on freedom riders) and more than eleven times the two-week high during the Little Rock crisis of 1957." (Thomas L. Hughes, "Soviet Media Coverage of Current US Racial Crisis," Department of State Bureau of Intelligence and Research memorandum RSB-92, June 14, 1963.)

Page 75. "…the phone lines were dead.": "I came back to my place and thought I'd try calling again, but... the phone wasn't working. We were cut off from the rest of the world." (Captain Third Rank Anatoly Andreev's diary, published in Nikolai Cherkashin, 'Povsednevnaya Zhizn' Rossiiskikh Podvodnikov' [Daily Life of Russian Submariners]. Moscow: Molodaya Gvardiya Publishing House 2000, p.111.)

Page 76. "…I was asking about the K-19.": (*K-19, The History*. www.nationalgeographic.com/k19/k19_html_main.html.)

Page 77. "He had the conn when a reactor coolant pipe burst…": "Captain Second Rank Vasily Arkhipov, a diesel-power man but an experienced submariner, took the conn." (Memoirs of Captain Second Rank Nikolai Zateyev, Commanding Officer of K-19, published in Peter A. Huchthausen. *K-19: the Widowmaker: the secret story of the Soviet nuclear submarine*. Washington, D.C.: National Geographic Books, 2002, page 120.)

Page 78. "The captain of the K-19 sacrificed his engineering crew…": (*Ibid*. Pages 128-132.)

Page 78. "Starpom stood his ground with a contingent of loyal officers and five pistols…": "I summoned…Captain Lieutenant Mukhin and ordered him…to gather the small arms…and throw them overboard, keeping only five pistols: for the commander, the starpom, Captains Second Rank Andreyev, Arkhipov, and Mukhen himself. This order was intended to discourage any attempts against my authority and was carried out immediately." (*Ibid.* page 134.)

Page 78. "…banned from talking about the incident.": "After he and his crew returned to Russia, they were sequestered and unable to contact family. They were told they were all suffering from mental illness due to stress. The words "radiation poisoning" were forbidden. A lot of these men died within a few months or years of the accident. Those who survived faced a lifetime of pain, both mentally and physically. It's a very tragic story." (Nikolai Zateyev's memorial @ https://www.findagrave.com/cgi-bin/fg.cgi?page=gr&GRid=11756871)

Page 79. "I read them and burned them for luck.": In a
BBC interview, recorded for a documentary, Arkhipov's
wife, Olga, alludes to her husband's possible superstitious
beliefs as well. She recalls walking in on Vasily burning a
bundle of their love letters inside their house, claiming that
keeping the letters would mean "bad luck". (Codi von
Richthofen, *Missile Crisis: The Man Who Saved the World*,
PBS Documentary, 2015.)

Pages 80. "We have deployed thirty-six medium range R-
12 ballistic missile batteries…": (Vitali A. Fokin and
Matvei V. Zakharov, "Report on Progress of Operation
Anadyr, 25 September 1962, Top Secret of Special
Importance for Premier Khrushchev, only copy, translated
by Gary Goldberg.)

Page 80. "…fifteen hundred men abandoned on the
beach…": (Dobbs, Michael. *One Minute to Midnight:
Kennedy, Khrushchev, and Castro on the Brink of Nuclear
War.* Vintage Books, 2009, p 7.)

Page 80. "The CIA tried to assassinate him many times.":
(*Ibid.* pp 8 – 14.)

Page 80. "President Kennedy is preparing a full-scale naval
invasion.": William Burr, and Peter Kornbluh. "*U.S.
Planned for Military Occupation of Cuba*," National
Security Archive Electronic Briefing Book No. 606,
October 16, 2017.)

Page 80. "…spearhead the new submarine base.": "The
shore submarine base of the 20th squadron was loaded onto
the ships of the Merchant Marine Ministry, arrived in Cuba
at Mariel harbor in October and remained there." (Vasily
Naumovich Agafonov, Captain First Rank, 69th Submarine
Brigade Commander Report [undated, circa December

1962, prepared by the USSR Northern Fleet Headquarters]
About participation of submarines "B-4," "B-36," "B-59,"
"B-130" of the 69th submarine brigade of the Northern
Fleet in the Operation "Anadyr" during the period of
October - December 1962, CARIBBEAN CRISIS,
Translated by Svetlana Savranskaya for the National
Security Archive).

Page 81. "I know Captain Nantenkov on the B-75,": The
submarine B-75 had 22 torpedoes, including two with
nuclear warheads. Captain Nikolai Nantenkov, indicated
this was his first experience with nuclear warheads.
(Svetlana Savranskaya, "New Sources on the Role of
Soviet Submarines in the Cuban Missile Crisis." *Journal of
Strategic Studies* 28:2, 2005: 233-59.)

Page 85. "Halt,": The story of being stopped at gunpoint
from entering a secured nuclear weapons space is a true
story that happened to me, the author, when I inadvertently
approached a nuclear weapon launcher during a drill on a
U.S aircraft carrier.

Page 86. "On June 30, 1908, near the Stony Tunguska
River in Siberia, a one-hundred-million-kilogram space
rock detonated in the sky.": (E. L. Krinov. *Giant
meteorites*. Pergamon Press, Oxford, 1966.)

Page 86. "Our scientists have completed multiple
expeditions to Tunguska, and I have seen a recent report.":
(V. G. Fesenkov. On the Cometary Nature of the Tunguska
Meteorite. Soviet Astronomy 5(4), 1962: pp. 441-451.)

Page 88. "The Irkutsk newspaper reported…": "… the
peasants saw a body shining very brightly (too bright for
the naked eye) with a bluish-white light.... The body was in
the form of 'a pipe', i.e. cylindrical. The sky was cloudless,

except that low down on the horizon, in the direction in which this glowing body was observed, a small dark cloud was noticed. It was hot and dry and when the shining body approached the ground (which was covered with forest at this point) it seemed to be pulverized, and in its place a loud crash, not like thunder, but as if from the fall of large stones or from gunfire was heard. All the buildings shook and at the same time a forked tongue of flames broke through the cloud. All the inhabitants of the village ran out into the street in panic. The old women wept, everyone thought that the end of the world was approaching." (E. L. Krinov. *Giant meteorites*. Pergamon Press, Oxford, 1966.)

Page 87. "It was the Evenki people who led Kulik's team of scientists to the impact site.": (Vladimir Rubtsov. *The Tunguska Mystery*, Springer, 2009.)

Chapter 5

Page 89. "Song of the Stormy Petrel": (Dan Levin, *Stormy Petrel: the Life and Work of Maxim Gorky*. New York: Schocken Books, 1986.)

Page 90. "Rig ship for heavy weather.": "The Atlantic was turbulent at this time of year. In order to maintain the average speed designated for the passage, we were forced to sail on the surface." (Ryurik A. Ketov, Captain First Rank, Russian Navy (ret.). "The Cuban Missile Crisis as Seen Through a Periscope," *Journal of Strategic Studies* 28:2, 2005: 217–31.)

Page 91. "SOSUS": "Another first in long distance detection was achieved in 1962, when the SOSUS station in Barbados detected a Soviet Hotel/Echo/November (HEN) class submarine as it passed through the Greenland-Iceland-United Kingdom (GIUK) gap. SOSUS was also proving its value to the aviation-based ASW community. Using the cueing from SOSUS and their own LOFAR-based sonobuoys, ASW patrol aircraft were becoming more effective at tracking adversarial submarines. Coordination with SOSUS, however, caused their tactics to undergo a good deal of refinement. Detections were being made at much longer ranges, and so the area of location uncertainty for the target sub was much larger by the time the ASW aircraft arrived at the original detection point than had been experienced before. This was particularly troubling when attempting to track diesel submarines, as they would only be snorkeling for a finite period of time." (Lt. John Howard, United States Navy, "Fixed Sonar Systems, The History and Future of the Underwater Silent Sentinel," *The Submarine Review*, United States Navy Naval Postgraduate School, Monterey, California Undersea Warfare Department, April 2011.)

Page 92. "…among hundreds of fishing boats…": "Of great help to us were the fishing boats on the Faroe-Iceland Ridge, of which there were several hundred. Maneuvering between them, we were able to move on the surface at 15 knots." (Ryurik A. Ketov, Captain First Rank, Russian Navy (ret.), "The Cuban Missile Crisis as Seen Through a Periscope," *Journal of Strategic Studies* 28:2, 2005: 217–31.)

Page 91. "Shackleton Maritime ASW Patrol Craft":(https://commons.wikimedia.org/w/index.php?curid=311637)

Page 93. "…spacesuits.": "I have to get ready for my watch, which means again donning my 'spacesuit,' which is pretty slow going." (Captain Third Rank Anatoly Andreev, Diary published in *Nikolai Cherkashin*, 'Povsednevnaya Zhizn' Rossiiskikh Podvodnikov' [Daily

Life of Russian Submariners]. Moscow: Molodaya Gvardiya Publishing House 2000, p.111.)

Page 93. "…sick feeling swamping over him.": "Day followed night, watch-rest-watch. Alik Mukhtarov is out of commission. He's been replaced by (illegible), while he is lying in bed and groaning." (*Ibid.*)

Page 93. "The bow glowed…": "The water is luminescent at this time of the year, especially in the Norwegian Sea, and that's quite a sight to see, even when this water is running off you in a luminescent cascade." (*Ibid.*)

Page 94. "…every seventh wave, a rush of bottle-green water…": "And the gale isn't even all that heavy, it's just the ocean surge. The bridge is still getting flooded." (*Ibid.*)

Page 95. "…sailors spread their legs to prevent rolling out of their bunks…": "You can't even get a good night's rest: you have to hold onto something even in your sleep, or else you'll fall off." (*Ibid.*)

Page 96. "Poli's prized typewriter slamming between the deck and the overhead…": The story of the disintegrating typewriter was my, the author's, true experience aboard a patrol gunboat in a violent storm north of Libya, when a seasick storekeeper abandoned his typewriter and left it unsecured in the supply office.

Page 97. "A pail of dish soap broke open in the galley…": Events in this paragraph and the next were borrowed from my, the author's, patrol gunboat experience in the Mediterranean.

Page 97. "…repeated impact of the hull pitch-slamming into the troughs between waves…": "Half a month gone.

We are sailing undersea. The pitching and rolling is terrible." (Captain Third Rank Anatoly Andreev, Diary published in *Nikolai Cherkashin*, 'Povsednevnaya Zhizn' Rossiiskikh Podvodnikov' [Daily Life of Russian Submariners]. Moscow: Molodaya Gvardiya Publishing House 2000, p.111.)

Page 98. "Waves whipped their faces, burning their eyes and filling their mouths with salt water…": "Our eyes are so full of salt they hurt. You can dodge one wave, but not all of them…We have a salty taste in our mouths all the time, there's no getting rid of it, as you get to swallow enough saltwater during your watch…" (*Ibid.*)

Page 98. "The protective clothing stank…": "…the smell I've come to hate most is rubber. I wasn't too crazy about it to begin with, but now -ewww" All the time I am up on the bridge, I have to be wearing this rubber suit, I can't even smell the fresh air for this stench…" (*Ibid.*)

Page 98. "The Captain forbade the use of fresh water for washing or cleaning because the crew had wasted so much water…": "…and we don't get any more freshwater for washing, we already wasted such a lot of it early on." (*Ibid.*)

Page 100. "…vicious seas in the North Atlantic…": "The Atlantic was turbulent at this time of year. In order to maintain the average speed designated for the passage, we were forced to sail on the surface. The stormy weather continued for virtually the entire voyage. Of great nuisance was a strong current into the starboard, which caused the boat to roll as much as 40–50 degrees…the pitching forced us to reduce speed to 6–8 knots, since the height of the waves reached 15–17 meters." (Ryurik A. Ketov, Captain First Rank, Russian Navy (ret.), "The Cuban Missile Crisis as Seen Through a Periscope," *Journal of Strategic Studies* 28:2, 2005: 217–31.)

Page 100. "Captain Dubivko faced a more serious problem.": "The only accident that slowed down our speed in the transit was the appendicitis operation on the instructor of the hydroacoustic service Pankov, which was done by captain of medical service Buinevich…The wardroom, where the operation was held, was cleaned with medical alcohol. The process of cleaning and the post-operation period resulted in a significant loss of time, because everything was done in the submerged regime at the speed of 3 knots. After that we were late with our deployment by one full day." (Aleksei F. Dubivko, "In the Depths of the Sargasso Sea," unpublished memoirs. *On the Edge of the Nuclear Precipice*, Moscow: Gregory Page, 1998. Translated by Svetlana Savranskaya.)

Page 101. "only long wave channels provided even marginal reception of the nightly broadcasts.": "Having passed the Faroe-Iceland ASW line, we found ourselves in what was, practically speaking, a radio vacuum: Moscow was reachable on neither short nor medium waves. Northern Fleet stations were completely blocked with radio interference, and the only audible voices were those of Murmansk fishermen." (Ryurik A. Ketov, Captain First Rank, Russian Navy (ret.), "The Cuban Missile Crisis as Seen Through a Periscope," *Journal of Strategic Studies* 28:2, 2005: 217–31.)

Page 102. "Slow, silent, and deep, the brigade sneaked past the next choke point, the Newfoundland — Azores Gap…": "Therefore, the massive deployment of antisubmarine forces at the defense lines Nordkap – Medvezhy Island, Iceland – Faroe Islands, Azores Islands – Newfoundland was deployed by the enemy after we have passed those lines... The fact that we were moving mostly in the surface regime, made their work easier, and enabled them to make assessments of the situation on the basis of the data from open radio intercepts. We did not just speculate, but we knew for sure that the deployment of the enemies' forces on the anti-submarine lines was carried out too late." (Aleksei F. Dubivko, "In the Depths of the Sargasso Sea," unpublished memoirs. *On the Edge of the Nuclear Precipice*, Moscow: Gregory Page, 1998. Translated by Svetlana Savranskaya.) "They arrived at the main ASW barrier between Newfoundland and the Azores, exhausted by storms and evading pursuit from fine-tuned organizations of shore-based ASW facilities and overflights by long-range patrol aircraft. The Americans moved late in closing the barrier, because the Soviets were past the 'ridge line.'" (Ryurik A. Ketov, Captain First Rank, Russian Navy (ret.), "The Cuban Missile Crisis as Seen Through a Periscope," *Journal Strategic Studies* 28:2, 2005: 217–31.)

Chapter 6

Page 103. "Cuban President Dorticós is raising hell at the United Nations.": (Osvaldo Dorticos, Video of the October 7, 1962 speech to the United Nations assembly, http://www.criticalpast.com/video/65675026297, United-Nations-assembly name-plate sit-and-speaks.)

Page 105. "I am third generation Naval Intelligence.": Second Captain Retired Vadim Pavlovich Orlov was the commander of the Special Assignment Group (OSNAZ) on the submarine B-59. He was "third generation naval and intelligence officer. His father – Navy officer Pavel Andreevich Orlov – was transferred to the Main Intelligence Department (GRU) of the General Staff during the Great Patriotic War. In 1945 Orlov's family was sent to the United States." (USSR, Memoir, "Recollections of

Vadim Orlov (USSR Submarine B-59): We will Sink Them All, But We will Not Disgrace Our Navy," (2002). Source: Alexander Mozgovoi, "The Cuban Samba of the Quartet of Foxtrots: Soviet Submarines in the Caribbean Crisis of 1962," *Military Parade*, Moscow, 2002. Translated by Svetlana Savranskaya for the National Security Archive.)

Page 105. "…World Series." (Baseball Almanac, 1962 World Series. http://www.baseball-almanac.com/ws/yr1962ws.shtml.)

Page 107. "Like sailors since the dawn of time, he thought of his lover.": "This morning my watch started at 8 A.M. (Moscow time), first thing 1 did was say hi to you via Orion, we have this constellation directly overhead now." (Captain Third Rank Anatoly Andreev, Diary published in *Nikolai Cherkashin*, 'Povsednevnaya Zhizn' Rossiiskikh Podvodnikov' [Daily Life of Russian Submariners]. Moscow: Molodaya Gvardiya Publishing House 2000, p.111.)

Page 107. "He pivoted to find Sirius to ensure that he did not mistake it for a search plane…": "Then, about 30 minutes after we emerged, the signalman again shouted: "Plane"" I looked and saw he was pointing to Sirius. But his Sirius looked exactly like my jet plane." (*Ibid.*)

Page 107. "A giant tuna…": "We were accompanied by a bunch of tunas for an hour, they kept up with us all the time. Where do they get the strength, I wonder? They only dive in for a second and then surface again with a powerful push." *(Ibid.)*

Page 107. "A large wave piled over the top of the sail…": "The bridge is still getting flooded. Our eyes are so full of salt they hurt. You can dodge one wave, but not all of them.

Even our rubber suits aren't much protection, we still have to dry our clothes after the watch even as it is, and just think what we would have done without them"" *(Ibid.)*

Page 108. "…Operation ORTSAC.": (Michael Dobbs, *One Minute to Midnight: Kennedy, Khrushchev, and Castro on the Brink of Nuclear War.* New York: Vintage Books, 2009, pp 17, 104.)

Page 109. "Operation ORTSAC in English is Castro spelled backwards." *(Ibid.)*

Page 109. "The brigade is assigned to deploy in a barrier due north of the entrance to the Turks Island Passage and take up combat positions in the Sargasso Sea." (Peter A. Huchthausen, *October Fury*, John Wiley & Sons, Hoboken, NJ, 2002. p. 79.)

Page 110. "Every American broadcast is in the clear…": "The US Navy at the time carried virtually all communications on radio via open text… We were at first skeptical about these transmissions, but as we started to listen to US radio stations, and compared their announcements with US ASW communique's, as well as with messages from home, we came to believe that these transmissions could be taken into account to determine where and when the ASW ships and planes would be located… From these transmissions, especially those between ships in carrier groups and between aircraft and shore facilities, it was possible to ascertain… the physical locations of search parties of surface ships, about their activities, about the discovery of submarines in the area and, most importantly, about specific orders given by US commanders. (Ryurik A. Ketov, Captain First Rank, Russian Navy (ret.), "The Cuban Missile Crisis as Seen

Through a Periscope," *Journal of Strategic Studies* 28:2, 2005: 217–31.)

Page 111. "We'll hide among the fishermen.": "Several hundred fishing boats on the Faroe-Iceland Ridge, provided submarine hiding places in the noise and clutter, maneuvering among them on the surface at 15 knots." (*Ibid.*)

Chapter 7

Page 113. "*On October 14, a tropical depression developed and stalled...*": (Gary E. Weir and Walter J. Boyne, *Rising Tide: The Untold Story of the Russian Submarines that Fought the Cold War*. New York: Basic Books. 2003, p. 75.)

Page 114. "Remind them how Admiral Fart Fokin arrived": The day before departure, the Soviet Navy's First Deputy, Admiral Vitaly A. Fokin and Northern Fleet Chief of Staff, Vice-Admiral A.I. Rassokha spoke to the crews. (Vasily Naumovich Agafonov, Captain First Rank, 69th *Submarine Brigade Commander Report* [undated, circa December 1962, prepared by the USSR Northern Fleet Headquarters] About participation of submarines "B-4," "B-36," "B-59," "B-130" of the 69th submarine brigade of the Northern Fleet in the Operation "Anadyr" during the period of October - December 1962, CARIBBEAN CRISIS, Translated by Svetlana Savranskaya for the National Security Archive).

Page 119. "Nobody was seasick; they were too afraid.": "We are sailing undersea. The pitching and rolling is terrible. Everyone's feeling very funny: the men don't get seasick but simply tired out by all this tossing." (Captain Third Rank Anatoly Andreev, Diary published in *Nikolai*

Cherkashin, 'Povsednevnaya Zhizn' Rossiiskikh
Podvodnikov' [Daily Life of Russian Submariners].
Moscow: Molodaya Gvardiya Publishing House 2000,
p.111.)

Page 120. "There is a lot going on, and it's difficult to
distinguish hurricane reaction from invasion and war
preparation.": "What's in store for us, how necessary is all
this? It all will, of course, become clearer once we get
there. We've been trying to tune in to the news, but we can't
get anything." (*Ibid.*)

Pages 120. "Captain Agafonov discovered patterns in the
American jamming schema …": "We ultimately found a
solution that facilitated our receiving and sending
communications in this shaky period of technical
difficulties. We adapted to the periods of 'cracks' that
jammed our radio frequencies, finding moments of clear air
and sending our radiograms in those windows." (Ryurik A.
Ketov, Captain First Rank, Russian Navy (ret.). "The
Cuban Missile Crisis as Seen Through a Periscope,"
Journal of Strategic Studies 28:2, 2005: 217–31.)

Chapter 8

Page 122. "*Jack Kennedy had a keen appreciation for the
vagaries of history. His experiences…*": (Michael Dobbs.
*One Minute to Midnight: Kennedy, Khrushchev, and
Castro on the Brink of Nuclear War.* New York: Vintage
Books, 2009, p. 31.)

Page 124. "…it was only a useless farm harvest report.":
"Moscow normally transmitted twice a day on the
broadcast, but the only real information was the domestic
news, how well the harvest was going in the USSR…"

(Peter A. Huchthausen. *October Fury*, John Wiley & Sons, Hoboken, NJ, 2002. pp. 233-234.)

Page 128. "They couldn't know the merchantman Iron Cavalier...": "The NAESS Cavalier has now been experiencing winds in excess of 80 mph for well over 24 hours. At 9am it reported winds of over 100mph, seas of 45 feet, visibility zero and rain and sea spray. Paradoxically, the ship was only 6 or 7 miles from the edge of the eye where winds were some 15mph or less." (U.S. Department of Commerce Weather Bureau, Hurricane Ella, October 14-22, 1962. Miami Weather Bureau Bulletin for Press, Radio and Television: 2pm EST October 19, 1962.)

Page 130. "Nothing about the Project 641 submarines was designed for operating in subtropical climates...": "We northerners, accustomed to working under low air temperatures and servicing equipment in trans-polar latitudes, were 'struck' by this tropical heat suddenly and unpredictably. Submarines of this generation were not equipped with refrigerators for keeping the full supply of provisions cold through the entire duration of the mission. There was an insufficient supply of fresh water for the crew, no air conditioning in the compartments – which would otherwise have facilitated the smooth operation of the boat's machinery – and most importantly, no one had experience in servicing equipment under such high temperatures." (Ryurik A. Ketov, Captain First Rank, Russian Navy (ret.). "The Cuban Missile Crisis as Seen Through a Periscope," *Journal of Strategic Studies* 28:2, 2005: 217–31.)

Page 130. "...fainting from heat stroke...": "My head is bursting from the stuffy air. ... Today three sailors fainted from overheating again. ... We are sailing with a risk of dropping down to six thousand meters. This is how much we have under [our boat]. The regeneration of air works poorly, the carbon dioxide content in rising, and the electric power reserves are dropping. Those who are free from their shifts, are sitting immobile, staring at one spot. ... Temperature in the sections is above 50 (122 degrees F). In the diesel – 61 degrees Celsius (141.8 degrees F)." (Captain Third Rank Anatoly Andreev's diary, published in Nikolai Cherkashin, 'Povsednevnaya Zhizn' Rossiiskikh Podvodnikov' [Daily Life of Russian Submariners]. Moscow: Molodaya Gvardiya Publishing House 2000, p.111.)

Page 131. "The air temperature rose to 113 degrees Fahrenheit, and 149 degrees in the engine compartment.": "While at first we were pleased with this change, our delight gradually faded and was replaced by a struggle against a blistering air temperature in the submarine and against the exhaustion of the crew. My men began fainting from heat stroke, and the increase in humidity started to affect the operating condition of the equipment. The average air temperature inside the submarine rose to 113 degrees Fahrenheit, and up to 144–149 degrees in the engine compartment." (Ryurik A. Ketov, Captain First Rank, Russian Navy (ret.). "The Cuban Missile Crisis as Seen Through a Periscope," *Journal of Strategic Studies* 28:2, 2005: 217–31.)

Page 132. "Carriers, destroyers and aircraft.": "Antisubmarine search groups led by the aircraft carriers USS Essex (CV-9), Wasp (CV-18) and Randolph (CV-15) entered the area of the Sargasso Sea. Shore-based ASW aircraft began a systematic search of the region." *(Ibid.)*

Chapter 9

Page 133. *"Gentlemen, today we're going to earn our pay. You should all hope…"*: (Michael Dobbs. *One Minute to Midnight: Kennedy, Khrushchev, and Castro on the Brink of Nuclear War*. New York: Vintage Books, 2009, p. 31.)

Page 133. "…swamped in heat and humidity.": "Already on the approach to the Sargasso Sea, near Bermuda, we felt a change in climate. The storms chasing us in the North Atlantic were replaced by a calm and high outboard temperature. At depths of 250 meters the water temperature reached 83 degrees Fahrenheit." *(Ibid.)*

Page 134. "…confirming the presence of the carrier group and active flight operations.": "According to the information from the radio surveillance group, and judging by the activities of the anti-submarine forces that were searching for submarines, we came to a conclusion that there were three or four aircraft-carrier based anti-submarine groups in the Sargasso Sea, as well as aircraft of shore patrol anti-submarine aviation, based in the airports of the Bermuda triangle." (Aleksei F. Dubivko, "In the Depths of the Sargasso Sea," unpublished memoirs. *On the Edge of the Nuclear Precipice*, Moscow: Gregory Page, 1998. Translated by Svetlana Savranskaya.)

Page 13. "Every word I picked up was in the clear.": "The U.S. Navy at the time carried virtually all communications on radio via open text, especially shore-based ASW aircraft guided by coastal reference points. We were at first skeptical about these transmissions, but as we started to listen to US radio stations, and compared their announcements with US ASW communique´s, as well as with messages from home, we came to believe that these transmissions could be taken into account to determine where and when the ASW ships and planes would be located." (Ryurik A. Ketov, Captain First Rank, Russian Navy (ret.). "The Cuban Missile Crisis as Seen Through a Periscope," *Journal of Strategic Studies* 28:2, 2005: 217–31.)

Page 137. "We'll need to ration the water.": (Peter A. Huchthausen. *October Fury*, John Wiley & Sons, Hoboken, NJ, 2002. p. 98.)

Page 143. "Captain Ketov on the B-4 received a Russian distress call while on the surface during the storm and decided to pass by the merchantman who had lost power and foundered in seventeen-meter seas.": (*Ibid.* pp. 94-95.)

Page 145. "Their skin reddened in reaction to the putrid moisture and dirt.": "The impossibility to wash off sweat and dirt led to 100% of personnel developing rashes in the most serious infected form." (Vasily Naumovich Agafonov, Captain First Rank, 69th Submarine Brigade Commander Report [undated, circa December 1962, prepared by the USSR Northern Fleet Headquarters] About participation of submarines "B-4," "B-36," "B-59," "B-130" of the 69th submarine brigade of the Northern Fleet in the Operation "Anadyr" during the period of October - December 1962, CARIBBEAN CRISIS, Translated by Svetlana Savranskaya for the National Security Archive).

Chapter 10

Page 147. *"missile gap."*: (Michael Dobbs. *One Minute to Midnight: Kennedy, Khrushchev, and Castro on the Brink of Nuclear War*. New York: Vintage Books, 2009, pp. 189-190.)

Page 147. "The United States amassed nearly 7,000 nuclear warheads, while the Soviet Union had only 500 in 1962.": (Robert S. Norris, *The Cuban Missile Crisis: A Nuclear Order of Battle* (October/November 1962), A Presentation at the Woodrow Wilson Center, October 24, 2012.)

Page 147. "The U.S. conducted over 1,000 nuclear weapons tests, totaling 298 megatons of yield, including 140 nuclear tests totaling 229 megatons of yield in 1961-1962. The Soviet Union conducted nuclear weapons tests on nearly 1000 devices, totaling 197 megatons of yield, including 135 nuclear tests totaling 38 megatons of yield in 1961-1962.": (Yang, Xiaoping; North, Robert; Romney, Carl; Richards, Paul G. (August 2000), *Worldwide Nuclear Explosions*, retrieved 2013-12-31.)

Page 147. "Their skin rashes deepened and became infected...": "Most of the crew developed open ulcers and painful rashes on their skin." (Peter A. Huchthausen. *October Fury*, John Wiley & Sons, Hoboken, NJ, 2002. p. 98.)

Page 148. "Crew members had lost weight, some as much as one-third of their body weight, appearing emaciated.": "People ate almost nothing. They lost approximately 1/3 of their weight." (Aleksei F. Dubivko, "In the Depths of the Sargasso Sea," unpublished memoirs. *On the Edge of the Nuclear Precipice*, Moscow: Gregory Page, 1998. Translated by Svetlana Savranskaya.)

148. "Tiny flying fish, dark and shimmery, flitted about...": "The flying fish are flitting all around. Now we've finally been able to take a better look at them. They are very small, no more than 10-15 cm, with wings, can fly for over 50 metres, darkish in colour, look green and absolutely transparent in the sun, very, very beautiful."

(Captain Third Rank Anatoly Andreev, Diary published in *Nikolai Cherkashin*, 'Povsednevnaya Zhizn' Rossiiskikh Podvodnikov' [Daily Life of Russian Submariners]. Moscow: Molodaya Gvardiya Publishing House 2000, p.111.)

Page 148. "Two satellites loomed...": "Tonight, I was lucky enough to see the two satellites at once, both ours and American. I've never seen them before." (*Ibid.*)

Page 148. "The brigade received new orders to proceed to a one hundred kilometer sector of the South Sargasso Sea...": "Around then, we received an order from Moscow to change course and proceed to an area with a radius of 50 miles in the southwestern part of the Sargasso Sea, and await further instructions. We did not expect such a 'blow' from the Navy General Staff." (Ryurik A. Ketov, Captain First Rank, Russian Navy (ret.). "The Cuban Missile Crisis as Seen Through a Periscope," *Journal of Strategic Studies* 28:2, 2005: 217–31.)

Page 148. "...received separate orders to proceed through the Caicos Straights on a dangerous solo excursion.": (Peter A. Huchthausen. *October Fury*, John Wiley & Sons, Hoboken, NJ, 2002. p. 82.)

Pages 150 – 153. "As though President Kennedy wanted everyone in the world to write down his words ...": (John F. Kennedy. "Cuban Missile Crisis: Address to the Nation." *American Rhetoric: The Power of Oratory in the United States,* 2 Dec. 2012. Web. 19 Nov. 2014.

Page 154. "We're not even heading for Cuba. Admiral Fokin Flatus gave us stand-down orders to some backwater sector in the southwestern Sargasso.": "Around then, we received an order from Moscow to change course and proceed to an area with a radius of 50 miles in the southwestern part of the Sargasso Sea, and await further instructions. We did not expect such a 'blow' from the Navy General Staff. From our vantage point, such a move was fatal – and this was when just one ASW carrier group was patrolling a strip of water 80–90 miles wide." (Ryurik A. Ketov, Captain First Rank, Russian Navy (ret.). "The Cuban Missile Crisis as Seen Through a Periscope," *Journal of Strategic Studies* 28:2, 2005: 217–31.)

Page 155. "With this announcement, the ASW pressure will intensify…": "President Kennedy, speaking on the radio, categorically declared that he would not allow Russian submarines to operate in US coastal waters and would use any means necessary to drive them out to beyond the 60th meridian west longitude. We felt this threat immediately reflected in the activities of the US Navy." (*Ibid.*)

Page 156. "The battery is charging slowly in this heat…": "The electrolyte is so hot it takes twice the normal time to charge." (Peter A. Huchthausen. *October Fury*, John Wiley & Sons, Hoboken, NJ, 2002. p. 190.) "Now a couple of words about charging the accumulator. Because the accumulator on the submarines of our model was not equipped with cooling technology for work in the conditions of sailing in the equatorial latitudes, the charging took very long because of the high temperature of the electrolyte, which reached 65 C. With such temperatures, the situation is aggravated by the fact that the electrolyte expels hydrogen very intensively. In order not to allow an explosive concentration and to reduce the temperature of the electrolyte to at least 60 degrees C, at which it was permitted to turn on the accumulator charge, we had to ventilate it intensively. The charging took 36 hours instead of normal 10 to 12 hours." (Aleksei F. Dubivko, "In the Depths of the Sargasso Sea," unpublished

memoirs. *On the Edge of the Nuclear Precipice*, Moscow:
Gregory Page, 1998. Translated by Svetlana Savranskaya.)

Chapter 11

Page 157. *"[Americans always] exaggerate the outside
threat..."*: (Sam LaGrone, "Soviet Perspective on the
Cuban Missile Crisis from Nikita Khrushchev's Son," *U.S.
Naval Institute News*, October 24, 2012.)

Page 157. "He brought the ship down to periscope depth
before dawn to give Oz maximum opportunity to evaluate
the tactical situation prior to the Captain's briefing.": "We
did not receive any information from the Main Navy
Headquarters, so we were trying to fish out various
information from the radio, which allowed us to come to
those conclusions. The work of the radio interception
group provided invaluable assistance here. Thus, according
to the information supplied by that group, it was established
that: President Kennedy announced the blockade of Cuba,
and warned his people on all-American open radio about a
possibility of a thermonuclear conflict with the Soviet
Union; the Americans were preparing a powerful
[airborne] landing on Cuba; our missiles with nuclear
warheads and the servicing personnel were already in
Cuba; special camps for future Russian prisoners of war
were being set up on the Florida peninsula..." (Aleksei F.
Dubivko, "In the Depths of the Sargasso Sea," unpublished
memoirs. *On the Edge of the Nuclear Precipice*, Moscow:
Gregory Page, 1998. Translated by Svetlana Savranskaya.)

Page 157. "They're using SOSUS to vector those damn
planes at our diesel rumble.": "Only one conclusion was
possible to draw: when the diesels were not making a noise,
no one heard us and ASW aircraft were not sent to
investigate acoustic signals. This meant that we were

located by seabed hydro-acoustic stations (SOSUS), which then dispatched the signal to shore-based command points, which in turn would send an ASW plane to verify the contact." (Ryurik A. Ketov, Captain First Rank, Russian Navy (ret.). "The Cuban Missile Crisis as Seen Through a Periscope," *Journal of Strategic Studies* 28:2, 2005: 217–31.)

Page 158. "The doctor had prescribed a chartreuse tincture that soothed his infected rash and knocked back the discomfort.": "Everyone's skin is covered with rash, some look like Indians -they put some (antiseptic ointment, bright green in color - Eds.) on their rash, and it got smeared all over their bodies because of the sweat." (Captain Third Rank Anatoly Andreev's diary, published in *Nikolai Cherkashin*, 'Povsednevnaya Zhizn' Rossiiskikh Podvodnikov' [Daily Life of Russian Submariners]. Moscow: Molodaya Gvardiya Publishing House 2000, p.111.)

Page 159. "He visited the ship's doctor …": "The men are feeling notably worse, a lot of them are ill…" (*Ibid.*)

Page 159. "The doc says he can no longer measure a man's temperature…": "Our poor doctor, he can't even take the patients' temperature, as there is no place on the sub where the air temperature would be under +38°C, so all thermometers read off-scale." (*Ibid.*)

Page 159. "Our water distillation plant output is down to ten liters per day….": (Peter A. Huchthausen. *October Fury*, John Wiley & Sons, Hoboken, NJ, 2002. p. 98.)

Page 159. "The enemy's chaos has self-organized.": "Beginning from October 22, a naval blockade of the island went into effect. To carry it out and to search for our submarines, the U.S. Navy employed over 200 combat surface ships, up to 200 planes of the base patrol aviation, four aircraft carrier search and assault groups with 50-60 planes on board and destroyers charged with discovering and destroying our submarines at the start of the military action." (Agafonov, Vasily Naumovich, Captain First Rank, 69th Submarine Brigade Commander Report [undated, circa December 1962, prepared by the USSR Northern Fleet Headquarters] About participation of submarines "B-4," "B-36," "B-59," "B-130" of the 69th submarine brigade of the Northern Fleet in the Operation "Anadyr" during the period of October - December 1962, CARIBBEAN CRISIS, Translated by Svetlana Savranskaya for the National Security Archive.)

Page 161. "Strike aircraft and carrier fleets dominated the Soviet assets.": "By this time, we had already passed the Bahamas and were approaching the straits between the Greater Antilles Islands. With every hour, we heard the pressure from the ASW overflights mount over our radio intercepts. During daylight, we didn't see an hour pass without the planes' lighting up on our Nakat surface search radar screens. From 22 October on, virtually the entire Nakat frequency range was jammed with signals from surface ships and aircraft radars." (Ryurik A. Ketov, Captain First Rank, Russian Navy (ret.). "The Cuban Missile Crisis as Seen Through a Periscope," *Journal of Strategic Studies* 28:2, 2005: 217–31.)

Page 162. "Captain Dubivko led the discussion regarding President Kennedy's blockade of Cuba…": "All this allowed us to make a conclusion about a possibility of a provocation on the part of the Americans. We increased our vigilance. The fact that the Americans concentrated 85% of all anti-submarine forces in the area of deployment of [our] four diesel submarines (information of the

Intelligence Department of the Navy) made carrying out our task on the designated positions extremely difficult for us." (Aleksei F. Dubivko, "In the Depths of the Sargasso Sea," unpublished memoirs. *On the Edge of the Nuclear Precipice*, Moscow: Gregory Page, 1998. Translated by Svetlana Savranskaya.)

Page 162. ". No explanations, no context, no additional information, and no sign of the mysterious B-75.": "On 22 October, the B-75 was detected by NATO antisubmarine forces while refueling near the Azores. It returned to Murmansk around 10 November." (Svetlana Savranskaya, "New Sources on the Role of Soviet Submarines in the Cuban Missile Crisis." *Journal of Strategic Studies* 28:2, 2005: 233-59.)

Page 163. "The Captain learned that the other captains experienced maritime flyovers…": "The captains learned of the first submarine sighting from a radio intercept from ASW aircraft. The location indicated that it was Shumkov on the B-130." (Aleksei F. Dubivko, "In the Depths of the Sargasso Sea," unpublished memoirs. *On the Edge of the Nuclear Precipice*, Moscow: Gregory Page, 1998. Translated by Svetlana Savranskaya.)

Page 163. "It's SOSUS, picking up our diesel signature and vectoring…": "After exchanging radio transmissions with Savitskii's B-59, we determined that no ASW planes approached us while we maintained communications at periscope depth, under the electric motors." (Ryurik A. Ketov, Captain First Rank, Russian Navy (ret.). "The Cuban Missile Crisis as Seen Through a Periscope," *Journal of Strategic Studies* 28:2, 2005: 217–31.)

Page 164. "An explosion in the water.": "ASW aircraft intensified their pursuit of submarine targets, testing any potential identification with the Jezebel sonobuoy system. Of course, once one had witnessed this system at work, experiencing firsthand what it was like on the receiving end of the depth charges, it was possible to somehow go about one's business with a good understanding of the situation." (*Ibid.*)

Page 165. "As his periscope broke the surface, he spotted two ships on the horizon near the blockade line ...": "Through the periscope I watched the Americans stop two transports, probably for an inspection. They are quite brazen about it..." (Captain Third Rank Anatoly Andreev's diary, published in *Nikolai Cherkashin*, 'Povsednevnaya Zhizn' Rossiiskikh Podvodnikov' [Daily Life of Russian Submariners]. Moscow: Molodaya Gvardiya Publishing House 2000, p.111.)

Chapter 12

Page 166. *"You just can't have this kind of war. There aren't enough bulldozers..."*: (Thomas M. Nichols, *No Use: Nuclear Weapons and U.S. National Security*, Philadelphia: University of Pennsylvania Press, 2014.)

Page 166. "The pressure to remain submerged in insufferable heat under the thumbs of ASW overflights mounted...": "By this time we had already passed the Bahamas and were approaching the straits between the Greater Antilles Islands. With every hour, we heard the pressure from the ASW overflights mount over our radio intercepts." (Ryurik A. Ketov, Captain First Rank, Russian Navy (ret.). "The Cuban Missile Crisis as Seen Through a Periscope," *Journal of Strategic Studies* 28:2, 2005: 217–31.)

Page 166. "Every hour of the first day of the blockade brought more aircraft and surface ship radar detections jamming the *Nakat* frequency spectrum.": "Airplanes and helicopters of anti-submarine defenses were searching for submarines round the clock, day and night. At night the anti-submarine aircraft were searching with radio-location stations, the work of which we could identify with our own equipment from a distance, which allowed us to avoid them by submerging early enough. By using this advantage, despite 5 or 6 urgent submergings a day on the diesel regime, we managed to fully charge our accumulator battery, which ensured the work in the submerged regime in the daytime." (Aleksei F. Dubivko, "In the Depths of the Sargasso Sea," unpublished memoirs. *On the Edge of the Nuclear Precipice*, Moscow: Gregory Page, 1998. Translated by Svetlana Savranskaya.)

Page 166. "Captain Shumkov reported that the B-130's damaged diesel engines needed repairs that could only be completed on the surface.": "In reality, at that time, all three diesel engines on the submarine "B-130" had broken down. In that hopeless situation, the submarine had to rise to the surface, which decamouflaged it and revealed the presence of other submarines." (*Ibid.*)

Page 166. "Captain Dubivko had a damaged acoustic decoy ejector on the B-36...": "Mozgovoi explains that B-36 had suffered earlier in a force 9 gale. The cover plate on the decoy ejector on the casing (outer hull) had been damaged. Repairs had not been possible due to the omnipresent aircraft and the boat's diving depth was limited to seventy meters." (Jan Drent. "Confrontation in the Sargasso Sea: Soviet Submarines During the Cuban Missile Crisis," *The Northern Mariner/Le Marin du Nord*, vol. 13, no. 3, July 2003: 1-19.)

Page 166. "The B-59 diesel cooling system was contaminated by salt water, packing glands were leaking, and the electric air compressors had broken down.": (Michael Dobbs, *One Minute to Midnight: Kennedy, Khrushchev, and Castro on the Brink of Nuclear War.* Vintage Books, 2009, p. 307.) "At the same time, during the operation serious technical deficiencies were discovered, which will be mentioned below. They emerged as a result of the fact that the submarines were not tested properly, were not used in working regime, and appeared to be insufficiently prepared for the intense operation in the conditions of the high temperatures of the water, air, and the high salinity of the sea." (Aleksei F. Dubivko, "In the Depths of the Sargasso Sea," unpublished memoirs. *On the Edge of the Nuclear Precipice*, Moscow: Gregory Page, 1998. Translated by Svetlana Savranskaya.)

Page 167. "…replacing it with a blue and white armband.": (Peter A. Huchthausen. *October Fury*, John Wiley & Sons, Hoboken, NJ, 2002. p. 77.)

Page 167. "The submarine-turned-steam-bath gave everyone multiple problems, especially with their feet.": "But the heat's been getting to us, and everyone as if right after a steam bath. We are beginning to feel the first consequences of such conditions. Everyone is having some sort of problem, mostly with their feet." (Captain 3rd Rank Anatoly Andreev's diary, published in *Nikolai Cherkashin*, 'Povsednevnaya Zhizn' Rossiiskikh Podvodnikov' [Daily Life of Russian Submariners]. Moscow: Molodaya Gvardiya Publishing House 2000, p.111.)

Page 168. "The men went directly to their bunks in exhaustion …": "I now have the following ration: after I am relieved from watch, I go straight to bed without breakfast, as it's a tiny bit cooler at that time; then, at lunchtime, I drink a cup of compote; at suppertime, a dairy meal and a cup of compote; and then evening tea, two cups. Freshwater is strictly rationed, only for cooking, and even that is and everyone is also thirsty." (*Ibid.*)

Page 168. "…crewmen developed intense thirst, while they steeped in their own perspiration, fingertips growing white and wrinkled.": "That's all everyone's talking about: thirst. Oh, how thirsty I am. It's hard to write, the paper is soaked in sweat. We are all looking like we just came out of a steam bath. My fingertips are completely white…" (*Ibid.*)

Page 168. "The B-59 had sailed into the enemy's lair.": "We are in the enemy's lair, and we can't reveal our presence to them, but they sense our nearness and are searching for us. They detected us yesterday, but we managed to escape. Something exploded somewhere, but at a distance from us, so we don't know how serious it was. But here, inside the sub, the situation is very serious." (*Ibid.*)

Page 169. "The Captain's anger swelled to rage that boiled within him, and he began tormenting his men when they needed to conserve strength.": "And in such a situation, when you'd think all this was bad enough, the commander's nerves start fraying around the edge…He's hard to deal with. I feel sorry for him and at the same time angry with him for his rash actions." (*Ibid.*)

Page 170. "He feared discovery.": "The worst fear of a submarine captain, according to the testimony of all four captains, was to be discovered and brought to the surface by an enemy ship. Not only was a discovery seen as utter humiliation, but even more importantly, it was a violation of their orders, which could bring severe consequences upon their return to the Soviet Union." (Svetlana

Savranskaya, "New Sources on the Role of Soviet Submarines in the Cuban Missile Crisis." *Journal of Strategic Studies* 28:2, 2005: 233-59.) "The captains believed they would be punished for not keeping the mission secret and allowing the US Navy to force them to the surface. However, senior Soviet leadership believed that the submarines sent to Cuba were nuclear powered missile submarines as initially planned, not diesel-electric submarines, not equipped for extended patrolling in the tropics. (Ryurik Ketov, Captain First Rank, Russian Navy. "The Cuban Missile Crisis as Seen Through a Periscope," *Journal of Strategic Studies* 28:2, 2005: 217–31.)

Page 170. "Moscow chose not to inform the brigade of the developing geopolitical or tactical situation to maintain the security of classified data.": "The situation was made worse by the fact that Moscow did not inform the captains about the developing situation, only giving them a general outline of the crisis and mostly reports on harvesting in the Soviet Union." (Svetlana Savranskaya, "New Sources on the Role of Soviet Submarines in the Cuban Missile Crisis." *Journal of Strategic Studies* 28:2, 2005: 233-59.)

Page 171. "…with organizing the crew for two-minute trips to the bridge for a navy shower and to gather and drink as much rainwater as their cupped hands could capture.": "One makeshift solution consisted of ventilating the submarine while the personnel washed themselves off with rain water in areas of waterspouts. We were hiding in squalls, where streams of fresh water were expelled by storm clouds created by constant temperature changes in the ocean and the air above it. We started to make use of this effect, at intervals of about 10–15 minutes. ASW Neptune aircraft could not enter these squalls, although they were evidently watching us on their radars." (Ryurik A. Ketov, Captain First Rank, Russian Navy (ret.). "The

Cuban Missile Crisis as Seen Through a Periscope,"
Journal of Strategic Studies 28:2, 2005: 217–31.)

Page 170. "Circling the B-59 before darkness fell, the plane
identified the Project 641 submarine, cataloging her as
contact C-19 on the surface 350 miles south-southwest of
Bermuda, northeast of the blockade line.": (Svetlana
Savranskaya, "New Sources on the Role of Soviet
Submarines in the Cuban Missile Crisis." *Journal of
Strategic Studies* 28:2, 2005: 233-59.)

Page 172. "...the B-59 had attracted the pursuit of the *USS
Randolph's* attack group of destroyers...": "...-submarine
"B-59" by carrier aviation and destroyers "Berry,"
"Lowry," "Beale," "Beich" (Bache), "Bill," "Eaton,"
"Cony," "Conway," "Murray," and the anti-submarine
aircraft carrier "Randolph." (Agafonov, Vasily Naumovich,
Captain First Rank, 69th Submarine Brigade Commander
Report [undated, circa December 1962, prepared by the
USSR Northern Fleet Headquarters] About participation of
submarines "B-4," "B-36," "B-59," "B-130" of the 69th
submarine brigade of the Northern Fleet in the Operation
"Anadyr" during the period of October - December 1962,
CARIBBEAN CRISIS, Translated by Svetlana
Savranskaya for the National Security Archive.)

Chapter 13

Page 174. *"We knew, one mistake and we would invite
disaster onto humanity...so we were careful."*: (Peter A.
Huchthausen. *October Fury*, John Wiley & Sons, Hoboken,
NJ, 2002. p. 131.)

Page 174. "The U.S. Strategic Air Command targeted...":
(Michael Dobbs, *One Minute to Midnight: Kennedy,*

Khrushchev, and Castro on the Brink of Nuclear War.
Vintage Books, 2009, pp 228, 281.)

Page 174. "The U.S. tested two nuclear weapons that day…
The Soviets air dropped 262 kilotons on Novaya Zemlya":
(Xiaoping Yang, Robert North, Carl Romney, (August
2000). *CMR Nuclear Explosion Database (Revision
3)* (Technical report). SMDC Monitoring Research.

Pages 175. "…a U.S. U-2 spy plane monitored the Soviet
nuclear tests at *Novaya…*": (Michael Dobbs, *One Minute to
Midnight: Kennedy, Khrushchev, and Castro on the Brink
of Nuclear War.* Vintage Books, 2009, pp 196-199.)

Page 175. "At 06:00, the CIA reported that five Soviet R-
12 nuclear ballistic missile sites in Cuba appeared to be
fully operational.": (*Ibid.* p. 207.)

Page 175. "Around midday, another U-2 pilot, US Air
Force Major Rudolf Anderson Jr., flew a recon spy plane at
70,500 feet over Cuba…": (*Ibid.* p. 242.)

Pages 176. "Starpom made the rounds after his watch and
found much of the crew gathered in the forward torpedo
room where the temperature was a bit cooler.": "I made the
rounds of the compartments, and the only one I saw was the
officer-on-deck. All the rest gather in the two places where
the temperature is slightly lower, about +40°C. I lay down
in Compartment One, hugging the [torpedo?]. It's getting
hard to breathe in here, too much C02, but no one wants to
leave, as it is slightly cooler here. I barely made it through
my previous watch. I feel faint all over, slightly dizzy…"
(Captain Third Rank Anatoly Andreev's diary, published in
Nikolai Cherkashin, 'Povsednevnaya Zhizn' Rossiiskikh
Podvodnikov' [Daily Life of Russian Submariners].
Moscow: Molodaya Gvardiya Publishing, 2000, p.111.)

Page 177. "The Captain decided they had escaped, and he took his ship deep to avoid MAD detection on a second flyover.": "Moreover, to successfully avoid any 'strong' sonar signal or capture by aircraft-mounted magnetometers, we had to submerge to sonic layer depths." (Ryurik A. Ketov, Captain First Rank, Russian Navy (ret.). "The Cuban Missile Crisis as Seen Through a Periscope," *Journal of Strategic Studies* 28:2, 2005: 217–31.)

Page 177. "Three of the fast, maneuverable, long-endurance Fletcher-class destroyers peeled off the carrier screen...": (Michael Dobbs, *One Minute to Midnight: Kennedy, Khrushchev, and Castro on the Brink of Nuclear War.* Vintage Books, 2009, p. 299.)

Page 177. "His fevered soul felt the boundaries of peaceful coexistence dissolve under the onslaught of the ticking clock.': "In those days, as the question of peaceful coexistence between the two systems was being determined, when the smallest provocation could tip the scales in favor of war, we were also concerned with the matter of our own safety." (Ryurik A. Ketov, Captain First Rank, Russian Navy (ret.). "The Cuban Missile Crisis as Seen Through a Periscope," *Journal of Strategic Studies* 28:2, 2005: 217–31.)

Page 177. "...fighting off the strangling surges of panic.": "The worst thing is that the commander's nerves are shot to hell, he's yelling at everyone and torturing himself. You can tell he's never before been on independent voyages: he doesn't realize he should be saving his own strength and the men's, too, otherwise we are not going to last long. He is already becoming paranoid, scared of his own shadow." (Captain Third Rank Anatoly Andreev's diary, published in *Nikolai Cherkashin*, 'Povsednevnaya Zhizn' Rossiiskikh

Podvodnikov' [Daily Life of Russian Submariners]. Moscow: Molodaya Gvardiya Publishing 2000, p.111.)

Page 179. "On the submarine, the Julie blasts could not be distinguished from tactical depth bomb explosions.": "In the course of search and pursuit of the submarines by anti-submarine warfare forces, they actively used explosive sources [sic] of the location systems 'Julie-Jezebel,' the blasts of which are impossible to distinguish from explosions of depth bombs." (Agafonov, Vasily Naumovich, Captain First Rank, 69th Submarine Brigade Commander Report [undated, circa December 1962, prepared by the USSR Northern Fleet Headquarters] About participation of submarines "B-4," "B-36," "B-59," "B-130" of the 69th submarine brigade of the Northern Fleet in the Operation "Anadyr" during the period of October - December 1962, CARIBBEAN CRISIS, Translated by Svetlana Savranskaya for the National Security Archive.)

Page 180. "There was only one escape option left for them, and he was ready for a fight.": "all the Soviet captains recalled their state of extreme tension and confusion in a situation where the war above could have begun any time while they were trying to evade their pursuers in the submerged position, with no communication with the outside world. The captains also anticipated that in the situation where the nuclear exchange either became inevitable or had already begun…the perception of the situation by the Soviet captains was shaped primarily by the limited and skewed information they received, and by their anticipation of a military conflict with the US, possibly even a nuclear exchange." (Svetlana Savranskaya, "New Sources on the Role of Soviet Submarines in the Cuban Missile Crisis." *Journal of Strategic Studies* 28:2, 2005: 233-59.)

Page 187. "The *USS Cony* lined up for a strafing run and pulverized the submarine with five more depth bombs, while all three destroyers banged away with their bow sonars.": "Arguably the most tense encounter between the Soviet and US navies occurred when the group consisting of the carrier Randolph (CV-15) and destroyers Bache (DD-470), Beale (DD-471), Cony (DD-508), Eaton (DD-510) and Murray (DD-576) were pursuing and forcing to the surface the Soviet submarine commanded by Captain Second Rank Vitali Savitsky with the 69th brigade chief of staff Captain Vasili Arkhipov on board." (*Ibid.*)

Page 187. "The depth charges exploded with spectacular power and proximity like a hundred-knuckled fist, damaging radio antennae in the sail.": "The Americans hit us with something stronger than grenades (depth charges) – apparently a practice depth bomb. We thought – that's it – the end. After this attack, the totally exhausted Savitsky, who in addition to everything, was not able to establish connection with the General Staff, became furious." (USSR, Memoir, "Recollections of Vadim Orlov (USSR Submarine B-59): We will Sink Them All, But We will Not Disgrace Our Navy," (2002). Source: Alexander Mozgovoi, "The Cuban Samba of the Quartet of Foxtrots: Soviet Submarines in the Caribbean Crisis of 1962," *Military Parade*, Moscow, 2002. Translated by Svetlana Savranskaya for the National Security Archive.)

"It is possible that depth bombs were actually used because three of the submarines suffered damage to the parts of radio systems antennas, which made reception and transmission of information substantially more difficult." (Agafonov, Vasily Naumovich, Captain First Rank, 69th Submarine Brigade Commander Report [undated, circa December 1962, prepared by the USSR Northern Fleet Headquarters] About participation of submarines "B-4,"

"B-36," "B-59," "B-130" of the 69th submarine brigade of the Northern Fleet in the Operation "Anadyr" during the period of October - December 1962, CARIBBEAN CRISIS, Translated by Svetlana Savranskaya for the National Security Archive.)

Page 190. "The war has already started up there, and we are down here doing somersaults. We're going to blast them now. We'll die, but we will sink them all. We won't disgrace our Navy or shame the fleet." (USSR, Memoir, "Recollections of Vadim Orlov (USSR Submarine B-59): We will Sink Them All, But We will Not Disgrace Our Navy," (2002). Source: Alexander Mozgovoi, "The Cuban Samba of the Quartet of Foxtrots: Soviet Submarines in the Caribbean Crisis of 1962," *Military Parade*, Moscow, 2002. Translated by Svetlana Savranskaya for the National Security Archive.)

Page 191. "We should release a single sonar ping in response to their depth bombs to indicate peaceful resolve.": "Savitsky was able to rein in his wrath. After consulting with Second Captain Arkhipov…he made the decision to come to the surface. (*Ibid.*)

Chapter 14

Page 191. "*It seems that what determines the choices a man makes in critical, life-threatening situations…*": (Peter A. Huchthausen, *K-19: the widowmaker: the secret story of the Soviet nuclear submarine.* Washington, D.C.: National Geographic Books, 2002.)

Page 196. "*A man does what he must—despite personal consequences…*": (John F. Kennedy. *Profiles in Courage.* New York: Harper and Row, 1964.)

Page 191. "He found no harm in Starpom's solution.":
"Mere chance prevented Savitskii from resorting to the use
of 'special weapons' at this time. A delay in diving time
and the prudence of the brigade's Chief of Staff Vasilii
Arkhipov – who happened to be on board – prevented the
combat operations which the B-59 could have initiated."
(Ryurik A. Ketov, Captain First Rank, Russian Navy (ret.).
"The Cuban Missile Crisis as Seen Through a Periscope,"
Journal of Strategic Studies 28:2, 2005: 217–31.)

Page 191. "Transmit one full power ping. ": "We gave an
echo locator signal, which in international rules mean that
'the submarine is coming to the surface. Our pursuers
slowed down." (USSR, Memoir, "Recollections of Vadim
Orlov (USSR Submarine B-59): We will Sink Them All,
But We will Not Disgrace Our Navy," (2002). Source:
Alexander Mozgovoi, "The Cuban Samba of the Quartet of
Foxtrots: Soviet Submarines in the Caribbean Crisis of
1962," *Military Parade*, Moscow, 2002. Translated by
Svetlana Savranskaya for the National Security Archive.)

Page 192. "The Captain brought the B-59 from the violent
underworld to the precarious scenarios of periscope
depth.": "Surfacing at night comes with certain risks
attached to it, and in this case the risk was ever more acute.
The overall uncertainty of the situation (the state of
relations between the USSR and US wasn't clear) and the
tactical circumstances at sea (the closely coupled surface
ships of the potential foe) placed the submarine in an
especially difficult position." (Ryurik A. Ketov, Captain
First Rank, Russian Navy (ret.). "The Cuban Missile Crisis
as Seen Through a Periscope," *Journal of Strategic Studies*
28:2, 2005: 217–31.)

Page 193. "When B-59 broached the surface": "8:50 pm.
Beale, Cony and others force B-59 to surface – its batteries

running low. It is surrounded by U.S. ships and illuminated with bright light. One of the destroyers has a band playing jazz. Savitsky understands that they were not in a state of war. Sub heads east on the surface, Cony, Beale, and Lowry circling around." (Svetlana Savranskaya, "New Sources on the Role of Soviet Submarines in the Cuban Missile Crisis." *Journal of Strategic Studies* 28:2, 2005: 233-59.)

Page 194. "They're signaling in Cyrillic. He says, 'Identify yourself.'" (Peter A. Huchthausen. *October Fury*, John Wiley & Sons, Hoboken, NJ, 2002. p. 170.)

Page 195. "Tell them '*korabl* X.'": (Michael Dobbs, *One Minute to Midnight: Kennedy, Khrushchev, and Castro on the Brink of Nuclear War.* Vintage Books, 2009, p. 327.)

Page 195. "The *Cony* sent a final question, "Do you require any assistance?": (*Ibid.* p. 318.)

Page 196. "…blinding blazes of brilliant white light to activate photoelectric camera lenses.": (Ryurık A. Ketov, Captain First Rank, Russian Navy (ret.). "The Cuban Missile Crisis as Seen Through a Periscope," *Journal of Strategic Studies* 28:2, 2005: 217–31.)

Page 196. "…they heard the reports of aviation cannons. Hundreds of rounds sliced into the roiling wake abaft the boat.": "When submarine "B-59" came up to the surface, airplanes and helicopters from the aircraft carrier "Randolph" flew over the submarine 12 times at the altitude of 20-100 meters. With every overflight they fired their aviation cannons /there were about 300 shots altogether…" (Agafonov, Vasily Naumovich, Captain First Rank, 69th Submarine Brigade Commander Report [undated, circa December 1962, prepared by the USSR

Northern Fleet Headquarters] About participation of submarines "B-4," "B-36," "B-59," "B-130" of the 69th submarine brigade of the Northern Fleet in the Operation "Anadyr" during the period of October - December 1962, CARIBBEAN CRISIS, Translated by Svetlana Savranskaya for the National Security Archive.)

Page 196. "'This ship belongs to the Union of Soviet Socialist Republics. Halt your provocative actions.'": (Michael Dobbs, *One Minute to Midnight: Kennedy, Khrushchev, and Castro on the Brink of Nuclear War.* Vintage Books, 2009, p. 318.)

Page 197. "When the *Cony* detected an open torpedo tube door...": (Peter A. Huchthausen. *October Fury*, John Wiley & Sons, Hoboken, NJ, 2002. p. 171.)

Page 197. "...their flashing light ripped out an apology for their aggressive behavior.": (*Ibid.*)

Page 197. "The *Randolph's* fixed-wing aircraft and helicopters flew over the submarine a dozen times at altitudes of twenty to one-hundred meters, training searchlights on the B-59's bridge, blinding the officers and lookouts." "...in the course of the overflight above the boat they turned on their search lights with the purpose of blinding the people on the bridge of the submarine." (Agafonov, Vasily Naumovich, Captain First Rank, 69th Submarine Brigade Commander Report [undated, circa December 1962, prepared by the USSR Northern Fleet Headquarters] About participation of submarines "B-4," "B-36," "B-59," "B-130" of the 69th submarine brigade of the Northern Fleet in the Operation "Anadyr" during the period of October - December 1962, CARIBBEAN CRISIS, Translated by Svetlana Savranskaya for the National Security Archive.)

Page 198. "He gulped so much sea air that he swooned and almost fell overboard.": (Michael Dobbs, *One Minute to Midnight: Kennedy, Khrushchev, and Castro on the Brink of Nuclear War.* Vintage Books, 2009, p. 317.)

Page 199. "He almost never had the opportunity to see his marks in person.": (Peter A. Huchthausen. *October Fury*, John Wiley & Sons, Hoboken, NJ, 2002. p. 174.)

Page 202. "After midnight, Oz appeared with a message from Moscow directing them to escape their American escorts, throw off their pursuers and move to a combat holding position near Bermuda.": (Michael Dobbs, *One Minute to Midnight: Kennedy, Khrushchev, and Castro on the Brink of Nuclear War.* Vintage Books, 2009, p. 318.)

Page 203. "…President Kennedy's message of congratulations on raising a Soviet sub.": "When the fact of the presence of our submarines in the Sargasso Sea became obvious, the activity of anti- submarine warfare was stepped up even more. From our radio intercept information, we knew that President Kennedy was informed that we had to come to the surface to charge our accumulator battery, that also meant that he must have known about submarines B-130 and B-59, which had to come to the surface earlier." (Aleksei F. Dubivko, "In the Depths of the Sargasso Sea," unpublished memoirs. *On the Edge of the Nuclear Precipice*, Moscow: Gregory Page, 1998. Translated by Svetlana Savranskaya.)

Page 203. "Raising hell. They didn't raise us.": "Submerged Soviet submarines essentially ignored the sonar and explosive charge signals. There were no reported instances of a Soviet submarine immediately surfacing upon hearing the signals. Soviet submarines surfaced because they needed to replenish air and batteries, or because they had some kind of mechanical problem." (Joseph F. Bouchard, *Command in Crisis: Four Case Studies.* New York: Columbia University Press, 1991, p.123.)

Page 203. "Have the mate break out a flag, not the Soviet flag, the big red Russian flag, and deliver it to the bridge." (Michael Dobbs, *One Minute to Midnight: Kennedy, Khrushchev, and Castro on the Brink of Nuclear War.* Vintage Books, 2009, p. 318.)

Page 204. "*Prinavlyet,*"…"*Prosnavlast,*": (*Ibid.*)

Page 204. "Captain Shumkov's under attack, and he's in bad shape.": (Peter A. Huchthausen. *October Fury*, John Wiley & Sons, Hoboken, NJ, 2002. p. 194.)

Page 207. "The *USS Murray* steamed alongside playing "*Yankee Doodle…*"": (Michael Dobbs, *One Minute to Midnight: Kennedy, Khrushchev, and Castro on the Brink of Nuclear War.* Vintage Books, 2009, p. 327.)

Page 210. "…throwing packs of cigarettes and Coke cans, and shouting "Russians go home.": (*Ibid.* p, 328)

Chapter 15

Page 210. "*Our commanding officer, Captain Savitsky, had a shadow aboard who was the brigade chief of staff, Captain Arkhipov.*": (Peter A. Huchthausen. *October Fury*, John Wiley & Sons, Hoboken, NJ, 2002. p. 173.)

Page 210. "The *starshy michman* and the torpedo men concocted a radar dummy out of wooden crates with reflective edges, crafted by attaching empty tins and foil.": (Ryurik A. Ketov, Captain First Rank, Russian Navy (ret.).

"The Cuban Missile Crisis as Seen Through a Periscope," *Journal of Strategic Studies* 28:2, 2005: 217–31.)

Page 210. "With no warning, under cover of darkness, the B-59 pulled the plug…": (Michael Dobbs, *One Minute to Midnight: Kennedy, Khrushchev, and Castro on the Brink of Nuclear War.* Vintage Books, 2009, p. 328.)

Page 210. "The Captain dove his boat to test depth and reversed course to confuse his tormentors.": (*Ibid.*)

Page 214. The B-130 had been surfaced. Forward sections of her damaged diesels had sheared and fractured the massive drive gears, blowing off the engines' gear boxes.": "A day after the B-130 was surfaced, they learned from her radio dispatches that all the submarine's diesel engines had broken down, and that the front sections had blown off. (Ryurik A. Ketov, Captain First Rank, Russian Navy (ret.). "The Cuban Missile Crisis as Seen Through a Periscope," *Journal of Strategic Studies* 28:2, 2005: 217–31.)

Page 214. "Captain Dubivko on the B-36 had broached the surface to snorkel in broad daylight less than eight kilometers from *USS Charles P. Cecil* (DDR-835)." (Aleksei F. Dubivko, "In the Depths of the Sargasso Sea," unpublished memoirs. *On the Edge of the Nuclear Precipice*, Moscow: Gregory Page, 1998. Translated by Svetlana Savranskaya.)

Pages 214. "Captain Second Rank Ryurik A. Ketov commanded the B-4 with the 69th Brigade Commander, Captain First Rank Agafonov riding aboard. The B-4 had tackled…": (Ryurik A. Ketov, Captain First Rank, Russian Navy (ret.). "The Cuban Missile Crisis as Seen Through a Periscope," *Journal Strategic Studies* 28:2, 2005: 217–31.)

Page 215. "He recognized that regular afternoon microbursts of rain often coincided with his communications séance to provide cover...": "They ventilated the submarine while the crew drank and rinsed in rain water from waterspouts. They learned to hide in squalls, where storm clouds streamed fresh water created by temperature changes at the air/ocean interface." (*Ibid.*)

Pages 215-218. "On November 3, Oz picked up a discussion of a New York Times summary of the events of the Cuban Missile Crisis: (Special to the New York Times, "Cuban Crisis: A Step-by-Step Review," *New York Times*, November 3, 1962.)

Page 216. "The next day *Tass* released a government statement...": *Tass* Largest news agency in the Soviet Union, government owned and operated.

Page 217. "On November 7, the B-36 damaged two of her three diesel engines due to human error...": (Aleksei F. Dubivko, "In the Depths of the Sargasso Sea," unpublished memoirs. *On the Edge of the Nuclear Precipice*, Moscow: Gregory Page, 1998. Translated by Svetlana Savranskaya.)

Pages 220. "On November 12, they received orders to proceed 500 miles north to an area near the Newfoundland-Azores....": "The period of 28 Oct. to 10 Nov. was nerve-racking, trying to remain undetected while recharging batteries. It became clear that snorkeling at periscope depth until only a 'strong' signal appeared on the Nakat was effective, because ASW aircraft employed a 'reduced' output signal scheme. They relied on visual means of submarine detection. We remained on station until 12 November, always prepared for combat operations... After 12 November, we all received orders to proceed 500 miles north on the US Navy ASW Azores-Newfoundland barrier.

President Kennedy declared on the radio that the US Navy would continue to surface our submarines." (Ryurik A. Ketov, Captain First Rank, Russian Navy (ret.). "The Cuban Missile Crisis as Seen Through a Periscope," *Journal of Strategic Studies* 28:2, 2005: 217–31.)

Page 220. "*Pravda* published articles on American bandits and warmongers. *Izvestia* ran headlines…": *Pravda* was the official newspaper of the Communist Party of the Soviet Union. *Izvestia* is a daily broadsheet newspaper in Russia.

Pages 223-224. "The return passage mimicked the initial route with stormy waters in the North Atlantic…": (Peter A. Huchthausen. *October Fury*, John Wiley & Sons, Hoboken, NJ, 2002. pp. 240 -259.)

Page 223. "…pending a full investigation.": "When the Soviet submarines returned to Murmansk, the captains were subjected to Soviet interrogations and inquiries by the Collegium of the USSR Ministry of Defense in Moscow. The authorities believed the captains violated orders and failed the mission. (Svetlana Savranskaya, "New Sources on the Role of Soviet Submarines in the Cuban Missile Crisis." *Journal of Strategic Studies* 28:2, 2005: 233-59.)

Chapter 16

Page 225. "*The crisis was not over.*": (Mikoyan, Serge, The Soviet Cuban Missile Crisis, Castro, Mikoyan, Kennedy, Khrushchev, and the Missiles of November, Stanford University Press, Chicago, Il., 2012. Translated and edited by Svetlana Savranskaya.)

Page 225. "The B-59 and B-36 made their way back to *Polyarny* …": (Peter A. Huchthausen. *October Fury*, John Wiley & Sons, Hoboken, NJ, 2002. pp. 240 -259.

Made in the USA
Columbia, SC
17 June 2021